CLOUD FARMING

CHONE YUM TSERING

Translated by
WU JIAMEI

Sinoist Books

Published by
Sinoist Books (an imprint of ACA Publishing Ltd).
University House
11-13 Lower Grosvenor Place,
London SW1W 0EX, UK
Tel: +44 20 3289 3885
Fax: +44 (0)20 7973 0076
E-mail: info@alaincharlesasia.com
Web: www.alaincharlesasia.com

Beijing Office
Tel: +86(0)10 8472 1250
Fax: +86(0)10 5885 0639

Author: Chone Yum Tsering
Translator: Wu Jiamei

Published by ACA Publishing Ltd in association with the Liaoning Children's Publishing House

Original Chinese Text © 牧云记 *(Mù Yún Jì)* 2017, Liaoning Children's Publishing House, Shenyang, China

English Translation © 2019, ACA Publishing Ltd, London, UK

ALL RIGHTS RESERVED. NO PART OF THIS PUBLICATION MAY BE REPRODUCED IN MATERIAL FORM, BY ANY MEANS, WHETHER GRAPHIC, ELECTRONIC, MECHANICAL OR OTHER, INCLUDING PHOTOCOPYING OR INFORMATION STORAGE, IN WHOLE OR IN PART, AND MAY NOT BE USED TO PREPARE OTHER PUBLICATIONS WITHOUT WRITTEN PERMISSION FROM THE PUBLISHER.

The greatest care has been taken to ensure accuracy but the publisher can accept no responsibility for errors or omissions, or for any liability occasioned by relying on its content.

Paperback ISBN: 978-1-910760-77-2
eBook ISBN: 978-1-910760-78-9

A catalogue record for *Cloud Farming* is available from the National Bibliographic Service of the British Library.

1

SPRING BREEZE IN LUNGSER VALLEY

Like a golden crown, the early morning sunlight lay over the top of the mountain and brought beauty and grace to the mountain's majesty and vitality, but the sunlight didn't linger there long. It descended little by little, as if wanting to rest upon every hill, every stream, and every swelling bud with its radiance. Soon, the golden yellow morning sun embraced the entire fields and hills as far as the eye could see, including the small valley named Lungser.

Lungser, though not deep, was rich with plant life and green grass, which presented itself in an auspicious and propitious manner. The ravages of a cold winter had caused the plants in this valley to have long lost their youthful beauty seen during past summer and autumn months, leaving the grass with only yellow and dry stems. The weather, after all, was getting warmer and warmer, and a faint light green, a symbol of nature's life, had begun to grow and blossom on the greyish branches of the plants. Near the roots of the grass, soil was slowly softening, while naughty wild thrushes chirped merrily in the trees, as if they could already smell the coming of spring.

Little Tashi stood inside the sheep pen, holding a dry twig tightly in his hand, as if ready to punish the naughty ones who wouldn't behave themselves when they went out of the pen. But, as he looked upon these tame and lovely sheep, he didn't have the heart to punish them. He threw the twig aside, spread his arms like a soaring eagle in the sky, and drove the flock out of the pen. His tiny mouth, filled with beautiful white teeth, was busy pouting and making hushing sounds while giving stern warnings. The flock, following his instructions, moved to the pen gate and darted out like terrified rabbits. A few vigilant ones were frightened by Dawa, who stood majestically beside the pen, and they jumped high over the fence, forming a beautiful curve against the sky, then fell to the ground, performed a somersault, shook their heads and rushed towards the flock as if nothing had happened.

"31, 32, 33, 34…" Dawa stopped his counting and said to Tashi in displeasure, "Tashi, couldn't you slow down a little bit and drive the sheep out one by one?"

Little Tashi retorted disobediently, "Look, the sunlight has already climbed the mountainside. It is not me who wants to hurry, but the sheep that are so eager to leave and eat the grass." As he said this, he laid down his arms and the sheep swarmed to the pen gate, appearing impatient.

"You little boy! Stop talking nonsense!" Dawa helplessly retorted, while snapping the half-closed fence wide open. Upon doing this, the remaining sheep in the pen squeezed out of the gate in an orderly mess, like white foam forming in a boiling teapot.

"Brother, don't you want to count them again as we usually do every morning and night?" asked Tashi. As he hurriedly ran out of the sheep pen, he bent down to pick up a small stone from the ground, preparing to drive the flock back.

"Forget it!" Dawa told him as he closed the fence after him, giving Tashi an impatient look. Dawa thumbed towards the small cabin behind him, signalling Tashi to tidy it up, and then he walked slowly towards the flock. Although Little Tashi nodded in agreement, he didn't go to clean the cabin at once, but instead he followed Dawa and the flock to the bank of the stream.

High above the sheep pen was a small cabin supported by a thick wooden beam hanging in the sky, where the roof was completely covered with yellowish-white weeds. The cabin looked shaky and shabby, having the resemblance of a very old man who was near to death. The wooden door and the front window were unsymmetrical, resembling a human face with slanted eyes and a distorted mouth. The cabin, however, displayed vitality, as the morning sunlight peered in from the hills and glittered on the cabin's frame, as if it had been gilded with gold.

As Little Tashi returned to the cabin from the bank, he lifted his right foot and kicked open the half-closed door with a grumble. The rickety cabin shivered slightly, though still managed to stand firmly still. The sound, however, startled the old dog chained beside the cabin, who pretended to be asleep. Hearing the noise, he immediately stood up and barked vigilantly.

The cabin was surrounded by walls of stone, which were not very sturdy. Near the window inside the cabin lay a square kang covered with two worn woollen rugs, appearing to be bumpy and rugged. Two leather jackets were also piled on top of the rugs, like an unfinished sculpture. Between the kang and the stove was a horizontal rod, and next to it stood a pillar with an old-fashioned oil lamp hanging down from it. A wok sat on the stove and resting on the edge of the stove were some bowls with clipped edges. In the corner of the cabin, a plastic 25kg water bucket and a dented dog bowl had been randomly placed. As Little Tashi entered the cabin, the sunlight slipped inside through the door and the shattered window, making the equipment especially eye-catching. Tashi looked up and saw several holes, large and small, in the roof where strong beams of sunlight filtered into the room. When looking through the holes to the blue sky, Little Tashi felt a fit of dizziness.

In the cabin, the stove beside the door looked like an open crooked mouth. One section under the kang had collapsed, which hampered lighting a fire in the stove, since the fallen stones would block the smoke from rising upwards, forcing it back into the room, making it difficult to breathe. Although the stove had problems, surviving in cold weather without using it would have been impossible, so a fire was lit in the stove by Little Tashi. Immediately, the entire cabin was engulfed by smoke coming out of the window, door cracks, the roof, and even from the crevices in the wall. It was as if the wooden cabin had turned into a big stove itself! However, the thick smoke, coming from different places, finally rose together and escaped through the holes in the roof and floated into the sky above. The cabin gradually cleared of smoke and the valley became alive with a breath of life as the smoke curled lazily upwards.

Uninvited animals, such as, weasels and wild cats would often visit this poor cabin when it was left unoccupied. Therefore, to prepare for this, whenever the two brothers left the cabin, they had to store the food they had, such as tsampa (or zanba, roasted highland barley flour), dried beef, brown flour, dried sauerkraut, made of the leaves of a yuan gen (a type of root vegetable, similar to turnip) and any remaining butter, into different bags and then hung in the room from a high place. Today was no exception! Little Tashi stood on his tiptoes, reaching for one of the bags, but he couldn't reach any of them and the bags, full or empty, collided with each other and dangled unsteadily. So, he took a small stool from beside the stove, stepped on it and took some of the bags down.

Birch branches were burning in the stove for heat, and as the flames sprayed out, the crackling sound of branches coming from inside the stove, caused by the heat of the fire, could be heard. Little Tashi squatted beside the stove, where he chopped the dried beef and sauerkraut leaves with his small and slightly rough hands, and then put all of it into the pot to stew. When he finished and stood up, he was covered with a thin layer of smoke. He shook his body, and the misty smoke danced from his clothes like many ghosts might do.

When Little Tashi left the cabin, the sun was shining on the bottom of the valley, where a layer of misty fog embraced everything with a symphony of colours: yellow, blue, purple and red. Sheep droppings in the pen, as if being fermented, were steaming, mixed with the strong odour of sheep, immediately filling the nostrils! Tying his leather jacket around his waist, Tashi began to shovel the sheep droppings out of the pen. Soon, the large sheep pen looked completely clean and Little Tashi, like a farmer, raised his head to look around while leaning on his shovel. He was tired, but very satisfied with the job he had just finished. As he looked around, his eyes fixed on the old dog sitting between the cabin and the sheep pen. The old fellow peered back at him with a dull and blurry look, even unwilling to bark at him. He simply stuck out his long tongue, licked the corner of his mouth in displeasure, as if to say: "Your old buddy is dying of hunger and you should do something about it".

Little Tashi grabbed a handful of the droppings beside the pen gate and threw it at the old dog. Despite the noise made when Tashi did this, the old fellow didn't dodge aside, but continued to stand beside the stake, and let the droppings fall onto his body, without moving a muscle. Little Tashi giggled but walked back into the cabin somewhat disappointed. He poured half a pot of boiled water into the old dog's bowl, added some grain, and stirred it with a wooden spoon. He didn't thin the food with extra water because of the old dog's unwillingness to play. Instead, he added two more handfuls of grain into the bowl as he stirred it.

The sun had climbed high above his head by now, and the forest on the opposite side was being blown by the wind, sending out a series of roars. While Little Tashi waited for Dawa to come back, the sauerkraut broth in the pot on the stove had long been ready and was giving off a rich aroma. Little Tashi sat on the stool and stared at the broth, tormented with hunger, as if a bug had made its way into his belly, making noises and scratching at his stomach continuously. Even so, he didn't have the heart to enjoy the delicious meal alone, so he swallowed hard, put the lid back on the pot, moved it to the edge of the stove and waited for Dawa.

Waiting for a while, Little Tashi fell asleep, leaning against the collapsed side of the stove. He had a dream in which he alone was farming the flock in a small valley where bushes and dry grass had thorns and thistles that were sharp enough to bite him. He worried that the flock would be hurt by them, so he cried out for Dawa, who was nowhere to be found. He had no choice but to try his best to drive the flock away from the bushes to the bare and smooth mountain ridge where the sheep could roam in safety and graze leisurely. Suddenly, a sparrowhawk dived from the sky, ferociously clawed a lamb, just as a tiger or a wolf would prey on a victim, and then soared back into the sky with its wings spread wide. The poor little lamb bleated desperately with his four legs flaying in the air. Little Tashi ran and jumped desperately, trying to save the lamb, but no matter how high he jumped and how far he reached out his arms for the lamb, he was unable to reach the sparrowhawk's claws. He cried and shouted, "Brother, the sparrowhawk took the lamb! The sparrowhawk took the lamb!"

"No, it is still in my arms," and with these words, Dawa suddenly entered through the cabin door, holding a baby lamb, followed by a ewe named Spotted Neck.

When Little Tashi saw the lamb in Dawa's arms, he rolled over, sat up and asked his brother with a pleasant surprise, "Brother, you saved the little lamb, didn't you?"

"What are you talking about? Nonsense!" replied Dawa since he had no idea of the bad dream Tashi had just had. Dawa continued speaking, "This is the first time for Spotted Neck to give birth to a lamb and I am afraid it would be too hard to take care of a young lamb on the mountain, so I brought it back here". He put the lamb down beside the stove, and the little guy stood unsteadily on its wobbly legs.

Smiling and with renewed assurance, Tashi replied, "Oh, I see!" as he ran to the little lamb, where he tenderly stroked its wet fleece. "Brother, this little guy has a white body and a black head, shall we call him Little Black Head?" Little Tashi asked Dawa.

Dawa answered, "Good idea and Little Black Head sounds pleasant." The newly named little lamb instinctively looked for his mother's nipple to nurse, but mistakenly nudged Tashi's belly and greedily sucked on the edge of his jacket instead.

"The firstborn is always like this. Hey, little fool, your mum is over here," Dawa said, as he grabbed Little Black Head from Tashi's side and put it under the ewe's legs.

When Little Black Head finally found her nipple, his tail shook as he contentedly sucked the milk with his little lips, making delightful smacking sounds from his throat. The delicate little lamb, strengthened by the milk, pushed against his mum's buttocks for more milk. This caused the ewe's two hind legs to unexpectedly move a few steps towards the stove where the pot holding the day's breakfast was sitting, causing it to spill. The delicious broth was now dripping all over the stove, while a cloud of dust floated in the cabin, appearing like drifting snowflakes. Seeing what happened, Dawa became angry and said, "Couldn't you place the pot in a safer place?"

"Where should I have put it?" Little Tashi retorted. He cleaned up the mess and said with a sigh, "What a waste! We don't have extra dry beef in the storage."

"A waste? Hurry up and fetch some water in the plastic basin," Dawa said with disappointment, as he pushed the ewe and Little Black Head out of the cabin.

"Why?" Little Tashi purposely asked, even though he knew what Dawa meant.

"If you don't want to have breakfast, stay away!" Dawa yelled.

Little Tashi then asked, "Brother, what's the date today?"

Dawa angrily replied to Tashi, "You boy! You don't take this seriously, do you? Why are you asking about the date?"

"No reason. I just want to know how many days have passed since we came here."

"Don't you have any brains?"

Dawa picked out the dried beef from the plastic basin and put it back into the pot. He sprinkled a few more sauerkraut leaves on top of the meat and continued to cook the stew. He poured a little boiled water into the bowls and began to make zanba while Tashi took out a bag wrapped in three layers of plastic that had a little butter in it. With much effort he was able to squeeze only a small amount out. He wanted to put the butter into the bowl but Dawa immediately stopped him when he saw it. "Don't be greedy!" Dawa told him, "We already have dried beef in the pot. Do we still need butter in the zanba? That's the only butter we have! Save it to put on our faces as a moisturiser. You should thank God for having some meat to eat now."

"No!" Little Tashi replied. He didn't care what his brother said to him. But, as he thought of the burning pain on his dry face with no butter to moisture it, he reluctantly put the butter back in the plastic bag.

It was noon, when they finished their breakfast. The two brothers walked out of the cabin together. Look, what handsome and capable brothers they are! Little Tashi, with his round head, dark and curly hair, big eyes, a small nose and mouth, and whose body was perfectly proportioned, wore a leather jacket made of sheepskin. Dawa had a long face, a pair of narrow eyes, a high nose framed over a pointed chin, and all-in-all, a tall figure. In contrast to Little Tashi, he was dressed in old cotton-padded jacket and trousers and wherever he went, he would carry a sling, called wu'duo in Tibetan, which is a strip of cloth tied around the waist as a tool to warn and manage the flock. Although they were brothers by birth, it was hard to imagine they were brothers from their appearance. All people agreed that Dawa looked like his maternal grandfather, while Little Tashi looked like his father. When they reached the stream, they both cupped their hands over their eyes, peering backwards at the mountain top. Against the blue sky, a mass of white clouds, appearing like scattered cotton, hung on top of the mountain. Little Tashi said to his brother eagerly, "Brother, look, the flock is over there."

"Did your eyes grow back into your head?" Dawa asked, sarcastically. Taking a closer look, he saw that it was not their flock since theirs had long disappeared and was nowhere to be found.

"Heh, heh!" Tashi laughed and said, "It is a flock from heaven."

"Nonsense!" Dawa, a little worried, cupped his hands around his mouth and gave a few cries which echoed back to them from the woods on the opposite side, and the sound then spread across the valley. The stream at the bottom of the valley was surrounded by bushes, but the stream that flowed from within the deep valley became wider as the snow and ice continued to melt, making the stream's water run even more swiftly than before. The sunlight shone on the stream which, as if it were wearing a beautiful dress sparkling with pearls, babbled away. The small ravine, eroded out by the stream year after year, looked charming under the sunlight. Every bush, every tree, and even every tender bud hidden in the soil were all happily stretching their delicate but growing bodies. If you listened intently, you could almost hear the faint murmuring of flowing sunshine mingling with the buzzing sound of the soil as it greedily absorbed the sunlight.

As Little Tashi looked at the back of the cabin where green buds were about to emerge from the once withered plants and bushes, he felt deeply moved. How tenacious these little lives were! Think of all the obstacles they had gone through from birth to the final maturity! Very soon, the entire mountain would be covered in green clothing made by these and all other plants in the valley. How beautiful it would be, Little Tashi imagined! A sweet smile rested upon his face as he pictured his sheep wandering in the green ocean of colour, while they happily grazed.

Meanwhile, Dawa, who had walked along the stream to the small ravine on the upper left corner behind the sheep pen, turned back and shouted to Tashi, "I am going to check the flock, remember to take care of Little Black Head and his mum."

"Ok, I will," Little Tashi answered, rushing back to the sheep pen from the stream, where he began to play with Little Black Head. The warm spring breeze floated down from the mountain top causing the weeds on the roof and the plants beside the sheep pen to gently dance, as if they had been longing for such an invitation. Nobody knew where those chirping birds, which used to be resting on the trees singing happily, were hiding. The cabin would have been quiet if it were not for the bleat of Little Black Head, who had slept lazily and soundly in the sunshine beside his mum. He added much playfulness and vitality to this serene picture when Little Tashi woke him up. Little Tashi smiled as this small and cute little lamb bounced and moved around, running and stumbling every few steps.

2
BATTLE AGAINST THE EAGLE

The next day, Little Tashi didn't know what time it was when he woke up in the morning. He lay snuggly in the warm jacket, reluctant to open his eyes. He buried his head under the pillow and drifted back to sleep for a little while, but he was thinking about the flock, wondering whether the sheep would get mad at him if he got up too late. He reached out for Dawa, trying to wake him up, but he felt nothing beside him, which shocked him. He raised his head immediately and looked around. The cabin was quiet, as if no one had ever lived there. Little Tashi hurriedly put on his patched, worn jacket, rushed out of the cabin and came to the sheep pen where he found no sheep except

Little Black Head and his mum. He looked up and saw grey clouds hanging over his head and shrouding the top of the mountain. The clouds, like ice beads formed after the winter glaciers melted, flew inside the mass of clouds secretly. Little Tashi knew this was not the real cloud but morning fog and when the morning mist faded away, today would be another sunny day.

The pen was closed tightly, which was a message left by Dawa for Tashi to take care of the ewe and the lamb. Spotted Neck, however, bleated impatiently when she saw Tashi, and butted her head on the pen gate a few times while Little Black Head curled up on the ground and slept soundly, looking like a vegetable-stuffed bun. Ewes were usually very tame, but when they become mums, they are vigilant and anxious, for their young lambs are still in danger, even if they were in the pen because wild cats and weasels could attack at any time. Seeing the eagerness of Spotted Neck, Tashi whistled all the way back into the cabin as if he had grown several years older.

Little Tashi cleaned the cabin, lit the stove and fed the old dog. After he finished all the work, the sun had emerged from behind the cloud and embraced every corner of the valley. When Tashi was about to prepare the breakfast, he found the zanba bag, hung high under the roof, had been taken down and placed in the corner of the cabin. It seemed Dawa had made some zanba with cold water and taken it with him to the mountain. Little Black Head and Spotted Neck bleated in the sheep pen at the same time. Tashi didn't have the time to enjoy a leisurely breakfast, so he made do with a quick bowl of zanba, took down the slingshot from the wall and the red scarf Dawa had found on the road, released Little Black Head and his mum from the pen, and drove them to the small ravine behind.

The small ravine behind the cabin was an offshoot of Lungser and shaped like a cupped palm. It was not deep, but its gentle slopes extended from its mouth to the far end, the lay of which was clearly displayed. On the shaded side of the ravine grew various bushes while the steep sunny side, with only some roots of yellow grass left, appeared to be smooth like a mirror. With no protection of tall trees and thick bushes on this sunny slope, the flock were quite vulnerable to eagles' sudden attacks. It was true that swelling buds all grew on the sunny slope and it was indeed a big waste if the flock were not allowed to graze there, but in lambing season, Dawa would rather go around in a large circle to the small valley on the upper left corner rather than to this small area behind, especially the sunny side, in case eagles would come to snatch lambs. In this small valley, out of her instinctive vigilance to protect Little Black Head, Spotted Neck seldom ate grass, which made Tashi's heart ache when he saw it. He hesitated, thinking about taking the mother and lamb to the sunny slope but at the same time he worried about eagles. After a while, his dewy eyes rolled quickly in his pink face, and he wondered, "My brother himself could look after dozens of lambs and I surely could take care of one lamb when I fix my eyes on it." Little Tashi, therefore, drove the two on, crossed the swollen bottom of the valley, and walked towards the sunny slope. Little Black Head and its mum, however, were somewhat unwilling to move forward as if they felt something ominous ahead of them. Little Tashi had to hold Little Black Head in his arms and walked in front and Spotted Neck had no choice but to follow him closely.

They finally arrived at the sunny slope and Spotted Neck couldn't resist the lure of the green buds and began to graze as she searched in the yellow grass. Tashi suddenly saw an eagle hovering above their heads and Little Black Head and his mum vigilantly bleated out of fear when they saw the eagle, but Tashi felt it hard to control his excitement and was eager to compete with it. The eagle, however, seemed to be so cunning that he could read Tashi's mind. He circled over their heads for a while, flew to the shaded slope on the opposite side and then disappeared in a minute.

Soon, Little Tashi's vigilance lapsed and he took out his slingshot from his bosom, looking for his target here and there. There was no vegetation or bushes around and wild thrushes and other birds were not stupid enough to put on a bold show in front of him either. Suddenly, a hamster jumped out of the grass in front of Tashi, ran half a circle and jumped back again. Tashi followed the hamster for a while and when the little creature reached its hole, it stood erect, stroked its whiskers with its two front paws, made a face at Tashi and darted back to the hole. Frustrated, Little Tashi gasped and plonked himself down on the ground to take a break. Just at that moment, he saw an eagle hovering low above Little Black Head and his mum. Spotted Neck circled around her baby trying to protect him. The eagle had plunged towards them before Tashi rushed to their rescue. Fortunately, the eagle failed at his first try but Tashi knew from past experience that the eagle would not give up easily once it had a target.

Little Tashi held the slingshot ready to shoot as he ran towards Little Black Head, but the eagle, not like a sparrowhawk who only pursued his immediate interests, just kept hovering above them. Tashi knew his carelessness almost killed Little Black Head, so he dared not leave them alone anymore.

The sun climbed slowly from above the forest to its upper right corner and the shadow of the sunny slope was folded inside the small valley. During this time, a pair of sparrowhawks and a big crow appeared above Spotted Neck and Little Black Head. Little Tashi scared them away with his slingshot, but they soon came back and hovered nearby, which made Tashi feel quite helpless. An idea occurred to clever Tashi. He tied the red scarf to Little Black Head and the sparrowhawks and the crow were all frightened away.

Probably carried away by the small victory, Little Tashi climbed to the mountain ridge on the right, squatted there and looked at the small path linking the ravine and the village. Flocks of sheep from the village all moved to grasslands far away and the entire Lungser valley, whose slopes were planted with crops, was a desolate place except for the two brothers. Little Tashi, however, looked at the path, hoping that someone could appear at the far end of the road and head for their sheep pen.

Little Tashi grew up in a happy family. He had grandparents, father and mother, and an elder sister, but since she married into a rich family in another village, Dawa had to drop out from the local school.

Little Tashi was brought up in pastures and he was full of admiration for Dawa when he was still at school because every winter and summer holidays, Dawa would bring back books and stationery and many other toys Little Tashi had never seen before. Little Tashi wanted so much to look at the books and toys but his parents never allowed him to touch his brother's stuff, saying that if he did so, Dawa would be scolded by teachers at school when he went back. So, he could only look at those things secretly and what made him feel even worse was that when Dawa went back every year, his parents would let him do anything he wanted and always gave him delicious food whenever available. When the holidays were over, Dawa would be treated to zanba with butter and dried beef that mum had stored in a leather bag hanging overhead. Therefore, since Dawa dropped out of school, Little Tashi had been eager to go to school to study. It happened that his family's pasture had to move to a grassland rented by strangers that year, which was a regulation of their village. Little Tashi's grandpa had some trouble with his legs and his grandma alone couldn't take care of all the crops in the field, so the village was very considerate and allowed their flock to stay in Lungser so that the back-and-forth trip between the pasture and the village wouldn't be such a burden. Before moving to the new pasture, Little Tashi's father who had long ago seen into Tashi's mind called him and asked:

"Tashi, you want to go to school, don't you?"

Little Tashi was surprised and said, "Dad, how did you know that?"

"Ha, ha, I am your dad."

"Yea, Dad, I want to go to school and I am really crazy about this."

"Yep, I understand, but you know, your mum and I have to go to the remote grazing area and if you go to school, how could your brother Dawa take care of the family flock by himself?"

"Dad, do you mean that I cannot go to school and have to help my brother with the flock?" Hearing this, Little Tashi became worried.

"No, silly boy."

"Then, what do you mean?"

"Look, Tashi. You need to help Dawa with the flock this year and if you do a great job and nothing should happen to our flock, I will send you to school when our pasture moves back. It all depends on your performance."

"Are you serious, Dad?"

"Of course, but you need to keep in mind that you must be your brother's right-hand man and take care of the flock without any loss."

"You have my word!" Little Tashi was so happy that he jumped a few times like a young lamb.

His father smiled.

To make his dream come true, Little Tashi, like a well-trained shepherd, kept his vigilance all the time in case something should happen to the flock.

When Little Tashi indulged himself in thoughts, a burst of frightened bleating from Little Black Head and his mum came from the hillside behind. Tashi jumped to his feet, followed the sound and saw that damned eagle had come back again. Obviously, the cunning fellow knew the red scarf around Little Black Head's neck was only a bluff and he was not afraid of that burning red at all. He swooped down from the sky again and again, and almost caught Little Black Head several times. Little Tashi ran like the wind to Little Black Head while the eagle, as if he knew it was his last chance to snatch the lamb, became wilder and once again he dived from the sky. Little Tashi ran to Little Black Head, but before he reached out his hand to grab him, the eagle had already spread its strong and powerful wings and roared down, the hay on the ground swaying in the wind from under his wings.

Quick as a flash, the eagle made a sudden dive forward before he touched the ground, and he seized Little Black Head tightly between his two sharp talons and took him away. Spotted Neck, with an innocent look on her face, lifted her head and bleated miserably towards the eagle, her short tail shaking in the wind like a flickering candle wick, but it was totally in vain. Seeing Little Black Head struggling between the eagle's talons, Little Tashi didn't know what to do but out of desperation he fumbled and grabbed a big stone from nowhere and threw it at the eagle. No one knew whether the stone hit the eagle, or the eagle was too nervous to balance, but the eagle released its talons and Little Black Head fell directly from a height of about 10 feet. The little fellow rolled over as he landed on the ground and then stood up unsteadily, bleating as if to say, "Mum, that was a close thing! I was almost caught by the eagle!"

It was an extremely degrading and ironic thing for any hunter to lose his prey because of a child and a stone. So, the eagle, as if full of shame and self-blame, lingered for a long time, flying to the sunny slope then to the shaded one, or down to the bottom of the valley or the summit of the mountain. The red scarf that had been tied around Little Black Head's neck was tangled around the eagle's claws and danced gently like a floating prayer flag as the eagle flew in the air; it was very eye-catching.

Little Tashi dare not lose vigilance again, nor dare he underestimate his rival, so he drove Little Black Head and his mum downhill where cypress trees had been cut down, leaving numerous uneven stumps scattered sparsely here and there in different corners of the lower part of the sunny slope. With bushes among the stumps and the open meadows, the mother and the lamb were safe here. The eagle, not reconciled to his defeat, hovered above their heads again, trying every possible way to get close to them to make another swoop, but the stumps blocked his huge wings and the frustrated eagle had no alternative but to reluctantly leave. He flew into the air, circled for a while and then soared towards the back of the mountain top with the red scarf on his claws floating lightly against the radiance of the setting sun, like a ribbon tied on a betrothal gift, or a red khata.

Although Tashi had saved Little Black Head, he could do nothing but watch as the eagle took Dawa's red scarf away. How would he explain this to Dawa? He was a little scared but when he looked at the mountain top where the eagle flew, some pleasant thoughts quickly replaced his worries. It was said that when you climbed up to the top of that mountain, you could overlook the monastery located at the bottom, and the school in the small town as well. They had been sheep farming in this place for dozens of days, but they had never climbed to the top of that mountain. Little Tashi had hoped one day he could do this and look down from the top to the valley far below to look at the monastery and the school!

In the evening, when Little Tashi drove Little Black Head and his mum back to the sheep pen, Dawa had not herded the flock back from the small valley. To please Dawa, Tashi gave the cabin a thorough cleaning, and then set the fire in the stove, mixed the flour and made a pot of delicious pasta. When Dawa drove the flock back, fenced them into the pen and entered the smoke-filled cabin, he found Tashi had prepared a delicious supper. He asked with a smile, "Hey, did you do something wrong?"

"Heh, nothing!" Tashi grinned at him.

Dawa sat on the bench by the fire, picked up the bowl and said, "Tell me the truth."

"Your red scarf has been taken away by the eagle," stammered Tashi.

With hesitation, Dawa asked, "Really? Where did it take it to?"

"Yes, it is true!" Tashi poured himself a bowl of pasta, and lifting the bowl to his mouth and said, "To the top of the mountain."

Dawa continued, "Why didn't you go after the eagle?"

"I worried about Little Black Head, in case some other birds would snatch him away."

It was a little cold that night, so Tashi and Dawa took Little Black Head into the cabin. At first, Spotted Neck kept crying in the sheep pen but later she stopped when she came to realise that Little Black Head was in the cabin with his two masters. Walking around in the cabin, this curious little fellow looked here and there and then Little Tashi put him onto the kang. Having been living with his mum in the sheep pen, Little Black Head became quiet at once when he felt the warmth of the kang. Throughout the whole night, he slept very soundly and quietly between Little Tashi and Dawa.

3
A VOICE SINGING ON THE MOUNTAIN TOP

The sun blazed brightly for days and even the piled snow in the opposite forest melted away, let alone the ice on the edge of the stream in the valley. Encircled by the plants around the sheep pen, green shoots sprung up in the shrubby wormwoods, and various insects wormed their way inside the melting soil, which attracted an increasing number of birds coming and waiting for them to come out. Their twittering echoed in the valley and made the morning extraordinarily lively.

A few days ago, Dawa's red scarf was taken away by the eagle. Little Tashi felt it had been his fault and worried about being scolded by Dawa, but he did not do that. Behind the mountain top was the grassland of Gonpa village and Little Tashi's flock would wander there to eat their growing grass whenever they were not watched. It was the season for green grass to shoot up quickly and the flock which had weathered a long winter appeared to be very excited and greedy and they wouldn't care about which grassland belonged to their master and which was another's as long as they could eat fresh and delicious grass. But could there be any herdsman willing to let another herdsmen's sheep graze in their pasture? They therefore would be very angry when they found this, and they would either grab the ram which invaded their territory out and drag it back to the village to slaughter or they would ask the master of the flock for a large sum of money as a penalty. To prevent this from happening, Dawa seldom led the flock to the mountain top, but today he, for the first time, decided to drive the flock there. Little Tashi was smart enough to know immediately that his brother wanted to get the red scarf back just as the old saying went the drinker's mind was not on the cup. If it were something different, Little Tashi would inquire further, but since today his wish to play on the mountain top for a whole day would become true, he zipped his mouth tight and asked Dawa nothing. The two brothers brought some food with them and released the flock from the pen, which seemed as if they had already known their masters' mind and slipped into the small valley voluntarily.

Little Tashi himself, like a bird released from the cage, ran merrily to the front of the flock to lead the way or flew back behind to urge them to move faster. He wanted to reach the mountain top without pausing once, but the flock were not so considerate of helping Little Tashi accomplish that. They stopped at the mountainside, scattering here and there, eating and walking leisurely like dispersed pearls. The flock marched slowly to the depth of the valley, young lambs gathering together, jumping happily, while a few goats, who were indeed not excluded from the flock, were so sensitive that they felt as if they were inferior to the others, and presented an air of being very humble. They formed a small group and kept a certain distance with the others, but they didn't have any intention of being separated away but followed behind, moving along when the flock crowded forward and stopping when the flock stopped to rest. Little Tashi and Dawa, stood on either side of the flock, crying out to manage the order.

Recently, Dawa would carry a copy of *Sitatapatra Scripture* strapped onto his shoulder wherever he went because his father would give him a test on it this time next year when they came back from the remote grazing area. Dawa sat cross-legged on the ground reciting for a while and then moved closer to the flock, squatted down and continued with his recitation. Little Tashi admired Dawa so much that he wanted to run to Dawa's side to look at that book; even if he could only take one look, he would be satisfied to the full, but each had his own work to do and could not leave his post as he wanted. Little Tashi hoped that he could read the scripture, but first he would need to learn to read. Thinking about the agreement with his father, Tashi tingled with excitement. He was waiting for that day all the time. Little Tashi, however, felt more bored than Dawa today and he laid on his back in the sunshine for a while or hid under the shadow of a tree.

Most of the men in the village could recite *Sitatapatra Scripture*, a scripture said to be helpful for relieving sufferings and avoiding evil spirits. For Dawa, though he could not recite it fluently, there was no problem for him to chant it through loudly. When they reached the hillside, Dawa murmured the scripture, then stopped when he finished the first half and clapped his palms suddenly, just like the men in the village did; a kind of showing off in front of Little Tashi. Father always said that this action should not be done so easily because whenever the palms clapped together, monsters would be driven away. Little Tashi wasn't sure whether Dawa had that power or not, but the flock nearby was startled by his action and raised their heads looking at him motionlessly. The small groups scattered on the sunny slope and shaded slope bleated and trotted back to the flock and slowly the flock climbed towards the mountain top leisurely like a cloud.

The mountain rose from the deep valley, like a dagger, shot in the blue sky while the mountain top, in the upper left hand corner presented itself as a narrow and gentle hill like the backbone of an elephant. In the middle of the hill lay a small lake surrounded by thorn groves; villagers named it Namtso. There was still a long period of time before the rainy season would come, so Namtso simply represented a small portion of its original size at the moment. Namtso, with the reflections of the blue sky, white clouds, and the bushes and the flock beside the lake, was like a beautiful scroll painting. Along the side of the lake grew the dense bushes filled with tiny golden sea buckthorn, a particularly sour yellow fruit that would leave a very sour taste and make the mouth start to water just by looking at it, let alone venturing to eat it. Walking a few steps along the lake towards the back of the mountain, one would find a thick forest, where growing there blocked the view.

Little Tashi and Dawa squatted on the slightly higher meadow beside the lake and began to eat their food. Among a small, independent group, Little Black Head followed the other lambs and horsed around for a while, and then he ran to the brothers, licking their hands or butting them with his hornless small head like a spoiled brat. After they finished eating, Little Tashi and Dawa came to a slope beside Namtso. They looked down through the branches of the pine trees where the fields and stream at the bottom of the valley just came into their view, as so did the small town with red tiled roofs and white walls and the magnificent monastery. The town hall and the monastery stood side by side with the kora route of the monastery dividing them into two sections. Dawa pointed at the golden-domed mani temple along the kora route, and said jokingly, "Look, isn't it the mani temple of your family?"

"Nonsense! That's Third Uncle's house," refuted Little Tashi.

Dawa continued, half jesting and half in earnest, "Doesn't Third Uncle look forward to the day when you could be adopted by him? And when that day comes, won't that mani temple be your family's house?"

"Nope! Hasn't Drolma, in Second Aunt's family, been adopted by Third Uncle?"

Little Tashi moved Dawa's hand in the direction of the school beside the town hall, saying, "I will go to school!"

Dawa said, "Third Uncle has become an influential man in the village and without a son in his family, how could he be happy?"

"Dad and I had an agreement," Tashi said confidently and mysteriously.

"What agreement? Tell me."

"No, it is just between me and Dad."

"Knock it off! Tell me!"

"All right, all right," Tashi spoke proudly, "Dad has promised me that, after I help you with the flock this year, and if nothing should happen to our sheep, he would send me to school next year!"

"Really? Dad is so nice to you!" Dawa said sourly.

"It is true, and Dad is kind to you too."

"Sure, we are his sons. But suppose something should happen to the flock…"

"Bah! Bah! You are cursing our flock, aren't you?" Tashi said very unhappily.

Dawa said, "Hey, maybe your dream of going to school is not that easy to realise. Remember, Second Uncle also wants you to be a lama."

"No way! I will go to school," replied Little Tashi, firmly

While the two brothers were still arguing with each other, a heavenly voice of a girl came from nowhere and they both believed that some fairy had descended to earth. They looked around and saw a few goats suddenly emerge from the meadow on the lower right corner of the bushes. They looked at each other and smiled.

Little Tashi looked at the school beside the monastery and said, "Brother, if our elder sister hadn't got married, you might still have studied there, right?"

"Yes, I would have already finished my elementary school then, but you are luckier than me for you are several years younger and you could go on studying at school," said Dawa with sad envy.

When Tashi and Dawa stood on the slope talking enthusiastically, the few goats in their flock sneaked into the grassland of the other village. Before they realised and were able to stop them, someone in the bushes on the lower right corner whipped these troublemakers towards Namtso, like tigers and wolves hunting for their prey. The goats darted out from the bushes and looked back in terror. Little Tashi and Dawa were wondering how a young lady with such a sweet voice could become such an uncontrollable beast, but they still secretly hoped that a young slim girl would appear in front of them. To their great surprise, it was a humped back old man, whose face was covered with scars, which frightened Little Tashi and Dawa quite a lot. The man waved a stick in his left hand, looked at them sideways and stammered, "Why did you drive your damned goats to our grassland?"

"It was only for a few minutes!" Dawa took Tashi's hand, ducked aside and asked, "Who are you?"

"Who I am is not important. What matters is your flock would eat a lot of our grass within a few minutes. Their mouths are scissors!" The humpback waved his stick as he spoke and chased after the two brothers.

After all, it was their goats that had intruded into the old man's grassland and eaten the grass, so the two brothers knew they had no reason to refute and fight back. They simply laughed aloud and retreated to the opposite side of Namtso thinking that the humpbacked old man might let them go. The old man, however, was still mad at them. He threw the stick on the ground, picked up a stone and hurled it at the flock which were frightened and fled, some shuttling in the bushes beside Namtso, and some fleeing toward Lungser. Little Tashi and Dawa had no idea what to do when suddenly, from the monastery at the foot of the opposite mountain, came the sound of Tibetan horns, and then the humpbacked old man, as if being shocked by electricity, clapped his hands and raised them above his head, praying for a while towards the direction of the monastery. He then took a string of beads, stood with his back to Tashi and Dawa, and plunged into the bushes in the grassland.

This small incident made Little Tashi very unhappy. Today, with Dawa, he at last had come to the top of the mountain but what he had encountered was not the wonderful thing he had imagined but an old man who would give him nightmares. He lost interest in everything around him. He played with Dawa along the lakeside for a while and then prepared to drive the flock back to the small valley in Lungser. All of a sudden, a rustling sound came from the bushes not far from them. The two brothers stared at it for a moment. A girl wearing a red scarf walked unhurriedly towards them, singing happily on her way.

As the girl came closer to them, Dawa stared at her. Her black hair was hanging, in one long slender braid, down to her shoulders. She had a pink face, a pair of watery eyes, a small mole on her nose and a petite mouth, lovely and fresh like cherries. Dawa was deeply attracted by her appearance while Little Tashi was surprised and happy when he saw the red scarf on her head. He opened his mouth and said, "Brother, the red scarf on her head…"

"Hold your tongue!" said Dawa, as he covered Little Tashi's mouth with one of his hands.

The girl came over to them and said, "Sorry about what just happened. That old man is my grandpa and he always treats people like that - everyone! Please don't take it to heart!"

"Ok, ok" Dawa answered happily.

"I found this beside the lake yesterday," said the girl as she took the red scarf from her head and lifted it in front of them. "Is it yours?"

"Yes!" Little Tashi blurted out.

Dawa winked at Tashi and said to the girl: "No!"

"Oh? Yes or no?" the girl asked eagerly.

"No," Dawa raised his voice and explained, "We are boys, why would we wear a woman's red scarf?"

"You are right. If someone is looking for this, tell them to come to me." The girl lowered her head with shyness and walked towards the bushes in front of her, looking back from time to time. Little Tashi shouted suddenly, "Sister, you are such a good singer!"

The girl stopped, a little bit excited. "Heh, heh, my grandpa always said my deceased mother had a better voice than me."

Little Tashi didn't understand her and asked, "Deceased mum? Brother, what does it mean?"

"I am sorry! He doesn't know any better," said Dawa, elbowing Tashi.

"Never mind! It happened long time ago." The girl walked on and then turned back smiling at them, "Good-bye!"

"Bye!" Tashi replied first.

Dawa stared at Little Tashi and then cupped his mouth with his hands, shouting, "If someone looks for the red scarf, where can we find you?"

"She is just in front of us and why did you shout so loudly?" Tashi answered, feeling his brother behaved in a rather intimate manner.

Dawa bent over and whispered to Tashi, "You'd better zip your mouth."

"My sheep pen is in the bushes on the mountainside below," the girl pointed at the bushes in the distance from which they saw smoke coming from a chimney there.

"What's your name?" Dawa asked.

"Call me Dekyi!" With those words, the girl had already gone into the bushes.

The flock arrived at the mountain top and, as if greatly cherishing such a rare opportunity, they strolled to the surrounding hills, the forests near the monastery for a while or ran to the lakeside, grazing and playing with each other to their hearts' content. Little Tashi and Dawa sat beside Namtso, moulding figures out of clay and Tashi had a lot of fun while Dawa seemed lost in thoughts and pre-occupied as if someone had stolen his heart, his eyes fixing on the direction where Dekyi had walked.

The sun was resting in the west far away, and the setting sun shone warmly on the lake where soft ripples glistered brightly. Tashi and Dawa, apparently in different moods, herded the flock back to the small valley behind them. The flock walked along the ridge and ran towards the bottom of the valley, like rolling stones, raising a cloud of dust that lingered in the air for quite a long time in the light of the sunset. When Little Tashi and Dawa reached the sheep pen, the twilight blurred everything at the bottom of the valley. The old dog kept barking, his voice carried a slight touch of complaint, as if to say, "I have been waiting for you a whole afternoon with an empty stomach while you seemed to have totally forgotten about me when you arrived on the mountain top." Dawa noticed that the old dog kept licking his lips, so he said to Little Tashi, "Tashi, go and light the stove; the old dog is hungry, and we need to feed him."

"I told you to go back earlier, but you didn't listen." Tashi complained.

Dawa said, "Nope."

"No? It was not until you watched Dekyi go to her home that you agreed to go back," Tashi said naughtily.

Dawa pulled a long face and urged, "Nonsense, go and do your work quickly."

The sunshine on the mountain top disappeared and the whole valley darkened gradually. Little Tashi had the fire burning in the stove and a film of smoke immediately filled the cabin while the old dog sat in front of the cabin, staring intently at the door waiting with all his heart for his food. Dawa, standing in front of the pen, counted the flock and then closed them back in, but clever Little Black Head remembered the warmth of the kang, and squeezed his small body through the fence after he finished his mother's milk. He followed Dawa like a small tail and circled around him. Dawa lifted him up as if holding a baby, kissed his lips, raised him above his head, turned full circle and put him down in front of the door. Little Black Head capered around and slipped through the door into the cabin.

4
A WOLF PACK ATTACKS

It was dusk, a few days later. The bottom of the valley was thrown into darkness as if the night had fallen early, though a golden crown was still hanging on the mountain peak. Little Tashi and Dawa were driving the flock back from the small valley to the left of the pen. When they passed through a trail in the thick woods beside the stream, the flock, as if frightened by something, scattered into the bushes beside the trail like white beans rolling in a sieve. Immediately, eager cries of ewes and young lambs separated from each other came from the bushes. Little Tashi and Dawa stepped closer and found a stout owl which stood on a twig beside the trail, motionless like a meditating Yaksha. The owl is a crafty bird and it always hid its ugly body so well that people seldom had the chance to see its true face and only heard a few low cries from deep in the forest. Little Tashi and Dawa felt it was ominous, so they picked up a stone from the roadside and threw it hard towards the owl.

It is said that the owl's eyes can only see at night and its vision therefore is blurred at the turn of day to night. From above the owl's meaty neck, knitted with feathers, which looked like a nine-eyed gzi stone, also called heaven pearls, stared a pair of villainous eyes. The owl didn't spread its wings and fly away immediately. The stone Dawa had thrown hit it right on its wings, so it flapped its wounded wings very reluctantly, flew awkwardly into the sky, circled in the air for a while and then landed on the top of a nearby tall pine tree. Then, as if expressing dissatisfaction about what it had experienced, the bird hooted in a very unpleasant and sad voice, making the gloomy and solitary valley full of loneliness, sadness and despair

Little Tashi and Dawa threw some stones at the owl, but all failed to reach the tall pine tree, so discouraged, they walked on, jumped over the stream and headed for the sheep pen. When they arrived at the pen, the flock had already come to the edge of the fence, some rams resting on the ground ruminating, while the frightened ewes lifted their heads bleating from time to time, as if asking the other ewes nearby about what happened just now. As for the young lambs, some played around the ewes, and some knelt on the ground with their front legs, lips touching their mother's breasts, small tails shaking all the time, and sucking the sweet milk.

Dawa stood at the entrance of the pen, counting the flock and Little Tashi herded the flock from behind. They counted several times and it seemed some of the flock were missing. Little Tashi suddenly found Little Black Head and his mum were not there. The brothers quickly drove the flock into the pen, closed the fence tightly, and retraced their steps to look for them, looking in different directions in the bushes. When they reached the pine tree where the owl rested, they found nothing but some wool hanging on the thorny twigs on the bushes; a mass of shining white.

At that moment, it was getting dark. A layer of pale grey cloud shrouded the valley and everything in front of their eyes was unclear, as if looking through the skylight of a building. In the darkness, the owl, seemingly having seen Little Tashi and Dawa's frustrated expression, burst out malicious hoots, from low to high, from husky to hysterical. The two brothers searched again and again in the bushes, along the trail, as if looking for lice in a fur-lined jacket, but nowhere could they find Little Black Head and Spotted Neck. The bottom of the valley was pitch black, as if it had been engulfed by black water. It seemed Little Black Head and his mum had got lost in the small ravine on the left, so Dawa hurried there to look for them. The flashlight he held kept twinkling in different corners of the valley.

Little Tashi returned to the pen, lit the fire and fed the old dog, and made himself something to eat. The owl's cry was still echoing in his ear, making him lose his appetite. Under the dark night, the restless air was suffocating, and the entire pen was in dead silence, and even the sound of the noisy stream softened a lot, as if waiting for something to happen.

The oil lamp hanging on the pillar of the cabin was gloomy, but the light drifting through the door frame and window seemed particularly dazzling outside. The fire in the stove had gone out, leaving a pile of red coals still warm. Little Tashi sat beside the stove and reached out his hands and feet closer to the coals, but he still felt frozen cold. Little Tashi was brought up in pastures and had certainly already experienced quite a lot, hadn't he? Tonight, however, was different. His heart leaped like a young lamb. Little Tashi began to be concerned about the silence of the old dog, so he went out of the cabin, looked at the stake to which the old dog was tied, who right now had curled up his body in the darkness, like a zombie

Little Tashi couldn't hold back any longer. He cupped his hands around his mouth and shouted a couple of times. Suddenly, a pack of uninvited visitors made a series of quick clicking sounds in the bushes on the opposite side of the sheep pen, which startled all the sheep in the pen. All bleating at the same time, they huddled in the corner. At this, the old dog stood and faced the sound, barking loudly, like he was firing belated shots. The unexpected pack then crossed the stream and fled to the forest on the opposite side. Frightened still, Little Tashi stood in front of the pen, thinking hard: the mysterious visitors seemed to be wolves, but wolves usually came out during midnight yet now it was shortly after dark, which was not the usual way they behaved. Could it be a group of wild boar coming down for some drinking water? Wild boar did like to move in packs, but they would always grunt after they were frightened, while the unexpected pack was so agile, like a gust of wind, and they made no sound from their noses and mouths except the clicking sound they made when they moved in the bushes

While Little Tashi was feeling confused, a few frightened sheep jumped out of the fence and ran back and forth along the pen. Little Tashi opened the gate angrily, held a stick, trying to drive those timid fellows back, but they refused to do so. When they were driven to the gate, they simply circled around the pen around and around, as if playing 'the wolf and the shepherd' game with him. Little Tashi nearly broke his neck trying to get them back and he was all wet with sweat afterwards.

It had been quite a long time since Dawa went to look for Little Black Head and his mum and Tashi had no idea as to what time it was. It seemed that even God didn't have the heart to see the embarrassment of Tashi anymore. Stars began to loom out of the clouds in the sky, and then more came out gradually. So, in the blackness of darkness, the silhouette of the forest opposite and the ridge behind were gradually visible and the frightened flock calmed down. They either lifted their heads as if meditating or curled up their bodies and lay there silently, humming slightly as if having eaten too much. The old dog, however, stood vigilantly beside the stake like a sculpture with the chain dragged behind in case, when something should happen, his master would blame him for it. There was no fire in the stove and the weak oil lamp flickered occasionally, but it was still burning like a warrior who was fighting against darkness.

Before midnight, from the forest opposite would usually come the cries of wild deer, owls, or even wild foxes, but tonight was soundless, particularly quiet, as if some terrible secret plans hid there. Little Tashi did not dare enter the cabin nor did he dare come out. Instead, he squatted at the threshold looking at the forest, feeling that something would come out from there. He awaited nervously as if his every move was ready for this possible event, but he was not sure what it would be, and an ominous feeling weighed heavily on his mind, like a rock. Time passed, and he felt a bit tired and sleepy, so he leaned against the wooden door to take a nap and in a moment, he dozed off and fell asleep.

In the dream, Little Black Head and his mum came back, but Dawa didn't. He waited for a long time but Dawa didn't show himself. After a while, from the bushes came a rustling sound and it turned out to be someone coming towards him. The figure stopped at the door and Little Tashi found it was his mother. Tashi ran to her, clung to her thigh and cried bitterly. Mother took him inside, set the stove and sat on the bench beside the fire, saying, "Look at you! Why did you cry like that?"

"Mum, when Dawa and I drove the flock back to the pen today, Little Black Head and his mum were missing, and he went to the mountain to look for them, but Little Black Head has come back while my brother hasn't. I am worried about him."

"Don't worry. Your brother is a little man now and he will be back."

"But tonight, the forest opposite is so quiet and I am afraid a beast will come out from there and eat him."

"Don't be afraid of beasts, we always have ways to control them."

"Do we?"

"Yes! Let me tell you a story and you will know what I mean."

"Great!"

"A long time ago, a goat fell into the bottom of a well and no matter how hard he struggled, he couldn't get out of it. Just as he was seized by fear and pain, a hungry wolf happened to pass by. When the wolf saw the goat in the well, he couldn't believe his eyes. He grinned at the goat and said, 'I am going to eat you.' The goat said, 'Wouldn't it be more convenient for you to eat me after you pull me out of here?' The wolf felt the goat was right. It would be wonderful to enjoy the goat leisurely after he dragged him out of the well. So, the wolf pulled the goat out of the well and then opened his mouth ready to eat…"

"…and the goat ran away?"

"No! The goat said to the wolf, 'Don't you think it is quite boring to eat only me? I have a friend; why don't you eat both of us?' The hungry wolf again felt the goat was right. That would indeed be the icing on the cake. The wolf, therefore, followed the goat to look for his friend. They walked one after another for quite a long time and at last…"

"What happened then?"

"At last, they saw an old horse stuck in the mire. The goat winked at the old horse and said to the hungry wolf, 'This is my friend'. The hungry wolf jumped to the horse's side, ready to bite. The old horse said, 'No rush! Rescue me from the mire first, and then, would it be more delicious if you eat me after I take a bath?' The hungry wolf felt it did indeed make sense. So, he saved the horse from the mire, brought him to the river's edge and cleaned all the mud from the horse."

"And then the goat and the old horse ran away?"

"No, they didn't! The hungry wolf said to the goat and the old horse, 'I haven't had any food for a few days and I am almost starving. Now I am going to eat you two.' The goat asked the wolf, 'Who do you want to eat first?' The hungry wolf said that although the horse was somewhat old, he had a large frame and he would eat him first. The old horse, with a flash of inspiration, raised one of his front feet and said to the wolf, 'It is only a matter of time that you will eat us, but your next life has to pay for what you do in this life. On my foot is a six-character mantra inscribed naturally and if you could chant it three times, you will not be reincarnated in an evil place'."

"How could the hungry wolf believe that?"

"Sweetheart, you are wrong. The hungry wolf firmly believed the old horse's words and when he lowered his head to check the horse's foot, the old horse forcefully kicked the wolf's head and the wolf died on the spot."

"How clever the goat and the old horse were!"

"So, you need to keep this in your mind that humans and animals both have their own advantages. Although we humans can speak, we are physically inferior to wild beasts and while animals are physically large, they lack wisdom. We must learn to use our strengths to compete with their weakness."

"Then I won't feel frightened when beasts come from the forest."

"No! You don't need to be afraid, even if some beasts come from the forest. Face them bravely!"

The cold wind suddenly sprang up and Little Tashi woke up out from the cold. It turned out to be a dream. Tashi half-closed his eyes and out of the corner of his eyes he saw a few glittering green fireflies. Fireflies were rare sights in the valley bushes. Little Tashi felt a little confused and then he found the fireflies in front of him were all in pairs. He came to realise suddenly that these are not fireflies but the eyes of some carnivores. He trembled all over with fear. He hid himself in the cabin, locked the door and kept reciting the Hayagriva mantra, thinking of the incompetent old dog outside and feeling like he would explode with rage.

Seconds and minutes passed by and a group of ghostly shadows appeared silently from across the stream. They seemed to be very confident about the situation in the sheep pen, weak and vulnerable as it seemed to be. They moved threateningly forward and in the gloomy twilight approached the pen, 300 steps, 200 steps, 100 steps. Little Tashi thought if he hid inside the cabin, he would neither save the flock, nor could he save his own life. Out of an instinct for survival, he fumbled for an axe from the woodpile in the cabin, ran out of the door and rushed towards the ghostlike shadows, as if possessed by a god or a spirit. At this time, the flock were kept in the dark and they all stood motionless, believing that Tashi was playing some boring game with them, while the old dog, who didn't believe that they were facing such a terrible threat, symbolically barked a few times behind Tashi's back and his voice was so friendly as if to win the favour of his little master.

Tashi rushed towards them without any hesitation until he was about 50 steps away. Pairs of twinkling green eyes in front of him turned into seven or eight ghostlike shadows which fled away when they saw Tashi. Tashi wanted to continue his victory and followed them to the stream, where the shadows stopped, and all the green eyes focused on him, as if they were going to attack back. Little Tashi stopped and threw the axe hard to the other side of the stream. The shadows didn't move when the axe fell to the ground heavily, instead, they put on an air of counter attack, panting in a terrifying manner. At this time, the old dog barked wildly, his chain straining, while Little Tashi suddenly remembered the dream he just had, the story about how the goat and the old horse defeated the hungry wolf. He knew he was no match for this pack of wolves with his bare hands and most possibly he would become their food, which might be far from enough for them to fill their stomach. He remembered the time he had spent in the summer pasture, where his parents always used a very good idea to drive away the wolf pack: the fire. He slowly retreated to the cabin, step by step. He fetched a pile of dry wood from the wood store and put it on the open ground in front of the sheep pen. Perhaps he was too nervous, but it was taking him quite a while to light the wood and he failed. Again, he took a handful of dried cypress branches and leaves beside the pen and placed them under the firewood. With a scratch of a match, he ignited the pile and it burned wildly at once, flames roaring and lighting the whole place.

Little Tashi heard the noise made by those ghostlike shadows when they fled after they saw the big fire, but Tashi felt it was not enough to work off his anger. He therefore picked a burning stick from the fire, held it in his hand and chased after them towards the stream. When he reached the lower area of the forest beside the stream, those shadows disappeared and after a while the howls of the wolves came from the forests on the hillside opposite and broke the silence of the entire valley, as if an evil person who had been careful not to do bad things finally revealed his true colours. After all, the most important thing to do in front of your natural enemy is to hide from them. All the sheep in the pen jumped to their feet immediately when they heard the howls and then crowded to the corner of the pen, none of them making any sound, even the young lamb knowing that silence was needed right now. One or two cries of the wolves were heard at first and then the howls of the whole wolf pack rose one after the other, as if the forest on the opposite side was packed with wolves.

Hearing this unscrupulous and dignity-trampling howls, the old dog barked out and his voice carried a kind of hatred. A moment later he felt the barking itself was not enough for him to express his anger. The old dog trailed the chain, circled around the stake, and cried out towards the opposite side. At this moment, Tashi cupped his hands around his mouth and shouted "hey" a few times with his immature voice. Suddenly, the two sounds in the valley collided with each other and made a loud crash, like the waves of the river flapping violently on the river bank. The whole valley trembled. About half an hour later, Tashi shouted himself hoarse while the confronting cries of the old dog and the wolf pack continued.

The firewood and even the dry willow branches used to drive the flock were used up, but the wolf pack showed no intention of leaving and their howls approached gradually from the far end of the forest to the bushes at the foot of the mountain just across the stream. Watching the impending arrival of the wolf pack and having no firewood available, Tashi was a little nervous and he didn't know what else he could do to drive those wolves away. He then saw the old dog dragging his chain and going around wildly beside the stake. The old dog was Tashi's last hope. He hurried to the stake, untied the old fellow from the chain and the old dog, unrelentingly, darted out, passed by the gate of the pen, ran across the stream, and fought bravely with the wolves there.

The old dog and the wolf pack battled with each other in the bushes across the stream for about half an hour. Then the sound moved from the bushes to the forest. Obviously, the wolf pack was at a disadvantage, but a moment later, the forest became silent and nobody knew whether the old dog had been bitten to death by the wolves or the wolves had been driven off by the old dog.

Like a sentry, Little Tashi stood in front of the sheep pen waiting for the old dog, totally forgetting that Dawa had gone to the mountains for the missing sheep. A rustling sound came from the bushes on the opposite of the stream. Tashi thought it was the old dog and went to meet him, but it turned out to be Dawa, holding Little Black Head in his arms, followed by Spotted Neck, the ewe. Tashi burst into tears the moment he saw them, "Brother…"

"What's matter?" Dawa asked with concern.

Tashi didn't know where to start as if he had experienced a whole year since Dawa left.

"The old dog went to fight with the wolves and hasn't come back yet," he said

"What? Why did you untie him?" Dawa asked anxiously.

"If I hadn't, the flock and I would have been eaten by the wolves."

Evening came and Little Tashi and Dawa went back to the cabin, finished supper and waited for the old dog, but at midnight the old dog still hadn't come back and they both believed that he might have been killed by the wolves. The two brothers were very sad and didn't sleep much that night, but the next morning when they got up, the old dog had come back, with wounds all over his body and he curled up and slept lazily beside the stake.

5
THE FATE OF THE PHEASANT EGGS

Little Tashi had become very nervous since the wolf pack appeared in the forest opposite, and he was more sensitive than ever to anything that happened there. He found when the sunshine fell on the bottom of the valley every morning, a group of dark blue, wild pheasants with red crests would flutter out from the forest and land on the crowded tree roots on the sunny slope to look for food. After sunset, they would fly back again to the forest.

The sun cast its golden rays all over the ground, and the birds, twittering on the trees, fluttered and fell on different corners of the sheep pen, as if having accomplished a mission and were now looking for food. In the morning, Dawa herded the flock to the mountain behind and Little Tashi waited for the wild pheasants when he had finished housework. Yes! The first pheasant flapped out from the forest, and then the second one, the third, and finally eight pheasants, large and small, apparently a big family, landed on the tree roots. For some birds, such as eagles and sparrowhawks, Little Tashi knew their flying speed and skills like the back of his hand, so when he saw the clumsy flight of these pheasants, as if they were inferior to other birds, he had some sympathetic and compassionate curiosity for them.

Little Tashi looked at the place where these pheasants flew from in the opposite forest, wondering what their nests looked like: would they be weaved with weeds the same as the other birds' or would they simply hide in a tree hole? His curiosity, like bubbles in water, rose one after another and grew bigger and bigger. Little Tashi crossed through the stream in front of the sheep pen and climbed towards the forest. The forest looked very dense from afar, but once inside, there was plenty of space between the pine trees standing upright inside. Varieties of unknown tall and short plants occupied this place and attempted to cling onto Little Tashi's body and wouldn't let him go. Tashi stepped on the soft and half-yellow lichen, trudged onwards and arrived at the upland part of the forest. He moved about in the woods, looking for the nests but he didn't find any and only came across some squirrels instead, which jumped out in front of his face and then jumped back like arrows. The squirrels finally stopped beside a sturdy tree, and then whizzed up to the tree top as if to make a parade of their abilities, leaving the branches above their heads shaking uncontrollably and dropping a few ripe pine cones reluctantly.

Squirrels, dressed in their fluffy yellow outfits, had small heads while their tails were larger than their bodies, but this didn't do any harm to their overall beauty; they were small and dainty, cute and lovely. Little Tashi suddenly felt sorry for his reckless intrusion when he saw the squirrels escape, yet strangely there was one standing under a big tree, its paws holding a pine cone shell, eating the pine nuts inside. When it saw Little Tashi, it was somewhat panic-stricken and threw the pine cone aside, but unlike the other squirrels, it didn't run away but stood erect, paws pointing in the air, as if wanting to say something to him. Little Tashi was more curious about this. He didn't mean to disturb the squirrel but he was wondering how wonderful it would be if he could catch one and bring it back to the cabin.

He moved closer and closer towards the squirrel, but the little creature's next move shocked Tashi. As if protecting a precious thing, the squirrel held its paws in front of the chest, as if to say, "Please do not break into this place". Little Tashi hesitated and from the corner of his eye he saw white bird droppings near the tree roots and when he looked up, he found the branches were covered with bird droppings and some dark blue pheasant feathers too. Little Tashi came to realise this was the place where wild pheasants landed to roost. They neither lived in a nest nor hid in a tree hole; their simple lifestyle made Tashi develop some sort of admiration for them. While Tashi was thinking sentimentally, he found that the squirrel near the tree root was gone.

He came to the tree and picked up the pine cone the squirrel had left and then he found a soft uplift of soil. He pushed aside the mound and saw, before his eyes, a pile of eggs ready to hatch. Little Tashi counted excitedly, a total of 11 eggs.

Little Tashi had often seen the eggs of sparrows, wild thrushes and even sparrowhawks in the bushes when he was younger. Those eggs were quite small, the size of a thumb nail and their colours were mostly earthen grey or speckled grey. He remembered, when his brother went back to the pasture one summer, they went to the bushes behind their tents to look for eggs of wild thrushes. They later roasted the eggs they had found when their parents were not at home. Mother found out about this later and gave them a lesson, "Are you two pretas (hungry ghosts)? You laid your hands on those eggs and even roasted them over the fire!"

"Not us!" Dawa argued.

"Who did it then?" Mother asked.

"A sparrowhawk attacked the nest and one egg was left there, so we brought it back," Tashi followed Dawa and lied to his mother.

"As the saying goes 'the whiskers of the cat would betray the cat if he had stolen the food'. Did the eggs themselves jump into the fire?" It turned out that the two brothers were so completely absorbed in eating the eggs that they forgot to clean away the egg shells. Mother pointed at the shells on their palms and scolded, "Who did it?"

"Tashi," Dawa answered with no shame at all.

Tashi was equal to the occasion and said, "Mum, it was Dawa who told me to do this."

Mother said to them, "Stealing eggs is nothing to be proud of at all. If you are truly capable, go and catch the cubs of tigers and wolves."

"Mum, it was my brother who asked me to do this," repeated Little Tashi in a tearful voice.

Mother continued, "Your brother will go back to school in a few days and you will not see him for at least half a year, but you didn't even try to say something on his behalf, instead, you simply threw the blame on him. Compared with eating bird eggs, the lie you just told was even more serious."

"Yes! Our teacher said children shouldn't tell lies," Dawa grimaced at Little Tashi.

At that time, it was Dawa who had come out with all these silly ideas, but because of his short stay at home with his parents and the fact that very soon he would leave home for school, Little Tashi became the one on whom his mother vented her anger. His mother didn't let him eat for a whole day and this had lived in Little Tashi's heart for a long time, like a scar that was unable to be wiped away.

Little Tashi stared at the small pheasant eggs, smooth and white like pebbles, and couldn't help but reach out his hand to stroke them gently. To his surprise, the eggs were still warm and Little Tashi couldn't tear himself away from them. He took out the eggs, one by one, from under the tree roots, but then put them back again. He wanted to bring those lovely eggs back, but hesitated because of that knot in his heart from the past experience. He didn't know what to do with them and after a while he thought he might ask Dawa for advice. He then shouted a few times to the ravine on the sunny slope opposite. Dawa didn't reply but some vigilant ewes bleated in return. Little Tashi climbed to a sparsely wooded slope and looked through the gaps between the branches at the ravine, where the flock scattered to different corners on the hillside halfway up the mountain. Dawa however was nowhere to be found. He shouted towards the opposite hillside once again, "Brother…"

"What's going on?" His brother appeared suddenly from the bushes behind the flock.

Little Tashi raised his voice and shouted again, "I've found a nest of pheasant eggs."

"Bring them back!" Dawa answered with some excitement.

Little Tashi asked in a daze, "How do I bring them back?"

"Stupid boy! Can't you work it out?" Dawa said impatiently.

An idea hit Little Tashi. He took off his leather jacket, put it on the ground, placed all the eggs carefully on the jacket, and tied it up with his belt. Going down the mountain, he saw the group of pheasants between the tree roots on the sunny slope opposite, among which there was one standing on the tree root cooing. A sense of guilt seized Little Tashi but he had never made any real contribution in the eyes of Dawa till now and these eggs could be regarded as compensation. For him, it was a chance he was unwilling to lose. He made up his mind, and carried the eggs in his jacket, staggered down the slope in the forest to the foot of the hill and back to the sheep pen at last. The moment he arrived at the gate of the cabin, the wily old dog shook his

THE FATE OF THE PHEASANT EGGS 37

tail and barked his welcome when he saw Little Tashi's cheerful appearance. Tashi kicked the door open and found Dawa had already returned from the mountain and was setting a fire in the stove. Little Tashi said with surprise, "Brother, you are even faster than the rolling stones."

"You did a great job this time," said Dawa with a big grin on his face, as he helped remove the jacket from Tashi's back.

Tashi said with some guilt, "The mother pheasant who gave birth to these eggs was crowing from the tree root behind."

"Nonsense. The male ones crow." Dawa said eagerly.

Together with his brother, Little Tashi picked out four eggs from the jacket and boiled them in the water. A moment later the eggs were well cooked and they each had two. They peeled the shells and gobbled them up. Afterwards they felt as if they had eaten nothing, which only whetted their intense appetites. Seven eggs were left, and so they each picked one again from the jacket, threw it into the pot and waited for it to be cooked. One of the eggs, however cracked and leaked a tiny egg yolk, as if it was moving. Little Tashi asked his brother in surprise, "Brother, what is this?"

"A baby pheasant, of course!" Dawa said calmly, "Look, its claws have already grown out."

"Ewww!" Little Tashi ran to the back of the cabin disgusted and threw up the eggs he had just eaten. He complained to his brother, "Why didn't you tell me earlier?"

"What a waste of such delicious food!" Dawa said with slight distain.

"No more eating!" Tashi ran back to the cabin, picked the eggs out of the pot, put them back in the jacket and tied it again with his belt.

"What are you doing?" Dawa asked with displeasure.

Little Tashi resolutely carrying the jacket on his shoulder, went out of the cabin and said, "I will take them back."

"Why do you do that?" Dawa grumbled.

Little Tashi almost reached the stream and then he turned around saying, "All their family are now looking for food on the sunny slope, but you asked me to bring them back. Since we have eaten them, all the sins would be put on me."

"You silly fool! Leave the cooked eggs here for they can't hatch now." Dawa said helplessly, as he stood on the threshold.

Little Tashi removed the jacket, untied it, took out the half-cooked three eggs and fed these to the old dog. He then carried the jacket on his back, hurried back to the stream, and within a minute he disappeared into the forest. When he climbed, step by step, the plants and shrubs along the forest kept biting his little face or his bare lower legs as if they had mouths. Little Tashi believed all these were punishments given by God for his evil doings and again he mentally blamed himself. Tashi worried all the way to the forest, "I have done bad things to the eggs and seven of them have been lost, am I bound to be punished in the end? And if it should happen, will it fall on my family's flock? And if something should happen to the flock, how could I explain to my parents? The agreement between my father and I is sure to be invalid." All these clueless thoughts lingered in Little Tashi's small head and the journey from the bottom of the valley to the pheasant nest seemed to be longer than before. Little Tashi struggled on his way and at last reached that big pine tree. He buried the remaining four eggs under the soft mound, but there was no warmth at all and the four pheasant eggs were as cold as ice.

Feeling like a guilty thief, Tashi was afraid of looking up for fear that the pheasant family might see him. Little Tashi arrived at the sheep pen, feeling relieved, but remorsefulness and self-blame tussled with each other in his heart, like two children. The old dog saw him and wagged his tail happily, his eyes seemed almost popping out, as if looking forward to getting delicious food from his master again. Looking at the insatiable expression on the old fellow's face, only God knows which nerve had been touched, Little Tashi picked up a stone from beside him, threw it at the old dog, and hit him right on his head. The old fellow didn't know what mistake he had made and wailed sharply.

The sun set, and sunlight at the bottom of the valley had climbed up to the hillside behind while Dawa had not yet driven the flock back. Little Tashi slumped on the threshold of the cabin like a wounded animal, staring blankly as if quietly waiting for something. From the sunny slope behind fluttered a group of pheasants who formed a queue in the air, flying towards the forest on the opposite side. Seeing that, Little Tashi felt his heart was eaten out. He imagined the sad look of the pheasant parents when they went back to the forest and found only four eggs remained. Tears swelled in his eyes and then fell like a broken ivory rosary, drop by drop.

6
GOING ON AN ADVENTURE

With the advent of spring, the sleeping land awoke; all kinds of birds and insects became active in the green valley and grass shot out of the bushes or in the meadows. Tonight, as Dawa drove back the flock to the sheep pen, it was getting dark, and the brothers hurriedly shut the flock in the sheep pen. Little Tashi, however, found Dawa was unusually excited, and saw him always casting his eyes to the small ravine behind, as if waiting for something. Little Tashi was confused and asked, "Brother, what are you looking at?"

"We have a guest tonight." Dawa answered excitedly.

Little Tashi felt rather confused, "Guest? What guest?"

"It's me," answered a shadow emerging from behind and answered, "the girl singing on the top of the mountain!"

"Sister Dekyi!" Little Tashi shouted happily.

Dekyi came over to them and asked, a little surprised, "You remember my name?"

"Heh, heh, my brother often mentions you," said Little Tashi, delivering a naughty look toward Dawa.

Dekyi then said to Dawa, "Are you both ready?"

"Yes, we are ready to leave in a minute." Dawa untied the old dog's chain from the stake, lead him to the gate of the sheep pen and then tied him there.

Tashi, like an outsider, was perplexed about what was going on here and asked, "Where shall we go?"

"Hasn't your brother told you?" Quite shy, Dekyi lowered her head to her chest and whispered, "We are going to watch a film in the town."

"Brother! You are really something! Why didn't you talk with me about such an important thing?" said Little Tashi with some dissatisfaction.

Dawa answered, "Am I your elder brother or are you mine?"

"I have a scarf on my head, but what if someone recognises you two?" Dekyi said.

"You are right," Dawa replied, "What shall we do then?"

"I have an idea!" Tashi ran back to the cabin, took some charcoal from the stove and emerged as he painted his face with it.

"Ha, ha, ha…" Dekyi bent double with laughter when she saw Little Tashi's appearance.

Dawa took the charcoal from Tashi and painted his face saying, "You boy, full of fresh ideas!"

Laughing and joking, they were ready to leave, but at that moment Little Black Head seemed to know his masters would have a long journey; he jumped from the warm kang and bleated eagerly. Little Tashi ran to him, held him in his arms and prepared to bring him along with them. Dawa stopped him and said, "We can't take him with us or he will be frozen to death."

"No, I want to. I couldn't leave him alone in the cabin, he would be too lonely."

Dekyi said, "You two just said that you didn't want to be recognised by your family, didn't you? Wouldn't it be more noticeable if you bring a lamb along?"

"Right, go and put him back," Dawa ordered.

Little Tashi holding Little Black Head, ran to the edge of the stream, turned back and said, "No, I want to take him with me."

"All right, then you go alone, Dekyi and I won't go," Dawa threatened.

Little Tashi had to turn around, took Little Black Head to the sheep pen and said, "Then I want to put him back in the sheep pen."

"All right, give him to me." Dawa took Little Black Head from Tashi's arms, lifted him up and put him back in the sheep pen across the fence.

The moon climbed up over from the mountain top opposite and its silver light shone on the slope behind. Although the moonlight didn't reach the bottom of the dark valley, its reflection on it made the valley bright and everything in it was clearly visible as if it were in the daytime. Dekyi and Dawa walked side by side, talking and laughing like two happy deer while Little Tashi followed behind like their shadow. Tashi looked at the red scarf on Dekyi's head and felt something in his mind and he wanted to tell her it was his brother's scarf, but when the words rose to his lips, he bit them back.

When they arrived at the foot of Lungser mountain, the moonlight, like white snow, covered the spacious valley, the only way that connected the village to the remote grazing area. In the middle of the valley flowed a river singing loudly, on each side of which lay fields planted with different crops, such as barley and lentils, whose pleasant smells filled the nostrils and made one feel very comfortable.

They reached the brightly lit village in a short time. Though painted with charcoal on their faces, they worried their grandparents and the other relatives might recognise them by their figures if they went straight into the village. They chose to walk around the village. At the back of the village were fields planted with crops, and for the sake of safety, they had to tread through the crops, which were still wet, and then walk towards the cement bridge at the far end of the village. On the bridge, they took off their muddy shoes and squeezed out the water. At this time, the moon shone on the river under the bridge, halos glittering faintly on the surface of the water. Dawa used to study as a fifth grader in the elementary school in the town centre. When his elder sister got married, however, the family was short of hands. Due to this but also because he was now the eldest child in the family, his father wanted him to drop out of school and came back home. Dawa, of course, refused firmly and often ran back to school. Later, Father went to his school and argued with teachers for quite a long time and finally brought Dawa home. But it was said that on that day when Dawa passed through the cement bridge, he threw his backpack, filled with stationery and various books, into the river out of anger. Little Tashi looked at the gleaming river in front of his eyes and remembered the scene when the water had carried away Dawa's school bag. He was feeling sad and somewhat relieved because now he would have the opportunity to go to school in place of Dawa who had thrown his school bag away. He was in a very contradictory mood anyway, and he couldn't help asking Dawa, standing beside him, "Brother, why did you throw your bag into the river?"

"Since I was not allowed to go to school, why should I keep it?" Dawa said.

Little Tashi said, "You could keep it for me when I could go to school."

"It is only your dream. No one knows whether you could go to school or not."

Dekyi came alongside and asked, "What are you gabbling about? We'd better hurry or the film will be over."

"Ok, let's go." Dawa put on his shoes and stood up.

Dekyi stood up and she and Dawa walked side by side to the town while Little Tashi followed. When he looked back reluctantly at the river, he stepped into a puddle and fell with a cry. Dawa and Dekyi ran back to him and impatiently helped him up, and then they continued to move forward. It seemed the film had already started and along the way they seldom met any people. When they arrived at the town, the sound of film's shouts and fighting sounds came from the woodworking factory.

When they entered the big iron gate of the factory, and arrived at the open yard, they could see nothing but the back of people's heads, tall or short. Like gophers, they dug their ways into the crowd and managed to squeeze in through a narrow passage. On the second from the front row of logs, Little Tashi and Dawa sat on either side of Dekyi. It was the time for the film to change reels and among the crowd were a man and a woman looking like cadres who were eating sunflower seeds noisily. The woman, who had long hair, raised her head, sniffed and then covered her nose saying, "What a strong gamey smell!"

"And also, the stink of sheep droppings," interrupted the man.

Suddenly a scornful voice burst out among the crowd, "Did I just smell a stinky human here?"

"Exactly, this choking smell of soap smells poisonous," a man in the crowd cut in. The crowd exploded with laughter.

The female cadre jerked her mouth and said, "How annoying!"

The male cadre said, "Won't you just shut up? How can you take offence at these people?"

A huge white cloth hung between a pair of rafters and in the lower left corner beside the cloth was a rectangular black box, from which thunderous noise came that was out of sync with the moving shadows on the white cloth. At first Little Tashi was afraid of looking up at the moving figures for fear that they would fall and smash on his head, but after a while he adjusted himself to the shaky pictures on the white cloth.

The Forest Centre in the town often showed films to the local people. Today's film was *Shaolin Temple*, which was shown many times, but people enjoyed watching it, and it was replayed over and over again. Little Tashi stared at the monks' kicks and blows, leaping on the roofs and vaulting over walls on the white cloth, and he felt they had nothing in common with the lamas who chanted scriptures solemnly in Choekhor monastery. Tashi got quite dizzy and had contained his bladder for quite a long time and wanted Dawa to take him to pee in the outside field. At present, Dawa sat shoulder to shoulder with Dekyi, watching the movie intently, as if he didn't hear Tashi's call for help. Tashi therefore stood up and gestured to Dawa. At this moment, a rock thrown just behind his back hit his head and Little Tashi had to bury his head, his bladder almost bursting. He had no choice but to lower his head and crawl through the crowd like a four-legged animal.

Little Tashi reached the corner of the gate of the woodworking factory, left a puddle there and gave a comfortable shudder. He passed by the town hall, and then came to the school gate, which was closed tight. He covertly went through a gap to the right of the mud wall and entered the school yard. In the middle of the yard stood a tall flagpole, behind which was a platform where a row of shabby flats stood quietly. Three or five rooms were lit up, and the lights shone on the open space. Obviously, it was the teachers' residence. Both sides of the flagpole were lined with a row of bungalows, which were apparently the classrooms. The iron gate opposite the flagpole was closed tightly, and everything in the school was seen clearly in an orderly array as the moonlight shone tenderly on the campus. Compared with the loud noise of the film in the woodworking factory, the serenity of the school yard appeared to be even more extraordinary.

Like a kitten who intruded on a forbidden place, Little Tashi came to the first classroom on the left. The blue classroom door was tightly closed, so Tashi climbed up to a window next to it and looked through the window pane. The moonlight shone through the glass into the classroom, where rows of benches were placed in an orderly fashion and portraits of some people hung on either side of the blackboard. Little Tashi's eyes were locked on a metal pencil box on a desk, which was glittering in the moonlight. With a touch of envy and a little worry, Little Tashi looked at that pencil box and thought about its owner: how could he leave such a cute little box here? Would it be stolen like those pheasant eggs? Just as he was lost in his thoughts, the school's iron gate opened with a grumbling noise and someone entered. Little Tashi was shocked by the sound; he jumped off the window and slipped through the gap on the wall of the school like a mouse.

Little Tashi squeezed back to his spot in the woodworking factory and found Dekyi's red scarf was placed on her seat. Dawa stared at him for a moment, as if to say, "Naughty boy! Where have you been? Someone almost took your spot!" Little Tashi sat down and looked up at the screen. A new movie named *The Decisive War!* was playing. He was fascinated by the picture of soldiers dashing forwards, though he didn't know which troops were the People's Liberation Army and which were Kuomintang's troops. Tashi picked up the red scarf, sat closer to Dekyi and held the scarf to his nose smelling continuously. A faint sweet scent of resin struck his nostrils and Tashi simply couldn't imagine it was the same scarf he had lost. Suddenly, someone snatched the scarf away and Little Tashi looked to his right and found it was Dawa. A little bit angry, Dawa scratched his cheek with his right forefinger to shame Tashi, and then pointed at the screen in front. With his head slumped over his chest, Little Tashi's heart pounded and he was so ashamed of himself. After a while, he forgot about this and held his face up watching the movie. But he was preoccupied and could not concentrate. When the movie went on to the second half, the critical moment of the decisive battle between the Kuomintang (KMT) and the Communist Party of China (CPC), all the other viewers were holding their breath and staring at the screen while Little Tashi couldn't get his mind off that pretty pencil box. He suddenly stood up and squeezed through the crowd.

The moon in the sky was naughty too. It entered the clouds hiding for a while or revealed its lovely bright face from between the clouds, spreading its silvering light down. Little Tashi went out of the woodworking factory and arrived at the right hand corner of the school wall. Like a very experienced burglar, he went through the gap and entered the school once again. Outside the quiet school campus, the bright moonlight lit everything. Little Tashi sneaked towards that familiar classroom, climbed up to the window and looked inside. The moonlight had moved on and the pencil box, though not glittering like before, was still lying solemnly on the dark desk. Little Tashi stared at it for a long time, feeling so excited as he thought about the day when he could go to school after he finished helping his brother with the flock and after his father came back from the remote grazing area. Suddenly, a beam of light moved across the campus and at last locked on his body. Before Little Tashi had time to jump from the window, a shadow leapt at him and captured him on the spot. It was a female teacher with short hair.

"What are you doing here?" she asked fiercely.

"I…" Little Tashi was speechless temporarily.

She went on, "You are a thief, aren't you?"

"No, I am not. My brother and I…we came to watch the film." Little Tashi stammered with nervousness.

"Why didn't you go to watch the film instead of sneaking in here?" asked the teacher sternly.

Little Tashi answered with a trembling voice, "I want to look at the pencil box."

"Pencil box?" the female teacher's voice softened a lot.

"Yes."

"Why?" the teacher continued.

Little Tashi faltered, "Because…"

Just at that time, a group of people rushed in through the iron gate, all talking about the film. Hearing this, Little Tashi pricked up his ears in the direction of the factory, where no film sound could be heard any more. He was afraid that Dawa and Dekyi might not find him, so he jumped away from the window when the female teacher was not looking and then squeezed out through the gap in the wall behind.

When Little Tashi went back to the woodworking factory, most of the viewers had gone and only a few in the back were still hanging around near their seats in the dazzling lights as if they hadn't enjoyed it to their hearts' content. He stood in front of the huge white screen and shouted, "Brother… Brother…" until suddenly someone slapped him in the face from behind. Little Tashi looked carefully and found it was Dawa who right now was ready to charge towards him again like a guard dog that couldn't be stopped. Luckily, Dekyi stopped Dawa. Little Tashi wailed and said in a pathetic voice, "Why did you hit me?"

"Where have you been? Why didn't you sit here watching the film?" Dawa asked angrily.

"I went to the school."

"Are you stupid? Why did you go there at night?"

"I…" Little Tashi wanted to explain, but his words stuck in his throat because he felt so wronged.

"What if you were recognised by someone? And how do you explain this to our family?" said Dawa as he grabbed Little Tashi by the shoulder and dragged him out.

"Dawa, don't do that," Dekyi shouted behind him.

The moon had risen to the upper corner of the sky, and its light on the bottom of the valley gradually dimmed. With increasing clouds covering the moon, the silvery bottom of the valley became darker. The three of them avoided people who went back to village in small groups, as if they had the plague. They crossed the cement bridge, made a circle around the village, and went back towards Lungser. Along the way, they all remained silent, a sharp contrast with the happy scene when they had been on their way to the movie a few hours ago.

7
CHISELLING A SIX-CHARACTER MANTRA

Since their last trip to the town to watch the film and after seeing that pencil box on the desk, Little Tashi was crazy about using the charcoal left in the stove to draw various patterns on the walls, windows, and cabin door. Of course, most of what he wrote were some Tibetan letters learned from Dawa. He could only write the first 20, and what he wrote always appeared uneven, sprawling, and disproportionate, some even larger than his head while some tinier than his little finger. But Little Tashi enjoyed doing this and had a lot of fun.

When Dawa drove the flock back every day, he would find the cabin in a mess with all the graffiti inside and outside, like a witch's house. Dawa would pull out a handful of dried alyssum beside the pen, and scrub the patterns and scribbles as he scolded Little Tashi. But the very next day, Little Tashi, as if by magic, restored the entire cabin to its original messy appearance with even more writing everywhere, leaving no empty space at all. Dawa had no choice but to scare him saying, "If you continue doodling like this, I won't teach you the last 10 letters." Little Tashi then improved his behaviour and seldom did he draw those letters inside or outside the cabin. Dawa thought Little Tashi had learned how to behave, so he taught him the rest 10, one by one.

A few days later, Dawa found the foldable knife he usually tied to his belt was missing. He checked with Little Tashi, who said he hadn't seen it. Dawa searched the entire cabin but could not find the knife anywhere. He thought he might have dropped it when he herded the flock on the mountain, so he went to the mountain, searching every inch of the grass field. It was like looking for a needle in a haystack, but in vain. Dawa felt sad for quite a few days.

A few days later, Dawa discovered some unidentified patterns on the willow bark covered with green foliage around the sheep pen. He thought that might be teeth marks left by weasels and hamsters, so he just ignored them. Later he found the bark of various trees in the opposite forest were also full of similar patterns, which made him very confused. He narrowed his eyes and looked at them carefully and found these patterns askew, somewhat like Tibetan letters, but he could not figure out what kind of smart animals could do this?

During these days, Dawa found Little Tashi was a little bit strange, which aroused his attention. So, one day, after he drove the flock from the pen to the small ravine, he slipped back and hid behind the cabin, to watch. Little Tashi hurriedly finished all the housework, crossed the stream like a rabbit, and went into the opposite forest. Dawa followed him, careful to keep a distance with him.

In the opposite forest, Little Tashi stood in front of a birch tree, took out something from his chest and began to carve on it, closely watched by Dawa who was hiding in the bushes. Dawa jumped out at him, like an eagle preying on a young lamb. He caught Tashi on the spot and asked, "What are you doing here?"

"I am practising writing," replied Little Tashi biting his lower lip and he lay on the ground face down, unwilling to admit defeat.

Dawa stared at Little Tashi, eyes wide open, and said, "These trees are living things, how could you carve letters on them?"

"Who cares? I want to practise writing letters." Little Tashi clasped his hands tightly under his body, as if trying to hide something.

"What is in your hand?" Dawa tried to turn Tashi's hand over but failed. He therefore rolled Little Tashi's sleeve up to the arm and pinched his thin wrist saying, "Does it hurt? You carve letters on the bark and you will feel it yourself."

"Ouch!" Little Tashi leapt up from the ground like a spring, the knife in his hand falling directly to the ground.

"You have stolen my knife!" Dawa lifted his clenched fist, ready to hit him while Little Tashi stumbled to the nearby bushes like a wounded deer. As he fled, he turned and shouted, "You beat me every day and I will go and tell Mum and Dad in the remote grazing area."

At first Dawa was very angry but later when he thought that the reason why Tashi did this was because he wanted to learn Tibetan letters, his anger softened. Little Tashi ran back to the remote grazing area, he couldn't take care of the flock by himself. His anger faded away, like a balloon shrinking down slowly after being pierced by a needle. At last, he even felt a little bit guilty, so he went into the bushes, following Little Tashi and begged for his forgiveness. Little Tashi, however, didn't appreciate his efforts and dodged here and there in the bushes. As Little Tashi and Dawa played a game of cat and mouse Dawa suddenly stumbled upon a stone; he rolled over and fell to the ground. His legs hurt badly. Dawa looked at the tilted rock in front of him, his eyes almost popping out in great anger, but just at this very moment, Dawa felt a flash of inspiration and found a way out. He shouted, "Tashi, don't be mad at me. I had a good idea for you to practise writing letters."

"Huh, I don't believe you," Little Tashi said naughtily.

"Do you remember when we were in the summer pasture? With our Second Uncle and the others, and the big rock beside the spring?" said Dawa, getting up.

Little Tashi responded quickly, "Chisel the six-character mantra on the stone?"

"Yes, why shouldn't we?" Dawa added as if he had found a great secret, "This could not only help you with your writing but also it is an act of benevolence."

Little Tashi asked innocently, "Really? Then how to do that on the stone?"

"I have an idea." With these words, Dawa found Little Tashi was already standing by his side.

When Dawa went back after he had checked the flock in the small ravine, Little Tashi had prepared a pot of pasta. The two brothers finished their meal quickly, and then began to prepare proper tools for their huge project. It was not an easy task to chisel on a stone and Little Tashi had no idea about Dawa's plan. Dawa brought out an axe from the firewood room, removed the wooden handle from the iron hole, and then from under the mattress on the kang, he fumbled and brought out a rusty and broken pair of scissors and held them in his arms. Then, the two passed through the bushes behind the sheep pen and arrived under an old cypress tree, surrounded by various plants, at the foot of the mountain. A clear spring ran under the tree, surrounded by short bushes. Besides the spring there was a patch of meadow flourishing with flowers. When they arrived, the two brothers dug out a few stones and then began to chisel on the stones.

With the sharpened edge of the axe, Dawa wrote the mantra on a flat stone that looked like a rolling board, and then began to carve busily. He hadn't ever learned how to carve, but the strokes of each Tibetan letter on the stone looked correct and beautiful, and like a professional engraver, he never dropped any of the stone scraps. Little Tashi beside him was busy writing Tibetan letters with the scissors on a large stone slab, the same size as his head. Every time he hit the stone hard with the scissors to chisel strokes into the slab, the situation would be either the slab rolled to the side or the stone in his hand tilted to one side. Little Tashi didn't lose heart at all, instead, he dropped his head and repeated the same work quietly. The two brothers were engaged in their work for almost half a day. Dawa then stopped to wipe the sweat from his forehead and then turned to check on Little Tashi, who at present had already chiseled quite a lot on the slab. Dawa didn't recognise any of the letters on Little Tashi's stone and it seemed he had carved a human face on the slab. Dawa said to Tashi, jokingly, "Look at your stone. You are simply carving ghosts."

"What does carving ghosts mean?" Little Tashi asked.

"When I was still at school, my teacher told us a story. Once a man went to ask a thangka painter what the easiest thing was to paint. Can you guess what the painter answered?"

"People?"

"Wrong. Ghosts."

"Why?"

"Because no one has ever seen a ghost, so it would be quite all right no matter how you draw it."

"Do you mean I am drawing a ghost?"

"I couldn't identify anything else but a ghost."

Little Tashi's feelings were hurt, so he took another stone from the pebbles covered with algae piled beside the spring and chiseled again. Dawa regretted being such a big mouth after he had told Little Tashi this story because when he turned back to look at his own work, it was scrawling, though faintly recognisable from its shape. He was ashamed and at the same time a little bit scared. The six-character mantra was the mercy mantra of Avalokiteshvara that included all the great blessings of dharma, and if he missed one stroke or a character he chiselled was disproportionate, that would be a sin indeed. Dawa therefore, like an inexperienced but unyielding engraver, buried his head again and carved on the stone carefully.

The clicking sound of the two brothers' carving played wonderful music at the bottom of the valley and the opposite forest echoed in a melodious way, although sounding a little messy. Little Tashi's sharp ears captured a different clicking sound, which to be frank should not be very surprising, however the strange thing was that when the brothers raised their tools to carve on the stone, that mysterious clicking sound appeared at the same time and when they both stopped their work, that sound stopped too. And if Little Tashi hadn't told Dawa this, Dawa wouldn't have heard this sound. Dawa had felt guilty and when he heard this sound, he shivered and had goosebumps all over. The two brothers raised their heads and looked around suspiciously and then their eyes converged at the same time on a tall and thick pine tree on the left. It turned out to be a woodpecker drumming the bark noisily for insects. Its shovel-like head crest remained motionless as if nailed on its head when it was busy hammering the bark with its sharp beak. Dawa and Little Tashi looked at each other, smiling with some relief.

Compared with the tapping sound of the woodpecker, the carving sound of the two brothers, however, seemed to have stolen the show, so the bird pecked the bark with greater passion, as if being electrified. Little Tashi put the scissors aside, took off his shoes, soaked his bare feet in the water, and then grabbed two pebbles, the size of a fist. He deliberately struck the pebbles against each other, making fun of the woodpecker, which was indeed stupid enough to take it seriously and pecked the bark more wildly. As if worrying about lagging behind, its clicking sound changing into rapid knocking. What's more, the bird would stop halfway and turn around to look towards Little Tashi and then continued pecking frantically. The stubbornness of the silly bird tickled Little Tashi's fancy, and he laughed out loud and then turned back to ask his brother, "Brother, the woodpecker has a sharp beak, why is it fond of pecking the insects behind the tree bark?"

"They are said to have done bad things in their past lives, so they are reincarnated as woodpeckers. They will be hungry if they don't peck the wood until they feel dizzy and uncomfortable after they tap the bark to get the insects."

"They have only themselves to thank for that," Little Tashi said sympathetically.

Dawa said in an adult tone, "Second Uncle always says there is in fact no other hell in our world, and this is part of the hell."

"What about us?" Little Tashi asked.

"Part of the hell as well. Man is a perpetually wanting animal and that's why they are so painful. Such as you, aren't you expecting to go to school every day and worrying about losing the chance at the same time?"

Little Tashi went on asking, "What about the sheep of our family?"

"It is said that they are particularly lonely, and even if they are in the flock, they will always feel insecure, hence they have the name deng'zhuo, which means lowering their heads all the time."

"It seems we need to chisel more of the mantra to accumulate good virtues," Little Tashi said as if he had understood a great truth.

"Om ma ni pad me hum"

Dawa finished the last character of the mantra, turned around and said to Little Tashi, "Tashi, stop teasing that silly bird, come over here."

"What's up?" Little Tashi ran over to him.

"I've already done with the chiselling and now that you are the future scholar in our family, please finish the small circle above the last character," said Dawa as he held Little Tashi's hand helping him with the last stroke of the mantra. Little Tashi did his work meticulously and after he finished, he was overcome with emotion and felt as if he had done a very sacred thing. He thought if he could go to school, he would read as many books as he could and then he would be able to explain Buddhist scriptures like Second Uncle or teach students at school like that short-haired female teacher.

At last, on the meadow, just as monasteries did, Little Tashi and Dawa placed the carved stones in the middle of a stone pile and lifted them up facing the spring. To their surprise, a slender white snake suddenly climbed out of the algae-covered pebbles in the spring, crawled to the front of the stones with the mantra on them, hoisted itself and flicked its tongue out, like an arrogant emperor making a tour of his palaces. Then it circled the stone pile a few times and slipped back into the spring at last. Standing there motionlessly, Little Tashi and Dawa didn't know whether it was a bad omen or a good one. Since then, however, Little Tashi and his brother were obsessed by carving the mantra on stones. When they were not herding the flock, they would work on any stones they could find and then pile them beside the spring, like addicts. For some time, the entire valley echoed with the clicking sound of stone carving by the two brothers.

8
THE FLOOD

Little Black Head had grown from a staggering, furry little meatball to a strong and muscular young sheep, but he had been accustomed to sleeping between Little Tashi and Dawa and enjoyed doing that. One night, after the two brothers had penned in the flock, finished their dinner, and went to sleep on the kang, Little Black Head, shaking his head, played with them for a while, and then, exhausted, stretched his legs and slept comfortably. Little Tashi and Dawa snored. The sky at that time was clear and the moon hung high in the sky, but when it was very late at night, dark clouds gathered suddenly, lightning flashed and thunder rolled. The two brothers were startled by the noise and raised their heads to take a look, and Little Black Head stood up drowsily at the same time. The thunder roared, deafening, and the lightning flashed in the night sky like silver satin making the whole world turn black then white, which was indeed very terrifying. Then, the whole world seemed to collapse, wind blowing, heavy rain pouring down and the cabin creaking above their heads, as if it would fall apart at any time. Little Black Head had never experienced such a horrible thing in his life, and he shook his tail and bleated all the time. He then suddenly fell and emitted a string of tiny droppings and a few drops of urine. Little Tashi and Dawa were panic-stricken too and huddled together with a leather jacket covering their heads. Then they found Little Black Head was circling on the kang, so they pulled him over and hugged him inside the cover too.

The old dog tied outside the cabin couldn't withstand the attack of the heavy storm and howled bitterly, but after a while, the sound of thunder, rain and wind mixed together and suppressed the cry of the old dog. The flock in the sheep pen remained silent as if they were enduring a disaster. Ewes and young lambs that used to bleat noisily were soundless too, like they were shutting their mouths during a fast. When Little Tashi and Dawa worried about the inside of the cabin, a lightning bolt appeared abruptly on the upper left corner of the forest, and immediately the cabin was brightly lit, inside and out. Shortly afterwards, a loud bang exploded in the bushes behind the sheep pen, leaving the whole earth quaking. The trembling cabin, like an old man who had suffered from stroke, tilted to the left, by about 30 degrees and the gale slammed the door wildly.

Little Tashi blacked out and, when he came to, his ears were ringing. After a while, he could hear nothing but a humming sound. Then he recovered, and in the darkness, he reached out for Dawa but found that he was no longer under the jacket beside him. Little Tashi put on his leather jacket, jumped off the kang, and went out of the cabin. He found some sheep had jumped out of the pen and run to the foot of the mountain after being frightened by the heavy rain and thunder. In the heavy downpour, Dawa was standing in front of the pen screaming and gesturing at him, but Little Tashi couldn't hear anything as his ears were still ringing. Through Dawa's gestures he understood what Dawa meant. He went back into the cabin and tried to find the raincoat, but he didn't remember where they had put it as it hadn't rained for quite a long time. He then grabbed the flashlight from the kang, trotted to the pen and handed it to Dawa while he went to the pen gate to stop the flock. Little Black Head, however, cried bitterly on the kang, so Little Tashi ran back and whispered in his ear, "Little Black Head, don't be afraid. Stay here and wait for us, we will be back soon." Little Black Head shivered on the kang, his whole body went limp from fear. Little Tashi pulled him over, then hugged and kissed him, saying, "Little Black Head, be brave! All the lightning and thunder will pass quickly but we shepherds will not." He then put him back on the kang and slipped out through the door. Little Black Head remained silent, standing nervously on the kang.

At this time, the thunder and lightning moved from Lungser to somewhere else and the faint lightning could only be seen on the horizon behind the mountain on the right, while the thunder was dull, like a monster who deliberately suppressed its cry in its throat. Little Tashi, who was still frightened, stood in front of the sheep pen for a while, his legs trembling and his whole body drenched, looking like a scarecrow. Suddenly, he felt his calf was warm as if something was licking it. He looked down, and it was Little Black Head who had slipped out of the cabin and circled around him as if to cheer him up. Just at that moment, the bleating of the flock pierced Little Tashi's ears, especially the non-stop cries of those goats, sounding as if their throats had been cut. Little Tashi picked up Little Black Head hastily, put him back into the cabin, shut the wooden door tightly and fastened the door chain. It was still raining, and the wind was blowing too, but everything seemed to relent a little. Little Tashi stood at the gate of the pen for a while like a statue of a Dharmapala (a protector of Buddhist dharma) while Dawa was driving the runaways back from the foot of the mountain and finally they managed to fence them into the pen.

The frightened brothers, although they had encountered bad weather quite often in the past, had never seen such a tempestuous stormy night with such thunder and lightning. Outside, the rain continued and when they went back to the cabin, Little Black Head stood beside the door waiting patiently like a little hero, which gave the two brothers a warm feeling. They squeezed the rainwater out of their clothes, held Little Black Head and went to sleep on the kang. Listening to the tickling sound of the rain drops, Little Black Head soon fell asleep and then the two brothers slept as well.

When they woke up the next day, it was still raining moderately outside. The roof of the cabin leaked and the puddle inside the cabin had grown into a small lake, with bowls, chopsticks and shoes floating on the surface. The water even flowed to the kang and when Little Tashi and Dawa woke up, half of their bottoms were soaked in the puddle. Little Black Head happily played in the pool when he woke up. Dawa got up from the kang, put on his clothes and went out of the cabin while Little Tashi didn't feel sad at all when he saw the entire cabin was full of water. Instead, he dunked himself in the pool and, in high spirits, played with Little Black Head. He then heard the sigh of Dawa outside the cabin, so he ran out to have a look. Good heavens! The stream in front of the sheep pen had changed into wild flood tumbling in the river bed, the bushes beside the stream were buried under the flood and the roots of some had been pulled out.

Later Little Tashi found what Dawa was amazed at was not the horrible flood in front of them but the cypress tree in the upper left corner of the sheep pen. It used to stand at the foot of the mountain, but now it was split in half by the thunder. Dawa said, "That was the cypress beside the spring where we chiselled the six-character mantra for the first time."

"How could this happen like this?" Little Tashi stared in surprise and then said, "Is it the case that we have annoyed the dragon underground?"

"I am afraid so, but if it is so, why didn't the thunder strike us?"

"Bah! Bah!"

"I told you not to scribble on the stone. The mantra shouldn't have been used, but you just wouldn't listen!"

"But it wasn't me who did this beside the spring. I didn't know how to do it at that time."

"The problem is one of the most important strokes was done by you!"

Little Tashi and Dawa were arguing with each other and the old dog who had gone through a stormy night, put his tail under his hind legs and huddled up, looking like black maize bread. But he didn't neglect his duty and raised his head suddenly to bark towards the flood. Little Tashi followed the bark and saw a man in a raincoat coming towards them on a horse. The worried face of the horseman turned to them and then the man jumped from the horse and limped towards the flood. Little Tashi stared at him and then exclaimed excitedly, "It is Grandpa! Grandpa!"

"Yes, it is Grandpa!" said Dawa as he ran towards the flood.

As the two brothers rushed to the flooded stream, one after another, the flood became wilder like a giant yellow beast which crashed against the bank and splashed onto their bodies violently. Grandpa led the horse to the flooded stream, waving his right hand to motion to them not to come forward. He then took off his shoes, rolled his trousers up to the crotch, and prepared to cross the flooded stream. But the rising flood water stopped him, so he had to ride the horse again and crossed the stream.

Little Tashi came over to hold the reins as Dawa helped Grandpa get down from the horse. Dawa then took over the reins from Little Tashi, and walked the horse to the sheep pen and tied it to the fence. Grandpa picked up Little Tashi, raised him high above his head and put him down slowly. He came to the sheep pen with a smile on his face and looked at the flock saying, "Your grandmother was really worried about you last night. The flock is unimportant, but she was afraid that the flood would sweep you away. So, that's why I am here. She drove me out of our home before dawn to check on you."

"Did it rain heavily in the village as well?" Little Tashi asked innocently.

"Yes!" Grandpa answered with fearful panic.

"Then it might not be our fault," Little Tashi said to himself, as he looked at the split cypress tree in the corner of the pen.

"Look, such a large cypress tree has been struck by lightning like this! Thank the 'Three Jewels' (or 'Three Treasures': the Buddha, the fully enlightened one, the Dharma, the teachings expounded by the Buddha and the Sangha, the monastic order of Buddhism that practices the Dharma) that have blessed your peace and safety." Grandpa clapped his hands in devotion, raised them to his forehead and began to murmur scriptures. Little Tashi said, "Grandpa, brother and I chiselled the six-character mantra over there…"

"Tashi, what are you talking about? Hurry and invite Grandpa into the cabin." Dawa interrupted him.

When Little Tashi led Grandpa to the cabin door by his hand, Little Black Head slipped through the door and bounced happily in front of them, as if welcoming Grandpa. Grandpa held him up and raised him high above his head saying, "Look, how strong this young lamb is! You two did a great job!"

Dawa tied up the horse and went inside the cabin, and began scooping water out of the cabin with a plastic bucket. Grandpa sighed, "What a cruel heart your dad has to let you live in such a shabby cabin." With these words, he took off his raincoat, launched into the water and began to scoop water out of the cabin with a pot. Little Tashi joined them with his bowl.

When they had drained all the water out of the cabin, the rain finally stopped and the clouds in the sky began to move southwards, like water bubbling in the pot. The flock in the sheep pen seemed hungry and bleated over and over again. Dawa was tidying up inside the cabin, so Tashi and Grandpa let the flock out and drove them to the small ravine behind the cabin. By noon, a few holes appeared in the clouds above their heads and the sun emerged from one of these holes and shone on the smoking cabin, which at present was steaming like a cooking pot on the stove. Today, Grandpa brought with him some pancakes, made by Grandma, and some Chinese chives and apples as well. They had a generous lunch. The old dog, tied to the stake, also suffered the attack of the storm yesterday, so Little Tashi made him a large bowl of hot zanba porridge as a treat.

The horse tied beside the cabin had to be fed with care because it was Third Uncle's prized possession, named Blackhawk, the best racehorse in the village. Third Uncle was well known for showing off in the village and every year he would take Blackhawk to various horse races and Blackhawk had won him many honours. Blackhawk, therefore, only ate white beans and millet and sure enough Grandpa had brought these for him from home. They all came out to feed Blackhawk. Dawa asked, "Grandpa, Third Uncle himself doesn't have the heart to ride Blackhawk so how could he let you ride him here today?"

"Only for Tashi!" Grandpa said with a pained expression, curling his mouth towards Tashi.

Dawa asked, "Isn't Jiri the youngest daughter of Second Aunt, adopted by Third Uncle? Why should we give Tashi to him?"

"Well, you should know how conceited your Third Uncle is! God didn't give him a son and he didn't want to have a live-in son-in-law and insisted on having a man who would be the head of the family," said Grandpa, frowning.

"No, I want to go to school," Little Tashi said with an innocent look.

Grandpa said to Dawa, "After you dropped out of school, the village cadres came to visit us several times and they wanted Tashi to go to school."

"They are not coming, are they?" Dawa asked.

Grandpa said helplessly, "It is said that Third Uncle bought them off and they didn't come to visit anymore."

"Dad said he would send me to school when they come back from the remote grazing area if I help my brother with the flock and if nothing should happen to the sheep," said Little Tashi in a forceful tone, though he buried his head in his chest.

"Alas, there is your Second Uncle too. He wants you to be a lama and I am afraid it is very hard for your father to make a decision," said Grandpa as he looked at Blackhawk and stroked its head.

In the afternoon, the flood turned from a raging beast into a tender animal. When night fell, however, the three were afraid that Blackhawk might be stolen, so they walked him into the sheep pen. The young lambs were extraordinarily excited when they saw such a huge giant among them and thronged to shuttle through Blackhawk's strong legs, which was quite dangerous as any one of them could be stepped on by Blackhawk's hooves. They had to lead Blackhawk out of the sheep pen and tie him beside the old dog. The old fellow had once worked for Third Uncle and he could be regarded as an old buddy of Blackhawk, but probably Third Uncle had lavished too much care on Blackhawk, so the old dog didn't keep old friends in mind. When Blackhawk was tied beside him, the old fellow shook its tail in an unfriendly manner towards him and barked as if Blackhawk had invaded his territory. They all worried, what if the old dog got mad and bit Blackhawk on the behind? That would indeed drive Third Uncle mad. They had no other choice but to lead Blackhawk into the cabin. It was a small cabin with a low doorway, even a tall person would have to stoop to get through. Blackhawk, who was used to holding his head high, had to follow Grandpa's instruction, and so he lowered its noble head and ducked through the door with a hurt look.

9
RELEASING A GOAT IN THE MONASTERY

In the next few days, Grandpa was haunted by worries. He accompanied Blackhawk every day for fear that the horse might eat something that he should not eat, or would be bitten by some wild beast. He finally decided to go back to the village. Based on the Tibetan calendar, the Choekhor monastery would have almsgiving in April and Little Tashi's family planned to set a goat free during this festival. Grandpa led Blackhawk, walking ahead, while Little Tashi took the chosen ram and followed behind. At the bottom of the valley, they walked along the trail beside the river bed that had been destroyed by the flood, to the mouth of Lungser.

It was a sunny day and the sun hung high overhead. Grandpa and Little Tashi arrived at the mouth of the valley and under the dazzling sun, they saw the green crops waving gently in the soft warm wind. They walked along the path through the field towards the village, but the ram was seduced by the crops and dragged Little Tashi into the field and grazed heartily. Little Tashi strained every muscle to try to pull it back but failed. Grandpa didn't realise anything was wrong until he had ridden Blackhawk for quite a long way. When he turned around he saw the tug of war between Little Tashi and the ram. He rode back to them and shouted at the ram in a commanding tone a few times, but this greedy fellow simply ignored Grandpa and buried its head, still eating. Grandpa had to jump off Blackhawk and pull the ram back from the field with Little Tashi. Little Tashi walked in front holding the rope around the ram's neck tightly while Grandpa, leading Blackhawk, followed behind. Walking for a while, Little Tashi turned back and saw Blackhawk holding his head high and Grandpa limping along beside. That was such a contrast! Little Tashi was concerned about Grandpa and said, "Grandpa, please ride on Blackhawk."

"Yes, you are right. That would be a big loss of face for a horse like Blackhawk if I don't ride him," said Grandpa as he put a foot in a stirrup and jumped onto the horse's back. Blackhawk, however, hopped and threw Grandpa off on to the field beside the path and if Grandpa hadn't held the rein tightly in his hand, he would have had a very nasty knock.

"Grandpa, are you alright?" Little Tashi dropped the rope on the road and hurried to help him up.

"Don't worry. Though I couldn't walk easily, I am still hale and hearty." Grandpa rose to his feet, walked back to Blackhawk, put his left foot into the stirrup and sat on Blackhawk's back. The old ram stood still in the middle of the road when he saw the thrilling scene, as if terrified. Little Tashi hurried back to the ram, grabbed the rope and led the goat, Grandpa on horseback following behind. Little Tashi wondered what was the problem with Grandpa's legs since he was still very strong. He turned back and asked, "Grandpa, what has happened to your legs?"

"Well, it has a long story, and it happened during the Cultural Revolution. The Red Guards forced me to kneel down on the ground to receive public criticism, which is the cause of my knee problems."

"Who were those Red Guards?"

"A bunch of impulsive young people."

"Why did they do this to you?" asked Little Tashi, his black eyes glittering in his innocent face.

Grandpa said, "To destroy the four olds."

"What is the destruction of the four olds?" asked Little Tashi.

"The destruction of the four olds refers to the destruction of old customs, culture, habits, and ideas," Grandpa recited a long paragraph, like he was memorising the scripture.

Little Tashi said, "I don't understand."

"It is alright if you don't understand. In short, the olds were regarded as bad at that time. You know, during that period of time all the sutra recitation halls in the monasteries had been destroyed and all the lamas had been driven home."

"Then why do we have so many recitation halls now? And, so many lamas?"

"Because they were wrong at that time and now everything has been restored to its original appearance."

Little Tashi chatted with Grandpa on the way and when the village was around the corner, a greenish-blue cuckoo landed on the willow beside the road and began chirping melodiously. Little Tashi often heard the singing of cuckoos, but he never saw a real one, so he was overjoyed when the bird appeared, whose singing was so clear and sweet, so pleasant and sonorous. He had thought cuckoos were larger than wild pheasants or sparrowhawks yet the real thing was this bird, not much larger than a yellow warbler or a thrush. He felt it an auspicious sign to encounter a cuckoo and therefore said, "Grandpa, will all the families doing almsgiving in the monastery release a goat?"

"Nope."

"Then why should we do this?"

"To accumulate goodness."

"Why should we accumulate goodness?"

"Because it will not only bless our family but also benefit mankind."

When Little Tashi and Grandpa arrived at the village, the sunshine fell on the well-proportioned village and wisps of smokes rose continuously from the chimneys into the sky. Prayer flags, tied on the wooden shelters on each household's roof, flapped and a burning smell pervaded the street. Third Uncle, who had gold teeth in his mouth, waited somewhat impatiently at the end of the village and when he saw Blackhawk, he came to greet him as if they were brothers who hadn't met each other for 10 years, and then he walked Blackhawk away and disappeared down the gloomy street. When Little Tashi and Grandpa reached home, First Uncle's family, Third Uncle's family, Aunt's family and the relatives of mother's brother's family had all gone to the monastery, except Grandma who was waiting for them at home. Together, they plucked a few hairs from the goat, tied the hair on some unknown and newly planted fruit trees in the yard and went straight to the monastery. Grandpa limped on, but he worried that the goat dragged by Tashi might escape, so he himself led the goat and Little Tashi and Grandma followed behind.

They passed by a straight path in the field of green crops down the village, came to the cement bridge at the foot of the opposite mountain, and went through the small alley into the town. A variety of music and pop songs came from the shops on both sides of the road and the street was alive with people coming and going. When they passed the school, Little Tashi couldn't help stopping to take a look, but only a small window in the upper part of the green iron gate was open. Little Tashi looked at the school through the door and the students happened to be assembled on the playground performing the Kordo dance. (Kordo also means singing and dancing in a circle in the Tibetan language, and it is one of the three Tibetan folk dances.) Little Tashi was so jealous that his staring eyes almost popped out of his head. A moment later, his grandmother pulled him back and said, "We'd better hurry up. Your Grandpa is far ahead."

"Grandma, let me stay here for one more second, please!"

"If you are destined for a better fate than going to school then no one can steal it away. And if not, what's the use of looking at it through the door?"

"I must go to school!"

"Then you could look at it when we are back but right now we really don't have time."

Grandma coaxed Little Tashi to the door of Second Uncle's room in the monastery and the relatives from other villages all crowded inside and outside the room. They surrounded the goat commenting now and then as if it were the first time for them to see a goat, while no one paid any attention to Little Tashi, as if he had been totally forgotten, although he had just came back from the sheep pen in Lungser. Little Tashi hid in the corner, silently missing his parents who were now in the remote grazing area. When Second Uncle saw him unhappily hiding in the corner, he pinched his red face as he used to do and said to him affectionately, "You and Dawa have been really working hard!"

"It's ok." Little Tashi bit his lips, pretending to be strong.

"Come over, I have something delicious for you." Still pinching his face, Second Uncle took Tashi to the shrine in the inner room of the abode. He then took a green apple from the fruit placed in front of the shrine and handed it to Little Tashi, saying, "If you become a lama in the future, you could have the chance to eat this."

"Heh, heh, heh!" Little Tashi smiled shyly.

Second Uncle continued, "You can eat a lot of delicious food given to lamas and have some money too."

"But I want to go to school and after I finish college I can find a job, earn a salary and buy a lot of delicious food," said Little Tashi.

"Even if you could go to school, and even if you could earn a salary, there is no chance for you to accumulate goodness."

"Why can't I?"

"You will get married, have children and spend time looking after your family, having no time to do good."

"Aren't doctors and teachers doing good for others?"

"That is not the same thing. If you become a lama, your life could obtain…" Second Uncle, waving his arms, explained quite a lot to Little Tashi, who however wasn't interested and even grew tired of listening to this. He then asked, "Second Uncle, could you give me three yuan?"

"What do you want to buy?" Second Uncle asked with disappointment.

"I want to buy a pencil box and exercise books when I go back."

"Your parents agree to send you to school?"

"Dad told me if I could take care of the flock with my brother, he would send me to school."

"I don't think your father would be so stupid!"

Second Uncle's face clouded a little bit, but he still fumbled three yuan from his robe and handed it to Little Tashi. When the uncle and the nephew came out of the room, the expressions on their faces made a sharp contrast, one happy and the other sad. Just at this time, Third Uncle riding Blackhawk arrived in front of the house with apparent superiority. He then jumped off the horse, led Blackhawk into the yard, tied him there and forced his way through the crowd. When Second Uncle saw Third Uncle, he said to him very seriously, "Gold Teeth, why did you come so late? The recitation has begun in the hall. Go and get some men to lead the goat there."

"Okay!" Third Uncle squeezed out of the crowd and deliberately shouted, "Where is my son? Where is my son?"

"Stopping talking nonsense. His parents haven't decided yet," said Grandma who was in the crowd, holding Little Tashi in her arms.

"Mother, don't forget, if my brother doesn't give me Little Tashi, I won't regard him as my brother either," said Third Uncle as he was preparing to hold Little Tashi, who however despised him and dodged aside, which embarrassed Third Uncle a little bit. All the relatives present giggled non-stop and Second Uncle cut in and said, "What are you talking about? Tashi will follow me and become a lama."

"Brother, times have changed. Nowadays, how many children are willing to become lamas?"

"Nonsense! It is not the children who don't want to but their short-sighted parents."

"Nope. Now everyone can earn money and live a happy life, and even some lamas in the monastery practise usury all over the place."

"How could you slander so venomously? That is just a few of them."

"Also, if we don't have money, how will we do almsgiving in the monastery? I am afraid if so, we couldn't even afford the food for lamas."

"Just because you have a little money in your pocket, there is no need to stink of it. Be cautious or no one will go and read scriptures in your home."

The whole family burst into laughter as Second Uncle and Third Uncle argued with each other, half jesting and half in earnest. Finally, Grandma said, "The Third, how could you talk to your elder brother like this? He is a lama anyway."

"Mother, Second Brother is the living Buddha in our family, and how dare I argue against him?" said Third Uncle as he went out of the door, shouting at some other uncles and cousins, adding, "Boys, come with me." Third Uncle and a few boys walked ahead with the goat and Grandpa, Grandma and the women in the family walked behind.

There was the philosophy college, the medical college, the Kalachakra college and so on in the Choekhor monastery, amongst which the Kalachakra college was the smallest with no more than 100 lamas living there. When donors came for almsgiving, it would still take half a day to read the scriptures. When it was the time for a meal to be served in the afternoon, the goat, with small pray flags of various colours tied all over its body, hairs and ears, was placed next to the recitation hall where a few older goats happened to be, which at the very beginning remained wary of the newcomer and butted it in an unfriendly way, but after a while they accepted it. From now on, the old ram of Little Tashi's family would have a life of complete renunciation in the monastery.

After the release ceremony, the family of Little Tashi, as the donor to the monastery, could pay tribute at the sutra recitation hall. When it was about noon, with Grandpa holding khata and Tibetan incense in front, the other males in the family, the maternal grandfather, Third Uncle, male cousins, maternal uncles, uncles-in-law, brothers-in-law and Little Tashi, followed behind holding khata and Tibetan incense too, and then the females in the family, Grandma, Second Aunt, sisters-in-law, aunts-in-law and female cousins. The whole family marched in procession through the door at the right hand side and entered the gloomy hall. The auditorium hall was illuminated by butter lamps placed around the hall and hundreds of lamas sat cross-legged on the rugs placed there neatly and orderly, whose loud and clear chanting of scriptures echoed in the hall and in the sky outside. The entire monastery was filled with a sacred and solemn atmosphere. Little Tashi in the midst of his family members looked at statues made from gold, silver, copper, wood or mud and murals of Buddha painted with rich colours, either with kindly faces or infuriated ones, and he, imitating the adults, clasped his palms, and kowtowed to the statues and murals, one by one. When he arrived in front of the gold-plated statue of Great Buddha in the middle of the hall, he offered khata and the yuan Second Uncle had given to him as the support money to the Great Buddha and kowtowed again and again. After that, he followed the procession and turned left. The whole family was bursting with happiness and satisfaction after they had paid tribute to the Great Buddha and gone back to the entrance of the sutra recitation hall.

After lunch, a lama with a moustache came to the crowd sitting on the ground and began to give five yuan to each of them. He then hung a talisman of different colours, yellow, blue, red or green, around everyone's neck as a blessing. Talismans of different colours had special meanings. Yellow was for a lama or the elders, blue for men and green for women; there was no strict requirement for red which could be given to both men and women. The lama with moustache hung a red talisman around Little Tashi's neck, whose mind was on the five yuan, and after the lama put the money in his hands, the distressed young fellow found peace in his heart. At that moment, an old man in rags named A'la came to the crowd and the lama with moustache hung a yellow talisman around his neck. This old man came from the upper village and was said to have been a living Buddha in the past, but his family didn't take good care of him and he therefore became a wasted talent. At present he was homeless, living on the offering food in the monastery and clothes discarded in the sky burial. The whole family greeted the old man with kind jokes when they saw him.

Little Tashi, however, kept thinking about the money he'd been just given all the time. With the three yuan from Second Uncle, he now had eight and he was yearning for the return trip. He wanted to look at the school as much as he could, but after the almsgiving was over, the sun had already sunk in the west. When Little Tashi went back with his grandparents and the other relatives, the school had long been dismissed and the iron gate was closed too. Little Tashi dived into the shop next to the school, ready to buy a pencil box exactly like the one he had seen in the classroom on that film night. That kind of pencil box cost three yuan and Little Tashi thought for a moment and felt a pencil box was not enough, so he also bought a pencil and an exercise book with squared paper. With these, Little Tashi seemed to have become the richest and happiest person in this world and along the way his heart, like the red talisman around his neck, was flying brightly.

Little Tashi would go back to Lungser tonight, so he hurried back to the village. When he arrived at the sheep pen, night fell. Dawa closed the flock into the pen and Little Tashi hung the prayer flag on a pole in front of the pen gate after he sprinkled the blessed holy water, fetched from the monastery, into the pen. In a moment, this brand new flag fluttered in the wind. When he entered the cabin, he took out the delicious food offering from a plastic bag for Dawa and the bright red talisman too. Dawa wore the talisman around his neck and sat beside the stove eating heartily. Little Tashi saw Little Black Head shake his tail and circle around in front of him, and he wondered what he could give to him. From his jacket he took out a bag which contained a few blessed long and thin talismans for sheep that were barren or those that were ill. He opened the bag, picked out a red one and tied it around Little Black Head's neck. The little fellow jumped merrily as if he understood the love his master had for him.

It was getting dark and Little Tashi, like a man with newly acquired wealth who didn't know how to splash his money, squatted on the kang, held a pencil and copied the alphabet on the exercise book carefully under the dim light in the cabin. During that night, inspired by Little Tashi, Dawa and Little Black Head were also very excited, and they stayed with him as he practised writing and didn't go to sleep until midnight.

10
THE SWAN COUPLE

Since Little Tashi and his grandfather released their goat in the monastery, Little Tashi had constantly thought about the monastery. He shared a lot of new things he had seen in the town with Dawa when he came back, hoping to persuade him into herding the flock on the mountain top and then he could look at the school and the students attending class at the foot of the mountain. Dawa used to be quite unwilling to drive the flock to the mountain top in case they grazed on the grass in other villages and caused problems but after he met Dekyi, especially after they had secretly gone to watch a film in the town, Dawa's will had become as soft as clay that could be modelled into any shape that you wanted.

One day, Little Tashi and Dawa drove the flock to the small ravine and climbed along the mountain ridge to the top of the mountain. The vast mountain top seemed to have taken on a new look. The two brothers walked among the plants and trees covered with dew, refreshed by the clean air floating into their noses. Standing on the high, steep slope, they gazed at the small town and monastery at the foot of the mountain, but unfortunately the entire valley behind was embraced with thick but evenly distributed fog and it seemed as if you could step on the morning fog and reach the mountain top opposite. The two walked along the path on the hilltop and arrived at Namtso, where green bushes flourished beside the lake, colourful flowers bloomed and various birds chirped noisily on the twigs of the bushes.

The lake rose and the water had come up from the middle of the lake to the shore, clear and pure, like a mirror placed horizontally above the mountain top, and crystal green, like a beautiful turquoise painting. The white clouds overhead fell into the lake, as if Namtso had become part of the sky. The sun glittered on the water, and a pair of swans played leisurely in the middle of the lake, ripples left behind them forming a beautiful oval, swaying lightly on the surface. What a breathtaking picture! The flock had reached the side of the lake and scattered in threes and fives, like pearls dispersed along the lake. The arrival of the flock disturbed the carefree birds in the bushes and they twittered as they flew up, which brought the bustle of the entire mountain top to its climax.

While Little Tashi was fascinated by the great gift of nature beside the lake, he noticed that Dawa was somewhat anxious, looking back from time to time at the grassland of Gorpa village behind him. At that moment, the swans swam towards them, shaking their heads and dancing on the surface of the water, as if completely absorbed in their own affairs. Little Tashi giggled when he saw that and said, "Brother, Namtso is very large, why don't they play alone while nestling against each other?"

"How should I know?" Dawa answered, a little shyly.

Little Tashi said innocently, yet knowingly, "The way they play with each other looks like something, doesn't it?"

"Stopping talking nonsense. Watch the flock and don't let them run over there. I will go and check whether we have some guests in the cabin," said Dawa standing up.

"Guests? Ha, ha, ha, I am afraid you are going to see someone!" Little Tashi smiled wickedly.

Dawa came to the other side of the mountain top, looked down and found the bottom of the valley was rather dark and quiet. He then felt something pulling his stomach downward, so he squatted among the wattle woods, held his breath and emptied his bowels, after which he felt relived a little. He turned back and looked at his poop, feeling disgusted. He thought, "I am not handsome at all, how could Dekyi have a crush on me? And how could I let her know my feelings?" When he was lost in his thought, a lizard crawled from the grass onto his leg and startled him so that he gave a short scream.

After Dawa left, someone sneaked out of the bushes behind and covered Little Tashi's eyes with hands, "Guess who I am?"

"Do I need to guess?" Little Tashi answered naughtily, "You are Sister Dekyi".

Dekyi appeared in front of Little Tashi like an angel, "Ha, ha! You little boy!"

"Sister Dekyi, why didn't you sing today?" asked Little Tashi with some surprise.

Sadly, Dekyi replied, "Since we all secretly went to the film, my grandpa keeps a firm grip on me, like the way he watches the zanba bag."

"Why did you come here today?"

"To visit you."

"I am afraid you are looking for my brother, aren't you?"

"Well, where is your brother? Why isn't he here?"

"Look, the cat is out of the bag," said Little Tashi with a smile, "Didn't he go and look for you?"

"Oh, I didn't see him," Dekyi said nervously with a flushed face.

The wind on the top of the mountain was indeed different from the one at the bottom of the valley, the former was like a stranger who simply passed by and then came back slowly in the near distance, while the latter was like an old acquaintance whom you probably would not encounter for quite a long time but would be unwilling to let him go after meeting with each other. Suddenly, a gust of wind blew from the top of the mountain and took the red scarf around Dekyi's head away. The two chased after it for a while and at last Little Tashi got it back. He tied the red scarf around his head and ran towards the lake side, looking back halfway and saying to Dekyi, "Am I looking good?"

"Boys shouldn't wear women's stuff or bad luck will come." Dekyi reminded him kindly.

"I welcome bad luck," said Little Tashi, mischievously.

"Nonsense! Give it back to me quickly," said Dekyi as she caught up with Little Tashi.

Little Tashi stopped when he arrived at the lake side and gave the scarf back to Dekyi. Sincerely, he said, "Sister Dekyi, do you know who the owner of the red scarf is?"

"No, I don't know. I found it on a slope on the other side," said Dekyi as she put on the scarf.

Little Tashi looked around for a while, then put his mouth to Dekyi's ear and whispered, "It is my brother's."

"No way! How could he wear a woman's scarf?" said Dekyi with surprise.

"It has a long story," Little Tashi, like a story teller, told all the ins and outs of the red scarf. "In fact, my brother found it at the mouth of Lungser, and I wore it secretly one day but unfortunately the eagle…"

Dawa suddenly appeared from the bushes behind them and scolded Little Tashi. "You little brat! You do have a big mouth, didn't you?"

After Dawa came back, the three fell silent and the tension mounted. At that time, they found the flock in the bushes was dwindling and it seemed that some of them had slipped onto the grass of Dekyi's village.

Dawa stared at his younger brother with a sullen expression and said, "Tashi, go and drive the flock back quickly."

Dekyi immediately came to Tashi's rescue. "It's alright. My grandpa has gone back to the village today."

Dawa said to Tashi with a commanding look, "No, it is not ok. Each village has its grassland and how could we steal from others?"

"Ok, I will do it," said Little Tashi and stood up without any hesitancy. Had it been on another day, Tashi would have never agreed to do this, but he felt guilty about what he had just done.

Little Tashi whipped into the bushes behind. The bushes, formed by rhododendrons and cypress trees, looked to be densely woven from afar, but once entered, there was still plenty of room to move around. In the bushes, Little Tashi heard a rustling sound of some sheep walking on the mountainside, and then hurried to follow them. He, however, felt apprehensive and hesitated a little bit because it was after all the grassland of the other village, and his heart was thumping, as if he had got butterflies in his stomach. When he remembered that Dekyi's grandpa was not here, he was much relieved. He ventured to move on and rushed towards the sound of the flock.

Down the mountainside, there was a marshy grassland that connected the forest and the bushes, and the flock, as if deliberately revealing where they were, slipped onto the meadow and bowed their heads grazing in a leisurely manner. There happened to be no fog below the marshy grassland and from here the rivers, fields, dirt roads in the distant mountain and the small town and the monastery at the foot of the valley were clearly invisible, as well as some part of Gonpa village. Little Tashi was afraid that people of Gonpa village might see the flock, so he picked up stones, showered them on the flock and drove them to the bushes on the mountain top. Then he hid quietly in the space between the meadow and the bushes, gazing towards the monastery. He happened to see the goat his family had released in the monastery following some elders who were turning the prayer wheels on the circumambulation. He shouted out in delight.

He thought the old goat would not feel lonely since it had become a real delight for all the people who came to turn the prayer wheels, but maybe one day it would run back to the pen in Lungser when it thought of the flock, thought of Dawa and him. But he also felt, since the old ram had become the released goat, the deified goat, how could it be worldly-minded still? Little Tashi stared at it for a while and then moved his eyes to the town school. On the campus hung a red flag, similar to the prayer flag in his family but, probably because the wind at the bottom of the valley was not as strong as the one on the mountain, the flag didn't flutter in the air but flapped a little in the breeze. The campus was empty, except for a few teachers moving around and students might have classes right now. The bottom of the valley was not very far away but the sounds of the river automobiles, and cries of people mixed together made it difficult to distinguish sounds from each other. Very soon, the sound of reading aloud broke through the mingling noises and reached Little Tashi's ears clearly, filling the young fellow with envy and made him anxious to climb down the mountain and join them in the classroom. The monastery and the town were so close to each other that although Little Tashi was very reluctant, he couldn't help but cast his gaze on the mani temple donated by Third Uncle and then broke out in a cold sweat. Third Uncle travelled through lanes doing jewellery business and made a lot of money; his Blackhawk had found no match for miles around, but Third Uncle had not been content with what he had, and just like the gold teeth he had in his mouth, he always wanted recognition from others. What confused Little Tashi most was why didn't Third Uncle have a child since he had donated such a big mani temple to the monastery?

With mixed feelings of joy and sorrow, Little Tashi led the flock to

Namtso and the morning mist at the bottom of the valley had dispersed gradually. The blue sky was cloudless and the green land surrounded by mountains was bathed in the solitary sunlight as if it were covered with a thin layer of golden yarns. Little Tashi drove the flock to Lungser and then he came to the bushes beside the lake, secretly. The golden sunshine fell on the middle of the lake, ripples on the surface glittering and the swan couple nestling against each other. Dawa and Dekyi sat side by side beside the lake, looking at the swans in front of them, as if they were confiding something to each other. The whole scene presented itself as a beautiful picture.

> *On the surface of Yamdrok Yutso lake,*
> *With goslings, mother goose swam,*
> *No calling for mum, little goslings,*
> *For it reminds me of my mum.*

Little Tashi sneaked into the bushes behind them, eavesdropping for a while. Dekyi sang this folk song in a low voice and Dawa applauded in a shy manner and said, "Your singing is so sweet!"

"I am not that good at singing, but this song used to be the one my mum liked to sing the most," said Dekyi wistfully.

"Why?"

"Everyone who went on a pilgrimage to Lhasa was said to sing this song when they passed the Yamdrok Yutso."

"The journey to Lhasa was too long ago and when the pilgrims saw such a beautiful scene, it simply evoked strong memories."

"It might be, but I just couldn't understand why should swans live in pairs instead of living in a group?"

"They might not want to be disturbed."

"Swans are probably the most punctual birds and they always arrive at the same time every year and fly away at the same time as well."

"Yes, this time next year they will fly back again with little swans."

"There are so many different kind of birds but why are swans the most beautiful?"

"When I was still at school, I always heard a story called *The Ugly Duckling*."

"Brother Dawa, tell me the story please."

"It was said that a goose had given birth to an ugly duckling and all the other ducklings looked down upon him, and even the mother goose turned away from him. The ugly duckling was very sad. Later, the ugly duckling met a group of swans and he admired them so much that he followed them every day. After a period of hard life, the ugly duckling finally became a real swan."

"I want to be this ugly duckling."

"Yes, the ugly duckling will become a beautiful swan."

Little Tashi had not intended to bother them, but it was his nature to be naughty and it was hard to change it. He threw a stone heavily into the lake and the swan couple was startled and clattered noisily while beside the lake, Dawa and Dekyi stood up in panic yet kept a certain distance, as if to hide something, but after a while smiles of happiness reappeared on their faces.

11
THE SCAPEGOAT

For days on end, Dekyi's family's flock of sheep would run from the other side of the mountain to the small valley, and sometimes they would even go down the mountain to the ridge that flourished with bushes behind the sheep pen and the small valley to the east. The two flocks mixed together, unwilling to part from each other, and Dawa and Dekyi became inseparable too, as if tied together by an invisible rope. Little Tashi always had a feeling that things would go wrong if they continued like this. He reminded Dawa a few times but Dawa simply turned a deaf ear to him. Every day Little Tashi would kneel beside the kang and practise writing the alphabet in his exercise book. Now he could write not only the 30 Tibetan letters but also the numbers from one to 10 he had learned from his brother.

One day when the night had just fallen, Little Tashi and Dawa fenced the flock into the sheep pen. They didn't feel any wind, but the prayer flags in front of the pen gate were fluttering noisily all the time and the old dog barked at the opposite path a few times as if he himself couldn't understand why he did this. The two brothers felt something might go wrong, but they didn't know what it was all about. They went back into the cabin and lit the fire in the stove. In the twilight, a cloud of smoke rose from the roof of the cabin and a touch of life was finally added to the restless air.

The horns on Little Black Head had grown longer and this lovely young lamb had changed into a big one which began to sleep with his mum in the pen and only occasionally slipped into the cabin and snuggled with Dawa and Tashi for a night on the kang. The cabin therefore, seemed to lack a certain vitality, but the two brothers could sleep soundly during the night without worrying about Little Black Head.

Bang!

Suddenly, a stone hit the roof of the cabin heavily and the cabin trembled a bit. Little Tashi and Dawa, though feeling somewhat nervous, thought it might be a rolling stone from the mountain and ignored it. One of them was rolling the dough on the edge of the kang, and the other was boiling water beside the stove.

Bang!

After a while, another stone hit the cabin and this time the cabin creaked after trembling for a while, from which you could tell how forceful the hit on the roof had been. At this moment, the old dog, dragging its chain, began barking towards the ridge behind. Little Tashi and Dawa went out of the cabin and saw a shadow standing on the ridge behind the cabin. In the twilight, they couldn't see its appearance clearly, but from its body shape and movement, it was obviously Grandpa Humpback. When he came over to the two brothers, Dawa asked him in surprise, "Grandpa Humpback, what did you come here for?"

"What did I come here for? Where is my goat?"

"What goat?"

"A ram is missing from my flock and I could not find it anywhere on the mountain."

"But neither of us has ever seen it."

"These days my cheeky Dekyi always drives the flock to your grassland and the entire Lungser is a desolate place except for you two. So, to whom else should I go and ask?"

"Then please come down to check our sheep pen."

"That's exactly what I am thinking right now."

The old dog barked at first and then he noticed his masters were talking with this ugly old man, and he therefore suppressed his voice and remained silent; God knows whether it was because he was scared, or simply out of courtesy. Grandpa Humpback came to the gate of the pen, pulled it open with his left hand and looked inside for a moment. It seemed he didn't find his ram, so he went into the flock like a clumsy brown bear. The flock saw a stranger inside their group and began to run back and forth, which greatly dazzled Grandpa Humpback and made it completely impossible for him to find his ram. He said ironically as he walked out of the pen, "The thief wouldn't hide his stolen goods in his own sheep pen."

"Look, I told you so. Now is there nothing you can do to regain your reputation?" whispered Little Tashi to his brother.

Though Grandpa Humpback looked as if his five sensory organs were not working, he did have sharp hearing. He shouted furiously, "What are you muttering about? Never dare to think about transferring the stolen goods. Where on earth did you hide it? I will find it, dead or alive."

"No, we haven't. Why don't you believe us?" Dawa glared at Little Tashi beside him and then turned to this old man with a jerky smile.

Grandpa Humpback, quite assertive, went into the cabin and walked about, finding nothing unusual. He then checked the roof of the cabin, the bushes around the pen, and even both sides of the stream on the opposite but found no clue at all. The old man was unwilling to give up. He returned to the pen gate and asked, "Where did you hide the stolen goat?"

"We didn't steal your goat, and that's the truth."

"You'd better tell me the truth, or I will report to your village. Then it won't simply be an issue between you and my family but one between two villages."

"Grandpa…" Little Tashi was ready to say something for fear that things should get worse, but the words stuck in his throat as he glanced at Dawa.

"What's matter, boy? Tell me. You know no one should tell lies, adults or kids."

Dawa said helplessly, "Well, go ahead and out with it."

"Grandpa, my brother and sister Dekyi are in love with each other, how could we steal your goat?" said Little Tashi innocently.

Grandpa Humpback ground his yellow teeth, "What did you say?"

"He said…" Dawa wanted to change the topic but failed to find a proper word for the time being.

"I heard it and you should not tell lies!" said Grandpa Humpback as he suddenly grabbed Dawa with his left hand, held him down to the ground, slapped him a few times on his face and stammered angrily, "I knew there was something strange though Dekyi never admitted it. Well, you two confessed without being pressed."

"Grandpa Humpback, we have done nothing! We are innocent!" said Dawa as he managed to escape from his grip.

"You are a toad who tries to eat swans!" Grandpa Humpback chased after him and said viciously, "If you dare come back tonight, I will take off your legs and make a cripple out of you!"

"Grandpa Humpback, why did you beat my brother?" Little Tashi cried, feeling grieved for his brother and also very guilty about his big mouth.

"How bold you are! Not only meddling in my family's affairs but you also stole our goat!"

Grandpa Humpback chased Dawa to the forest and then he walked back slowly, talking to himself, and vanished into the small valley behind. Looking at his disappearing back, Little Tashi felt Grandpa Humpback resembled a crawling beast, though he couldn't exactly figure out what kind of beast it was. He wondered how the ugly Grandpa Humpback could have such a beautiful granddaughter like Dekyi. He was quite sure that Dekyi must have inherited her beauty from her grandmother.

Goodness knows where Dawa hid or whether Grandpa Humpback lay in ambush nearby or had climbed over the mountain and gone back to his cabin. Little Tashi had no idea about what to do. He went back silently to the cabin and squatted on the threshold, waiting for a while. Nothing was stirring, there was only the croaking of frogs and chirps of grasshoppers from the dark bushes on the opposite and also the gurgling sound of the stream in the near distance. Little Tashi crossed the stream, reached the mountain road and, lowering his voice called softly towards the forest, "Brother, where are you?" There was no response in the darkness, except that a fox looking for food nearby was startled and jumped from the bushes. Little Tashi had to go back to the cabin. The oil lamp was still burning dimly, but the fire in the stove was out. Little Tashi sat at the edge of the kang waiting for his brother and in a minute he fell asleep. When he woke up, he found himself lying on the kang and it was his brother who had put him there. Little Tashi peeked at his brother and said, "Brother, why did you come back so late?"

"I thought Grandpa Humpback had hidden behind the cabin," said Dawa, as if still frightened.

Little Tashi said, "Brother, what have you done to sister Dekyi? Why did

Grandpa Humpback get so mad at you?"

"I did nothing!" said Dawa, as he extinguished the dying oil lamp.

Little Tashi continued, "You must have done something bad to sister Dekyi."

"We only dated a couple of times," said Dawa in a pathetic tone as he buried his head in his leather jacket.

Little Tashi asked, "Brother, do you like sister Dekyi?"

"Huggggh..." Dawa snored. Goodness knows whether he was simply pretending, or he had indeed fallen soundly asleep.

The next day, when Little Tashi and Dawa got up and went out of the cabin, ready to let the flock out of the pen, they found a group of vultures resting on the ridge of the mountainside behind the pen. They drove the flock to the small valley and then climbed onto the ridge to check what was going on there. It turned out that these vultures were pecking on a broken body of a dead ram. They drove off the vultures and searched for the remains of the ram in order to bring these to Grandpa Humpback to prove their innocence, but the vultures had only left some limbs and the head of the ram, and they had no choice but to bear these to the mountain top. They had thought Grandpa Humpback or Dekyi would be herding sheep on the mountain top, but nobody was there. Looking from the top of the mountain, they could see part of the pen of Dekyi's family on the ridge of the mountainside surrounded by bushes at the left corner. Dawa said to Little Tashi, "You take the limbs and the head to their pen and tell them we didn't steal their goat."

"I dare not. Grandpa Humpback will kill me."

"Compared with losing his goat, he hated me dating Dekyi more. You go and see him; he wouldn't do something horrible to you."

"Let's go together."

"Why are you being so annoying? Had it not been for your big mouth, Grandpa Humpback wouldn't have been so mad at me."

"No! Even if it is so, I am afraid to go."

Little Tashi had to go to Dekyi's pen after he argued with Dawa for almost half a day. He went through the bushes that were flourishing with rhododendrons, from the mountain gap towards the pen. The nearer he approached her family, the more nervous he was, and his heart thumped so violently that it seemed that it was about to jump out of his throat. He panted when he arrived at the edge of Dekyi's pen. On the sunny slope below the pen stood a little cabin with a roof, and considering the materials, structure and style, the two brother's cabin was no match to it. Little Tashi stepped on the grass beside the pen and stood in front of the cabin, whose door was half-open, but it was silent inside, as if it had been vacant for quite a long time. In front of the cabin lay a mother dog like a corpse, with three lovely puppies playing beside her. The dog raised her head, barked a few times when she saw Little Tashi and then put her head down to carry on sleeping.

Seeing that, Little Tashi thought no wonder such a dog didn't take good care of the flock! "Is anybody here?" he asked in a low voice. Perhaps his voice was too low as no one answered, but Little Tashi seemed to hear that someone was crying inside the cabin. He pricked up his ears, listening carefully, feeling the sound was quite familiar. So, he asked again, "Sister Dekyi, is that you?"

"Who is out there?" shouted Dekyi from inside the cabin.

"It is Little Tashi."

Dekyi walked out of the cabin, wiping away her tears and asked, "Why did you come here?"

"Is your grandpa at home?" asked Little Tashi, nervously.

"No, he is out," Dekyi shook her head.

"Look…" hearing that Grandpa Humpback wasn't at home, Little Tashi's voice became a little higher. He held the head of the ram up and asked, "Do you recognise this?"

"What's this?"

"The head of your lost ram."

"Where did you find it?"

"On the ridge behind our pen."

Dekyi ran over to him and looked at the head carefully with a mixed expression of joy and sorrow on her face, and then she placed the ram's head on the horizontal bar in front of the window and led Little Tashi into the cabin. The dog smelled the meat and got up from the ground. She came to the ram head, sniffing. The three little puppies followed their mum and smelled with their tiny noses. One of the puppies was probably choked by the smell of blood and kept sneezing.

Little Tashi entered the cabin and looked around curiously. Everything inside the cabin was in order, and even the pot and bowls on the stove were placed in a tidy manner. On the kang, quilts and leather jackets were stacked neatly, and on the wooden box inside the cabin stood a temporary statue of Buddha, in front of which were placed some sweets and a burning butter lamp. Dekyi put a basket of buns in front of Little Tashi and poured a bowl of the black tea that her grandpa loved for him to drink. Little Tashi held the bowl, enjoying the bun and the tea, but he was still worried for fear that Grandpa Humpback might suddenly appear from somewhere. He asked nervously, "Sister Dekyi…?"

"What?"

Little Tashi had wanted to ask about her grandpa, but he changed his mind and said, "I heard you crying just now, what happened?"

"Well, last night when my grandpa came back, he gave me a good scolding, right to my face," said Dekyi, mournfully.

Little Tashi said, somewhat guiltily, "I am sorry for that."

"Why?"

Little Tashi buried his head into his chest and dares not look at Dekyi. "I told your grandpa about you and my brother yesterday."

"It's not your fault. You know, since I was born, I have been left behind with my grandpa and that's why he has been very strict with me." Once Dekyi opened her mouth, she became excited.

Little Tashi asked, "Then, where did your grandpa go?"

"Grandpa at first thought it was your brother who had stolen the goat, but he felt he might be wrong after he had gone to your pen. So, he went to visit the living Buddha in the monastery early this morning, for some advice."

Little Tashi then asked with some eagerness, "Does that mean your grandpa doesn't blame my brother anymore?"

"It's hard to say," said Dekyi, worried.

Little Tashi said, innocently, "I have brought the ram's head over and it helps, doesn't it?"

"I am afraid it might make the whole thing more suspicious."

"What should I do then?"

"A ram's head can't prove anything. Take it back with you and pretend as if nothing has happened."

Little Tashi felt confused, as if he had received a heavy blow on his head. He didn't know whether it was correct or not for him to bring back the head and the limbs, but he had to listen to Dekyi's plan and so he headed for the mountain top with the remains of the ram.

12
MOTHER YELLOW WARBLER AND HER CHICKS

Dawa rarely herded the flock to the mountain top after he had been accused by Grandpa Humpback. Instead, he always drove the flock to the small ravine on the upper left or the steep mountain ridge on the right. Little Tashi, therefore, could only do his "homework" near the pen. One morning, when he woke up, it had rained moderately the night before and the rain, dripping down from the leak in the roof, dropped onto his notebook and blurred the letters and numbers he had written down. He left the notebook in the sun on the fence but forgot to take it back during the night. The next day, unfortunately, some sheep with growling stomachs, seized and ate the notebook and only a few damaged pages were left. Little Tashi was very sad for a few days and was no longer interested in practising writing anymore.

One day, a bored Little Tashi came to fetch some water in the small stream with a plastic bucket and when he looked at his own reflection in the crystal-clear stream, he saw some discharge in the corner of his eyes and wiped them away. Then he saw his fluffy and slightly curly hair on his head; he folded his hands up and dipped into the water, ready to wash his hair.

He then saw a white cloud in the blue sky had crowned his head in the reflection and he would rather he look a little bit ugly than spoil the beautiful picture. He thoroughly enjoyed this image as if he had entered a quiet and tranquil Shangri La when suddenly two startled yellow warblers flew out of the wattle bushes between the sheep pen and the stream.

Disappointed, Little Tashi raised his head and looked at the two birds, believing there was sure to be a nest hidden inside. He threw the plastic bucket beside the stream, came close to the bushes, looked inside and indeed, there was a yellow warbler's nest, inside of which three eggs that were about to be hatched, lay silently. Bored, Little Tashi felt a strong desire for the nest, but he urged himself to leave at once. When he held the bucket and went back to the cabin, he turned back and spotted a sparrowhawk hovering above. Little Tashi picked up a stone and threw it towards the sparrowhawk, but it seemed the hawk didn't fear it at all and dived towards the nest. When the mother yellow warbler saw this, she hurriedly covered the nest with her soft wings to protect the eggs, chirping loudly as if cursing the hawk and asking him to stay away from her nest and the father yellow warbler flew into the sky like a fighter and hit the hawk with his body. The battle between the father and the fierce hawk was like the battle between an egg and a rock, but each dive of the imperious hawk was blocked by the father yellow warbler. The enraged sparrowhawk landed on the nearby willow, shook his head and stared with fierce, deadly eyes at the father yellow warbler that perched on the edge of the bird's nest.

Little Tashi was stunned by this breathtaking scene and he didn't know how to deal with it for the time being. The sparrowhawk right now was hovering in the sky, but it was obvious that his target was not the eggs in the nest but the father yellow warbler that dared to challenge him. The father was also equal to the occasion and flew from the wattle tree to the willow, displaying an air to fight. The sparrowhawk swooped down from the sky and fought with the father yellow warbler. The father, though fighting bravely, was no rival to the sparrowhawk and a few rounds later his feathers fell like drifting snowflakes. A moment later, the yellow warbler father fell from the willow branches and hit the ground heavily. In a rage, Little Tashi took out his slingshot and shot at the sparrowhawk but the sly sparrowhawk dodged and disappeared quickly. Little Tashi ran to the willow tree and found the battered father yellow warbler struggling on the ground for a while and then he died, with his tiny beak and claws open. Poor father yellow warbler! Though he had managed to protect the eggs in the nest, he had died so tragically but heroically.

Seeing this, Little Tashi ran back to the cabin, grabbed his slingshot, went back to the bushes again and shot a few times in different directions to vent his grief. However, he failed to hit the sparrowhawk but startled the sparrows and thrushes on the willow trees nearby, causing them to twitter noisily and fly aimless over the branches. Little Tashi picked up the body of the father yellow warbler from under the willow and planned to feed it to the old dog but the grieving mother yellow warbler seemed unwilling to let her lover's body be ravaged. She flew over from the nest, fell beside the father and crowed with grief. Little Tashi knew the wisest choice for him to make was to leave this sentimental place at this moment. He turned around and headed for the pen but only a few steps away, he heard the grieving tweets of the mother yellow warbler. He looked back at once and saw the mother yellow warbler was pushing the dead body to the stream with her tiny beak, in fits and starts. When she reached the edge of the stream, she pushed the dead body of the father into the water. There was no heavy rain for days and the stream was neither wide nor deep, but the slight waves lifted the body of the father yellow warbler anyway and carried him away at last.

This incident sowed self-blame and sympathy in the young heart of Little Tashi because his mother often told him that all living things were born equal, birds or insects, tigers or leopards, and we shouldn't hurt birds and insects and we shouldn't be afraid of tigers and leopards either. For days, Little Tashi looked quite upset; Dawa had seldom seen him like that. He asked the reason but Little Tashi simply shook his head and said nothing. Dawa didn't inquire into it further anyway. Since then Little Tashi took his slingshot with him all the time and hung around the nest to protect the mother yellow warbler and her babies, and he wouldn't allow anything or anyone to approach the nest, no matter whether it was a sparrowhawk, black eagle, a weasel, or even a crow.

Nothing is impossible for a willing heart. A few days later, in the nest among the wattle bushes, the baby yellow warblers opened their yellow beaks wide and cheeped eagerly as they emerged from their shells. Little Tashi was so eager to see these little fellows, but when he thought of the thrilling scene on that day, he dared not to step closer. Every day after he cleaned up the sheep pen and finished all the housework, he would come close to the nest, quietly listening to the tweeting of the baby birds. The mother yellow warbler also regarded Little Tashi as one of her family members and whenever she went back to the nest with insects, she was not afraid of Little Tashi who squatted on the ground looking at them. Each time when the mother came back to feed her babies, the three little chicks all chirped eagerly and Little Tashi was very envious when he saw that. In the past when Dawa studied at school, Little Tashi lived and grew up with his parents and sister in the remote grazing area, so when he saw the happiness of the bird family, he couldn't help thinking of his mother whom he hadn't seen for a long time. Tears burst forth from his eyes.

One day, he watched the mother yellow warbler feeding the three baby birds and amid their merry chirps, Little Tashi lay on the meadow beside the wattle tree and fell asleep. In a dream, he went back to the remote grazing land but there was nobody in the pasture and no cattle in the barn. Little Tashi thought his parents must have been taken away by the wolves and he trembled with great fear, crying loud and searching for them everywhere. He searched all the neighbouring grassland but in vain. Then he climbed over the mountains, crossed the deep furrows, and walked through the dense forests and narrow valleys. Suddenly, he saw their cattle gathering on the edge of a cliff and it seemed they were going to fall to the abyss. Little Tashi cried bitterly as he ran to the cliff but when he reached there, all the cattle fell off the cliff.

At that time, he found his mother was calling him at the foot of the cliff. He jumped off the cliff without any hesitation but when he was falling down, he felt terrified and woke up from this nightmare, shouting "Mum!" all the time. Dawa happened to arrive at the gate of the pen and heard Little Tashi's cry from the meadow below, so he came to him and asked, "Hey, Tashi, are you alright?"

"I had a nightmare."

"Don't you know what time it is? Why didn't you set the fire and cook?"

"I will do it straight away."

Little Tashi ran out of the meadow and found the three lovely baby birds setting on the edge of the nest, so lovely and charming. He waved to Dawa and signalled him to come over quietly. Dawa came gently to Little Tashi and asked in a low voice, "What's the matter?"

"Look," Little Tashi pointed at the three little birds on the branches.

Dawa said contemptuously, "Just three baby birds! I don't see anything special about them."

"They are no ordinary baby birds," Little Tashi told the whole miserable story about the mother yellow warbler and her babies to Dawa.

"Why didn't you tell me earlier?"

"I am afraid one more pair of eyes means more danger to the baby birds."

"You boy! You are starting to grow up!"

"Heh, heh, heh…"

"Though you have done a good deed, empty bags cannot stand up! Go and set the fire!"

In the next few days, the three baby birds grew thicker feathers and they began jumping here and there on the wattle branches, and then fluttered down to the ground, learning how to fly. They made progress every day and before long, they could not only fly back to the nest from the ground but had also learned how to peck insects.

The young birds had been hatched and they had also learned how to be independent, so Little Tashi lost his vigilance for sparrowhawks. But one afternoon when the sunlight shone lazily on different corners in the valley, a sparrowhawk flew from the near distance and hovered maliciously above the nest of the mother yellow warbler and her babies while all the other birds and insects were hiding in their nests enjoying the coolness. Little Tashi pulled back the rubber bands of his slingshot, ready to shoot the sparrowhawk but he wanted to see first how the three young birds faced the enemy which had killed their father. The sparrowhawk hovered above the nest for a while and then swooped down. Now, the three young birds were not to be bullied anymore. Under the command of their mother, they flew here and there among the wattle branches and made the attack of the sparrowhawk futile. The sparrowhawk spread his claws and charged towards one of the young birds, which dodged aside cleverly while the sparrowhawk fell and got himself stuck in the thorns of the wattle trees. He thumped for a while but failed to get away and then was caught by Little Tashi who happened to be around.

Little Tashi caught the sparrowhawk, pricked with thorns all over his body, tied his feet with a thin string of rope and locked him in the cabin, waiting for Dawa to bring judgement on him. After Dawa came back, Little Tashi's heart softened and he persuaded Dawa instead, "Brother, look at the thorns on his body. He has parents and children too. Let's set him free, shall we?"

"No, we can't let him go like this."

"Then what should we do with him?"

"The sparrowhawk, though he committed a hideous crime, we couldn't punish him ourselves. The old dog hasn't had meat for several days, let's feed it to him."

"What if the old dog doesn't eat it?"

"The old dog will lick his mouth when he smells the meat, how could he refuse to eat?"

"Feed it alive to the old dog?"

"Of course."

Dawa tied the rope around the sparrowhawk's claws on the old dog's stake and threw the hawk to the old fellow. The old dog smelled the struggling poor bird and lay on the ground somewhat unsatisfied, as if to say he himself was a dog and how could he eat this for nothing? Little Tashi said, "Hey, this sparrowhawk indeed has a blessed life!"

"Nope. The old dog didn't even look at it."

"You won't kill the bird yourself, will you?"

"No, I won't. Eating this carnivorous devil will bring more sins. Let it go."

"Will it come back again and prey on innocent birds later?"

"Even if it doesn't, the other sparrowhawks will."

"Why?"

"Because sparrowhawks are birds' natural enemies."

"But eagles, black eagles, wildcats and even we kids would kill birds, does it mean that we are all the natural enemies of birds?"

"Not really. There is a story about it."

"Brother, tell me the story, please."

"A long time ago it was said that sparrowhawks were horrible man-eating birds which only preyed on little children. A couple had a son and they took good care of him and never let him be alone. But during the busy season, they had to work in the field, so they left their son in the yard when they worked in the field."

"The son was eaten by the sparrowhawk?"

"Yes. When the couple came back home from the field, they found their son had been eaten. They were crushed by the death of their son and refused to go out for a few days, thinking about how to take revenge for their son. The farmer was a wise and far-sighted person and he thought even if he could kill the sparrowhawk this time, they would still come and hurt people. So, he came up with a good idea.

"What was his idea?"

"The farmer went and found the sparrowhawk and instead of getting mad at it, he said to the devil quietly, 'You like eating kids, do you? Eating children is no fun indeed. Let's make a bet and if you win, you can eat me, but if you lose, you promise you will not eat children from now on.' The sparrowhawk asked the farmer what they would bet on."

"Yes, what did they bet on?"

"The farmer took out a stone skull he had long prepared and placed it on the ground, saying, 'If you can peck the human skull to pieces, you win and if not, you lose.' The arrogant sparrowhawk nodded his head at once and then he came over to the skull and began to peck on it with its hook-like beak. It turned out that the sparrowhawk failed to peck down on any piece, let alone smash it."

"The sparrowhawk was sure not to admit his defeat, wasn't it?"

"No, the sparrowhawk, as an unruly carnivorous bird, felt the shame of losing face and his dignity in front of the farmer and he promised him that from now on they would never eat human children, but…"

"But what?"

"Though we human beings have escaped the disaster, birds have to suffer. Sparrowhawks began to eat bird eggs and baby birds from then on."

"So, the poor father yellow warbler died for us humans too!"

"Sort of."

"We humans should keep our promise. Let's set it free."

The two brothers untied the rope on the sparrowhawk's claws and released it back into the sky. Within a moment, the lucky fellow had flown to the forest opposite.

The three baby birds grew healthy and stronger every day and Little Tashi could occasionally came to look at the nest in the lively wattle trees when he accompanied his brother herding the flock or after he finished the housework. But one day, when Little Tashi held the plastic bucket to fetch water in the stream, he felt the wattle trees that used to be so lively were strangely silent.

He was curious about this and came closer, quietly, to take a look. The nest on the branches was empty and it had been spoiled by other birds already. It seemed that the three baby birds had moved to other places to build their nests and find their food when they grew up. Seeing the messy empty nest, a feeling of loneliness arose in Little Tashi's heart and he who hadn't seen his mum for quite a long time squatted on the ground shedding silent tears.

13

VENTURING TO THE REMOTE GRAZING AREA

It had been five months since Little Tashi left his parents and he missed them more and more. Every night he would dream about them, so he made a plan to go to the grazing area without letting on to Dawa.

That morning, Dawa got up very early, woke Little Tashi up as usual and then they went out of the cabin together. Little Tashi ducked into the pen and drove the flock out while Dawa stood at the gate counting the sheep. Dawa bent his body and herded the flock to the small valley behind and then he turned back, saying to Little Tashi as if he had felt something, "Tashi, wait for me after you finish cooking. Don't run off."

"Yes, I will!" said Little Tashi a little sadly as he watched Dawa's leave. "Brother, what do you want to eat today?"

"What's the matter, why do you ask that?"

"Nothing. I just want to know what you want to eat, zanba or pasta?"

"You decide."

"Ok."

Dawa drove the flock away. Little Tashi hurried back to the cabin, finished the housework, and efficiently made a pot of Dawa's favourite pasta. He quickly finished one bowl of pasta and placed the pot beside the coal that was still warm inside the stove, and after that he searched in a corner of the cabin and found the damaged sheets from his notebook left by the sheep. He wrote down two characters, "Dad" and "Mum" and put the paper on the wooden door, hoping Dawa would know where he had gone when he came back with the flock.

Little Tashi left the sheep pen, crossed the stream, passed along the small path and marched towards the mouth of Lungser. From afar he saw the flock heading from the small valley to the mountain ridge on the left while Dawa followed at the very end of the flock like an old man. Little Tashi felt remorseful and guilty. He stopped and found himself in a dilemma: if he didn't go, he would miss his parents, and if he should go, he felt indebted to Dawa. What should he do? After a while, Little Tashi comforted himself and said, "It's alright. The young lambs have grown up and I will be back from the grazing area within a couple of days." He then climbed down the mountain quickly towards Lungser like a rolling ball.

When he reached the entrance to Lungser, he turned left and walked a little further, where a mani stone pile lay quietly marking the boundary of the valley and the village. Little Tashi passed through the small path in the valley for about half an hour and then he stopped at a narrow opening. There was a water mill ahead. Grinding machines were available in the village and most of the villagers would use the grinding machine to make zanba flour and wheat flour. Some senior villagers, however, didn't like the flour made by the machine, so Little Tashi's maternal grandpa operated this water mill. Little Tashi thought if he passed by the water mill, he would probably be caught by his grandpa who, of course, would never allow him to go to the grazing area and leave Dawa alone in the cabin. He therefore turned towards the bushes on the mountain, a large circle indeed, and when he crossed through the woods that thinly covered the hillside in front of the water mill, he saw smoke coming out from almost everywhere in the water mill: the door, the window and even the waterwheel, making the entire water mill a burning stove filled with smoke. His maternal grandpa came out of the mill suddenly with flour on his hands, forehead and on the tip of his nose, and he stooped on the road coughing a few times as he wiped his tears. He then looked up in the direction of Little Tashi, which startled him a lot. He hurriedly went into the woods and hid in the bushes for fear that his grandpa might have seen him. His movement, however, was heard by the old man who thought it might be the beasts hunting in the mountain. The old man shouted towards the mountain a few times and then ducked into the water mill again.

Little Tashi's heart pounded heavily as if he had butterflies in his stomach and he climbed down the small path in the ravine with fear and continued to head for the deep valley. At this time, all the flocks in the village had moved to the summer pastures in the heart of the valley. Little Tashi enjoyed the beautiful scenery along his way. A crystal-clear river crossed the road, a moderately wide road was quiet and deserted, a variety of birds' twittering, occasionally mixed with some cries of other animals, came from the forests on both sides of the road, golden trollius flourished by the roadside, as if a yellow carpet was spread over the ground, bees sang among the flowers and butterflies danced amongst the flowers. Little Tashi was overwhelmed by all these beautiful scenes in front of his eyes, but he was restless and worried whenever he arrived at the entrance of each ravine of the valley or the cattle ranch in someone else's winter pastures. Third Uncle was repairing his house, so he had hired a group of people in the village to cut trees on some slopes in the valley and at present they were all busy working there. Little Tashi didn't want to see Third Uncle because last time, when he had gone to the monastery with his paternal grandpa, Third Uncle said in front of the whole family that if Little Tashi's father didn't let him adopt Little Tashi, he would never regard him as his elder brother. This had become a heavy burden in Little Tashi's heart and therefore whenever he reached a small pass, he would immediately hide in the bushes on the roadside as long as there was some sound around.

At noon, Little Tashi walked quickly on the road at the bottom of the valley, as if he were an animal hiding from a hunter. Suddenly someone up in the woods shouted a few times to warn passers-by that the wood in the forests were being felled. A moment later, the sound of something tumbling down the path in the mountain sounded and some logs without branches and bark rolled down the mountain like dead bodies.

When the mountain returned to its tranquility, Little Tashi turned around the foot of the hill and continued towards the valley. When he reached the stream, he stopped and hid behind a willow tree surrounded by bushes. Third Uncle was there blowing the fire inside a stone pile. His sweaty forehead was covered with smoke. Third Uncle bit his lower lip, which exposed the gold teeth in his mouth and he also occasionally licked his teeth with the tip of his tongue. Little Tashi thought only Third Uncle could be so narcissistic. When he moved his contemptuous look from his uncle and prepared to leave quietly from behind the willow trees, his feet touched some twigs lying on the bushes alerting Third Uncle who thought he might come across a rare animal. He jumped from the ground, took out a gun, and walked step by step towards Little Tashi. Little Tashi hastily imitated the cries of a sand grouse and Third Uncle was disappointed when he heard this. He then turned back and left.

Little Tashi rushed towards the deep ravine and along the river at the bottom of the valley. When he reached a fork in the road, a few yaks hurried over, with the tongues hanging out, from a narrow path ahead. He was encountering yak thieves and wondered whether he should hide or just pretend not to see them and continue on his journey. As he wondered what to do, two riders appeared from behind the yaks. One wore a cheap, unlined Tibetan garment, the other was dressed in leather jacket and trousers, neither were wearing masks. Little Tashi knew they were not yak rustlers but cattle traders. Little Tashi therefore stood aside to let them pass. Smiling at him, the two riders drove their yaks and headed in the direction of Little Tashi's village.

It wasn't easy for Little Tashi to see his parents. He had crossed two main passes and he didn't know how many lay ahead. In the afternoon, the sun above his head had hidden in the west and Little Tashi arrived at an open place with grasslands on its upper part and forests on the lower part which had made itself a dividing line between summer pastures and winter pastures. Little Tashi had to cross the colin on the opposite hill, enter the grassland of another village, and then climb over another hill, he would arrive at the remote grazing area. When he reached this open place, he passed along the mountain ridge, covered with various bushes, and arrived at the basin of the mountain, the sun had sunk. There were three pastures of the village in this basin, one of which was his elder sister's.

Little Tashi hadn't planned to visit his sister, but when he came to the basin, he was spotted by his sister's dog. The animal barked at him wildly, dragging an iron chain behind. Little Tashi crossed the pass quickly and disappeared behind it while unexpectedly the dog broke loose from the stake and charged at him. As a child of a herdsman, Little Tashi knew there was only one way to cope with such an urgent situation, that is by lying perfectly still on the ground and playing dead. His sister's dog, though not big, was very aggressive and the moment he sprang on Little Tashi, his force carried a gust of wind, lifting the hem of Little Tashi's clothes. The dog circled around

Little Tashi and sniffed his face as if to check whether he was dead or not. At this moment, his sister who was milking nearby placed the milk barrel on the road and came over. She yelled at the dog and drove it away.

She was surprised to find it was her younger brother, Little Tashi. She hurriedly helped him up and asked, "Tashi, how could you be here?"

"Heh, heh," Little Tashi smiled slightly as he looked at his sister.

His sister said with fear, "Still laughing? You almost scared me to death!"

"I want to…" Little Tashi didn't know how to tell this to his sister.

"You want to go and see Mum and Dad, don't you?" His sister had already guessed it.

"Yes."

"What about your brother? Have you told this to him?"

"Nope."

"Hey! You are naughty indeed!"

Three tents stood alone on the slope close to the mountain basin with crowds of yaks and sheep flocks scattered nearby and his sister's tent was on the far end. His sister held his hand and took him back to the tent and on their way the milk barrel was knocked over and milk spilled all over the ground. The dog at first followed behind like a child who had admitted his mistake and then he saw the milk on the ground and began to lick greedily. In the tent, his sister set the fire in the stove and began to boil milk for him.

Tents in Tashi's neighbourhood were usually built with some rafters hammered into the ground in a large circle and then the cover, made of cowhides, would be placed over it, with a skylight in the door curtain. His sister's tent was different, it had one beam, one pillar and a cover, and the skylight was on the roof of the tent. Inside his sister's tent, Little Tashi glanced here and there. The tent didn't have a high ceiling but was quite spacious and in the middle stood a stove supported by three iron rods, each with hooks. To the right of the stove was a simple couch with mattresses of suru tree branches and two padded leather cushions on it, while on the left was a variety of iron and wooden barrels and cans. At the far inside of the tent was placed a horizontal wooden bar on which were a wooden box filled with butter, some bulging woollen bags and some saddles. Little Tashi moved his eyes from different corners of the tent to his sister who was busy boiling milk for him. She had been married for more than two years and it was said that there were more than 100 yaks and fertile fields of tens of mou in her family; sort of a rich family in the village. His sister had been living on the pasture land since she married and in Mum's words, his sister did the work of two people, milking and herding all by herself, and that's why he rarely saw her since she married. In Little Tashi's memory, his sister didn't talk much like his father, but she was somewhat defiant and unruly, while now she had become mild and capable around the home, like his mum.

It was getting dark and the barking of dogs came sporadically from different hilltops. His sister fumbled and brought out a china bowl from nowhere, washed it hastily, poured a bowl of steaming hot milk into it and put it in Little Tashi's hands. The milk was a bit hot, but Little Tashi, like an experienced shepherd, held the bowl in his hand, pursed up his mouth and took a sip of the tasty and delicious milk. When his sister looked at him as he drank the milk, a happy smile appeared on her face. She then went out of the tent and continued her milking work. When it was pitch dark outside, she went back to the tent and began boiling milk again. She chatted with Little Tashi as she turned the handle of the milk separator. She said, "You didn't tell this to your brother before you left, and he will be worried about you."

"I wrote him a letter," Little Tashi answered proudly.

"A letter? You don't go to school, how could you write a letter?"

"I learned from my brother."

"What did you write then?"

"I wrote "Dad" and "Mum" on a piece of paper and then put it up on the cabin door."

"That was a good idea, but don't you think it would be miserable for your brother to be alone?"

"Sister, he is not alone."

"Oh? He has someone to be with him?"

"He met a girl from another village."

"No way! You brother is only 13."

"You are just 16, aren't you?"

His sister crouched down in front of the milk separator and kept turning the handle and the separator buzzed happily. Little Tashi asked, "Where is my brother-in-law?"

"Third Uncle hired him to cut trees. Didn't you meet him on your way?"

"I did meet Third Uncle but didn't see my brother-in-law, but I don't want to see Third Uncle anymore from now on."

"Why do you say that?" asked his sister. "You are going to be adopted by him and he will be your dad."

"No, I will go to school."

"Your brother has already dropped out of school and as for you, perhaps Mum and Dad won't send you there."

"Dad and I had an agreement. If I can help my brother take good care of the flock, he would send me to school next spring when the grazing area should move back to our grassland."

"Then why didn't you help your brother and not leave him alone? You know, you leaving for remote grazing area without permission was a kind of breach of your agreement."

"But I miss Dad and Mum."

"If you want to go to school, you'd better go back and keep you promise, it is only by doing this that you could have the opportunity to study."

It had been quite a long time since Little Tashi last saw his sister and the two had a long chat and it was already midnight when they went to sleep. Although Little Tashi had a lot of things on his mind, he didn't linger on those things like adults usually did and he fell into sleep the moment he lay on the pillow while his sister couldn't. Like any rich family, her husband's family had a lot of rules and even if she worked hard, uncomplainingly, she could never please them, which filled her with a lot of grievances. Tonight, she was both excited and sad to meet her young brother whom she hadn't seen for ages and she therefore was wide awake.

The next day, the burning red glow appeared on the eastern mountain top, by which the rising sun showed its face. The basin where his sister's tent located was not very high, but from there you could still see the mountains far away. His sister had already driven the cattle back from the neighbouring area before daybreak and at dawn she had finished all the milking work. She went back into the tent, made a bowl of zanba with butter and warmed a pot of milk for Little Tashi. Little Tashi ate the zanba as he drank three bowls of milk and then kept hiccupping all the time. His sister didn't force Little Tashi to make the choice as to where he would go, leaving him to decide. Little Tashi however gave up the idea of going to see his parents; instead he wanted to go back to Lungser helping to herd the flock with his brother, which pleased his sister very much. Before he left, his sister made another bowl of zanba with butter, put it in a plastic bag and sent Little Tashi to the road at the foot of the mountain. Upon leaving, she said to him, "Tashi, Dawa must be mad at you this time. Bring this zanba to him."

"I will," answered Little Tashi.

His sister continued, "Dear Brother, Mum and Dad are in the remote grazing area far away from home and there is only Grandpa and Grandma at home. Your brother has to take all these things into consideration at the same time. So, when you go back, try your best to help him with the flock."

"Sister, I won't let you down," Little Tashi said firmly.

When he reached the turn at the bottom of the valley, Little Tashi looked back and saw his sister standing on the roadside, watching him as she wiped her tears. He felt a little bit sad, but as he turned back, he disappeared like a flying deer on the road that flourished with plants at the bottom of the valley.

14
THE FLOCK TRAMPLES THE CROPS

Little Tashi left his sister with much reluctance and when he walked on the gloomy road at the bottom of the valley he thought he had committed an unforgivable sin. What if something happened to the flock? Even if his brother should forgive his foolish decision, the loss indeed outweighed the gains. He hurried back as fast as he could as if he had grown a pair of wings. When he passed by the place where Third Uncle and his men cut trees yesterday, he didn't make a detour this time, but didn't meet them either. Little Tashi knew Third Uncle never wasted money in business and since he had paid for a few strong men to work for him, he would never leave them idle or he himself might bring them along and cut trees on the mountain. When Little Tashi reached the water mill, its door was half open and a creaking sound came out continuously, as if a giant beast was hiding inside. Little Tashi stopped on the road in front of the water mill and tiptoed to the door, and looked into the room. His maternal grandpa was busy working beside the millstone, his body bent and covered with white flour like a snowman. Little Tashi wanted to say hello but the old man was so busy and didn't even look up at him, and he also felt what he had done was nothing to be proud of. He turned back and continued his journey to Lungser.

On the road opposite Lungser was a small slope where piles of mani stones stood and from where small ditches on the sunny slope of the bushes and the dense forests on the shaded slope at the bottom of Lungser could be seen. It was about half an hour's journey from the mani stone piles to the village and when Little Tashi arrived at the stone piles and took a rest beside them, the sun had just climbed to the top of the mountain behind, far from sinking in the west. Little Tashi looked at their sheep pen guiltily. Though he couldn't see the pen, the mountain ridge behind the pen was very clear in his eyes.

Suddenly Little Tashi heard a burst of bleating from somewhere and he looked around for a while but didn't see any flock. He pricked his ears to listen again and seemed to hear a few more. Then, from the corner of his eye, he suddenly saw a flock appear in the place where the bushes and fields met at the lower left corner beside the river. He was confused and wondered whose flock had run into the field. If the flock was not driven out of the field immediately, how terrible it would be when the patrols from the village should find this. Little Tashi's brain swung as fast as the wooden gear of the water mill and then he stepped into the field of crops and rushed towards the flock like a flying arrow. When he reached the flock, he was very surprised to find it was his family's.

He ran about from the bushes beside the river to the field, breathlessly driving the flock towards the inside of Lungser. When they fled there, he stopped and counted the sheep and found there were only fifty of them, twenty were still missing. He had to drive them to the ravine for the time being and went back to the river's edge to check the sheep footprints. At the river bank, he found the footprints of the flock went down to the river and when he was about to chase after them, Dawa suddenly showed up behind him. Little Tashi waved his hands towards Dawa and shouted excitedly as if he had found the most important thing in the world, "Brother, I found the footprints of the flock!"

Smack! Smack! Dawa came over and slapped Little Tashi across his face.

Little Tashi grumbled, "Why did you beat me?"

"Why? Couldn't you have at least let me know where you were going? I thought you had been eaten by wolves!" Dawa yelled angrily.

"I did tell you," said Little Tashi, in a pathetic tone.

"When did you say that? I looked for you everywhere and because of you we are in trouble now," Dawa said, as he searched the footprints.

Little Tashi wailed, "I did write you a letter and put it up on the wooden door."

"Wrote me a letter? Are you out of your mind? Do you know how to write a letter?"

"I wrote "Dad" and "Mum" on a piece of paper with pencil."

"There was no such paper on the door. It must have been blown away."

Dawa said this to Little Tashi as he ran straight down to the river while Little Tashi had wanted to give him the zanba his sister had made but when he looked up, Dawa was far ahead and he had to follow him closely. When they arrived at the mouth of Lungser near the village, the flock that was trampling on the field was spotted by a few men who came to patrol the fields. Little Tashi and Dawa ran towards the field and Dawa arrived beside the flock first with Little Tashi closely behind. When the two brothers drove the flock out of the field and hurried towards Lungser, the patrol from the village stopped them and circled the flock in the flat land there. The men stood around them and there was no possibility for the sheep to escape. Both Dawa and Little Tashi pleaded, held their thumbs up, "Please excuse us this time!"

"If all farm animals of each household were to spoil the crops like this, how could we harvest in the autumn?" It seemed there was no use pleading with them.

The two brothers said unanimously, "We promise the flock will never trample the crops again."

"Your flock dared to trample crops in broad daylight and now it is too late to say anything. You boys know what fine you need to pay according to village rules. Go and call the adults in your family," said a middle-aged man with a goatee beard.

Little Tashi said, "My parents are both in the remote grazing area"

"Then, ask your grandparents to come here," said another man.

Dawa said, "Grandpa and Grandma have gone to pray in the monastery at this time."

"Then ask your great Third Uncle to be here," said Goatee.

Little Tashi said, "Third Uncle is cutting trees in the mountain."

"Borrow the money from your relatives in the village," Goatee said.

"Relatives…" Little Tashi was interrupted by Dawa.

"Stop it, I will go."

At that moment, the flock seemed quite aware of the situation they were in and they no longer ran about but gathered together, lying on the ground ruminating quietly. Dawa crossed the bridge and ran towards the village and the patrol men looked at each other smiling, as if to say they hadn't come in vain. Little Tashi didn't understand why they could be so mean since they all belonged to the same village. He asked, "We live in the same village, why do you treat us like that?"

"Just because we are in the same village, we should do our work according to village rules."

"Last time when Grandpa and I went to the monastery, there was livestock from other families in the field at the lower part of the village," said Little Tashi.

Goatee continued, "Boy, you know, yesterday we slaughtered a sow in a field at the lower part of the village, and the day before yesterday in the field where your flock trampled crops we cut a cow's tail…"

"The flock did trample the crops, but they didn't eat crops like pigs and cattle."

"Hey, stubborn boy! All flocks in Dungkar village have moved to summer pastures and your family's flock is the only one that still stays in the autumn pasture in Lungser."

"Our pasture is on the grassland outside the village," argued Little Tashi.

"The grassland outside the village does not belong to your family alone! As for your family, everything is done based on the spirit of taking special measures for special problems. I have no idea what your Third Uncle has done to lick the village chief's boots," interrupted another man.

"The flock belongs to my family and Third Uncle is simply a business man. He doesn't even have a yak or a goat tail," refuted Little Tashi with annoyance. He didn't want to talk about Third Uncle but when he heard someone ridicule him, he felt somewhat uncomfortable.

Goatee said, with a significant look, "Doesn't it mean your family bullies others, relying on your Third Uncle's power?"

"No. My family is not Third Uncle's," retorted Little Tashi, unhappily.

The man smiled lightly and said, "Well, it is said that you will be adopted by him, isn't it? Then you will be a member of his family."

"No. My dad promised to send me to school the next spring after my family moves back to the grassland in the village."

After a while the sun had already fallen in the west and the dark shades shrouded them like a black robe, the gloomy bottom of the valley making a sharp contrast with the golden sunshine on the opposite mountainside. The patrol men walked around the flock impatiently and then they deliberately kept a certain distance from Little Tashi and gathered on the other side of the flock, whispering secretly. Little Tashi had thought they were planning to let him go, so he ran over to them and asked, "Could I drive the flock away?"

"Stop daydreaming! If your brother doesn't come back, we will have to drive the flock to the village and let the village chief decide how to punish you," said Goatee.

Little Tashi pleaded tearfully, "Please! Don't report this to the village, otherwise my dad won't send me to school when he knows this."

"Then who will pay the fine for your family?" said Goatee.

"Please wait a little longer and if my brother doesn't come back, I will go and find Third Uncle. I know where he is," said Little Tashi, honestly.

Time passed by slowly. The sunshine climbed from the opposite hillside to the mountain top which was therefore covered with faint golden light and looked like a faded golden crown; the river at the bottom of the valley ran onwards at the same rhythm but its sound seemed to grow much louder; willow trees and the other plants around Lungser danced gracefully in the slight breeze. A blast of coldness came and lingered in the air, biting Little Tashi and making his teeth chatter continuously.

The patrol men drove the flock by force in front of Little Tashi's eyes and when they were going to cross the bridge and lead the flock to the village, Dawa and Grandpa appeared on the small slope on the opposite of the small ravine, one after another. In the twilight, Grandpa fumbled and took something from his pocket and handed it over to Goatee, saying, "Look, the boy's father is in the remote grazing area and I only have that much right now. Please accept it."

"Only 20 yuan? That is too little," said Goatee as he looked at the people around him.

One said, "If it were five yuan per goat it would be at least a 100 yuan."

"Well, we are in the same village and in a sense, we are all relatives. Please excuse us this time," pleaded Grandpa.

Goatee said, "Though we are related in a way, we are no better than your third son. And also, your family takes advantage of your third son's power and herds your flock in Lungser, which the other villagers all complain about. I am afraid 20 yuan won't convince them at all."

"You don't know the reason why we herd the flock in Lungser. Last year, their sister was married and there was only me and their grandma at home. I have problems with my legs and so we have asked permission from the village. And, their dad has donated a statue of bodhisattva for the mani Lhakang in the village to express our thankfulness." Grandpa told them the whole story.

At this time, it was getting dark and the entire bottom of the valley was blurred in the twilight. They couldn't see each other's faces except the shadows in the darkness. They all remained silent and at last Goatee said, "At least we need to report this to the village chief."

"No need, let them go." A man's rough voice suddenly came from a dark slope, it was the village chief who had finally come.

Goatee said, "Village chief, they…"

"Let them go at once. It is dark, and they have to drive the flock back to the sheep pen," said the chief quietly.

Although the patrol men from the village were quite reluctant to let them go, it would be improper to make things difficult since the village chief had spoken. So, they took the 20 yuan and followed the chief to the village, complaining. In the darkness, Grandpa warned Little Tashi and Dawa not to let the flock trample the crops again and after he sent them off, he stood there for a while and then dragged his right leg that was as stiff as a piece of wood and limped towards the village.

When Little Tashi and Dawa herded the flock to the Lungser pass, the other sheep had already gone back to the pen. Along the way, they were silent, spitefully refusing to speak to each other. Dawa took off the sling from his waist and whipped it above his head to drive the flock on and the sheep hastened their steps breathlessly on the small road in Lungser. Little Tashi quickened his steps too but still fell behind Dawa. It was after all his fault and he wanted to please Dawa, who right now didn't give him any chance to do that. When they were very close to the sheep pen, Little Tashi caught up with Dawa at last and he said, "Brother, don't be mad at me and I promise I will never slip away from the sheepfold again."

"None of my business. Just go wherever you want to go," said Dawa who was still annoyed at Little Tashi.

Little Tashi said, "Last night I slept at Sister's family home."

"Huh! You did run very fast" Dawa said unwillingly, "Sister should have driven you out and let you stay overnight in the field."

"Brother, look, my running away this time has some gains anyway," said Little Tashi as he shook the plastic bag filled with zanba in front of Dawa.

"What's this?"

"Sister made this especially for you," said Little Tashi, proudly.

Dawa said, "Give it to me quickly!"

"Are you still mad at me?" Little Tashi asked, naughtily.

Seeing the zanba, Dawa's attitude softened a little and he said, "Stop talking nonsense. No one would still get mad with delicious food available."

"The sheep pen is around the corner and I will give it to you when we arrive there," Little Tashi began to tease Dawa.

Dawa grabbed the bag eagerly from Little Tashi and ate heartily, saying, "Haven't had zanba with butter for a long time. Sister was always the one who cares about me most."

In a while, they arrived at the stream opposite the pen and the sheep bleated happily when they heard the greeting bleats from the pen, as if they hadn't seen each other for a few months. The old dog barked his welcome too. They shut the flock in the pen, went into the cabin and lit the oil lamp, and they were on good terms as before.

15
WORSHIPPING THE MOUNTAIN GODS

On 19 June, according to the Tibetan calendar, men in every household in the Jangkhok valley would bear prayer flags, riding horses or walking on foot, to worship mountain gods on a mountain top in the Jangkhok valley. The two brothers, however, could not leave the flock in Lungser to worship mountain gods, but there was one, General Jiri, on the top of the shaded slope across from the sheep pen. Usually people in the village would go to worship mountain gods on 21 February but at that time Little Tashi's family had been in winter pastures and was unable to do this. So one morning, just after daybreak, the two brothers set out on the journey. As instructed by Grandpa, they carried prayer flags, lungta, zanba and cypress branches for a ritual ceremony and drove the flock toward the small, shaded valley opposite.

The slopes of the small shaded valley were covered with dense forests, the other side was grass. The flock climbed up the mountain as fast as they could, regardless of the steep mountain road, as if summoned by a god. Very soon, they reached the top of slope. When they arrived there, different hills climbed up to the higher mountains, layer after layer like a ladder and the highest peak was where the prayer flags of General Jiri were located.

The two brothers cut a small tree, as thick as Little Tashi's lower leg, peeled its bark and made a pole with some leaves still attached to the top.

Then they each carried one end of the pole and followed the flock, climbing up towards the direction of General Jiri on the mountain top.

They climbed the mountain in fits and starts and finally arrived at their destination. Halfway, they looked back and Namtso lake, on the top of the opposite mountain became smaller and smaller. They found Dekyi's flock was grazing leisurely beside Namtso. Dawa shouted excitedly towards the opposite hillside like a ram in rut, but there was no reply and Dawa became very upset. Little Tashi thought Dawa had stopped dating Dekyi due to Grandpa Humpback, so he took the opportunity and asked, "Brother, didn't you say you won't see sister Dekyi anymore?"

"I mean I don't want to see her grandpa."

"But you told me that the last time I went to her pen."

"Now it is not me who doesn't want to talk to her; it is she who is unwilling to talk to me."

"Sister Dekyi asked me to give you a message that she didn't want to see you again, but I did not dare tell you this."

"That's why I didn't go to see her."

"You have a good chance today."

"Why?"

"Didn't you see her flock beside Namtso?"

"But she didn't even want to show up to talk to me."

"Try again and I promise she will show up within three minutes."

"No, she won't."

Dawa shouted again and just as Little Tashi had said, Dekyi came out from the bushes beside the lake and the two began singing songs to each other. Little Tashi didn't quite understand what they were singing about and also felt a bit embarrassed to be the listener, but later he joined in and made up folk songs with Dawa, singing happily towards the opposite hillside. For quite a while they sang so merrily and when they turned around to look at the flock, they had already reached the peak. The two brothers stopped singing and climbed up towards the mountain top.

The mountain peak where General Jiri was pointed upwards like a spear but when they climbed up to the top they found there was a labtse, or prayer flag, surrounded by iron wire and the flock scattered around it like a broken ivory rosary. The moment they reached the peak, the prayer flags fluttered in the air and a feeling of reverence rose in their hearts. Dawa piously performed bsang (a smoke offering or purifying with incense) and other actions to worship the mountain gods while Little Tashi could do nothing but stand quietly watching because he had never done this before and didn't quite understand the ceremony. White clouds wandered overhead on the heavenly mountain top and Little Tashi felt he could snatch them with his bare hands. As he looked back, Namtso seemed to be resting on the hillside and when he moved his eyes to the far bottom of the valley, he saw their village was encircled by a patchwork of green and yellow fields. Under the blue sky, range after range of hills stretched for miles, unfolding on a magnificent scale like huge waves of the vast ocean. Little Tashi asked, "Brother, why is the mountain god called General Jiri?"

"General Jiri used to be the subordinate of the mountain god Anye Machen and he ventured into the land of demons, conquering monsters and goblins single-handedly and finally settled here and became the mountain god of our village."

"Is Anye Machen the mountain god of some village or a certain tribe?"

"Anye Machen is not the mountain god of some village or a tribe; he is the head of all Tibetan mountain gods."

"Then General Jiri must be very valiant."

"In the past, our grandpa was a member of a horse caravan. Once when they were on their business trip to Lhasa, they met some bandits. Grandpa prayed to the mountain gods for help and in a dream, he saw a man wearing a coral hat protecting them all the way. He believed that man must be General Jiri and that's why our family feels particularly thankful to General Jiri."

"Where does General Jiri live?"

"Maybe in the labtse"

"Will he see us burn cypress branches, put up prayer flags and shower lungta for him?"

"Certainly, he will."

Dawa burned the bsang and a thread of smoke rose quickly into the sky in the wind. The two brothers tied the prayer flags to the head of the pole and leaned it against the wire fence around the labtse, and then they held a wad of cypress leaves tightly in their hands, praying as they scattered the leaves in different directions. Dawa raised his hands and began to kowtow after he finished all this. At this sacred and solemn moment, Little Tashi heard Dawa praying, "General Jiri, please clear away all the obstacles on our way and make me and Dekyi the happiest couple in the world." Little Tashi felt it was very improper for Dawa to say this at such a sacred moment, so he turned back and stared at Dawa angrily. When he thought again, he felt the worship of mountain god was to realise one's dreams and there was nothing wrong in Dawa making his wish. Little Tashi then scattered the leaves around, kowtowing as he narrowed his eyes and prayed, "General Jiri, please bless our flock and wish me good luck that I could go to school early next spring."

They solemnly held up the pole with its prayer flags and walked clockwise around the labtse three times after they kowtowed and prayed in front of it. The wind on the mountain top was so strong that it almost blew down the pole they held in their hands. When the two brothers finished the ceremony and managed, using all their might, to put the pole into the labtse, a gust of wind suddenly roared in and prayer flags fluttered solemnly again in the wind, making the surrounding flock look up towards the labtse, as if inspired by such a grave atmosphere. Dawa and Little Tashi were both overjoyed when they saw this. They took out lungta from their pockets and showered them into the air as they circled around the labtse and said, "Lhagyal lo!" (Tibetan, meaning "God wins") The lungta drifted down like snowflakes and then fell on the nearby mountain top gradually. Some lungta dropped on the heads of some sheep and the timid ones ran away while some stood still watching the flying lungta as if receiving the blessings and when the lungta fell to the ground, they came close to sniff a bit but did not eat it.

Little Tashi looked at this solemn scene and suddenly felt a little uneasy as he thought of the dream he had had that morning. He said to Dawa, "Brother, I had a dream this morning."

"What dream?"

"In the dream, I was walking on an endless road. I walked on and on for a very long time and there was nobody there, except me. Willow trees by the roadside laughed at me and stones crawled in front of me to block my way, and…"

"…and a pack of wolves followed behind, right?"

"Brother, how did you know that?"

"I often had a dream like this, but I don't dwell on it like you for I simply forget it."

"I just couldn't forget it. You know, later I met a short-haired female teacher on the road and she…"

"Ha, ha, ha, boy, you go on making up the story. So, the short-haired teacher took you to school, didn't she?"

"Nope. She took me to the school gate and when we were about to enter, two transparent figures fought against each other in front of me and I simply couldn't move a step. The short-haired female teacher urged me ahead and said if I didn't hurry up, we were going to be late. I tried to walk on, but I just couldn't break through."

"Er, you did have a complicated dream. And then?"

"And then I opened my eyes and looked at it again. The two transparent figures became two clouds of light, one white and one black. They just fought against each other in front of the gate, not letting me in."

"So, did you get in in the end?"

"Nope. Can you imagine what the white one and the black one turned into at last?"

"No idea."

"The white one became Second Uncle and the black one became Third Uncle."

The sun had moved overhead after they finished worshipping General Jiri. Bathed in the sunlight, the land was restored to its tranquility. Standing on the top of the mountain, they looked towards Dungkar valley and saw floating smoke and some shimmering figures on the distant hilltops. The two mountains, one at the mouth of the valley, and the other on the right in the innermost part of the valley, worked side by side to protect this land. At this time, some sheep slipped into the thorn bushes below the labtse and Dawa took off his sling and fired stones at them to drive them back. The sheep immediately ran out of the thorn bushes and went back on their way towards Lungser.

Little Tashi pointed at a distant mountain ridge, to the east and said, "Brother, look, that is the remote grassland and our pasture should be there."

"Yes, but I heard the farm manager this year is not easy to get along with and Dad and Mum must have suffered a lot."

"Why should we move there every few years when we have such a huge grassland?"

"Dumb head! You don't know this? Our grassland is not enough to feed cattle and sheep."

"I hope next spring comes early."

"When did you learn to think about our parents? You only care about going to school."

"Didn't you only think about Sister Dekyi, every day?"

Little Tashi and Dawa chatted as they walked down. A rabbit darted out suddenly from the bushes and the two brothers chased after it like rolling stones, although they didn't have any intention to hurt it. The rabbit kept running on the open grass in front of them and suddenly a black eagle appeared in the sky and swooped down behind their backs. Dawa said, "We should stop the black eagle."

"Why?"

"Rabbits could be dependants of General Jiri," said Dawa as he stuffed stones into the sling.

"Then what about the black eagle?"

"I don't know, but today we could not let it snatch the rabbit anyway."

"Brother, hurry up, the black eagle is diving down again."

The black eagle swooped down, snatched the rabbit in its sharp claws and flew away. Dawa waved the sling high above his head and fired the stone at the eagle. Goodness knows whether the stone hit the black eagle or the black eagle was frightened by the snapping sound of the sling; the rabbit dropped down straight from the claws. The black eagle trembled in the air and almost hit the ground, and then he spread its wings, flew back up into the sky and disappeared in a minute. The moment the rabbit fell to the ground, it rolled over, ran backwards and then lopped away towards the labtse.

16
GOING TO SCHOOL AS A STOPGAP

When they were fast asleep on the kang, Little Tashi and Dawa were awoken by the neighing of a horse. They squinted and looked up from the pillow. The cabin was in darkness, but it was much brighter outside as the morning light shone on the shabby window.

"Open the door!" A middle-aged man was knocking at the door.

Dawa got up from the kang, put on his leather jacket and asked, "Who is there?"

"It's me," said the man anxiously.

Confused, Dawa prepared to open the door while Little Tashi put on his leather jacket and said groggily, "It is Third Uncle."

"Oh, Third Uncle! What has brought you here?" Dawa opened the door, "Come on in."

"Why shouldn't I come here?" said Third Uncle looking back at Blackhawk tied beside the pen as he entered the cabin.

Dawa, with fearful panic after Third Uncle came in, said, "The old fellow! He didn't even bark just now. If thieves should come, we wouldn't know at all."

"I gave the old dog to your family. Though it has been three years, he would never forget his old master, would he? He even wants to wag its tail to greet me, so how could he bark at me?" said Third Uncle proudly.

Everything was blurred in the cabin and Little Tashi could barely see the tall figure of Third Uncle. Though he couldn't see his face clearly, he could imagine the picture of Third Uncle's gold teeth when he opened his mouth as he talked. Third Uncle came to the kang and said, "Tashi, get up quickly!"

"What's the matter?" asked Little Tashi.

Third Uncle said, "Go to school!"

"Go to school?" Little Tashi couldn't believe his ears!

As he walked towards the outside, Third Uncle said, "Yes, go to school!"

"You mean you agree to let him go to school?" Dawa asked in surprise.

Third Uncle didn't answer but said, "Hurry up. Blackhawk doesn't want to wait anymore."

It was dawn and the silhouettes of the forest opposite and the trees at the bottom of the valley became clearer and clearer. Dawa and Little Tashi were both stunned by the sudden news. They went out of the cabin, and sure enough, the old dog wagged his tail continuously when he saw his former master as if he wanted to give Third Uncle a hug. Third Uncle took something out of his saddlebag and fed it to the old dog as he stroked its head. Then he went back to Blackhawk, quickly jumped on his back and said, "Tashi, get on the horse, quickly."

"Brother…" Little Tashi didn't know what to do and looked at Dawa in panic.

"Go and get on the horse quickly!" Dawa said firmly to him.

Little Tashi rushed towards Blackhawk, grasped his mane, put his left foot in the stirrup and jumped onto the broad and strong back of Blackhawk.

Third Uncle spurred Blackhawk forwards, crossed the stream in front of the pen and rode away, humming a tune all the way. With mixed feelings of joy and sorrow, Little Tashi looked back intently at Dawa who was standing at the pen gate seeing him off, at the flock in the pen and at the old dog and the cabin. He just couldn't believe he had departed from them like this.

Blackhawk galloped on steadily as if his four limbs were moving wheels and it was very comfortable to sit on his back. Very soon the uncle and the nephew arrived at the mouth of Lungser and Third Uncle couldn't help feeling elated and asked Little Tashi proudly, "What do you think about Blackhawk?"

"He is good." Little Tashi was still in a daze after his dream was realised overnight and he didn't quite understand what his Third Uncle referred to and so replied absent-mindedly.

Third Uncle looked back at Little Tashi and asked, "Do you want to ride Blackhawk often in the future?"

"If I should go to school, would I have the chance to ride horses?" Little Tashi had now recovered himself and answered in a low but forceful voice.

"Ha, ha, ha!" Third Uncle laughed wildly on the horseback.

Blackhawk quickened his steps and rushed towards the village with his head high. The uncle and the nephew remained silent, like a quarrelling father and a son. When they arrived at the village entrance, Little Tashi broke the silence and said, "Third Uncle, should we tell Grandpa and Grandma about my going to school?"

"No need. I have told you that we must go directly to school or we will be late," answered Third Uncle, coldly.

They crossed the bridge via the small path below the village and then galloped towards the school in the town. The people they met on their way all looked at Blackhawk with admiration, some even whispering to each other and watching them until they were far away. They arrived at the school gate when the morning sun was falling on the town at the bottom of the valley. Some teachers came to meet them the moment they saw them. Among them was a fat man with a large head. He asked with a smile, "Gold Teeth, is this your son?"

"Yes, Mr Principal, now I give him to you." Third Uncle didn't get down from the horse but answered as he rode Blackhawk in a circle.

The fat man with a large head patted Little Tashi on the shoulder and said, "Good, don't worry about him."

"Go with them and listen to your teachers," said Third Uncle.

Little Tashi protested to the fat man, "I am not his son."

"What did you say?" The fat man was surprised at Little Tashi's reply, but he didn't ask why and gave an order to the teachers beside him instead. "Take him in."

Some teachers nodded and came over to take Little Tashi into the campus. Blackhawk became arrogant in front of these teachers, as if to show off his abilities and even Third Uncle had to follow his lead and let go of the reins. The moment Blackhawk galloped away, Third Uncle turned back to Little

Tashi and said, "Tashi, I have my hands full tonight and can't come to pick you up. You must go back home by yourself after school."

Little Tashi had sneaked into the campus in the moonlight and peered into the school through the school gate, so he was very familiar with the layout, but today it was the first time for him to be there as a student and he was very excited. The teachers led him into a classroom where there were only a dozen students dressed in worn clothes like him, among which were even two little lamas in robes. A few more came and all of them looked like rough kids hanging around in pastures or street corners, not the slightest resemblance to an ordinary student at school. Just then, the fat man came into the classroom followed by a few teachers and he said to them, "Today, some leaders will come to inspect our school but some of our students have gone to the monastery and become lamas, and some have been herding cattle and sheep in pastures. So, you are called here to serve as stopgaps and after the leaders leave you may go home."

"Oh!" Little Tashi understood at last. He wasn't a real student in this school but a stopgap. Little Tashi was very angry but since he had already come it was not proper for him to leave at once. He therefore sat in the corner, quietly waiting for the leader. Like Little Tashi, the other children invited here all appeared shy and nervous in this strange new world and they simply sat on their seats waiting silently for that special moment.

Ding-dong-dong.

The bell rang and students in the other classrooms all ran outside to line up for the radio calisthenics, while the children in Little Tashi's classroom were at a loss, having no idea about what they should do. After a while, the students finished the radio calisthenics and some played in the yard while some came to lean on the windows of Little Tashi's classroom, laughing and pointing at them, which made Little Tashi even more annoyed.

About half an hour later, a car stopped at the school gate and some people got out of the car, including a tall, thin man wearing a pair of sunglasses. Apparently, he was the leader, with all the others surrounding him. The principal, who had been waiting at the school gate, presented the man and the other people with a khata, one by one and then led them into the campus.

The principal showed them around the classrooms and when they arrived in front of the classroom where Little Tashi sat, the principal slipped into the classroom through the door and spoke to the 'students' like an experienced tour guide. "Students, today, it is an honour for us to have Mr Yang, the deputy director of the county education bureau at our school and inspect the enrolment of school-age children. Let's stand up and warmly welcome our leader."

The children, as they had rehearsed already, stood up immediately and applauded warmly. Deputy director Yang walked through the aisles between the desks smiling, stopping occasionally to look at the textbooks and assignments on the 'students' desks. When he stopped beside a student's desk, he suddenly turned back and said, "Principal Dan, which grade are these students in?"

"Director Yang, they are first graders, class two," answered the principal, with a smile.

The deputy director took off his sunglasses and said, "Well, why do some of the students have grade two textbooks?"

"Director Yang, you know our school is in a remote area and textbooks usually cannot be handed over on time, so sometimes the juniors have to borrow textbooks from the seniors," stammered the principal.

The director glanced at a person behind him and said, "Xiao Wang, write this down."

"Yes," said a young man called Xiao Wang, as he wrote what the director just said in his notebook at once.

The deputy director asked, "Well, how many students in your school?"

"260 children, but the actual number is 250," answered the principal nervously with sweat on his forehead.

The director said, "Good job!"

"Director, without the bureau leaders' support, we could not achieve this," said the principal, gratefully.

The deputy director walked around the classroom in high spirits and stopped beside each student, asking about their study. When he finally came to Little Tashi, he asked, "Hi, what's your name?"

"Tashi," answered Little Tashi.

The director continued, "Which village do you live in?"

"Dungkar village," Little Tashi pointed at the village on the opposite side of the river.

"How do you feel about school life?"

"I am not a student here," Little Tashi lowered his head and replied absent-mindedly, "I am a shepherd boy!"

Little Tashi spoke the truth and laughter burst out in the classroom.

The director asked in astonishment, "What did you say?"

"Director Yang, this child is very shy and when he sees you, he is so nervous that he says the wrong thing," said the principal, coming over to explain.

"What did he say then?" asked the director.

The principal did not know how to answer and stammered for quite a while. At last he said, "He said he was so scared that he almost peed his pants!"

Laughter exploded again because all the children in the classroom knew the principal was lying.

The deputy director pinched Little Tashi's cheek and said, "Don't be nervous! Study hard and be a useful man when you grow up, do you hear that?"

"I will study hard when I can go to school next spring," Little Tashi said earnestly.

Students in the classroom burst into laughter again at Little Tashi's reply to something completely different to what the director had just asked.

Hearing them laughing, the director asked the principal, "What did this boy say just now?"

The principal hurriedly made up a story and said, "He said no matter how hard he tries, he just cannot catch up with his classmates, but he was greatly encouraged by what you told him just now and he said he would study harder and make progress every day!"

The principal's lie made everyone laugh again.

Standing behind the director, the principal stared at the whole class, placed his index finger on his lips, signalling them not to laugh at it anymore.

"Ha, ha, ha, Little Tashi is clever and smart and you all need to learn from him," said the director with a smile. He then walked to the desk in front of the blackboard, stood facing the students and said solemnly, "Students, don't be nervous. Just like you, I began my study as a first grader and at last I graduated from a technical secondary school. But you have better chances than me and you could all go to study at college in the future. Study hard and make progress every day, won't you?"

The director finished his speech but the whole class was silent. The principal immediately applauded nervously and said to the students, "Why don't you applaud and say 'Yes'?"

"You should tell us when to say 'Yes'," said a boy who was one of the older students.

The principal wiped his sweat and said, "Applaud, now!"

"Yes!" cried all the students at the same time.

The director and his men hurried to the reception room of the school to have a feast, and then they got back into the car and went to the next inspection site. In the afternoon, all the enrolled students continued their class while the dozens of stopgap students were released. Before they left, each of them was given two yuan. It was said that the director was very satisfied with Little Tashi's performance and he highly praised the school's quality education, therefore two yuan was given to each of the students as a reward. The other children immediately rushed to the shops on both sides of the school, buying things with the money but Little Tashi didn't want to go with them. Instead, he went to the shop to the left of the school gate alone and bought a pencil and a notebook and a small book with pictures.

Though Little Tashi felt cheated, he was very satisfied with what he had earned today when he held the pencil, the notebook and the booklet. He told his grandpa and grandma everything when he returned to the village and they were both unhappy with what Third Uncle had done that day but it was no use crying over spilled milk. In the afternoon, they prepared some food for Little Tashi and Dawa and taking the food with him, Little Tashi went back to the pen in Lungser.

When he came to the pen in the evening, Dawa had fenced the flock back in and was preparing food for the old dog. When he saw Little Tashi slip into the cabin smiling at him, he was shocked and asked, "Why did you come back?"

"I was a student for just one day," said Little Tashi.

Dawa said, "Oh, I see. I was wondering how Third Uncle could send you to school"

"But I got two yuan as a reward today," said Little Tashi, with a big grin on his face.

Dawa said, "How could you be so lucky for being a student for just one day? When I was at school several years ago, we had been told that we would be given six yuan, a kind of financial aid, but we had no further news."

"They told us some county leader would come and inspect the enrolment of school-age kids, but the number of eligible students submitted by the school does not agree with the number of enrolled students. So, that's why we were there today," said Little Tashi.

Dawa said, "Then you were dismissed when the leader left, weren't you?"

"Yes and the other kids all bought some delicious food with the money and I bought these." Little Tashi placed the pencil, the notebook and the booklet with printed pictures in front of Dawa.

Dawa said, "It seems you will have your heart set on reading and writing from now on and won't help me with the flock. Well, you might as well go to the remote grazing area now."

"Brother, don't worry. I will help you and I promise I will protect every sheep, even their tails," said Little Tashi excitedly.

Dawa said, "All adults tell us the Han people trust in notes and we Tibetans trust in promises. You shouldn't trifle with your promise."

"Surely I won't!" said Tashi as he fiddled with his precious stationery.

17
SHEEP STEALER

The next morning, it was drizzling with rain. Dawa put on his raincoat and drove the flock to the small ravine as usual. After a while, as the mountain fog gradually faded away, billowing grey clouds appeared and the sun showed faintly through the gap in the clouds. The rain stopped slowly.

Little Tashi cleaned up the sheep pen, went back to the cabin, and prepared to feed the old dog. The water was boiling and Little Tashi looked at the steaming pot and then looked around the cabin, having no idea about what to cook. As he worried about this, he suddenly remembered the xiase (also called duoma, a kind of zanba made during Buddhist services) that Second Uncle had given to him. (Tibetans would make zanba in different shapes and after services, duoma, or xiase, is provided for people to eat.) He fumbled in the corner of the cabin but found they all looked somewhat mouldy with teeth marks left by rats. Anyway, it was not a bad idea to have a change today, so he didn't cook at all, but sat there waiting for Dawa.

Some of the boiling water in the pot spilled out from under the lid, and some turned into steam and disappeared. Little Tashi kept adding water with a wooden spoon to the pot and in a minute the pot was boiling again. Little Tashi's stomach was growling, but Dawa had not come back yet. Little Tashi went to the stream and looked back at the small ravine, but nowhere could he see the flock and Dawa. He thought Dawa would probably go to meet Dekyi and, if so, he had no choice but to wait patiently. Little Tashi bottled up his anger and went back to the cabin. He looked at the xiase and leaned over to take a sniff; the mouldy stuff smelt good! He pinched a small piece from its apex and put it close to his mouth, but he suddenly realised that Dawa had herded the flock to the mountain very early in the morning and now, although the rain had stopped, Dawa must be wet from the rain and dew on the grass and bushes on the mountain. Little Tashi didn't have the heart to eat it alone, so he finally put the xiase down.

Bored as he was, he remembered the notebook and pencil he had bought in the town, so he knelt beside the kang and began to copy alphabet letters on the notebook.

Page after page, Little Tashi devoted himself entirely to his practising and soon the notebook was filled with Tibetan characters. In the Tibetan writing system, there were 30 characters, each having a special meaning. Interestingly, the second character 'ka' means 'mouth' and the fourth one, 'ang' means 'me'. Little Tashi also found that if he put characters with different meanings together, he would have sentences with simple but different meanings, as if by magic. He was absorbed in doing this and felt very excited. Not knowing how long it had been and what time it was now, Little Tashi simply felt the light that was slipping through the door and window become thinner and softer. The old dog outside barked wildly; he would not usually exhaust his energy for no reason. Little Tashi continued his work but occasionally he looked up, listening to the outside carefully. Then he heard the voice of a middle-aged man.

"Excuse me, is anyone at home?"

"Who is there?" Little Tashi stood up alertly.

The middle-aged man answered, "We are looking for our missing yak."

"Looking for your yak?" asked Little Tashi as he ran outside and saw two masked men crossing the stream and walking towards the sheep pen. One was short and the other was tall.

The short man asked, "Have you seen a yak in the mountain?"

"No, I haven't," said Little Tashi as he wondered how a yak could appear in the empty mountain as all flocks had moved to the summer pastures. He immediately became wary of the two strangers.

"Don't be afraid. We are cattle traders and yesterday we lost a yak at the mouth of Lungser. That's why we come here to look for it." The tall one remained silent while the short one continued talking to Little Tashi.

"Oh, I see," replied Little Tashi as he knew the mouth of Lungser was the only way for the cattle traders to make their trip and he therefore relaxed his vigilance.

The old dog barked at them madly, but the two masked men seemed to have no fear at all. They passed the gate of the sheep pen and strutted towards the cabin. Then the tall one said, "We have been searching for the yak for the whole morning without eating and drinking. Could you give us something to eat?"

"No, my brother said never to let any strangers into our home," replied Little Tashi.

"Well, we don't need to enter your cabin and we just want some food to eat and then we will go away." The short one suddenly asked with concern, "Where is your brother?"

"He is herding the flock on the mountain," replied Little Tashi. He then asked, "Why did you ask about my brother?"

"It is not safe for you to stay here alone. The autumn is coming, the best season for cattle and sheep to grow fat, and thieves are everywhere. You should be very careful!" said the tall man.

"Thank you and we will." Little Tashi was a little suspicious of the two masked men who seemed in quite a hurry but what they said was true after all. "Just a second," he said, "and I will get you something to eat."

The old dog kept barking at them and the iron chain around his neck clanked noisily as he yanked it. Little Tashi handed a small piece of xiase to each of them and they were very satisfied and said a lot to express their gratefulness. When they were about to leave, the short one suddenly pinched a bit from the xiase in his hand, spat on it and threw it to the old dog, who smelt it and gobbled it up at once. In a minute, the old dog became very quiet like a soldier having been disarmed. The two strangers muttered as they looked at the sheep pen and headed off into the valley.

Looking at their backs, Little Tashi thought they were kind indeed. He ran back to the cabin and knelt beside the kang to continue his 'homework'.

At dusk, Dawa began to drive the flock back from the mountain top. On his way back, he waved his sling to herd them to the hillside and then the sheep climbed down the mountain voluntarily. The flock roamed on the meadow in front of the sheep pen for a while and went back into the pen in an orderly way. At this time Dawa came back, grinning broadly.

Worried, Little Tashi asked, "Why didn't you come back today?"

"What's wrong with that?" answered Dawa cautiously.

Little Tashi said, "Aren't you hungry, not eating for a whole day?"

"I had some wild fruit on the mountain," said Dawa as he walked toward the sheep pen.

"Wild fruit?"

"Yes."

"Ha, ha, ha…"

"Hey! You dare to laugh at me?"

"I am afraid you didn't feel hungry at all when you met Dekyi," said Little Tashi, naughtily.

Dawa rolled his eyes towards Little Tashi, but he didn't carry on arguing with him. He hummed merrily as he went to the sheep pen and shut the gate tightly. Little Tashi shouted, "Brother, why didn't you count the sheep?"

"I followed the flock all day long and there is no difference whether I count it or not."

"If we don't check in the morning and in the evening, what if…" said Little Tashi.

"Why do you talk so much nonsense?" said Dawa as he walked towards the cabin. "I am starving! Couldn't you cook me something to eat?"

"Didn't you just say you had wild fruit?" Little Tashi began to roast some xiase on the stove.

Dawa had waited a long time to meet Dekyi and Little Tashi had practised writing alphabets for a whole day, so they both felt tired, but when the smell of the roasted xiase reached their noses, they both gobbled it up heartily. When Dawa had almost finished half of his food, he asked Little Tashi why there were only half of the xiase left. Little Tashi told him the rats had stolen it and Dawa didn't enquire further. When they were both full, they went to bed and fell asleep the moment they put their heads on the pillow.

During the small hours of the morning, the sheep in the pen suddenly dashed about and a few even jumped out of the pen, leaving the entire sheep pen in chaos outside and inside. Dawa and Little Tashi were woken by the noise at the same time and when they took the torch and went out to check, they found a few sheep were running around aimlessly outside the pen. They hurriedly drove them into the pen and searched around with the torch but found nothing suspicious. Dawa cupped his hands around his mouth and shouted a few times and the echoes from the opposite forests added something extraordinary to the vast shadow of the night. The old dog was startled by the shout and stood beside his stake, barking for a while and then he curled up and became silent again like a meat burrito. Dawa and Little Tashi found nothing unusual, so they went back to the cabin and slept again.

When they woke up the next morning, everything looked all right except that Little Black Head kept bleating in the pen, but neither of the two brothers paid attention to him. They drove the flock out of the pen and began to count, and it seemed there was one missing, so they counted again, but the result was the same. Little Black Head walked out of the pen and bleated anxiously, which finally caught the two brothers' attention. They looked into the pen and found Spotted Neck was gone. Little Tashi said, "I told you so. We should count the flock twice and you just didn't listen. Now, what should we do?"

"Where did Spotted Neck go?" said Dawa to himself.

Little Tashi asked eagerly, "Could she have run into Dekyi's flock yesterday?"

"I don't think so. Her flock didn't come to the mountain top yesterday," Dawa raked his brains but could not work it out.

Little Tashi jumped up and asked anxiously, "Where on earth did she go then?"

"I am sure I didn't miss any of them on the mountain yesterday. And yet, it is a little bit strange here," said Dawa as he looked at the fence of the sheep pen.

Little Tashi looked flustered and said, "Last night…"

"Yes, I am thinking about it too," Dawa frowned.

Little Tashi said, "But we both came out to check and there was nothing wrong."

"Yes, and what's more, the old dog didn't bark at all," said Dawa who could not make it out either.

The whole thing was very strange, and the two brothers began to search in the bushes around the pen to see whether it could be some wild animal that had dragged Spotted Neck away. Brown bears usually liked doing this, but it would not be so kind to take only one ewe away and even if a bear did this, there should be some traces of fighting and remains of the dead body. The brothers searched in the bushes beside the sheep pen, checked along the stream and they even went to look in the lower part of the forests opposite, but still found no clue at all. Dawa suddenly found footprints of two men in the mud on the path and asked, "Tashi, did you see any strangers yesterday?"

"Yes, two of them," answered Little Tashi.

Dawa asked surprised, "When did you see them?"

"Yesterday, two men came to our pen to look for their missing yak," replied Little Tashi.

Dawa was greatly shocked and said, "Looking for their yak? How could it be?"

"They said they were cattle traders and they lost one yak when they drove the cattle towards the mouth of Lungser. Then they came all the way here to look for it," answered Little Tashi.

"My silly brother! They were lying to you," Dawa rolled his eyes and continued, "What did they look like?"

"They were both masked and I didn't see them clearly." Little Tashi became nervous and added, "From the way they spoke, it seemed they were not locals."

Dawa asked, "What did they say to you?"

"Brother, I lied to you last night. The rats didn't eat the xiase at all. I shared some with the two men when I saw them thirsty and hungry," said Little Tashi full of self-reproach.

Dawa said with discouragement, "You let the wolf into the pen!"

"What should we do?" said Little Tashi sadly.

"What should we do? Nothing! Beasts with tails will always leave a trace while thieves without tails would wipe their footprints even if they leave some on the ground," said Dawa as he hurried towards the flock.

Little Tashi stood there kicking himself. He cupped his hands around his mouth and shouted towards the mountain, "Hey, you ungrateful thieves! I shared our food with you, why did you steal my Spotted Neck? Come out, you shameless thieves! Give my Spotted Neck back!" The valley reverberated with his rebuke but after a while it returned to its tranquility.

18
BOUND TO EACH OTHER

Without anyone noticing, in the woods opposite the sheep pen, the leaves of the birches turned yellow; the turbid stream became clear, becoming thinner and thinner as well. Funghi grew in the forests on the shaded slope or in the bushes on the sunny slope, and various wild berries, all turned ripe. The green earth had changed into a colourful world.

This season, herds and flocks in Dungkar village or in the remote grazing area all moved from summer pastures to autumn pastures, that is, from mountain top to the foot of the mountain. Autumn pastures, in a sense, were temporary transitioning areas between summer pastures and winter ones, so herdsmen usually spent less time, only about one and a half months, in the autumn pastures. While in autumn pastures, herdsmen started getting busy helping with breeding and castrating young bulls.

Though Little Tashi's family didn't have many yaks, it was still hard work for his parents to do alone. Work generally started in April, but his family was so busy this year that the work had been delayed. A few days ago, word from his parents came that they wanted Dawa to help with the castration work in the remote grazing area. As the time for Dawa to depart was approaching, Little Tashi was very uneasy. How would Dawa explain Spotted Neck to their parents? It had been his fault and suppose Dad was mad at him and agreed to let Third Uncle adopt him or sent him to Second Uncle's monastery, he would probably never have the chance to go to school! The more Little Tashi thought about it, the more scared he felt and he almost went mad from the sadness.

One evening, Dawa smelled something delicious from afar when he drove the flock back from the small valley behind the cabin. It was still early for supper. Dawa left the flock free on the open field between the pen and the stream and went into the cabin to have a look. Little Tashi had cooked a pot of wild herbs and it smelled so tasty with some minced leek leaves in there too. It seemed Tashi had run to the forest and picked a lot of fresh mushrooms as a special treat for Dawa. Dawa said, "Hey, what happened? Do you have some guilty secrets?"

"No! You are going to the remote grazing area soon and I just want to cook some delicious food for you," said Little Tashi.

Dawa said teasingly, "Well, you have some secrets, do you?"

"Brother, could you do me a favour?" murmured Little Tashi.

"What is it? Tell me."

"I…" said Little Tashi as he bowed his head.

Dawa said, "Well, I guess I know what you want to say."

"I know. It was my fault that…" Tears welled up in Little Tashi's eyes.

Dawa asked, "So what do you want me to do?"

"Could you take responsibility for the loss of Spotted Neck?" Little Tashi looked at his brother eagerly.

Dawa raised his voice on purpose, "You want me to cheat our parents?"

"Brother, I have no choice! I truly want to go to school!" Little Tashi cried out.

Dawa said chivalrously, "Well, I am your brother, right? I won't put the blame on you; anyway, I should be responsible for it too."

"Thank you, Brother," said Little Tashi as he wiped his tears.

Dawa then said, formally, "But after I leave, you must take good care of the flock. If anything should happen to the flock again, don't expect me to get you out of the trouble."

"You have my word!" Little Tashi became excited at once.

The day for Dawa to depart finally came. That morning, when the sun just climbed up to the top of the hill on the opposite, Dawa got up. He thrust some food he had prepared the night before into his bosom, warned Little Tashi over and over again, and then headed for the mouth of Lungser.

Little Tashi got up too. The sunlight rested on the mountain top behind, and later paced down slowly, but on that morning, the sunlight seemed to be more impatient than it used to be and soon it reached the bottom of the valley, shining warmly on the cabin and the sheep pen. The snow on the roof and the fence of the pen melted, forming a turbulent stream running high.

After Dawa's departure, Little Tashi, instead of relaxing his efforts, worked harder. When Dawa was here, they usually counted the flock like this: one person stood at the entrance of the pen and one went inside to drive the flock out. But how would Little Tashi do this by himself? He didn't want to repeat the mistake he had made and even if he was the only one staying here, he would never relax his vigilance and he would do his job well. He thought for a while and then an idea struck him. He opened the pen a little, slipped inside, and stood beside the doorway. Then he drove the sheep out one by one so that it would be quite possible for him to count precisely. Little Tashi counted once, and yes, it was the right number. They used to have 89 before Spotted Neck had been stolen.

Little Tashi drove the flock to the bushes at the foot of the mountain and then came back to the cabin. He at first set a fire in the stove; a cloud of smoke rose into the sky from the roof. The bark of birch trees crackled in the fire, sending off a unique, fragrant smell. Little Tashi held the bamboo broom, went into the pen and began to clean piles of sheep droppings. The droppings, like mischievous lambs, rolled to the corners of the pen, but Little Tashi was not impatient at all and like an adult, he swept all the droppings into a pile beside the pen gate, without missing one piece.

After he finished the work, Little Tashi's forehead was full of sweat but he didn't take a break; instead, he went to the cabin, ladled out two scoops of coarse grains from the flour bag and poured them into the old dog's bowl. He had second thoughts and added one more scoop, then ladled some boiling water from the pot into the bowl, stirred it until it was smooth and placed it in front of the old dog who was crouching beside the stake. Recently, the clever old dog felt guilty about his negligence of Spotted Neck and had no appetite for his food. Today, he was frustrated when he looked at the steaming hot food in front of him, licked the corner of his mouth with his large tongue but was unwilling to get up. Little Tashi knew what he was thinking. He squatted down, stroked his head and comforted the old fellow, "Spotted Neck was my fault too. Cheer up and eat your food!"

"Woof, woof…" cried the old dog, as if he was telling his young master how useless he was.

"I know you are feeling sad, but it's time for you to pull yourself together. Brother has gone to the remote grazing area and we are the only ones left here. If you don't keep up your spirits, how could you help me take care of the flock?" Little Tashi was more and more excited as he said this.

Hearing the words, the old dog stood up as if he understood Little Tashi's good intentions and in a minute, he had finished his food. Looking at the old fellow who ate his food so pleasantly, Little Tashi went back to the cabin with great satisfaction. He sliced some butter, put into the bowl and made a large bowl of zanba, and then pinched what he left after breakfast into lumps, placed them into plastic bags and put them into his bosom. He would stay with the flock and wouldn't be back very soon.

Little Tashi, like Dawa, tied the sling around his waist, closed the cabin door tight, went to the gate of the pen and looked towards the back of the mountain. Most of the flock had already slipped into the left side of the ravine with only some goats and the old and weak sheep following behind.

With sudden inspiration, Little Tashi ran to the old dog, removed the chain from the stake, and led the old fellow towards the stream. Having been tied to the stake for such a long time, the old dog was overjoyed by such liberation that he didn't know how to express his gratitude but kept shaking his tail and jumped up occasionally to lick Little Tashi's face.

They crossed the stream and arrived at the lower part of the forest. Standing there, Little Tashi turned around, looked at the sunny slope, cupped his mouth with his hands and shouted at the mountain ridge on the opposite. He was warning the birds and beasts not to get at his family's flock because the old dog and he would stay and protect the flock all the time. When they reached the small ravine on the ridge, the flock scattered and grazed leisurely and some had almost climbed to the mountain top. Little Tashi felt it was very inconvenient to lead the old dog by the chain, so he put it down and said, "Listen, don't run about!"

"Woof, woof…" The old fellow spun around Little Tashi excitedly when he was released.

"If you meet a stranger and bite them, there would be serious consequences!" said Little Tashi, as if he was talking to an old friend.

The old fellow seemed to get the point. He shook his tail and spun around

Little Tashi at first, then goodness knows where he fled, but when Little Tashi gasped as he climbed to the top, and drove the flock to the mountainside, the old fellow followed behind him again with his tongue sticking out.

The afternoon sun was softly warm. Little Tashi came to lie on the mountain ridge that swelled up like the bridge of a nose between the two ravines. He looked at the dancing clouds, floating eastwards in different shapes in the blue sky, thinking they must pass by the remote grazing area. Had Dawa arrived there by now? What were Mum and Dad doing right now? Suddenly, a cloud stopped over him, as if listening to his mind. Little Tashi shouted at the top of his voice, "Aunt Cloud, please take a message to my parents; tell them I am doing my work quite well and they don't need to worry." As the words fell from his lips, echoes came from the opposite forests and the clouds over him rushed eastwards a little, and then stopped as if they had heard him and were listening.

Little Tashi felt his Aunt Cloud could pass the words directly to his parents, so he shouted again, "Dad, you must keep your promise when next spring comes!" Once again, his words echoed from the forest and soon the entire valley was full of Little Tashi's voice. Out of vigilance, or loyalty to his young master, the old dog barked as well and made the sound in the valley even louder.

As if in a dream, Little Tashi talked with the white cloud in the sky and finally he fell asleep. In his dream, he was not farming the sheep but the clouds all over the mountain. He drove the clouds into the pen, closed the door, and then let them out to the mountain. The dream was short, but he felt it had been several months, and then he was wakened by the sudden noise of the flock as they ran about in a confusion. He looked up quickly and found the flock was fleeing in a flurry, among which was the old dog fighting with a jackal. Little Tashi summed up all his courage and rushed toward them. The jackal, though physically smaller than the old fellow and very frail and thin like a shadow, was no less savage than any huge beast and it seemed the old fellow didn't have any advantage over it. When Little Tashi reached them, the cunning jackal fled toward the bushes opposite while the old dog chased after him unrelentingly; the sound of dry twigs snapping came from the bushes.

At night, when Little Tashi and the old dog drove the flock back and counted them, Little Tashi found Little Black Head limped a little. Tashi grabbed him and checked him; it turned out that the damn jackal had bitten his buttock and if it were not for the old dog, Little Black Head would probably suffer like his mother had experienced. Little Tashi took Little Black Head to the cabin, scraped a bit of charcoal from the back of the pot, spread it on Little Black Head's wound and kept him inside. Little Black Head, who used to sleep between Dawa and Little Tashi, had grown up to be an energetic young lamb and he bleated all the time as if he was somewhat embarrassed. Little Tashi embraced him and gave him a kiss and Little Black Head stopped bleating and followed Little Tashi wherever he went as if deeply moved by his young master.

Little Tashi lit the stove and boiled a pot of porridge for the old dog. He tied him beside the pen after the old fellow had heartily eaten his food. He looked around; the moon hid behind the cloud in the gloomy sky; the bottom of the valley was shrouded in the pitch dark and, usually in such a dark night nothing, whether lonely souls, ghosts, thieves or hunting beasts, large or small, were rarely seen coming out, so the pen is relatively safe tonight. Little Tashi went back to the cabin and put Little Black Head, who couldn't fall asleep for quite a while out of either excitement or nervousness, on the kang. Little Tashi was unwilling to put out the oil lamp and he didn't fall asleep until a gust of wind from the door chinks blew it out.

19
THE MOON HANGS OVER THE MOUNTAIN TOP

The next morning, Little Tashi drove the flock to the ravine on the left, and in the evening, he drove them back from the small path covered with vegetation to the pen after they had stuffed themselves with grass. On the way back, Little Tashi heard the continuous hooting of two owls from the forest and he felt it quite strange. Why didn't owls call when Dawa was still here yet now they hooted so loudly when Dawa was gone? Did they know he was alone at the moment and it would be quite easy for them to take advantage of him? Although he was wondering like this, he bravely finished counting the flock and closed them in the pen. The old dog stood drowsily on the step in front of the cabin with his huge tongue hanging from the corner of his mouth, his eyes glued to Little Tashi for fear that he would disappear suddenly and leave him alone to take care of the flock in Lungser.

Yesterday, the old dog had performed brilliant exploits, but he maintained a noble manner, showing not the slightest pride. Little Tashi knew he was waiting for a big dinner as a treat. He, therefore, put two handfuls of coarse grain in his bowl, stirred it with his right index finger and carried it to the old fellow. The old dog stuck out his tongue and ate pleasantly, some of the porridge flowing down from its mouth and dripping onto the ground. Little Tashi thought this would never be enough for the old fellow, so he ran back to the cabin and ladled another scoop, but still he felt it not enough. He at last scooped a large handful of coarse grain, poured into the old fellow's bowl and stirred it till smooth. Then he clapped his hands with satisfaction. The old dog licked the thickened porridge and his ears that pricked up a moment ago drooped and clung to its head from contentment.

Darkness came. The moon in the east had not risen and the bottom of the valley between two mountains looked quite dark. Little Tashi lit the oil lamp hanging on the pillar in the cabin and in a second the gloomy cabin became brighter. Looking at the dim outlines of the utensils in the cabin, Little Tashi sensed something strange, and what's worse his ears became extraordinarily sensitive as if the long-accumulated ear wax had been removed. When the hoots of owls faded a little bit, coughing sounds like the ones an asthmatic patient usually made, came from the opposite forest, and in all directions. Little Tashi wondered, but after he listened for a second, the sound was a little familiar and reminded him of a memory in the past. It was several years ago, when he went to the mountain hunting for the first time with his father. They hid in a private place and then Father suddenly put his index finger to his lips signalling him to be quiet and asked him to listen attentively.

Shortly afterwards, some coughing came from the bushes on the ridge. Little Tashi remembered he had been very scared at that time and clung to his father's thigh and dared not move at all. To his surprise, his father shot at the direction of the sound with a semi-automatic gun he had hidden at home and after a moment, a wild deer tumbled down from the bushes and the others fled. As they came close to check, they found a poor female deer lying there, sprawling on all fours and her eyes rolled back, dead. Little Tashi asked his father why he shot the wild deer when they were bleating. His father told him when deer are in heat, they lose vigilance easily, which Little Tashi had once seen with Dawa and Dekyi and he hoped these two would never encounter a hunter like his father. When he was recollecting his memories, bleats of the wild deer disappeared, but a variety of strange sounds came one after another and made the solemn forest dismally spooky.

Little Tashi ran out of the cabin, untied the old dog from the stake, took him inside and closed the door behind, hoping the old fellow would be the bodyguard for him and Little Black Head. But the old dog refused to get onto the kang after he was led into the cabin; instead, he ran restlessly in the cabin, butted the door open with his head and went back to its stake at last. Little Tashi ran after him and coaxed him into the cabin again while the old fellow ran back to its spot the same way he did last time. Little Tashi tried several times but all failed, so he had to hold Little Black Head in his arms and went to sleep on the kang.

The moon rose to the right of the ravine. The silvery moonlight sprinkled its light on the sheep pen and the small cabin; shadows of the fence around the cabin stretched out long. In the opposite forest, noises of owls and wild deer all faded away, and the sheep slept silently in the pen, most of them making no sound except a few that were chewing the cud slightly after eating too much, occasionally panting a little bit. Little Tashi put Little Black Head beside him, but this young fellow stood there unwilling to sleep and licked his wound from time to time, probably because it was painful. Little Tashi held him gently and blew his wounds a few times. Little Black Head shook his tail at first, as if quite enjoying this. When Little Tashi felt his neck and arms somewhat soft, he blew out the oil lamp and the crystal moonlight on their bodies became brighter, and the shapes and movements of them were clearly seen as well. With the moonlight all around, Little Black Head at last lay down beside Little Tashi. He rested his head in Tashi's arms and formed a conch shell. Soon, he fell asleep quietly. Little Tashi, who had been busy for a whole day, was relieved; he snored the moment his head touched the pillow. In his dream, he went to the remote grazing area with Dawa, but his parents greeted Dawa warmly yet didn't even say hello to him. They placed in front of Dawa the zanba with butter, fresh curd cheese and some white steamed buns that are usually available during the new year celebrations, while Tashi had nothing in front of him. Little Tashi was very sad. It seemed his existence was hollow, and his parents were indifferent and ignored him. He believed his parents were punishing him because he had made a mistake and lost Spotted Neck. Thinking about this, Little Tashi squatted at the corner of the tent beside the door, clasped his thighs and cried bitterly. In the past, when he was blamed, or even punished, by his father for his small mistakes, his mother would come to comfort him immediately, but today, even as he cried so sadly and alone, his mother didn't even look at him once.

Little Tashi cried at the thought. This time, his father was sure to give him to his annoying Third Uncle out of anger and that means he would never have the chance to go to school. Little Tashi went out of the tent and at that moment a cloud appeared in the sky and he began sending the message he had left for his parents yesterday. He was very curious. Why did Aunt Cloud arrive so late? Then he wondered, since his parents paid little attention to him, how could Aunt Cloud impress them with the message he left yesterday? When he was still at a loss about what to do, his father rushed towards him angrily, from behind and slapped him across the face. Little Tashi woke up from the nightmare, but he couldn't see anything in the darkness, which was completely different from the time before he fell asleep. As he recovered some of his vision, he found in a blur that it was Little Black Head whose tiny mouth was pressing his face.

Though it was only a nightmare, Little Tashi felt pain when he woke up, as if his heart had been pierced with thorns. When he was still feeling apprehensive, a sinister wind blew in gusts outside and the prayer flag standing at the entrance of the pen fluttered violently. Then the cabin door squeaked open a bit and, distraught, Little Tashi jumped up from the kang, ran outside and looked at the sky and found the mountain top opposite was covered with a layer of cloud. After a while, the wind stopped, and the prayer flag stopped as well. Little Tashi went back to the cabin and went to sleep again but when he began to doze off and was about to fall asleep, the door squeaked open again. This time, Little Tashi was in a panic. He pulled up his leather jacket and covered his head and, after a while, he felt something moving gently towards him. He was so scared that he lifted a corner of his jacket to glance around the cabin quickly. The cabin was brighter from the moonlight after the clouds on the mountain top had moved away. Little Tashi gave a long sigh of relief and jumped off the kang.

Little Tashi came to the door quietly and looked outside. He soon found something on the dead tree next to the stream swaying back and forth. He looked intently at it, it was shadowy, like a gust of a tornado or a woman's long hair. Little Tashi snapped the door shut and then turned around to look at Little Black Head, who seemed to be startled by the sound and had opened its eyes to stare at him, as if he couldn't understand why his young master was so secretive.

The immediate image that popped into Little Tashi's mind when saw the horrible scene, was the tragedy that had happened to their neighbour. The mother-in-law and the daughter-in-law could not get on well with each other. Once, after a quarrel, the daughter-in-law ran to the small woods in the inner side of Lungser and hanged herself. All the villagers said the daughter-in-law was now a ghost and whenever they passed by the mouth of Lungser they would inevitably panic. This had happened a long time ago and Little Tashi never feared this before, but tonight, when the 'ghost shadow' appeared in front of his eyes, he got scared.

Little Tashi climbed back to the kang and covered his head with the leather jacket again while Little Black Head, also startled, tucked up his head inside the jacket. Little Tashi and Black Head hid inside the jacket, but this didn't work, and they became more frightened. Little Tashi therefore sat up on the kang, cross-legged and began reciting silently the six-character mantra. Adults always said the six-character mantra is the essence of all dharma but to eliminate evil spirits and resist demons and ghosts you must recite the mantra of Hayagriva. Again, Little Tashi recited the mantra of Hayagriva silently.

Little Tashi chanted the mantra as he stared at the door out of the corner of his eye, fearing that the wooden door would open again by itself. The door, as it turned out, squeaked open again after a while and this time much wider than before. Little Tashi's heart was almost in his throat and he lay huddled up in the kang while Little Black Head was startled too and hid behind his young master. This was the third time and Little Tashi felt it very unusual. He thought it was not enough for him to recite the mantra of Hayagriva only, he needed to write it down. He lit the oil lamp carefully and then took out his worn pencil and dog-eared notebook from under the cushion on the kang and prepared to write down the mantra of Hayagriva.

Dawa had once taught him the Mantra of Hayagriva, but the mantra was overlapping Sanskrit and after he wrote the first character 'weng', he forgot the rest of it. So, he had to write down the relatively complete six-character Mantra with a pencil on his notebook, and under the dim light, his handwriting sprawled across the page with no form at all. When he finished, Little Tashi grabbed some zanba from the bag, chewed it in his mouth, and then tore the page with the mantra from the notebook, spat the zanba paste on its back and pasted it on the outside of the door.

Little Tashi returned to the cabin and again the chilly wind began to blow and something on the roof blew down on the ground with a clatter while the door was shut close. Little Tashi and Little Black Head huddled under the jacket at the corner of the kang, but when they looked through the window chinks, the haunted dead tree outside was obscured by the sheep pen and the bright moon was hanging over the mountain top opposite.

Through the window, Little Tashi could clearly see the moon above the mountain top, which looked like a cheese painted in the sky. In the past, Little Tashi often looked at the moon and he only knew it was simply a white circle with some vague patterns inside, and he didn't study it then. Tonight, when he looked at the moon, he suddenly felt that the vague pattern inside the moon was moving. In their village or in pastures, whenever they encountered good days in the calendar, villagers would all claim there was a bodhisattva in the moon and they would bow their heads excitedly or even be moved to tears. Little Tashi always looked up to see the moon, but he could see nothing except some vague patterns. It was said those who couldn't see the bodhisattva in the moon had no blessings, so Little Tashi would follow the adults and claim he had seen the bodhisattva and begin talking about what the Buddha looked like.

Tonight, Little Tashi looked at the moon again and again and he found the pattern in the moon moved slightly and what surprised him most was the pattern gradually became a person's head. He stared at it intently and the human head portrait became his mother: two thick braids on her head, wrinkles on her forehead, a pair of not-so-big eyes, straight nose and even the dimples on her cheeks, all clearly seen in the moon. No matter how he looked at it, he felt it was his mother who was opening her eyes and staring at him affectionately, as if saying, "Tashi, mother misses you, but you must take care of the flock!" Seeing that, Little Tashi's nose twitched and tears streamed down from his eyes, some dribbling onto Little Black Head's head and making the young fellow look back to see Tashi's tired face. Tashi thought, what if he had a pair of wings and fly to the moon to meet his mum? After a while, a layer of cloud covered the moon and his mother's face disappeared too. Little Tashi wiped away his tears and said firmly to Little Black Head, "We are not afraid of beasts and thieves, let alone ghosts! Let's go to sleep." He slept on the pillow and after a while snores could be heard in the cabin.

20
SHEARING THE SHEEP

When Dawa helped their parents in the remote grazing area, Little Tashi had a few thrilling nights in the sheep pen, but fortunately Dawa came back three days later. When Dawa arrived, Little Tashi was driving the flock back from the mountain to the pen gate and preparing to shut them in. Little Tashi felt aggrieved when he saw Dawa. He grabbed a handful of sheep droppings from the pile beside the gate and threw them at Dawa; Dawa, though he dodged to one side, was hit right on the face by some of the sheep droppings. Dawa knew Little Tashi was playing with him like a spoiled child, so he didn't get angry with him.

Dawa looked at the flock he hadn't seen for a few days, his face blossoming with a bright smile like a flower, but in a minute, his attention was drawn from the flock to the mountain behind. Little Tashi standing beside him knew what he thought, but he was not in the mood for jokes; instead he told his terrible experience exaggeratedly to Dawa who on the contrary didn't show any sympathy for him, but doubled up with laughter. "A female ghost? Well, that's great! Today I will teach her a good lesson."

Little Tashi felt uncomfortable and wanted to ask Dawa whether he was laughing at him, but things had moved on and what Tashi cared about most at the moment was his parents' attitude about Spotted Neck. The words rose to his lips but when he was about to speak out, he said something else, "Brother, is everything alright in the remote grazing area?"

"Very good!" said Dawa.

Little Tashi asked, "What about Mum and Dad?"

"Good!"

Little Tashi continued guiltily, "Didn't they say anything?"

"What is 'didn't they say anything'?" Dawa asked purposefully, in a roundabout way.

Little Tashi said earnestly, "Something about me."

"You are beating about the bush! What you want to know is whether our parents blame you or not, don't you?" said Dawa directly.

Little Tashi grinned at him. "Yes!"

"Mum said nothing, but Dad said he would send you to Third Uncle," said Dawa solemnly.

Little Tashi whimpered, "Then I don't have the chance to go to school!"

"I am just joking! Our parents said the past was the past and they want us to take preventive measures to guard against possible troubles," said Dawa.

Little Tashi switched at once from grief to merriment, "That's great. I could go to school then."

"But Tashi, there's another thing. After the harvest, pastures on the village will move from autumn pastures to winter ones and at that time, Lungser will be a noisy place. Mum and Dad said it is of course important to keep wild beasts off, but it is more important to be aware of people walking on two legs." Dawa told Little Tashi all he had heard from his Dad.

At this time, from the top of the mountain came the singing of Dekyi. Little Tashi was marvelling at Dekyi's timing! He didn't hear her singing for a few days yet here it was again. The singing disappeared in a moment like the sunshine on the mountain top. Dawa had a new inspiration and he said, "Tashi, Grandpa and Third Uncle will come to help us with shearing the wool, could you tell this to Sister Dekyi and invite her to come to help us?"

"It should've been done in April! Why do it now?"

"Father said wool would cling to bushes if we didn't shear the sheep. Tell her, please!"

"Well, you should speak to me about my going to school then."

Dawa said unhappily, "You boy! Begin bargaining with me, will you?"

"Heh, heh!" Little Tashi laughed mischievously.

"All right, all right, go and tell her, otherwise, she is gone," said Dawa, eagerly as he looked at the mountain top behind.

Little Tashi and Dawa came to the bushes at the lower part of the forests. Little Tashi wondered, "No singing sound at all! Sister Dekyi might have gone back home."

Dawa replied hastily, "No, she is still here."

Little Tashi cupped his mouth with hands and shouted toward the mountain top, "Sister Dekyi, our family will shear the wool tomorrow; could you come to help us?"

"What did you say?" Dekyi's voice came from the mountain top suddenly as if by magic. "I didn't hear you clearly."

"Sister Dekyi, we are going to shear the wool tomorrow; could you come to help us?" Little Tashi shouted again, blood in his veins rushing to his face which was contorted at the same time.

"No problem!" said Dekyi, crisply.

The old dog raised his head and barked back a few times when he heard echoes of the cries of Little Tashi and Dekyi in the valley while the prayer flag in front of the pen fluttered as if inspired by them. The two brothers closed the flock in the pen, fed the old dog, ate the zanba and fresh curd cheese and then went to sleep.

The next day, Grandpa and Third Uncle, riding on Blackhawk, arrived at the entrance of the pen shortly after dawn. Dawa and Little Tashi got up quickly and hurried to go out and greet them. When they got off the horse, Third Uncle unloaded the saddle and his saddle bag from the horseback. Immediately, sweat oozing on Blackhawk's back turned into steam in the cold morning. This fellow stood there with ears sticking up on top of its head, shook his head back and forth, dilated its nostrils occasionally and spewed water out from its mouth to demonstrate his presence. Seeing Blackhawk's haughty and rebellious manner, Little Tashi thought Blackhawk and Third Uncle were somewhat similar. Third Uncle took the rein and led Blackhawk to the meadow between the pen and the stream to run around in a few circles. Little Tashi was puzzled and asked, "Grandpa, what is Third Uncle doing over there?"

"The horse couldn't stop and rest after it sweats, it needs exercising a little," explained Grandpa as he looked at Third Uncle.

Dawa sighed, "Well, people all say that Third Uncle loves horses the way he loves his sons. That is definitely true."

"Yes, there are only horses in his eyes," Grandpa said with a sigh.

Dawa looked at Little Tashi with a mischievous look and said, "There is Little Tashi too."

"Ha, ha, ha!" Grandpa tossed his head and laughed.

Little Tashi pinched Dawa's thigh in discontent, "Brother!"

The sunlight shone on the mountain top and then gradually stepped down. Carrying the saddle bag, Dawa walked ahead while Little Tashi supported limping Grandpa, following behind. They finally went into the cabin. In the saddle bag were snacks urban people liked to eat and some watermelon, green beans and bread as well. They set a fire in the stove and began to eat. Third Uncle was still busying attending to Blackhawk. Grandpa put his head out of the door and called impatiently, "Are you coming to train your horse or help your elder brother with the shearing work?"

"Okay, I am coming!" Third Uncle said as he led Blackhawk to the entrance of the pen and tied him to the fence. Seeing his former master, the old dog shook his tail, circled around the stake and made a low whistling sound, as he pulled his chain. Third Uncle entered the cabin as he looked at the old fellow, "Tashi, why didn't you take good care of our old dog. Look, he is nothing but skin and bones!"

"Huh, who belongs to your family?" Little Tashi muttered and whispered to his grandpa.

Inwardly unhappy with all this, Dawa thought whatever it was that Third Uncle had, it would always be good. He argued, "Third Uncle, we do feed the old dog every day." Sitting around the stove, Grandpa, Dawa and Little Tashi began eating breakfast while Third Uncle took out a rice sack from the saddle bag, poured some into a nosebag, and went out of the cabin to feed Blackhawk.

When the sunshine moved from the mountain top to the mountainside, they took out the binding rope and scissors and walked out of the cabin. At that moment, Dekyi, with the red scarf on her head, arrived shyly. Seeing so many people walking out of the cabin, she hurriedly covered her face with her sleeve and hid behind the cabin. Grandpa and Third Uncle cast their surprised look on Dawa, who was about to explain, somewhat awkwardly. Little Tashi said eagerly, "This is Sister Dekyi who farms sheep behind the mountain. We invited her to help with the shearing yesterday."

"Yes! Why did she hide there?" With his back to Grandpa and Third Uncle, Dawa secretly gave Little Tashi a thumbs up and then he came to the back of the cabin and said to Dekyi, "There is no need to be shy. Come out! This is Grandpa and Third Uncle."

Dekyi then came out shyly from behind the cabin and a sly smile appeared on Third Uncle's face. He said, "What a beautiful girl! Dawa, is she your girlfriend? You must have the knack!"

"What are you drivelling about? She is coming to help us while you are speaking for fun instead." Grandpa scolded Third Uncle and then turned to Dekyi, "Daughter, you have climbed the mountain and come all the way here so early in the morning. It is cold outside, come inside and have some hot food."

"I have eaten already," answered Dekyi as she hid behind Dawa, pulling her red scarf and murmuring in a voice that could hardly be heard.

"Well, let's begin our work," Grandpa said in a commanding tone.

Little Tashi stood in front of the door to block the flock while Third Uncle and Dawa, Grandpa and Dekyi all went into the pen. The flock scattered in chaos and eventually huddled in the corner of the pen. Some young lambs didn't know what was happening and bleated all the time thinking the flock wolves were coming; adult sheep, though disturbed a little bit, all squeezed into their respective spot consciously. Third Uncle and Dawa grabbed two adult sheep that needed shearing from the flock. They tied their legs with the rope; Dawa pressed the legs and horns and Third Uncle began to shear the wool with the sharp scissors. After a while, the two sheep were sheared as if a layer of skin had been taken off. They untied the rope and released the sheep from the pen while Grandpa and Dekyi finished the shearing in the same way, though they were a bit slower than Third Uncle and Dawa.

The sun had lay on the pen, above which a mist rose, and the smell of sheep's odour mixed with the smell of urine assaulted the nostrils. Outside were more and more sheep that had been sheared and they walked around a bit uncomfortably and smelled each other as if they had suddenly become strangers. At that time, Grandpa Humpback appeared on the ridge behind the mountain. When he saw Dekyi helping shear the sheep in the pen, he shouted at her angrily, "Dekyi, did the ghost drive you there? Come back at once."

"Grandpa, I am helping them shearing the sheep," answered Dekyi as she ducked out of the pen and turned to her grandpa.

"You simple-minded girl! Come to help others instead of doing your own housework," said Grandpa Humpback as he almost squatted on the ground.

"Ok, I will be back in a minute," answered Dekyi as she ran back to the pen and said, "I am sorry I have to go. My Grandpa is calling me back."

"Go back, kid. We are sorry to have brought you any trouble. Go back quickly," said Grandpa anxiously.

"Yes, Grandpa," said Dekyi as she ran back to the ridge.

Dawa walked out of the pen wanting to accompany her back but when he saw Grandpa Humpback standing on the ridge and staring down threateningly, he stopped and said, "Thank you!"

"It's alright!" Dekyi turned back, a slight smile appeared at the corner of her mouth.

When they finished the shearing, it was already the afternoon. Little Tashi and Dawa drove the flock to the foot of the mountain yet the flock, which had not eaten anything in the morning, were not eager to climb the mountain; instead they simply bowed their heads grazing silently. They, therefore, came to the meadow beside the stream with their food, eating while talking with each other. Little Tashi said suddenly, "We have so many delicious foods today, but Sister Dekyi didn't have the chance to share with us."

"Yes, just now I was thinking I had forgotten something, but I couldn't remember what it was. We should send her some snacks and watermelon," said Grandpa with regret.

Third Uncle, like a very experienced man, smiled at Dawa and said, "Don't worry, Dawa is sure to send some to her tomorrow."

"Third Uncle..." Dawa said shyly.

Little Tashi took the liberty and said, "If Brother doesn't go, I will."

"Tashi, don't worry about your brother. Go and check on Blackhawk," said Third Uncle as he looked worriedly across to Blackhawk who was tied up and grazing in the meadow behind the pen.

With his back to Third Uncle, Little Tashi disgruntled and said, "No!"

"Why do you always touch a sore spot?" Grandpa stared at Third Uncle.

"Enjoy your food," Dawa jumped up from the ground, "I'll go and see Blackhawk."

When it was getting dark, Grandpa and Third Uncle rode away on

Blackhawk. On the way, Grandpa turned back and said, "Dawa, the crops in the village are to be harvested in early August and you must come back to help me and Grandma at that time."

"Ok," said Dawa.

In a second, Grandpa and Third Uncle disappeared in the opposite bushes while Little Tashi shouted, "I will come too!"

"What's wrong with you, Tashi?" asked Dawa. "Don't you want to go to school?" he said meaningfully.

21

THE LOST RAM

As Dawa drove the flock back to the pen from the small ravine, it was getting dark. Little Tashi was playing scramble alone in the cabin. Hearing the cries of the flock, he went out to help Dawa counting the sheep. Dawa stood inside the pen while Little Tashi spread his arms and hushed the flock back to the pen in an orderly way. When counting, Dawa almost put his index finger on the buttocks of each sheep, but after he finished, he looked unpleasant and said it seemed one was missing. Again, Little Tashi and Dawa drove all the sheep out and counted one more time. Dawa said firmly, "Yes, one is missing."

"How could it happen? Didn't you follow the flock all the time?" asked Little Tashi disappointedly.

Anxiously, Dawa said, "I did. Come and help me check which one was lost."

"They all crowd in the pen and I can't see them clearly," said Little Tashi as he stretched his neck to explore the sheep pen.

"Wait outside; I will drive them out."

Dawa entered the flock and patted his thigh preparing to drive the flock out of the pen, but after these fellows rushed out and then were locked back in several times repeatedly, they seemed unwilling to cooperate and fled in all directions. At this moment, Little Tashi suddenly said, "Brother, don't drive them out, I know which one is missing."

"Which one?" asked Dawa, anxiously.

Little Tashi answered with assurance, "The breeding ram."

"Yes, it is him," said Dawa as he stood in the middle of the flock and looked around carefully.

Little Tashi was surprised, "Did you meet with wolves during the day?"

"Quite impossible. The wolves are not a gust of wind; how could I not see them?" said Dawa, with some conceit.

Little Tashi asked him, "So, on the mountain top today, did our flock mix with Sister Dekyi's again?"

"Right, they were mixed with each other, but when they were separated, no single one was missing," said Dawa, confused.

The sky gradually turned dark, the burning red sunset slowly disappeared behind the thick clouds, stars were all shadowed by the dark clouds. It was now the ewes' fertile period and the breeding ram was indispensable! If it had got lost or met with misfortune, it would be a very serious problem. The two brothers were very anxious but they had no idea for the time being, except to stand at the entrance of the pen, helplessly. When darkness completely shrouded the bottom of the valley and everything was in pitch darkness, the two brothers shut the pen and went back to the cabin with heavy hearts. Inside the cabin, everything was in darkness except the dim and slight brightness in the stove. They had no appetite at all. After feeding the old dog, they both went to bed early, preoccupied with their respective thoughts.

The window of the cabin did not have a smooth and bright glass but a piece of broken plastic, which was now rustling in the cold wind. Little Tashi and Dawa, who had been uneasy, were disturbed by the sound and they were both wide awake and tossed and turned in their bed. Little Tashi firmly believed that the breeding ram must be in Dekyi's flock, but even it were true, he was not sure whether Grandpa Humpback would allow them to bring it back. Little Tashi had so many questions in his mind, so he lay on his side and asked his brother, "Brother, Grandpa Humpback says the rosary every day but why does he get angry so easily?"

"It is said, many years ago, he had taken the lead destroying the monasteries and hurt many people."

"Grandpa's legs had been crippled by someone during that time. Could it have been done by Grandpa Humpback?"

"Nope."

"And then?"

"And then, policies on freedom of religious belief have been carried out; monasteries have been renovated, and more and more people choose to be lamas. Though it is history, quite a lot of people still expressed their disapproval or even hostility toward him overtly and covertly. Grandpa Humpback had been isolated and that's why he would be so bitter to everyone."

"Once when I went to pray in the monastery with Grandpa and Grandma, I picked a little mud from the wall of the Great Hall. Grandpa and Grandma were quite shocked when they saw this and said, since I damaged the sacred thing, I would be punished. Grandpa Humpback had destroyed the monastery, hasn't he received any punishment?"

"His wife, son and daughter-in-law, that is, Dekyi's grandma, father and mother, died one after another. Have you ever thought about why things would go like this?"

"Could it be a coincidence?"

"It might be. Don't you feel that he is very miserable? As a widowed old man, it is the most tragic thing for him to bury his own children."

"I never knew Grandpa Humpback had such a miserable life! But, Brother, I truly believe our breeding ram must be in Dekyi's flock."

"Me too!"

The next day, when they woke up, it was bright outside, but it was raining heavily. The rain must have begun late, at midnight or at dawn, since there was no leak in the cabin yet. Little Tashi and Dawa looked up from under the quilt, yawned almost at the same time and then got up.

They only had one raincoat. Usually on rainy days, whoever went to herd the flock to the mountain would wear it, but today, they had to climb the mountain together. Dawa, left the raincoat for Tashi. The raincoat fitted Dawa while on Little Tashi's body it looked quite loose and a little bit large, which however made it easier to keep out wind and rain. Dawa himself wore a plastic bag and then they hurried out of the cabin, released the flock from the pen, and headed for the small ravine behind. The old dog stood beside the stake, shook its tail and saw them off, his eyes filled with sorrow and loneliness.

They drove the flock to the hillside of the small ravine, turned to the ridge on the right and then moved toward the mountain top. The growing grass and the bushes on the hill had been drenched to either bow their heads or bend their bodies. As for Dawa and Little Tashi, their legs and feet had been soaked by the rain before the rain soaked their bodies, which made it difficult for them to walk. After a while, they reached the top of the mountain, where thick fog pervaded, and nothing further could be seen clearly except the flock in front of them. Gusts of wind blew over the mountain but the overwhelming fog, though dancing wildly in the wind, didn't clear away. Seeing this, Dawa said, "Tashi, call Sister Dekyi loudly and ask her whether our breeding ram is in her flock."

"You have a loud and rough voice, you do it," Little Tashi's teeth chattered with cold.

Dawa replied helplessly, "You know what will happen when Grandpa Humpback hears my voice, don't you?"

"Ok." Little Tashi cupped his hands around his mouth and shouted in a trembling voice, "Grandpa Humpback, is our breeding ram in your pen?" Little Tashi shouted a few times, but his weak and immature voice always echoed nearby as if it had been attracted by some sort of mysterious power in the fog and the whistling wind choked Little Tashi and made him unable to speak. In the heavy fog, the flock lost its way as well and began to bleat wildly, which made the two brothers even more anxious.

Seeing the way Little Tashi shouted and screamed in the wind, Dawa couldn't bear to let him continue but he said instead, "Tashi, perhaps Grandpa Humpback is not in the pen. Could you try calling Sister Dekyi?"

"Sister Dekyi, is our breeding ram in your flock?" Little Tashi trembled all over and shouted again.

There was no reply except the whistle of the wind around the ears. Dawa then said, "They probably don't want to respond, or they didn't hear it at all. You stay here to take care of the flock and I will go and have a look."

"Brother, the breeding ram is no ordinary sheep and in case it is in their flock, how could you drive it back yourself?" Little Tashi hid from the wind behind Dawa and continued, "We'll drive the flock with us. With its companions, it would be easier for us to herd it back."

"Sounds a good idea." Dawa felt Tashi's idea was great. He patted Tashi on his raincoat, which shook the rainwater out from the folds.

In the heavy fog, they drove the flock across the bushes on the lower right corner behind them, and headed for Dekyi's sheep pen. They had been walking in the bushes for a while and then the bleat of the sheep came suddenly from the fog below and the barks of dogs too. Yes, right on the lower ridge, the fence of the pen came into sight, and the blurred shape of Dekyi's cabin could be made out, below the fence.

Dawa and Little Tashi stopped the flock above the sheep pen and checked on Dekyi's flock. The breeding ram was there, shaking its long horns and following a ewe in a majestic manner. They looked at each and smiled. As they were about to walk towards the cabin, a dog with her puppies charged at them. Seeing this, Dawa shook his plastic bag a few times and the mother thought she had met a strong opponent and fled with her puppies.

The dog and her puppies went back to the cabin door and barked as if wailing to their master. Someone slammed the door open suddenly, it was Grandpa Humpback. He stepped out and asked, "Who is outside?"

"Grandpa Humpback, this is Dawa, the shepherd in Lungser. Our breeding ram is in your flock; could we take it back?" Dawa had wanted to let Tashi do the talking, but when he saw the miserable appearance of drenched Tashi, he himself did the job.

"You are here just at the right time! You've taken advantage of my granddaughter and your breeding ram dares do the same to my ewes!" Grandpa Humpback picked up some stones from his side and charged at them, like a crawling bear.

Dawa had thought Grandpa Humpback was ready to beat him, so he jumped into the bushes and Little Tashi dashed off as well. Grandpa Humpback, however, didn't chase after them, instead he entered the pen. The sheep in the pen became restless and ran about in confusion, like cats on hot bricks. Grandpa Humpback hit the breeding ram savagely with stones and the poor fellow ran around the pen like a chicken with its head chopped off. Frightened by what he saw, Little Tashi worried and cried, "Grandpa Humpback, please don't beat our breeding ram. If something should happen to it, our ewes couldn't give birth to lambs."

"I will beat it! No lambs are to be born in your flock anymore!" Grandpa Humpback chased angrily after the breeding ram.

Dawa couldn't bear to watch this anymore, "Grandpa Humpback, it is an animal and knows nothing about our world. Beat me if you want!"

"I'll beat it to death first, then I will deal with you," said Grandpa Humpback, furiously.

Grandpa Humpback chased after the breeding ram and beat it wildly and the poor fellow ran here and there breathlessly, his mouth frothing and eyes and horns bleeding. The sheep inside and outside the pen bleated all at once as if they didn't have the heart to look at this anymore. The breeding ram, perhaps inspired by the call from his own family, suddenly jumped over the 1.5 metre high fence and fell to the ground outside the pen. The poor fellow, though he stumbled a bit, stood on its feet quickly and ran towards his own family. Dawa and Little Tashi followed the flock instantly as if being electrified and drove them into the bushes and fled toward the mountain top. Grandpa Humpback still felt far from avenged and he jumped out of the pen and threw stones at Dawa and Little Tashi.

When they reached Namtso on the mountain top, the rain had stopped, and the heavy fog dispersed gradually. They took a rest for a while and then laughed like crazy as if they just escaped from wolves. Dawa, however, frowned and became silent after a while and Little Tashi asked, "Our breeding ram is back, why are you still unhappy?"

"No, I am happy," said Dawa with an awkward expression on his face.

Little Tashi continued wisely, "Are you mad at Sister Dekyi because she didn't come out to stop it?"

"Would it have worked, even if she came out to stop her grandpa?" said Dawa coldly.

Little Tashi comforted him and said, "Perhaps she was not in the cabin at that time."

The clouds in the sky didn't clear away completely, but the sun had already come out and rested on the top of the mountain. Clean and crystal blue, Namtso was a lovely place to relax and refresh, and a rainbow crossed over the lake, with one end resting on the slope full of cypress trees behind the monastery and the other on the bottom of flourishing Lungser.

22

HARVESTING SEASON

A few days later, the first day of August in the Tibetan calendar arrived and it was the day for the village to harvest crops. On that morning, when Little Tashi woke up, Dawa had already left. He stretched himself lazily and got up as usual. He went out of the cabin, looked up at the sky and found it was clear and cloudless as if it had been washed clean, but when he looked down, the ground was clothed in white frost. Elders in his family always said frost would do harm to crops and Little Tashi was a bit worried and kicked the frost with his toe to check how thick it was. It turned out to be a thin layer on the ground and probably it would melt under the sunshine. He sighed with relief.

Little Tashi gazed at the golden sunlight on the mountain top, took a deep breath of the fresh air, feeling refreshed. He stood inside the pen near the gate and the impatient flock walked out of the pen orderly as if to cooperate with Little Tashi's counting work. When the flock came to the pen gate, some older lambs knelt to suck the milk under the ewe's body, but they butted hard and pushed the ewe backwards continuously. With forelegs bowing and back legs stooping, some shook their small and delicate tails and were ready to poop and in a minute the sheep droppings fell to the ground like distorted black pearls. Steam rose when the frost melted, and clouds of mist floated in front of the gloomy pen gate as if someone poured boiling water there.

Little Tashi drove the flock to the small ravine and the sheep bleated on their way to the mountain. Listening to the chirping of various birds, Little Tashi began doing the housework, but he didn't keep his mouth closed and chanted one line in *Elegant Sayings* that Dawa had taught him.

The wise, when studying, suffer pains;
Without exertion, it is impossible to become wise.
He that is passionate for a small pleasure
Can never reach great peace.

When he finished the housework, the sunlight fell on the cabin and the pen and the flock, as if hurried along by something, climbed from the small ravine to the mountain ridge to the right of Namtso. Little Tashi ate some zanba quickly and followed the flock to the mountain. When he reached the ridge, the flock had arrived at Namtso, so he had to go on and follow them to the side of the lake on the top of the mountain, breathlessly.

The lake was as clean as the blue sky and if there were no ripples on the blue surface of the water, people would mistakenly think a small piece of the sky had fallen to the mountain. The brilliant sun blazed on the lake, where a faint light of blue, red, green and purple was reflected by a layer of mist there. Birds flew low over the lake. Namtso in the morning had an elegant and graceful appearance.

The flock, like snowflakes, scattered around the lake and some ewes bowed their heads drinking water, and some stared at their reflections in the lake, meditating quietly. A moment later, a fish jumped out of the lake and then fell into the water again. Some timid sheep were startled a few steps backward and then returned to the lakeside joining the fun again.

Mountains and hills are treasure lands;
Vast and endless the green forests are.
Terraces and golden wheats are dancing waves.
This is my lovely motherland.

A melodious and familiar singing voice wafted to Little Tashi's ears. He looked up excitedly but didn't see Sister Dekyi. He found her flock had already arrived at the edge of Namtso and joined with his flock. The breeding rams of each flock, however, followed one ewe together and behaved somewhat unfriendly to each other. Little Tashi looked intently at the bushes on the lower right corner of Namtso and although he couldn't see her, he saw her red scarf moving towards him. Little Tashi waited for her for a while beside the lake and suddenly Dekyi's voice was gone. He stood on the slope beside the lake and shouted, "Sister Dekyi, I am here!"

"Tashi, I am here," said Dekyi as she appeared from the bushes behind Little Tashi.

Little Tashi said disappointedly, "Sister Dekyi, why did you stop your singing?"

"How could I sing songs to you?" Dekyi replied with regret.

Little Tashi replied naughtily, "Heh! Heh! You must have thought my big brother would be here when you saw our flock, didn't you?"

"Nope," answered Dekyi shyly.

Little Tashi continued to explain, "My brother went back to the village helping with the harvest."

"When did he go there?" asked Dekyi, anxiously.

"He left the cabin before I woke up."

"Well, harvesting crops is the hardest job of the year and he happens to be up to that," said Dekyi worriedly.

Little Tashi said earnestly, "Not a coincidence. You know, my parents are in the remote grazing area; my elder sister has married and there is only Grandpa and Grandma at home. Who else can do the job if he is not going to do that?"

"You are right," replied Dekyi.

Little Tashi pressed his two index fingers together and stared at Dekyi, "Of course, things will be different if he had a wife."

"Why did you look at me like this," asked Dekyi as she lowered her head shyly.

"Oh, there is one thing. You were not in the cabin on that day when my brother and I went to look for our breeding ram in your sheep pen, were you?" asked the puzzled Little Tashi.

"No, I went back to the village helping my relatives harvest crops," replied Dekyi.

"Helping your relatives?" asked Tashi in surprise, "Don't you have your own crops?"

"Grandpa and I have been farming the flocks here, how could we have time to plant crops in the field?" said Dekyi.

Little Tashi continued his question, "What about your field then?"

"Grandpa donated our field to the monastery a long time ago," replied Dekyi.

Little Tashi asked curiously, "I remembered it rained on that day when we went to your pen, didn't it?"

"Once the harvesting date is scheduled, nothing could change it even if it is raining pocket knives," replied Dekyi.

"Why do people in your village scramble to do it?" asked Tashi, innocently.

"Because no one wants to lag behind and become the laughing stock of the village," replied Dekyi, sounding like an experienced rural woman.

"Oh, I see," said Tashi as he recalled that day, fearfully, "Your grandpa almost beat our breeding ram to death on that day."

"Sorry about that, but it was good news that he didn't inflict any wounds on you," said Dekyi in a helpless tone.

Little Tashi was confused and asked, "Why is your grandpa so unhappy and unwilling to let you and my brother become friends?"

"Because there are only two of us at home and he wants to have a live-in grandson-in-law, or at least have me marry a man in our village," replied Dekyi, though that was the last thing she wanted to say.

Hearing this, Little Tashi felt sorry for them and asked, "Does it mean you two have no hope at all?"

"I don't know," answered Dekyi, as tears welled up in her eyes.

Suddenly, the two flocks that used to hang about together in peace were in a chaos; it turned out that the two breeding rams were ready for a fight. They stood on the meadow beside the lake, rearing up on their back legs and ready to crash their huge horns into each other. Seeing this, Little Tashi said, "We have trouble now. Once breeding rams fight with each other, they won't give up easily. We should stop them!"

"It's not a big thing. Rams fight to decide who will be the dominant one in its territory. Leave them alone," said Dekyi quietly.

The two breeding rams kept a certain distance between them, made a big show of their strength for a while, and almost at the same time charged violently towards each other. "Bang!" The crash was so violent that they both bounced back. That was the first round. The two breeding rams started the second round, again the same act. Most of the sheep around them paid not the slightest attention to their fighting and went on eating while two uncastrated young sheep and some lambs were excited by the scene and began to run about, making themselves the cheering spectators for the two wrestling rams. Bang! Bang! Bang! The sound of the battle echoed in the valley and the fighting lasted longer and longer, the crashes grew fiercer and fiercer and the fighting postures became more and more ugly.

At last, the battle was over, with no winner and loser. The two breeding rams collapsed on their respective spots and glared at each other with bloodshot eyes, their horns and foreheads bleeding still. Some sheep ran along the mountain top to a spot beside the lake, a place that appeared smooth like a mirror since no bushes grew there. Little Tashi and Dekyi followed the flock there too.

Looking down from here, they could see Dungkar village clearly below. The village was located in open land at the bottom of the valley. On the hills behind the village were sparse forests, in front of the village ran a river, neither large nor small, the town and monastery were on the opposite side of the river. From here, they couldn't see the monastery, only some parts of the town. On the right side of Dungkar village was the Dungkar valley which extended gradually from the mouth of the valley. Around the village, and even in the inner side of the Dungkar valley, were fields planted with crops of different colours such as green and yellow. It was said that the village would harvest barley on the first day of the year, so all the villagers gathered in the fields, men and women, old and young, and cut the barley as they sang the harvesting songs.

Little Tashi strained his eyes to see the fields scattering in all directions for a long time and then found his grandpa, grandma and his brother in a field near the village. He shouted, but all the people in the fields were busy cutting the barley and paid no attention to him. So, he borrowed Sister Dekyi's red scarf and waved it in the air as he shouted. Dawa immediately saw it and waved his hand towards them. Little Tashi saw this and said, "Sister Dekyi, look, my family's over there and my brother is waving towards us."

"Yes, I already saw that," said Dekyi, excitedly.

Little Tashi was overjoyed and said, "Look, although Grandpa can't walk easily, he has done more than Grandma and Dawa have done combined."

"Look at the field beside your family's. A mass of people, at least 10, while there are only three in your family," said Dekyi, with some sympathy.

Little Tashi said to himself, "Yes, my family is rather short of hands."

"Look at the one beside the river! Isn't it your Third Uncle's?" said Dekyi.

"It is my Third Uncle's."

"I hear your Third Uncle has no children, so who is that girl?"

"She is Drolma, my cousin, the youngest daughter of my second paternal aunt. She has been adopted by Third Uncle since she was a child."

"Why does your Third Uncle insist on having you since he has already had a daughter?"

I don't know, but…"

"But what?"

"But if I could take good care of the flock with my brother this year, my father would send me to school the next spring. In that case, I don't need to go to Third Uncle's family then."

"But even if you are adopted by your Third Uncle, you could still go to school, couldn't you?"

"No, Third Uncle wants me to stay at home and run the family."

The sheep now ran to the hill behind and Little Tashi stood up and walked towards them. Standing in the middle of the flock on the hill, Little Tashi turned around and waved at Dekyi to join him. The town and the monastery appeared in front of Dekyi when she arrived on the hill. Little Tashi pointed at the goat standing on the stone staircase at the entrance of the Great Sutra and said to Dekyi, "Sister Dekyi, that's the goat our family has donated to the monastery."

"You brother always told me that."

Little Tashi smiled and said, "Why did my brother tell you everything? What else did he tell you?"

Dekyi nodded her head towards a golden-domed mani Lhakhang on the circumambulation and said, "You brother told me your Third Uncle donated that monastery. He is truly rich and generous."

Little Tashi retorted in displeasure, "Third Uncle likes showing off. To be honest, he is quite stingy."

"You might have a better life after you become his son," said Dekyi, in an earnest manner.

"No, I will go to school," said Little Tashi firmly.

"May your dream come true!" said Dekyi, as she looked at rooms of lamas at the foot of the mountain on the opposite side. She continued, "You brother said your Second Uncle is a lama in the monastery, so which room belongs to him?"

Little Tashi pointed at a room down the Great Sutra and said, "That one!"

"Why does it look so shabby?"

"My family doesn't have the money to repair the room for him, but my Third Uncle could and he has promised to do so. Two years have passed; nothing has happened yet."

"Why?"

"I don't know. Oh, Second Uncle wants me to be a lama!"

"Heh! Heh! You are so popular! Could it be because of you that they don't get on well with each other?"

"I don't know!"

"It is not easy for you to go to school, is it?"

"I know, but I will go to school," said Little Tashi as he pointed at the school in the town beside the monastery. "Sister Dekyi, that is the school I will go to."

"Why can't I see anyone there?"

"It is the summer holiday and students haven't come back yet."

"I will go to see you when you study there."

"Great!"

The sheep scattered around them and roamed leisurely. Little Black Head suddenly ran to them and laid his tiny mouth in Little Tashi's hand, as if asking for something. Dekyi took out a bun from her bosom, broke it into small pieces and put one piece into his mouth. The little fellow took a few bits and then sneezed uncontrollably. Apparently, he wasn't used to this kind of dry food. Dekyi felt Little Black Head was very weak and thin, and asked Little Tashi as she stroked his back, "Tashi, is he an orphan?"

"Yes, we named him Little Black Head. His mum has been stolen and he himself has been attacked by jackals. What a miserable life he has had!" said Little Tashi, sadly.

Dekyi was worried and said, "You and your brother should take good care of him, otherwise it is difficult for such a delicate lamb to survive the winter."

"He has lost his mum and if something should happen to him, how could I explain this to my parents!"

Little Black Head freed himself from Dekyi's arms and ran back to the flock as if he knew they were talking about him. With something on their minds, Little Tashi and Dekyi were both silent for a while.

Clouds appeared in the sky over the monastery. Little Tashi broke the silence and said to Dekyi, "Sister Dekyi, those clouds look like sheep flocks, don't they"

"Very similar. They might be the sheep flock in heaven."

"Will there be a shepherd to take care of them?"

"I don't know."

"If there is no shepherd in heaven, won't they be stolen by thieves or eaten by wolves?"

"Perhaps there are no wolves there."

"Then I want to farm the flock in heaven."

"You don't want to go to school?"

"I will go to school."

"Then why do you want to farm the flock in heaven?"

"Since there are no thieves and wolves in heaven, I don't need to take care of them. Doesn't it mean I could go to school?"

23
AN ACCIDENT

Harvesting crops is the most back-breaking task of the year. It is usually when the night fell and the sky was full of stars that Dawa could return to the sheep pen. Every day after Dawa got up and went back to the village to reap the crops, Little Tashi dare not slack off and he did his work more carefully. He would get up quickly, finish all the housework, carry his food and follow the flock to the mountain, keeping his eyes on the sheep all the time.

When Dawa came back after a day's work, he only briefly asked about the flock and then went to bed, snoring immediately. Harvesting crops was time-consuming and laborious: reaping barley and wheat first, then green beans, potatoes, rapeseed and yuan gen. In short, it took seven or eight days to finish the task and Dawa had blisters on his hands and was noticeably thinner after the work was done.

After harvesting, all flocks and herds in the entire, deep Dungkar valley would move back from the autumn pastures to places near the village, a temporary transitioning on to the winter pastures. There were no strict rules about where to farm the flock during transitioning and the villagers simply piled into the place where fresh and high quality grass was available. Lungser, of course, was one of the best choices. Soon, the entrances of small valleys in Lungser would be filled with black tents.

AN ACCIDENT

Some villagers had planned to move next to Little Tashi's pen, but they finally changed their mind and moved to other places as they found Little Tashi's flock grazed in this valley for the entire summer and there was not much grass left. Later, a dozen or so flocks moved back to Lungser, that is to say, one in five of the flocks in the villages squeezed up there. Lungser, the most serene corner in the mountain, had become a place full of hustle and bustle except for the small valley where Little Tashi's pen was located. The small road beside the forest on the opposite side of Little Tashi's sheep pen was alive: cattle and sheep flocks passed through back and forth; someone came along looking for missing sheep and cattle; and within a few days the small road surrounded by bushes were broadened out.

These days, Lungser was packed with herds of cattle and flocks of sheep: in small valleys behind the mountain, on mountain ridges beside valleys, along the edge of Namtso, on the mountain top or even in the forest on the opposite side. As night fell, the noise of bleating sheep, moos of cattle, barks of dogs and cries of people rose and fell from entrances to valleys, as if tranquility at the moment was a luxury. Only when the night settled in and the sky was studded with twinkling stars was the entire Lungser area restored to its serenity.

Dawa and Little Tashi followed behind their flock, making unremitting efforts to take care of them. They, however, were turned to for help quite often after the other villagers moved their flocks here. Because they lived in the same village and were related to each other in a sense, they found it hard to say no. Dawa therefore had his hands full with helping a family in the upper part of the valley find a missing cow or a family in the lower part find a runaway sheep on the grassland of the other village. Taking care of the flock was entrusted to Little Tashi at last. He had to follow behind the flock all day long and felt bored indeed, but on the mountains, he could always spot some flocks of other families or even some kids who were farming flocks there, which comforted him a little bit.

One day, as Little Tashi was tending the flock on the mountain ridge behind the valley, a grey sheepdog suddenly appeared in the nearby bushes as it looked down searching for food. It looked up at Little Tashi and then was ready to go somewhere else, but Little Tashi mistook it for a lone wolf and began shouting at him. The dog became very angry and sprang straight for Little Tashi, who, based on his past experience, immediately lay down on the ground pretending to be dead. This, however, didn't work with the sheepdog which jumped on Little Tashi and bit him wildly. The flock nearby started bleating and fled out of fear. After the sheepdog jumped on Little Tashi, it played with its prey as if Little Tashi was a scarecrow. All of a sudden, the sheepdog and Little Tashi rolled down the steep slope of the mountain ridge and didn't stop until they reached the bottom, even though clumps of bushes grew on this smooth ridge. The sheepdog pressed him to the ground with its forelegs and its jaws closed on his body tightly, showing not the slightest intention to relax. Probably it was because of nervousness or the fact that Little Tashi lay on the ground face down, he didn't even cry.

A middle-aged man who was walking along the road at the bottom of the valley happened to see this. He shouted towards the ridge opposite for help as he yelled at the sheepdog. The dog was startled by the man and, grumbling and sulking, it left Little Tashi alone.

After the dog walked away, Little Tashi rolled onto his back, feeling like a limp noodle. He didn't feel any pain, so he stood up and walked towards the direction where the flock had fled. The middle-aged man asked him loudly, "Hey, child, are you all right?"

"What?" asked Little Tashi.

The middle-aged man asked again, "Did that sheepdog hurt you?"

"No," replied Little Tashi trying hard to calm down as he found there were different sizes of dog bites on his calves, the back of his hands and his neck.

The middle-aged man said with concern, "But why do you walk with a limp?"

"Oh, it is only minimal abrasion," Little Tashi said calmly.

The middle-aged man said, "Anyway, there are many pastures in Lungser recently and sheepdogs. As a child, you should be very careful about this."

"Ok, I will. Thank you," said Little Tashi, gratefully.

The man added with concern, "Well, that sheepdog might still hang around nearby so don't provoke it anymore."

"All right, thank you. I will be careful!" Little Tashi said firmly.

The middle-aged man looked at Little Tashi from across the road for a while and then left. Though there were only some teeth marks and dog scratches on Little Tashi's body, the wounds began to ache. Little Tashi hid in the bushes beside him and cried out. He clapped his hand over his mouth, but the sound of crying slipped through his fingers.

Dawa was called out to help others again and Little Tashi knew that it was no use for him to go back to the cabin, so he gritted his teeth and followed the flock for the whole afternoon. When it was the time to drive the flock back to the pen, he limped like his grandpa as he drove the sheep down the hill

When he reached the sheep pen, he found the old dog spinning around the stake, whining and howling as if trying to tell him something or complain plaintively in front of his master. Little Tashi drove the flock to the pen gate and rushed to the cabin. Good heavens! The cabin was leaning forward and tilted to the side of the sheep pen like an old man who had had a sudden stroke. The cabin, fortunately, didn't fall over but looked like an animal which had been attacked by a wolf and then had his eyes pecked out by a crow, with its windows and door knocked over and part of the mud wall caving in.

Little Tashi totally forgot his pain when he saw the miserable cabin. He cautiously stuck his head into the room and found it had been turned upside down: pots and bowls on the stove and bedding on the kang were all in a mess, everything was covered with a thick layer of dust from the fire stove. Little Tashi bent forward to look and spotted some hoof marks left by yaks in the dust, and a big heap of yak dung on the wooden stepping stone at the door entrance! Little Tashi poked his finger into the dung and it felt still warm inside, and it seemed that the yaks just walked away after they had ravaged the cabin.

Little Tashi looked at this, unable to decide whether he should shut the sheep into the pen first or clean the mess in the cabin first. As he was standing in front of the cabin turning this over in his mind, Dawa walked towards the pen as he hummed a tune along the way from across the stream. He shouted from afar, "Tashi, why didn't you close the flock into the pen?"

"Brother, our cabin has been ravaged by yaks!" Little Tashi said with a tearful voice.

Dawa asked anxiously, "What? I don't believe it!"

"Come over and have a look," said Little Tashi.

Dawa rushed to the cabin and stood in astonishment when he saw it. Then he asked, "Where are the yaks?"

"They have already walked away when I came back," stammered Little Tashi.

"Oh heck! We are doomed," said Dawa in a panic.

"What's wrong?" asked Little Tashi as he felt Dawa seemed to pay less attention to the cabin and more to the whereabouts of the yaks instead.

"The yaks have licked the soil with salt at the corner of the wall and an excessive amount of that would lead to a swollen belly, which would probably kill them in the end," said Dawa apprehensively.

Perhaps the wound pain made Little Tashi slow to react. He asked anxiously, "How could this happen?"

"Don't you remember the case of our yattle? Last year, it had run into someone's house to lick the soil and eventually died of a bloated stomach," explained Dawa.

Little Tashi suddenly remembered what had happened last year and with a panicked expression on his face, he said, "Yes, I remember, so what should we do now?"

Dawa said worriedly, "When it comes to the damage of the cabin, the yaks' lives should take precedence. And if a yak dies, we have to pay half the price of the yak!"

It was getting dark and the two brothers set about cleaning the mess at once. Dawa reframed the window and the cabin door and jacked up the collapsed part of the mud wall on stones while Little Tashi drove back the scattered flock and closed them into the pen as he counted the number carefully.

When they finished their work, it was pitch dark. It was not until they tidied up the messy cabin and lit the oil lamp that Little Tashi uttered a loud cry of pain as he bit his lower lip. Dawa came to check on him and was stunned at the wounds on his body. He asked, "What has happened to you?"

"Brother, I was bitten by a sheepdog," said Little Tashi in a pathetic tone.

Dawa asked, "Where did you meet the dog?"

"On the mountain ridge behind us," murmured Little Tashi.

"Why couldn't you be a little bit more careful? Did you provoke it? Sheepdogs rarely attack people for no reason," asked Dawa.

"Yeah, it was in the bushes at first and I had thought it was a wolf, so…"

The old dog suddenly barked outside. Out of curiosity, Little Tashi ran to the cabin door, opened it carefully and looked outside, regardless of his wounds. A woman appeared in front of the pen gate all of a sudden, she didn't say anything but just looked around sneakily. Little Tashi fled back in horror. Dawa asked surprisingly, "What's wrong?"

"A female ghost is outside," Little Tashi gasped rapidly.

"Nonsense!"

"It is true," Little Tashi insisted, still full of fear.

The old dog barked more fiercely and loudly, and the rattling of the chain burst out as he rushed forwards dragging the chain behind him. The cabin was in dead silence and the two brothers waited inside. Suddenly an unpleasant and tinny voice jangled in front of the cabin door, "Is anyone at home?"

"Who is it?" Dawa asked in a loud voice.

The woman answered, "Why didn't you lock the door? My yak licked the soil in your cabin and now it is dying of a swollen belly!"

"We are very sorry. My younger brother was out herding the flock on the mountain and I…" Dawa stood up beside the stove and replied as he walked out of the cabin.

Little Tashi interrupted, "But your yak almost knocked our cabin down!"

"Your cabin? Someone abandoned it a long time ago and it should have been pulled down earlier. It is unbelievable that your family would let you boys live here," complained the woman, angrily.

"We didn't mean to do this!" Dawa comforted her in a soothing tone, "What about your yak now?"

The woman cried as she answered, "What about my yak? It is suffering from a severe pain and going to die of a bloated stomach!"

"Er, what about my going to the village vet for some medicine tomorrow?" suggested Dawa, in an understanding tone.

"Go to see the village vet tomorrow? We don't even know whether it will live through the night!" yelled the woman, becoming more and more excited.

"Madam, we are awfully sorry! Please tell us what we should do?" said Dawa, helplessly.

Sobbing, the woman said, "You know, this female yak has been giving birth to calves for about six or seven years in my family."

"Madam, your yak won't die," said Little Tashi, sadly.

The woman raised her hand and slapped her thigh, crying bitterly, "What should I do?"

It was a moonless night and the sky was covered by a cloak of dark clouds. A gust of wind rose suddenly at the bottom of the valley, blowing the nearby plants so they swayed silently while the singing of the flowing stream on the opposite sounded louder. The old dog felt some gravity in the woman's crying, so he stood beside the stake quietly. Profound silence! Even gasps couldn't be heard. The flock that had roamed on the mountain for a whole day, however, slept soundly in the pen, ruminating and snoring occasionally.

24
BY NAMTSO LAKE

The next day, Dawa got up at daybreak and hurried to the town's veterinary clinic to buy medicine while Little Tashi stayed on the kang for a while before he got up. The wounds on his neck and hands were minor injuries and the two bites on his calf had already healed. Little Tashi looked at the two bites in his calf, feeling no pain only numbness and he knew it was because he had bent his legs and curled up his body the whole night as he had been sleeping. Little Tashi put on his leather jacket and got off the kang as he tied his belt, but the piercing crying of the woman with a long braid, last night was still ringing in his ears.

He released the flock from the pen and rushed them to the foot of the mountain. The flock bleated as it climbed the mountain and Little Tashi went back to the cabin to do housework. The wounds in his calf began aching as it regained feeling, so he walked to the stove, removed the bandage from his calf and smeared some charcoal powder, scraped from the back of the pot, on the wounds. The wounds hurt, but after a while, the pain reduced a little bit, probably a kind of psychological effect.

The firewood had burned out in the stove; the final steam had escaped from the partially covered pot; the cabin was quiet, inside and outside. The sunlight sifted into the cabin through the window and the door chink, shining on the kang and the stove. Instantly the swirling dust floated in the air like numerous fairies, and a warm atmosphere pervaded the entire cabin. Little Tashi sat on the stool made of willow branches beside the stove, bent his head down and picked the scabs off the wounds, clear snot dripping down from the tip of his nose, long and glittering in the sunlight.

All of a sudden, a fat male gopher marched into the cabin, as bold as brass, entering through the crannies between rocks at the corner of the cabin, as if he had arrived at an uninhabited territory. Inside the small cabin, this tiny fellow strolled along the wall and then ventured to climb onto the stove. Little Tashi sat as still as a statue, dark eyes rolling and following the movements of the gopher.

The male gopher reached the stove, held his paws in front of his chest, his two black bean-like eyes blinked vigilantly and then he turned around and squeaked towards the stone wall, as if delivering a secret message to his companions. As it was, a female gopher came out of the cranny followed by four or five baby gophers. When the pups were inside the cabin, they scampered and chased after each other having a lot of fun. The mother leaped onto the stove as she saw the father standing by the pot and, side by side, the parents stood by the pot and looked at the huge thing in front of them, as if talking about how to get into it and eat the food inside. There was a short distance between the pot cover and the stove, so when the father gopher jumped toward the edge of the pot, he fell heavily on the stove and squeaked anxiously, as if to say, "My dear wife, you are slender and now it's your turn to check on the pot to see whether there is some delicious food for our little ones."

The mother gopher immediately leaped onto the pot cover, investigated the pot through the narrow passage under the cover and turned back to the father gopher, squeaking disappointedly as she found there was only a whole pot of warm water. The father gopher stood up on the stove, waving his paws as if telling her to try to find something to eat from the pot; even some crusts would be good enough for the pups. At this moment, the baby gophers climbed onto the stove one after the other, squeaking eagerly for food. Hearing the sound, Little Tashi had goosebumps all over his body and the wound pain grew worse, but he developed some sympathy for those lovely creatures. He looked up at the bags, blackened with smoke, over his head and wondered what he could give to this gopher family. They had already run out of butter and zanba and all they had left was the coarse grain for the old dog and some black flour. He stood up from the stool, wanting to get some food from the bags for the gopher family but his action startled the family and they all fled into the holes in the corner before Little Tashi realised.

Little Tashi totally forgot his wounds. He mixed some black flour with water in a bowl, placed some in front of the holes and went out of the cabin. The sun already hung high above his head. Little Tashi reached the pen gate and looked back for a while. There was no flock on the mountain, but a strangely shaped cloud appeared on to the ridge close to Namtso and then climbed down the mountain towards the bottom of the valley, like a fairy who descended from the heaven and settled down in the human world. Whenever Little Tashi saw those soft and pure clouds, he would feel an indescribable delight. Some sheep were hiding in the clouds, so he walked along the small ravine behind and climbed the mountain hurriedly.

When Little Tashi arrived at the mountain top, flocks of sheep and herds of yaks were everywhere, and his flock joined the other flocks. Little Tashi crossed through the flocks and reached the shore of Namtso. The sun was shining warmly. A few girls lingered by the lake with their skirts tucked up, some squatting by the side of the lake and some dipping their feet to check the temperature of the water. No one ventured to go swimming in the lake, for it was autumn after all, while in the middle of the lake four or five naked boys were frolicking noisily. Little Tashi went over to the lakeside and gazed. He had been alone in the mountain during the entire summer and it was indeed an exciting thing to see so many friends here. He knew the boys, who all lived in the same village as him. Just as he was looking at them, a boy swam out along the bottom of the lake and yanked him into the water suddenly. Little Tashi fell into the lake head first with a flop and almost drowned, and the kids around all giggled. In the lake, Little Tashi joined their play and as the water became warmer, the girls beside the lake went into the lake at last. They divided into a boys team and a girls team and engaged in a water fight, which startled the yaks and sheep that came to drink water from the lake. They retreated a few steps, then came back and went on drinking with their ears pricking up vigilantly. Flocks came and went and the cheers and laughter over Namtso drifted far, like a breeze.

The sun started to set in the western portion of the sky and they had already played in the lake for several hours. With mud all over their bodies, they came out of the lake, dressed themselves, gathered on the gentle meadows by the lake and played the game 'the wolf and shepherd', similar to the game 'the eagle catches the chickens'. Little Tashi was chosen to play the wolf but he refused and wanted to play the shepherd, so another boy nicknamed "Crooked Face" became the wolf and all the other kids were sheep. All the 'sheep' stood behind Little Tashi in a line as he tried his best to protect them from Crooked Face the 'wolf' who was running to catch them. Though they were all extremely tired by now, still they enjoyed the game very much. Crooked Face suddenly said, "We have played this game for quite a long time, it's a little bit boring, isn't it? Let's try something different. What about playing armies?"

They went to look for dry branches in the bushes beside the lake and made toy guns, setting out to play the battle between the Eighth Route Army and the Japanese invaders, as they had seen in the film. Eight in total, they divided into two teams playing respectively the Eighth Route Army and the Japanese, with the division between the flocks in the upstream and the downstream of Lungser as the border. Little Tashi joined the upstream team as the downstream side had more members, though in fact his flock didn't belong to either side. No team wanted to be the Japanese, so they each assigned a member to play 'rock, paper, scissors' to make an unbiased decision and the upstream team won and was the Eighth Route Army and the downstream team was the Japanese. To shame the Japanese army, they picked up some dyed stones and painted X marks on the faces of those who played the Japanese soldiers.

Before they began, they set up the rules. Everyone should place their food on the high slope beside the lake and each team was to launch the attack towards the higher slope from either side of the lake. The team which occupied the higher slope first would be the winner and enjoy the food alone while the team which lost could only go back home with empty stomachs. When they were ready, a fierce battle began. Who was going to win decided who could eat the food, so they all fought against each other violently, carrying their wooden guns, holding the mud grenades and marching and shouting towards the slope. Finally, the Japanese side won. The team circled around to enjoy the food, but the Eighth Route Army team questioned that, based on the film, how could the Japanese army win the battle at last! They argued with each other and engaged almost in a hand-to-hand combat.

A few kids from Gonpa village emerged from the bushes by the lake at that moment. They reached the side of the lake, looking quite timid as they found several yaks in their herd had slipped into Lungser. Nervously, they watched the quarrelling sides, before asking the fighting teams if they could enter the grassland and drive their yaks back. The kids of Dungkar village stopped their fight and blocked their way. Crooked Face asked, "Why do you herd your yaks on our grassland?"

"Your sheep and cattle come to ours quite often," one of the timid children said, falteringly.

"No way! When did our cattle and sheep go to your grassland?" shouted all the children of Dungkar village together.

"We don't want any trouble, we just want to drive the yaks back," explained a Gonpa village boy with a long neck.

Crooked Face said boldly, "Impossible! You have to pay the fine!"

"No, you bully! Our sheep and cattle did go to graze in their grassland, didn't they?" said Little Tashi as he took a step forward with his hands on his hips.

Angrily, Crooked Face yelled at Little Tashi, "Shut your stupid mouth! When did our cattle and sheep slip into their grassland?"

"My flock did this summer," said Little Tashi, earnestly.

With his hands on his hips, Crooked Face came over to challenge Little Tashi, chest to chest, "Hey! Are you a traitor? How could you help others at our expense?"

"Why should I want to be a traitor? I just speak the truth!" replied Little Tashi, biting his lower lip.

A girl, who looked like a boy, from their village said innocently, "You are indeed a bogus foreign devil! You are a traitor!"

All the other kids in his village burst into gales of laughter as they looked at Little Tashi.

Little Tashi said, "As a small village, Gonpa doesn't have many grasslands, and that's why you dare to bully them. If you had guts, go and bully the kids of Sibpa village and Kongjo village!"

"I am sure to give them a lesson if they dare to herd their cattle in our grassland!" said Crooked Face.

Little Tashi refuted, "You are just bluffing! When the flocks move to the summer pasture I am wondering whether you dare to drive the cattle to graze in their grassland! If so you are asking for trouble!"

"Coward! Coward! Coward!" all the other kids of the village surrounded him and shouted together.

A girl from Tashi's village whispered, "Little Tashi said the right thing. When summer comes, we don't have enough grass on our grassland, so we sometimes sneak into the grasslands of Kongjo village and Sibpa village, for which we are often abused or even beaten."

"Whoever has the largest grassland is the boss. They deserve to be bullied since their grassland is smaller than ours!" said Crooked Face.

Little Tashi argued angrily, "The flock of my family grazed on the grassland of Gonpa village many times during the winter and I won't allow any of you to bully the kids of their village. Whoever dares to do that, I will ask my brother to teach him a lesson."

"Hope you have the guts to do that!"

Crooked Face patted Little Tashi's head, expressing his contempt towards him but Little Tashi showed no timidity and wrestled with him immediately. They were about the same age and all the other kids didn't stop them but watched intently, with occasional laughter. It was a fight without a winner or a loser and they at last collapsed on the ground breathlessly.

At this time, the burning sun hid in the clouds, and shadows hung over the entire Namtso; the cattle and the sheep cast glances at these noisy kids as they drank beside the lake. When Crooked Face and Tashi wrestled with each other, the three timid children of Gonpa village secretly made a detour around the bushes by the lake, like rats hiding from a cat. A lanky boy from Dungkar village shouted suddenly, "Stop fighting! The three brats are driving their yaks!" They pulled them apart and Little Tashi and Crooked Face looked as if they just escaped from a cave, hair in disarray and scratches on their faces, although none serious, no real harm done anyway. The two followed the other kids sullenly. The lanky boy, like Crooked Face, was ruthless; he blocked the way of the three Gonpa kids, gave each of them a kick, and then the other children joined in. Little Tashi came to the aid of the trio and said with his arms wide open, "Stop beating them!"

"Why?" asked the lanky boy.

Little Tashi made up a lie and said, "They are relatives of Sister Dekyi."

"Who is Sister Dekyi?" asked a girl.

"My future sister-in-law, my brother's future wife," answered Little Tashi with a solemn face.

Goodness knows what touched the nerve of everyone but all the other kids laughed. At this moment, a melodious singing voice came from the bushes behind and as they turned to take a look, a beautiful young lady with a red scarf on her head was walking towards them.

25
THE FIRE

It was a cloudy day. Dawa was asked by a villager to help with castrating a bull in the early morning. When Little Tashi got up, he came to the pen gate, ready to release the sheep from the pen, but the breeding ram was chasing after a ewe, which stirred up the flock and all the sheep ran about in chaos. The sheep jumped and ran about inside the pen and the breeding ram stamped down on Little Black Head, almost smothering him to death. Little Tashi was furious with the big fellow, wondering why it picked on the poor orphan! He picked up a stick at the gate, went into the pen, and waved his stick at the ram, trying to beat it on its bottom. The ram, though tall and strong, was quite agile and dodged aside smartly. He ran back to the flock, looked back and stared at Little Tashi, shaking its horns as if to demonstrate its authority in an imposing manner.

The breeding ram escaped Little Tashi's sudden attack while another ram beside it was unlucky enough to be hit on the bottom. The poor fellow jumped up instinctively and butted a hole in the bushes above the fence, through which it squeezed to the outside followed immediately by some other strong rams. The other sheep ran about in the pen as they witnessed the misbehaviour of their pen fellows and then went through the half-opened gate of the pen. Although Little Tashi stood up for Little Black Head, this innocent young lamb wasn't angry at all; he got up from the ground, followed the flock out of the pen, capering merrily outside the pen. Little Tashi, however, regretted having been so reckless when he saw the hole in the sturdy pen. He checked the fence and wanted to do something, but it was not easy to mend the hole at once, so he went out of the pen disappointedly and drove the flock to the shadowed ravine of the opposite forest. In fact, the flock climbed the mountain voluntarily as they bleated on the familiar road. The grass in the forest was not high quality, but after a long summer it had been kept intact and the flock, tired of grazing on the sunny slope, seemed to quite enjoy the change. Moreover, it could be a supply in the cold winter to let the flock occasionally graze in the shaded ravine.

It wasn't very cold, to be honest. Little Tashi drooped his head and cleaned up all the sheep droppings in the pen, but he didn't feel warm after finishing doing all the work. He lifted his head, looking at the grey clouds in the sky, with a look of disgust. Then he went into the woodshed, fetched out a machete and took it to the foot of the mountain behind the cabin. He cut a bunch of thorny chaste tree branches, dragged them one by one to the pen fence and began to fix the hole. He patched over the hole in the fence with the branches making sure they fitted the hole according to the fence's width and length. His hands were covered with scratches from the thorns, as painful as if being pricked by a needle, but he didn't have time to attend to this. Hot and sweaty, he was busy with the repair work, even unable to spare his hand to wipe off the tiny beads of sweat on the tip of his nose and his forehead. Fixing and repairing, Little Tashi finally mended the hole with his clever hands.

The old dog kept howling as he watched Little Tashi, busy working with the fence, as if laughing at his young master for his silly work, like carrying coals to Newcastle, while in fact the old dog was not in such a poetic mood but just felt hungry and was asking for food. Little Tashi muttered, not knowing whether he was complaining about himself or about the old dog, as he went back to the cabin. In a while, the stove was set up by his small hands full of wounds and a thin cloud of smoke slipped through the weed-covered roof. In such a cold and melancholy winter, the thin cloud of smoke from the roof in the desolate ravine inevitably generated a sad feeling of loneliness. Soon, the old dog enjoyed a pot of hot food, though not a rich one, and then he curled up beside the stake to doze contentedly

Presently, however, the old dog lifted his head sharply and barked towards the shaded ravine, as if finding something unusual. Little Tashi did not rush out to check what's going on outside, instead he sat beside the stove calmly and finished a large bowl of zanba pasta first. He then went out of the cabin, shielded his eyes with his hands, gazing at the shaded ravine opposite. On the upstream of the shaded ravine gathered flocks of sheep, apparently not only the flock of Little Tashi's family. It seemed many families on both sides of the entrance of Lungser had driven their flocks there, as although many small bushes flourished, it was endowed with many grassy meadows.

"Tashi, come on, your flock is climbing the mountain," some of his village pals shouted at him from the shaded ravine.

Little Tashi replied, "All right, I will be right there."

"It is frozen cold here, bring the matches," another boy in the shaded ravine shouted.

"No problem!" Dawa never allowed Little Tashi to bring any matches to the mountain, but today Dawa was not at home and Little Tashi did it on his own will.

Little Tashi slipped on a pair of rubber shoes, put the matches in his pocket and rushed towards the forest. In the forest, snow was heaped up everywhere, but in a minute, Little Tashi had climbed to the hillside and reached the upstream, shaded ravine.

There was a big moss-covered rock midstream in the shaded ravine, where Little Tashi's friends were waiting for him. The moment he arrived, they gathered a large pile of dry branches from the bushes nearby and excitedly, they struck the matches and lit a fire. The dry branches burst into huge flames immediately in the cold, dry air. The friends sat around the fire, and the light shone upon their faces, glowing and radiant. How warm and cosy it was to sit by the fire on the mountain in such a cold and gloomy winter! They felt warm after a while, but their growling stomachs were such an annoyance that they all looked around, trying to find something to eat. How could it be possible for them to get some food on such a barren mountainside at this time of the year? So, they rushed into the forest below to capture sparrows and other birds, which turned out to be another failure. Disappointed, they walked back to the fire when Little Tashi suddenly remembered the xiase in their cabin. He said, "Cheer up! I have something delicious for you!"

"What is it?" They asked him eagerly.

Little Tashi smiled and said, "Do you want to eat?"

"Definitely! Go and get it!"

"Look, my sheep flock are nearing the top of the mountain," said Little Tashi as he pointed at the mountain top, "let's divide the work. Some stay here taking care of the fire; some drive the flock back from the mountain top and I will go back to get the food."

"Great idea!" shouted the other kids as some of them had already rushed to ascend the mountain to drive the flock back.

Like a swift fawn, Little Tashi tumbled through the snow-covered forest and in a while he reached the bottom of the valley. He panted as he fumbled out from a corner in the cabin a plastic bag of xiase which looked mouldy and smelt bad. Little Tashi knew they would smell good and taste delicious when roasted over the fire. He quickly tucked the bag into his bosom and went back to the mountainside.

Some children had already driven Little Tashi's flock back when he returned. He divided the xiase into small parts, sandwiched butter that had been dyed red inside and distributed to each of them. Some had once seen this in different religious rituals, but never eaten it before. Looking at the food, they all gave a look of disgust and after they ventured to try a little bit, they almost threw up. Little Tashi, however, had experience. He roasted the xiase over the fire and then ate it heartily, and his friends around couldn't resist the temptation when they saw the way he ate this and just like him, they began to roast them over the fire and eat them and even those who just now felt like throwing up began to eat with relish.

To roast more xiase, they kept adding dry branches into the fire and it burnt more and more fiercely. No one even noticed when the dry bushes beside them caught fire and, at first, they thought it was nothing serious and they even chased each other holding a burning stick for fun. Soon, unfortunately, the fire went wild and dark smoke blew up and covered the sky above. They at this time began to realise something was wrong and they cried out in panic like a troop of monkeys, having no idea what to do. Luckily, some smart and brave children stood up and ordered everyone to stay calm and fetch snow from the forest to put out the fire. They rushed to the forest, fetched heaps of snow with their jackets and spread it over the fire, but the snow they fetched from the forest was far from enough, like adding a tiny bit of salt into a large pot of broth, it didn't slow down the fire at all and it burned fiercer instead.

Whipped by the wind, the fire continued to spread like scuttling mice, burning more and more furiously, and the crackling sound of the burning bushes nearby broke the silence of the entire Lungser. Little Tashi and his friends were frightened by such a horrible fire and cried out as they huddled with each other, and even the smartest boy didn't know what they were supposed to do. Adults farming flocks on the opposite sunny slope were alarmed by the big fire and they yelled all the way as they ran towards the shaded ravine from all directions in the valley. As soon as they reached the fire, instead of scolding these troublemakers, they first took these frightened children to a safe place away from the fire and then some tried their best to put out the fire and some prayed to the mountain god for blessings. All of Lungser was in chaos!

Clouds of dark smoke shrouded Lungser, the fire had spread to the mountain, the sheep fled in confusion as they bleated in panic. What a horrendous scene! Some clumsy sheep didn't notice the fire and continued grazing leisurely until they themselves caught fire and bleated desperately as they fled about or even lost their mind and jumped into the fire. Soon, a strong burning smell filled the choking air adding a touch of desperation. At that moment, herdsmen came in all directions and began to fight the fire. People yelled to each other as they took what they could find trying to put out the fire; some even took off their leather jackets and their trousers to beat the fire, but it seemed all in vain.

Most of the sheep had escaped from the upstream area of the shaded ravine to the surrounding forest, but those that had scattered on the top were still grazing as usual, totally unaware of the impending danger. The only way to save them was to break through the fire, run to them and drive them back. Some young villagers, regardless of the big fire, dashed at the mountain, but only a few of them made it while the rest of them were forced back. Moreover, those who had reached the upstream part of the ravine found it was impossible to drive all the sheep back! There were too many of them and even if equipped with wings and three heads and six arms, they were no match for the raging fire!

Little Tashi was also in the crowd, trying his best to fight against fire. He was blackened all over from the dark smoke, the hair hanging down over his

THE FIRE

forehead was burnt by sparks shot from the fire. The anxiety in his mind, like a raging fire, became stronger and stronger and almost drove him mad. He knew it was impossible for them to conquer such a fierce fire with their bare hands! He suddenly remembered the trip to worship the mountain god General Jiri that he and Dawa had made last summer. Overwhelmed with a sudden passion, he clapped his hands, raised over his forehead and prayed, "General Jiri, please put out the fire for us, bless my flock and bless all the flocks in our village!" Perhaps General Jiri was deeply moved by Little Tashi's earnest plea for it was like a miracle that the wind changed direction and blew downwards before Little Tashi could finish his prayers. The fire ceased to spread to the mountain top and began to die down. Encouraged by this, people rushed towards the fire, lined up and took anything that was available to fight it: sticks, scarfs, leather jackets, trousers or even the shoes on their feet. Upon hearing the news, more and more people came and pitched into the battle. Many hands make light work. At dusk, the fire upstream of the shaded ravine had, finally, been put out.

Assessing the fire damage, there were three sheep burned alive and dozens were injured. Little Tashi's flock that had scattered on the mountain top narrowly escaped the disaster with only two sheep injured. Little Tashi, however, was still occupied with mixed feelings of apprehension and fear: it was he who had brought the matches to the mountain, it was he who had offered the xiase and if there had been no xiase, his friends wouldn't have kept adding branches to the fire, which was eventually out of control. In short, it had been his fault. Little Tashi nearly broke down as he turned over all these things in his mind. He suffered great agonies as he drove the frightened flock back from the forest and minutes later, Dawa arrived at the pen, all his clothes scorched by the fire and covered in soot. Little Tashi had thought Dawa would give him a good beating when he came back home but to his surprise, Dawa didn't scold him. Instead, he said to him with a sad look, "It is a miracle that we didn't lose any sheep but as for the dead sheep and their masters, it is indeed very pathetic!"

"It is a blessing of General Jiri," said Little Tashi timidly.

"It could be."

"Brother, I made a huge mistake. Please forgive me!"

"What huge mistake?"

"It was I who had brought the matches to the mountain."

"I knew it."

"You won't be angry with me, will you?"

"What's the use of getting angry?"

"Will they blame me for that?"

"Who do you mean will blame you?"

"Those who had lost their sheep."

"Of course, they are mad at you! They could skin you alive! But what I am worried about is the county government will send police to investigate the fire."

"Why should the police be sent here?" asked Little Tashi innocently.

"To arrest arsonists like you."

"No! Brother, I am so scared!" Little Tashi's legs began to quake as he heard this.

"Well - that depends," warned Dawa, "but dry and windy winter weather always make conditions perfect for wildfires. From now on, you must remember not to light a fire, for any reason, in the forest."

Little Tashi felt relieved a little bit as he heard this, and he solemnly promised, "You have my word, Brother! I will never do this again!"

"You stay at home and I am the watchman on the mountain tonight," said Dawa, as he put on his jacket and left the cabin.

It was said that all the men in the village went to the mountain on that night to keep an eye out for anything suspicious, in case small sparks hidden in the bushes might lead to big fires. Little Tashi was seized by a strong sense of guilty for the whole night, his little heart beat fast as if it would jump out of his chest. He wondered still: "Dawa is my brother and although he could forgive me, how could those who have lost their sheep, and the police, do the same? What will they do to punish me?" Little Tashi was full of these worries, hoping the horrible fire would disappear at once, with not even a small spark left on the mountain. Wondering idly, he stayed awake for almost the whole night.

At daybreak the next day, Little Tashi walked out of the cabin and gazed at the mountain opposite where heavy smoke billowed still but had thinned out, and even began to clear compared with what it was yesterday. By noon, thin smoke could only be seen floating into the sky from some corners on the mountain and people who came to fight the fire from the villages began to go back home, one after another.

In the next few days, Little Tashi was on tenterhooks all day long and the days felt like years. He was afraid that the villagers who had lost their sheep would punish him, he was afraid that the county forest public security service would send police to arrest him. What an embarrassing and horrible thing it would be! As soon as someone appeared on the far end of the mountain road opposite or the sound of footsteps came to his ears, he would be in an agitated state of mind, feeling very uneasy. To his relief, the families did not come to blame him aggressively because, after all, their children had some responsibility for the big fire on that day too, but when would the forest public security send police was still unknown, which had become an affliction haunting Little Tashi all the time. But, as the saying goes, 'a fall into the pit, a gain in your wit', Little Tashi was smart to keep this in his mind; he would never touch matches, nor light a fire on the mountain again.

26

ANIMOSITY BETWEEN BROTHERS

It was getting colder and colder as the winter solstice approached. On the shaded slope of Lungser, leaves of every hue fell from the trees in the wind, all the plants by the stream at the bottom of the valley began to wilt. Bramble bushes and the like on the sunny slope enjoyed more sunshine than those on the shaded one, and took off their autumn outfits according to the laws of nature, their branches turning sharper. At this time of the year, a yellowish desolate winter replaced the golden harvest season gradually and at last Lungser was dressed in a brownish-yellow, a valley of yellow grass indeed.

The flocks of sheep at the mouths of the small valleys in Lungser moved back to the winter grazing areas one after another. Someone who farmed sheep alone in the ravine or the poor people who herded cattle would drive the flock back to the village to survive the cold winter and drove them back to the mountains near the village the next day. Lungser was in dead silence as if it had suffered from a terrible ravage, all its ravines, streams, forests and even small bushes taking on a suffocating desolation.

Whenever a flock moved away from Lungser, Dawa would always be asked to help with the moving as if he were a grown up and he was indeed quite busy these days. It was understandable, on reflection, because herdsmen lived on grass and once they became neighbours, it was the right and proper thing to help each other. Little Tashi was seized with a strong feeling of loneliness recently which made him helpless and frightened, no matter whether he drove the flock to the small ravine behind or to the sunny slopes on either side. Unlike the gentle and considerate summer, winter in Lungser was freezing cold. The cold weather cut at the face like a sharpen knife, menace lurked everywhere in this deserted valley, hungry wild beasts, like wolves and jackals, became more aggressive and fiercer because of the shortage of food. The flock, as if it had already realised the might of the chilling coldness, gathered in the small ravine, unwilling to climb to the mountain top and even if they reached the hillside, they would go back to the bottom of the valley in twos and threes, roaming at the mouth of Lungser.

One day, the brothers drove the flock to a grove of willows at the bottom of the valley. When they played at the edge of the river, they suddenly saw a river otter. The brothers hurriedly chased after it. At that time, animal fur clothing reform in Tibet had not taken place, the otter fur was very valuable. The brothers still remembered the year before last when their sister got married and their father sold two rams and one ewe to buy an otter fur so that their sister could have it sewn onto the collar of her pulu robe.

The river otter was an amphibious animal which had an adorable appearance and was very agile. When it saw the brothers, it could have swum away quickly; it didn't however but ran along the stream for a while, then looked back at the brothers as if to tease them deliberately. Dawa and Tashi seemed to have found their confidence too and ran after it like hunters chasing their prey. When they followed it to a small gully at the deep valley, the brothers were a little breathless, while the otter disappeared as if the chasing game was over.

Then Little Tashi remembered their flock was still grazing at the bottom of the valley, so he reminded Dawa, "Brother, our flock won't run to the mouth of Lungser, will they?"

Dawa was still thinking about the otter. He replied, "You go and check the flock and I want to look for the otter." Little Tashi was a bit dissatisfied with Dawa. He stretched himself out on the ground like a deflated leather bag and said, "You go and check it if you want. I don't want to do that."

Dawa said at once, "Do you know how much does an otter fur costs? If we can catch one, its fur will redeem four lost Spotted Necks!" Hearing that, Little Tashi jumped to his feet and ran quickly toward their sheep pen like a gust of wind. Little Tashi, like a flying arrow, chased after the flock along the small path at the bottom of the valley and when he arrived at the mouth of Lungser, he found the flock was very close to the village, as if they were going to an appointment together. Little Tashi quickened his steps, managed to arrive beside them in time and began to drive them back.

On the road leading to the deep valley appeared a group of shepherds herding a group of yaks, their looks and the goods on the back of the yaks revealing that they should be on their return trip from the remote grazing area. Little Tashi took the initiative to greet them, "Excuse me, are you coming from the remote grazing area?"

"Yes, what's the matter?" said a man with an oblong face.

Little Tashi asked eagerly, "Is everything right with our pasture?"

"Who are your parents?"

"I am the son of Manba's family."

"Oh, yes, I remember. Everything is good in your pasture."

"When will flocks in Forest valley move back to our village grassland?"

"After the early spring, I guess."

"How many days it will be before the early spring start?"

"50 days and more."

"Great!"

A man with a round face cut in, "Oh, we have something for you from your parents, butter and curd cheese for the new year celebration."

"I have to drive the flock to Lungser, would you please take these to the village and give the food to my grandparents?" said Little Tashi.

"Your flock is still in Lungser? The new year is coming, so why don't you move back to the village?"

"My brother said it is better to stay in the valley than in the village."

Some of the shepherds said together, "There are no crops in the field, what's the difference between staying in the valley and going back to the village?"

"Well, I will talk about this with my brother when I see him," replied Little Tashi.

Among them, a man suddenly said, jokingly, "Hey, aren't you going to be adopted by your third uncle?"

"Yes! I will go to school when the early spring comes."

"Ha! Ha! Ha!" laughed the shepherds as they continued their journey.

The sun sank west, and its sunlight slipped to the hillside, glowing like a bronze-red apron tied around the mountain and the blue sky. Little Tashi ran to the gloomy bottom of the valley to drive the flock back, where the biting wind blew heavily. Little Tashi, however, was consumed with the conversation he had just had with those herdsmen and, based on his past herding experience in the last year, he felt if the flock should stay in the Lungser for the whole winter, there were sure to be many unexpected and unavoidable disasters. If so, that would spoil all his efforts of the past year and he would fail to keep the promise, and of course his dream of going to school would never be realised. When he reached the sheep pen, he rushed to Dawa after he shut the flock inside the pen and said, "Brother, let's drive the flock back to the village."

"Why?" asked Dawa in confusion.

"The other families have already done that."

"Do we have to follow suit? What if someone wants to jump into the river to kill himself, do we still need to follow?"

"What if those feeble sheep should freeze to death in the pen?"

"Impossible!"

"What if wolf packs attack the flock?"

"Impossible!"

"What it sheep stealers come to steal them?"

"Impossible!"

"Brother! You just kept saying 'impossible, impossible', but have you ever thought what if something should happen to the flock? Maybe you don't care, but I want to go to school!"

"Who said I don't care! Isn't it our family's flock?"

"Brother, I know what you are thinking about. Sister Dekyi is here and you don't want to leave her, do you?"

"Nonsense! Don't you know it is only your wishful thinking to go to school. When our parents come back from the remote grazing area, you should go directly to Third Uncle's family."

Little Tashi was four years younger than Dawa. In his mind, Dawa was always a good brother who was heroic and fearless; although he occasionally quarrelled with Dawa, he always respected him, listened to his words and accepted his advice. This time, however, what Dawa just said hurt him so much that his respect for him disappeared suddenly. Little Tashi bit his lower lip, clenched his fists, waved them in the air, charged at Dawa and hit him heavily on his chest. It caught Dawa totally by surprise that Little Tashi would be so mad at him and he fell to the ground, but he didn't rise from the ground to hit back at once while Little Tashi hardened his heart and punched Dawa's body. Dawa had thought his younger brother just let loose on him his anger but at this moment he knew he did it in earnest. He therefore jumped to his feet and tussled with him. To Dawa's surprise, Little Tashi, who used to be as meek as a lamb, acted like a powerful breeding bull this time and he couldn't gain any advantage over him at all, which was indeed a disgrace for an elder brother. Finally, Dawa, with all his strength, tossed Little Tashi to the ground and punched him quite a few times on his face. Little Tashi rolled around on the ground and burst into passionate weeping.

Seeing them wrestling frantically with each other, the old dog barked anxiously as if trying to stop them from fighting; the flock around was shocked to see this as well and fled in all directions after they had been in a daze for a while. Frail Little Black Head came to Little Tashi, sniffed him and bleated, as if trying to say, "You brothers! Is it worthwhile to punch each other like that?" Little Tashi sprang to his feet, kicked Little Black Head and flung him afar, then he turned around heading for the stream where he turned back and shouted, "I am leaving! I will go to the village and tell our grandparents all what you have done!"

"Get lost! Leave me alone!" yelled Dawa as he glared at him.

"And I will tell Grandpa and Grandma everything about you and Sister Dekyi," whined Little Tashi.

"If you have the guts, go and tell them!" Dawa became impatient when he heard this.

It was getting dark and everything became blurry in the valley. If nothing had gone wrong, Little Tashi would now be in the cabin with Dawa, but Little Tashi was so mad this time that he dashed all the way along the small road at the bottom of the valley, his cries reverberated on the sunny and shaded slopes in Lungser. It was pitch dark when he reached the mouth of Lungser. One by one, stars came out in the sky, staring at Little Tashi curiously as they blinked at him naughtily. The stream flowing from the mountain in Dungkar valley ran along the path making gurgling sounds along the way. Though stars twinkled in the sky, the visibility in this spacious bottom of the valley was poor, and the biting wind chilled him to his bones.

Little Tashi often travelled at night but tonight he felt somewhat scared and he didn't know why. Could it be because he had quarrelled with Dawa and ran away from the cabin? When he reached the intersection of the small path of Lungser and the road leading to the village, a sand grouse, with a flutter of wings, flew out of the bushes beside him all of a sudden. Little Tashi who was running on the road with avid attention was so terribly frightened by this sudden noise that he shivered, had goosebumps all over and was almost scared out of his wits. He became very suspicious and sensitive and his ears could pick up any subtle sounds in the darkness and his eyes could see any formless shadows. Characters in ghost stories flashed through his mind involuntarily, each having a distinctive but scary face. He always heard a rustling sound behind him, as if someone followed him stealthily, but when he summoned up his courage to look back there was nothing except darkness, which indeed sent shivers up and down his spine. He arrived at the outskirts of the village at last but the prayer flags in the village, put up for the deceased, fluttered suddenly in the sky, making the ghostly quiet and empty night extraordinarily frightening. Hearing this, Little Tashi who had already been terrified all the way was seized with more fear.

When he arrived in the village, lights in each household reflected through the windows into the courtyard, so bright as if it was during the day, but when he was in front of the door of his family, it was dark inside, and the door was tightly barred. He peered through the door but saw nothing. He knocked at the door for quite a long time and finally his grandma came out of the inner room and asked, "Who is it?"

"Me," said Tashi, as he cried grievously.

Grandma was surprised as she recognised Little Tashi's voice and she asked, "Little Tashi, why did you come back? What has happened?"

"I…" Little Tashi was still wailing outside the door.

Grandma was so frightened by his cries that her mind went blank and she even forgot to open the door for him. She just stopped beside the door and spoke from inside the yard, "Come and tell me what has happened?"

"My brother beat me!" complained Little Tashi.

Grandma relaxed a little bit as she moved to the inner side of the door, asking worriedly, "Why did he beat you?"

"Grandma, open the door first! I will tell you in a minute," said Little Tashi as he stopped crying.

Suddenly the sound of his grandpa's coughs came from the inner room and then his yelling too, "Old woman, who is it?"

"It is Little Tashi and he is back," answered Grandma as she opened the door, hands still trembling.

Grandpa said impatiently, "Don't dilly-dally then! Go and open the door for him!"

"Are you all right?" Grandma managed to remove the door lock, opened the door and asked Little Tashi as she looked at him. "You frightened me out of my wits! Are you hurt?"

"I am ok," said Little Tashi.

Grandpa shouted again from the other room, "You old woman, stop nagging! It is so cold outside, why don't you let him in first?"

Little Tashi felt half relieved when he saw his grandma, who then took his hand, walked through the hallway and entered the inner room. There were no lights inside the room except an old-fashioned lamp with a glass shield sitting on the crossbar of the stove, flickering. Under the dim light, Grandpa sat cross-legged on the kang turning a prayer wheel fastened between two posts beside the shrine, a brazier with burning coals placed in front of him. When he saw Little Tashi, he asked him with excitement and worry, "Tashi, why did you come back to the village at this hour of the night?"

"Why not turn on the bulb?" asked Little Tashi instead.

"It broke a few days ago. We have bought a new one but neither of us know how to change the bulb," said Grandma as she went over to the counter to fetch a bowl.

"Tashi, you didn't answer my question!" Grandpa stopped pulling the chain on the prayer wheel, which itself was still spinning creakily.

Little Tashi had no choice but to answer, "My brother beat me!"

"Why did your brother beat you?" asked Grandpa as he stretched his neck trying to listen to him clearly.

"The other families all moved their flocks in Lungser back to the winter pastures; those who farmed flocks near the village have driven their sheep and cattle back to their home as well. So, I suggested we drive our flock back to the village. Brother was so mad at me when he heard this that he beat me."

"Come over here! Did you get hurt?" asked Grandpa as he moved his behind off the bed and sat on the edge of the kang.

Little Tashi tiptoed to the kang, leaned over towards Grandpa and said heavily but with a touch of reluctance, "No, I am ok."

"Why did you run back then? Isn't it so pathetic of your brother to be in the cabin alone?" said Grandpa as he cast a look a Little Tashi under the dim light.

"Uh-huh!" said Little Tashi as he lowered his head, his anger melting.

Standing beside the stove, Grandma interrupted, "You old man! Let him have some hot zanba porridge to get warm first."

"Oh, yes! Go to your grandma and have some hot zanba porridge," said Grandpa as he stroked Little Tashi's hair affectionately.

Little Tashi went over to the stove, took a bowl of steaming porridge from his grandma, took a sip and raised his head asking, "Grandpa, let's move the flock back to the village, shall we?"

"Your brother is after all some years older than you, so listen to him, will you?"

"There is a reason why my brother wants to stay in Lungser!"

Grandma asked, as she added boiled water to his bowl. "What reason? Tell us and we will back you up."

"If I tell you this, my brother is sure to beat me again!"

"What happened?" enquired Grandpa as he looked at Little Tashi.

Grandpa and Grandma stared at Little Tashi, he deliberately left them hanging there for a little while and then said, "After I tell you this, keep it between us, will you?"

"Of course, we will!" said Grandpa and Grandma with a smile as they exchanged looks with each other.

Little Tashi put down the bowl on the stove, looked around cautiously and whispered with his hands covering his mouth, "Brother has a girlfriend in the grassland behind Lungser! That's why he doesn't want to go back to the village."

"He does?" asked Grandpa.

"As true as I am sitting here!" said Little Tashi firmly, lowering his voice.

"Which village does she come from? How old is she? What does she look like?" Grandma posed a series of questions, excitedly.

Grandma's questions confused Little Tashi for a moment. He thought for a little while and said, "She comes from Gonpa village, she is the same age as my brother. And she is very beautiful!"

"Don't you want to have a sister-in-law?" asked Grandpa with a broad smile on his face.

"I want to have a sister-in-law!"

"Don't you want to go to school?" added Grandpa.

"I want to go to school!"

"Then you'd better listen to your brother!" Grandpa burst out laughing as he finished his words, his laughter resounding around the room.

With a contemplative look on her face, Grandma asked, "Whose daughter is she?"

"I heard her parents are both dead and she only has a grandpa, a hunchback," replied Little Tashi.

Grandpa chimed in, "The girl who came to help with sheep shearing?"

"Yes, it is she."

"She is a very good girl!" praised Grandpa.

"But I heard her grandpa had taken the lead in destroying monasteries and humiliated people in sessions in the Cultural Revolution," continued Little Tashi as he wondered why Grandpa could accept Dekyi without any objection.

Grandpa frowned, as if recalling the past humiliations he had suffered, but after a while, slowly but very forcefully, he said, "Well, forget it! Let bygones be bygones!"

"Right! Let bygones be bygones!" Grandma grinned but said with a displeased look, "Is the girl willing to marry your brother?"

Little Tashi said, "It seems to be, but I heard her grandpa objects to it."

"Times have changed and seldom is an arranged marriage practised nowadays! As long as they want to live with each other, nothing will stop them," said Grandpa as he cleared his throat.

That night, sleeping on the kang alone, Dawa was angry, aggrieved and regretful and he almost stayed awake throughout the night. As soon as dawn came the next day, he released the flock from the pen and decided to look for Little Tashi, but he knew he could not leave the flock unattended. He hesitated and didn't know what to do. In the distance Grandpa and Little Tashi suddenly appeared on the small road, Grandpa taking Little Tashi by the hand as he limped towards the pen.

27

THE SNOWY DAY

It snowed heavily the whole night. The next morning, when Dawa and Little Tashi got up, it was freezing cold inside the cabin where the biting wind sneaked in through the door, the window and the crevices in the stone wall. The two brothers crept under the bedclothes again, snuggling down to get themselves warm, like two hedgehogs. It was not until the sun moved from the mountain top to the hillside that they rose up lazily. Their hearts were overflowing with excitement when they saw the white snow outside through the window. Horrible as the cold weather was, it was the first snow this year after all!

Little Tashi's heart overflowed with great joy. He put on the patched leather jacket and ran out of the cabin. What a beautiful world of ice and snow! On this windless day, the prayer flag stood high in front of the pen gate, hanging down from the pole; the old dog curled up his body sleeping beside the stake like an ice statue, and even didn't bother to glance up at his young master but only rolled his eyes to indicate that he had spent the whole night in the snow. The sheep huddled with each other in the corner of the pen to warm themselves up, all covered with a blanket of snow. Little Tashi heard the wild thrushes singing melodiously in the nearby trees, he took a deep breath of the cool, fresh air and sang aloud like the wild thrushes, but his voice sounded like a terrible scream as if a man who didn't know how to blow the horn blew it for the first time. The flock, probably unable to put up with Little Tashi's singing, bleated one after another, and chunks of snow slid off the roof as well.

The sun shone warmly on the cabin and the pen, its golden rays were extraordinarily glaring in the sky. Little Tashi trod on the deep snow, which crunched under his feet. He picked some wool from the fence beside the sheep pen, spun it into thin thread, tied it above his eyes and went back to play in the snow. He stepped on the snow back and forth, leaving a trail of footprints like tyre tracks of a tractor; he had a lot of fun and shouted at the cabin excitedly, "Brother, come out! It is so beautiful here outside."

"I am here," answered Dawa as he stood between the old dog and the pen, peeing on the bushes, the sound of his stream was absorbed by the thick snow. He later turned around to check on the flock in the pen, and then on the old dog who was lying on the snow miserably. He said to Little Tashi, "The old dog has slept in the snow for the whole night and is almost frozen to death. Go and set a fire in the cabin. Cook something for him to warm him up."

"Come over here and let's play for a while," pleaded Little Tashi, as he was still having fun in the snow.

Dawa opened the pen gate and said, "Stop fooling around. I am about to drive the flock to the sunny slope behind."

"Brother, look!"

Little Tashi made a snowball and threw it at Dawa who turned around and tried to deflect it with his left hand. The ball failed to hit him, but the snow splashed into his neck. "Ouch!" yelled Dawa. He bent down, trying to dig snow out of his jacket collar and then he made a snowball and rushed towards Little Tashi, who, like a mouse, sneaked into the cabin and shut the door quickly. The snowball hit the door heavily, spraying around.

In a minute, a cloud of cooking smoke rose above the roof. Dawa drove the flock out of the pen after he finished the counting. The moment the flock walked out of the pen and stepped on the deep snow, the adult sheep were all busy with relieving themselves. As they moved on, droppings like black pearls were scattered on the white snow, leaving rugged tracks while young lambs gathered together butting playfully. Making hushing sounds along the way, Dawa drove them to the bushes behind the cabin.

When Dawa returned to the cabin, the fire in the stove was burning happily, the crackling sound of the firewood inside the stove and the flames were licking the bottom of the pot, filled the shabby hut with a warm atmosphere. Little Tashi brought a large bowl of hot food to the old dog, a treat for him for watching over the flock all night. As he hummed a tune on his way back to the cabin, he saw a magpie perched on the pen fence, chirping. He looked at the bird, wondering whether a guest would come to visit. He sheltered his eyes with his right hand to look around while there was nothing but the vast expanse of whiteness and the entire bottom of the valley was in silence like a deserted place. He turned back and went into the cabin, to eat beside the stove with Dawa. Suddenly, the flames inside the stove kept spraying out. Little Tashi put down his bowl, pointed at the flames and said, "Look, flames are spraying out , we are sure to have guests today!"

"Who would come to visit on such a snowy day?" Dawa said in disapproval.

The old dog barked outside the cabin and the two brothers did not stand up immediately to check what was happening. They listened and then heard someone walking towards the cabin door, snow crunching under his feet. The door was pushed open lightly and a lovely face wearing a red scarf came into view. It was Dekyi!

Dawa and Little Tashi quickly stood up and invited her to come in. Dekyi stomped the snow from her feet and entered the cabin, sitting beside the stove, a pair of black eyes glancing around the cabin from her rosy face. She warmed her rough little hands over the fire and Little Tashi asked her eagerly, "Sister Dekyi, you and my brother have an appointment today, don't you?"

"Nope," said Dekyi as she lowered her head.

"You are talking nonsense again! We haven't seen each other for several days, how could we arrange an appointment?" said Dawa as he took a bowl to get Dekyi something to eat.

Dekyi stopped him, saying that she had already eaten something.

"Sister Dekyi, have some hot water and get yourself warm," said Little Tashi like an adult.

"Ok, I could help myself," Dekyi rose to her feet quickly and poured a bowl of hot water for herself, and for the two brothers too.

The three huddled together beside the fire, Dekyi sitting in the middle with the two brothers on either side. Dekyi chewed a lump of tree resin loudly in her mouth, which crackled like the bang of firecrackers, a sweet scent of pine tree coming out of her mouth. Every time Little Tashi saw Dekyi, he would have a lot of questions and he asked, "Sister Dekyi, why did you come here on such a snowy day?"

"Look at this," Dekyi took out a pair of sheepskin hats from her coat.

Little Tashi grabbed one from Dekyi and asked, "You made these for us?"

"Yes! One of my family's rams was bitten to death by a jackal last month. That vicious jackal worked its way up through the ram's backside and ate up almost everything inside the ram, leaving the sheep skin intact. My grandpa decided to sell the sheepskin to a Hui merchant and I managed to get the hide of its four legs and some remnants before he noticed and made each of you a hat for the winter," explained Dekyi, slowly.

Little Tashi tried the hat on his head and blurted with some regret, "Oh, why is it a visor hat? Only my ears are covered."

"Do you have ears? Didn't Sister Dekyi say just now that she managed to make these from hide remnants? Say thank you!" said Dawa as he elbowed Little Tashi.

Little Tashi hurriedly corrected himself and said, "Sister Dekyi, thank you for all the trouble you have taken."

"You are welcome, and it is only a small gift," replied Dekyi as she looked round the cabin and stood up.

She first put things back where they belonged and then took off her shoes and climbed onto the kang, folding up their quilts and putting them away tidily. Then she climbed off the kang, took the broom and gave the cabin a thorough clean, including every nook and cranny. All the rubbish was cleaned out and the cabin that used to be quite messy was turned neat and bright instantly.

Watching her as she was busy working in the cabin like a housewife, Little Tashi whispered to Dawa, "Brother, look! How hard-working and virtuous she is! She is the one you should make your wife for life!"

"Easier said than done! Her grandpa would never approve this," said Dawa in a low voice.

"If you dare not propose this to her, I could help you," suggested Little Tashi, cool and collected.

"You boy? You couldn't even fix your own problem, not to say be a matchmaker for me," sniffed Dawa, scornfully.

Little Tashi asked in confusion, "My problem?"

"Yep, going to school," said Dawa.

Little Tashi however was very sure about this. "I will go to school in the early spring next year. We can bet on it!"

"Don't be so sure! We could talk about this in the early spring next year," replied Dawa.

Dekyi came back inside the cabin with the empty rubbish pail and saw the two brother's mysterious looks. She asked, "What are you two whispering about? A secret?"

"Oh, we are…" As Little Tashi wanted to say something, Dawa interrupted him and said, "We are talking about his going to school."

"Oh," said Dekyi, standing in the doorway, laughing as if she was lost in thought. The sun shone on the snow outside the cabin, and the reflection was white and dazzling. A thick blanket of snow covered the forest and the plants at the bottom of the valley, but the snow on the open areas in the sheep pen and small cabin melted and dark patches of the ground showed through. More and more wild thrushes came to find food in front of the sheep pen and the cabin while Dawa led Dekyi and Little Tashi to make snowmen beside the pen gate. Each of them made one according to their wishes. Dawa and Dekyi quickly piled up two snowmen, which, though looked a little bit clumsy, were what they each looked like. They looked at each other and smiled, happiness rippling in their eyes like waves. The snowman Little Tashi made looked like a man or an unknown utensil. Standing beside him, Dawa and Dekyi teased him but Little Tashi didn't care and he continued his snowman without haste. After a while, he finished his snowman, which looked like a woman with braids or a fully armed scarecrow. Little Tashi said it was the female teacher who often appeared in his dream. Later, they were bored with making snowmen and decided to do something different. They used a small wooden stick to hold a bamboo basket in the snow, scattered some zanba crusts under the basket and got ready to catch wild thrushes.

Wild thrushes are small, swift and smart and it seemed they had already known their small tricks. They therefore poked their heads under the bamboo basket, pecked the zanba crusts and then withdrew their bodies and flew aside immediately. They worked for quite a long time before they caught a greedy wild thrush. They brought it to the cabin, closed the door and the window and then released it free to play with it.

At this time, the sun was already above their heads. The three of them came out of the cabin, gazing at the mountain top behind. The flock was gone, or they might have ascended the top of the mountain. Dawa and Dekyi went to the small ravine to drive the flock. Little Tashi wanted to go with them but was rejected by Dawa, who at last gave the bird to him as a little compensation.

Standing in the doorway with the wild thrush in his hand, Little Tashi was full of admiration and warmth when he saw Dawa and Dekyi walk one after another on the mountain ridge where the piled snow began to melt. He drew out a thin line from the talisman around his neck, hung it around the neck of the bird and threw it into the sky, where it flew low, unsteadily in the sky for a while and then disappeared.

It was originally a bright and sunny day, but in the afternoon, it suddenly turned cold and grey clouds gathered overhead, where snowflakes came out sporadically and gradually fluttered across the sky. When Dawa drove the flock back in the evening, he was covered with snow and looked like a snowman. They quickly shut the sheep into the sheep pen and went to bed early.

In the early hours of the next morning, Little Tashi had a dream, in which he, together with Dawa and Sister Dekyi, was making a snowman in the open space in front of the sheep pen. The snowman he made physically resembled the female teacher he had met in school and was quite vivid after Little Tashi decorated it with stones for her eyes, nose and mouth. Dawa and Dekyi gave him the thumbs up to praise him as they all stood there looking at the snowman when the snowman suddenly rose to its feet and began to talk, "How are you, my dear friends!"

"Good heavens! Ghosts are coming!" The three of them were shocked and ran wildly towards the cabin.

The snowman shouted, "Don't be afraid! I am teacher Drolma, not a ghost. What can I do for you?"

Upon hearing this, Little Tashi came to his senses. When he piled up snow for the snowman, he made it according to the image of the female teacher in his mind unconsciously! So, he was not afraid anymore and stopped to talk to the snowman, excitedly, "Wow! It is amazing! Teacher Drolma, could you come and teach us?"

The snowman said, "It's my honour to be your teacher. Come with me."

"Teacher Drolma, where do you want to bring us to? We cannot leave here for we have to take care of the flock," asked Dawa.

Little Tashi retorted, "Isn't the flock shut in the sheep pen?"

"Are you blind or what? Who will shut the flock in the pen in the broad daylight?" replied Dawa angrily.

Little Tashi insisted on his words and added that Little Black Head was looking at them through the gap of the pen gate, and he continued, "Sister Dekyi, I trust you! Is the flock in the pen right now?"

"The flock is…" as Dekyi was about to say something, the snowman standing beside him, interrupted, "Don't worry, we won't go far. How about going to your cabin?"

"That is a good idea!" Little Tashi was so happy that he ran back to open the cabin door first and said, "Teacher Drolma, come in please!"

In the cabin, the three of them sat in the open space on the floor and Teacher Drolma took out a printed teaching syllabus and began to write on the wall. As if by magic, one small part of the wall changed into a blackboard which was full of the Tibetan characters written by Teacher Drolma.

"Ka, kha, ga, nga," Teacher Drolma started reading them one by one and they read aloud after her. Little Tashi had already learned these characters, so he finished reading the 30 Tibetan ones in one go before Teacher Drolma even came to the fifth one. Dawa was woken up by Little Tashi's reading aloud in his dream. He looked up and it was already dawn while Little Tashi was still sound sleep, reciting those 30 characters. Dawa had thought to wake him up, but he didn't have the heart to do so when he saw the smile on his little face, so he got up quietly and went out of the cabin.

28
THE YEAR OF THE RAM

It was very cold after the winter solstice. The edge of the stream at the bottom of the valley froze, animals hibernated and the cheerful tweets of birds that used to perch on the branches chirping noisily while hiding in their nests were rarely heard. The entire valley was filled with biting coldness. Amidst the dead silence, some crows croaked across the sky, leaving a suffocating desolation in this valley.

Yes, that was right. The year of the ram was about to arrive after such a long and cold December. The last day before the new year's eve, that is the 29th day of the Tibetan calendar, was gloomy and cloudy. The sky was always covered with grey clouds; snowflakes fell from the clouds continuously, it seemed the gods were unwilling to give blessings to a happy new year.

Even sheep stealers would stay at home celebrating the new year. On that night, Dawa and Little Tashi closed the sheep into the pen earlier than usual and, after they fed the old dog and tied it in front of the pen gate, they carried the cypress leaves and dried wormwood prepared for the new year and set out to the village. When they reached the mouth of Lungser, it was getting dark and sounds of firecrackers came from the village in the near distance.

In the twilight, the road stretched from the mouth of Lungser to the village like a faint white line and the fields on both sides of the road seemed to be more empty and desolate than usual. The cold wind slashed them across the face like knives as it whistled by and disappeared. The two brothers wore a thin layer of snow on their jackets when they were very close to the village and the smell of firecracker powder was flying in the air. It was completely dark when they arrived at the village, but the lights shone from each household, making the outside as bright as it were in daylight and a halo hung over the village in the sky. It was the convention for everyone to go back home early on the evening of the last day before new year's eve. Visiting friends was not allowed because when night fell each household would dispose duba (the dirt and grit particles collected during house cleaning) and it would be regarded as very unlucky if someone happened to see that. But when Dawa and Little Tashi came into the yard of their house, unloaded the cypress leaves and dried wormwood and walked into the brightly lit interior room and held their hands above their eyes, they found Third Uncle was in the room too. The three of them wore a look that presented nothing of new year celebrations but solemnity as if something had gone wrong. When Third Uncle saw them, he greeted them with a big grin and said, "Why did you come back so late? We have been waiting for quite a long time?"

"Third Uncle, why are you still here?" asked Dawa and Little Tashi at the same time.

"I have come to pick up Tashi! Your parents will be back from the remote grazing area in a few months and it is only a matter of time for me to adopt Little Tashi, so I think it might be quite right to take Tashi to my home tonight! You know on every new year's eve, I am the only man in my family to do this while the whole village lights the butter lamp, burns cypress leaves and worships mountain gods at midnight. If Little Tashi could go with me this year, we can do all these together tomorrow," said Third Uncle sadly, which was very unusual, as he spoke out his troubles briefly but clear.

Little Tashi walked to the stove, warmed his hands over the fire and replied sullenly, "No, I don't want to go!"

"Son, it's good for you to go back home now," said Grandpa as he turned back to place offerings in front of the shrine, with his mask on. "We can talk about it later," Grandpa added.

Third Uncle was getting worried, "How could I go back home alone? I want Tashi to go with me!"

"Son, you might as well go back first. It is still up in the air. Don't you think it is too early for you to say that?" said Grandma as she filled the melted butter into the lamp made of yuan gen. She couldn't get her hands dirty, so she leaned towards Little Tashi and touched his head affectionately.

Grown-up as Third Uncle was, he was stubborn like a naughty boy in front of his parents and he insisted, "No, I won't go home if I'm not allowed to take Tashi with me!"

"Nonsense! You have your wife and daughter at home waiting for you right now while you are here making trouble. Don't you think it is a shame?" scolded Grandpa, as he took off his mask in front of the shrine.

The firewood crackled in the stove, warm and cheerful while everyone in the room was silent and solemn, an air of tension prevailing. Outside the yard, sounds of firecrackers burst out in all directions in the village and it seemed some eager households began to dispose duba. Through the window, Dawa gazed at the colourful fireworks in the sky outside and said, "Third Uncle, our neighbours have started disposing of duba; it will be too late if you don't go back home right now!"

"Tashi, come with me, will you?" pleaded Third Uncle as he looked at Little Tashi eagerly, tears in his eyes.

Like an eagle that shifts position cautiously on the edge of a cliff, Little Tashi moved a step towards Grandma and replied firmly, "No!"

Grandpa was angry. He kept his temper and said, as if cursing him, "Stay here and wait as long as you want! Good luck for the coming year when you see neighbours dispose duba on your way back home later!"

"Son, listen to your mother, will you? We could talk about Tashi after his parents come back from the remote grazing area. Go back home now, otherwise it is indeed ominous if you happen to encounter duba on your way."

"Are we a family?" muttered Third Uncle as he walked towards the door and turned back saying, as if to look for a way to cover up his embarrassment, "What about tomorrow morning? Please?"

"Ok, I will bring him there," Dawa said in a half-hearted manner as he knew they would burn cypress leaves at the same place the next day.

Deafening firecrackers exploded in the village after Third Uncle went back, so they hurriedly gathered all the dirt in a wooden tub and asked Dawa to throw it out. Grandma closed the door the moment Dawa went through the yard and out of the front gate. Grandpa, together with Little Tashi, let off firecrackers behind Dawa's back, showing that they had already swept all the dirt and diseases of the past year out of their home and now they would greet an auspicious and peaceful new year.

Adults always told children that Father New Year would come to visit each household on new year's eve and children would always ask what he looks like. They would be told that Father New Year was an old man with white beard and he would also bring them many new year gifts. Every year, Little Tashi was eager to see this mysterious white-bearded old man, but he never saw him, so he didn't expect it anymore and began to look forward to something more practical during the new year celebrations. The dinner of the new year! A feast with three meals for the night and Little Tashi did have too much food that evening. After the meals, the family would light butter lamps placed in front of the shrine, on the stove and in the outside yard to worship the three treasures, the god of the stove and heaven, expecting blessings for a safe, lucky and peaceful new year. They, however, should go to bed early because in the early hours of the next morning the most beautiful woman in their family would feed the Naga. (A Tibetan new year festive custom. The hostess of a family will climb up to the roof and performs bsang and other ceremonies to worship the household Naga before daybreak for blessings.) Dawa wasn't married, Little Tashi's mother was in the remote grazing area, therefore Grandma had to take on the important task.

At about three o'clock the next morning, Grandma got up very quietly because Naga was said to be very shy and would not come to visit if he heard any noise. Grandma climbed to the roof, lit dried wormwood and spread on it some zanba and dried flower powders to feed Naga, which was the end of the ceremony. At dawn, all the men in the family would be dressed in festive costumes and perform bsang around the village, according to ancestral tradition, to every household. The field close to Dungkar valley behind the village was the place where Little Tashi's family performed bsang. It had snowed heavily last night and when Grandpa with Dawa and Little Tashi walked across the snow to the bsang place, there were no footprints on the vast and white snow, showing that they were the first to be there.

Under Grandpa's instruction, the two brothers swept the snow away from the place where they would perform the bsang, and then they set a fire and added cypress leaves over it. Soon, cypress leaves crackled in the fire, giving off a fresh and pleasant smell. They scattered offerings over the fire, such as zanba and ground dry flowers petals alike and started chanting new year congratulatory messages. The other families who would do bsang close to this place came over, one after another. Like the three of them, they started the ceremony. When the whole village finished bsang, they would form small groups and have a firecracker contest in different places to see whose firecrackers were the best and whose fireworks were the most beautiful, which indeed was the most sacred and auspicious moment of the year. Also, the household that had a new baby would bring fruits and scones to share with everyone, a blessing for a thriving family. The household that had a new daughter-in-law would surely bring something too, such as a bottle of wedding wine. Men in the village usually got married young, so the young men at the age of 17 or 18 generally married and had a family. They then began to tease Dawa:

"Dawa, why didn't you bring any wedding wine?"

"He is still a boy and how could he have a wife?"

"To find you a wife, your father even asked you to drop out of school! Why didn't you get married?"

"Wait a second. I heard he has a girlfriend in Gonpa village."

"Brilliant! Those who are capable would find wives themselves and those who are not have to find a matchmaker to do that for them."

"Hey, don't hide your wife in a secret place, now is the time for you to introduce her to us!"

Firecrackers exploded in all directions in the village, smells of gunpowder attacked nostrils along with smoke. It was nearly dawn, but Third Uncle didn't show up yet and Grandpa wore a very solemn look instead of the expected joy of the festival. It was after dawn when the whole village gathered together, exchanging good wishes and enjoying the new year's lucky food merrily, that Third Uncle ran towards them hastily, a handful of cypress leaves under his left arm and a leather sack with offerings in his right hand. He began to set the fire and do the bsang. The other men in the village chatted indiscriminately when they saw Third Uncle.

"Has the Father New Year of your family been blocked by the heavy snow?"

"Have all your offerings been eaten up by rats last night?"

"Hahaha! Are the meat tied under the beam unwilling to get down?"

"Have potatoes and vegetables for the dinner been frozen in the cellar?"

"Has your wife…"

It was the first day of the new year and whatever the other people said would be regarded as auspicious, and you couldn't get mad at heckling or even sarcasm.

Although Third Uncle was not angry, the look on his face was not in harmony with the festival atmosphere when he alone made a fire, spread cypress leaves and did the bsang. Anyway, he was a man who cared about keeping his dignity. Dawa and Little Tashi felt uncomfortable when they saw the other men in the village laugh at Third Uncle, so they both looked at Grandpa who, however stood among the crowd without any annoyed expression on his face. Dawa and Little Tashi were about to help him with the ceremony but Grandpa shook his head in the crowd, signalling no to them. The two brothers had no choice but to stand in the crowd watching Third Uncle being jeered at by the surrounding people. Little Tashi never liked Third Uncle, but he couldn't help feeling sympathy for him when he saw what he was suffering at the moment.

In the blue sky, the sun rose slowly from the east, its sunlight shining on the top of the hill opposite and grey smoke prevailing above the snow-covered village. In the gloomy village, women dressed in festival costumes carried buckets to fetch water from the stream in small groups; the old and the middle-aged usually went back quickly after their buckets were filled with water while the young wives and girls all took a break half way chatting happily, unwilling to leave. Amidst the sound of firecrackers and continuous laughter, the new year's day started.

When the men came back home from where they did bsang, the sunshine descended from the opposite mountain and reflected on the snow at the bottom of the valley, it was very dazzling. According to the local custom, visiting friends after breakfast on new year's day was not allowed, so the villagers all went to pay a visit to the living Buddha in the monastery. Dawa and Little Tashi, however, could only go back to the village in turns every day over the next few days because one of them had to stay in Lungser and take care of the flock. They played 'rock, paper, scissors' to decide who needed to go back to the sheep pen; Little Tashi won the game at last. Dawa quickly finished his breakfast and went straight to Lungser while Little Tashi, dressed in festival costume, together with Grandpa and Grandma, went to pay a visit to the living Buddha in the monastery.

When they arrived at the entrance of the living Buddha's palace, a long queue had already formed there, someone bearing a saddle bag, some holding a khata and note of large or small denominations, all standing still, waiting respectfully. A young lama who served the living Buddha stood in the doorway of the inner room, letting the believers in one by one. Standing between Grandpa and Grandma, Little Tashi was so excited that he bobbed his head as if he were beating a small drum. The long line moved forward, and it was their turn to go into the palace. After the young lama let them in, they walked on and at last reached a clean and comfortable inner court, where the living Buddha sat dignified in the chair in the corridor with a Tibetan wooden table in front of him.

In front of the living Buddha, Grandpa removed his saddle bag from his back, handed it over to another young lama and then knelt to kowtow before him, and Little Tashi and Grandma followed suit. Grandpa took out a khata and 10 yuan after he finished head knocking and presented these with respect on the table in front of the living Buddha, who in return stroked Grandpa's head gently with a scroll of scripture and Little Tashi and Grandma too. Then the young lama tied a thin red talisman around their necks and placed some canned plums into Grandpa's saddle bag. After all this was done, the three of them clapped their hands in devotion and walked backwards leaving the living Buddha's presence in full respect.

After they went out of the living Buddha's palace, Grandpa limped towards the circumambulation in the monastery closely followed by Grandma and Little Tashi. Compared with the other days, today many more people came to turn the prayer wheel on the circumambulation. When they arrived at the mani temple built by Third Uncle above the monastery, Grandma took out a new butter lamp from her bosom, lit it and placed on a counter under a mural. In other mani temples, they would usually leave after walking around the mani temple three times, but in Third Uncle's mani temple they didn't leave until they did it for more than 10 times. Then they walked along the circumambulation down to the monastery, passed through a narrow path and arrived at Second Uncle's abode, who had already left his door open as if he knew they would come. In the inner room, Second Uncle prepared for them freshly braised pork, momos (similar to dumplings or stuffed buns), biscuits, fruits and other delicious food. In the past they usually waited on Second Uncle whole-heartedly but today Second Uncle tied his robe around his waist and served them with bare arms. When the family enjoyed the delicious food together, Second Uncle looked at Little Tashi and asked him earnestly, "Tashi, are you ready to be a lama?"

"I..." Little Tashi wanted to say something but when he saw the food in front of him, he swallowed it back.

Second Uncle continued, "Father, I heard that you are preparing to send Tashi to school?"

"Well, no, but..."

Second Uncle asked, "When will Tashi serve the monastery as a lama?"

"Shall we talk about it when your elder brother comes back?" Grandpa suggested with some embarrassment.

Second Uncle complained, "Father, you were a lama before. How could you be so unenthusiastic about it? We all will die and when my day comes, to whom could I give this monastery?"

"Who said I am not enthusiastic about this? The problem is there are usually two or three children in one family, who always put children before their own lives. How could I decide Tashi's future since his parents are all here," said Grandpa, helplessly.

Second Uncle could hardly sit still, "Mother, why don't you say something?"

"I have been expecting Tashi to serve in the monastery as a lama since he was very young, but I love all my sons. Everyone has his own ideas, so tell me what I should say?" Grandma said as she started to weep.

"Old woman, it is the first day of the new year, stop crying!" Grandpa then said to Second Uncle, "Your younger brother has been pestering us to give Tashi to him while you want him to be a lama."

"Hasn't the daughter of my second sister been adopted by him? And, to be a common man in the secular society or be a lama in pursuit of nirvana, which is better?" argued Second Uncle.

Grandpa continued, "Your mother and I, old and useless as we are, have already stepped on the threshold of the Palace of Hades, so you might as well talk about this with Tashi's father after he comes back from the remote grazing area."

It was afternoon when Little Tashi and his grandparents came back from the monastery. At home, Little Tashi changed into his leather jacket and started for Lungser with some snacks. Along the way, the sound of firecrackers still echoed in his ears, and the tang of new year mixed up with smells of gunpowder and scent of delicious food lingered in the air. When he reached the mouth of Lungser, with much reluctance he looked back at the village, above which white clouds floated in the blue sky like blooming white corals. The clouds had no fixed shapes and changed their form with the wind, presenting a kaleidoscope of patterns. Little Tashi spotted one that looked very familiar, so he stared at it and found it resembled a scroll of scriptures. Feeling it was indeed some auspicious sign, Little Tashi was overjoyed and hummed a tune on his way back to the sheep pen.

29
CRIES UNDER THE FROZEN STREAM

During the new year season, there were various activities in the village such as horse racing, basketball matches, singing and dancing and firecracker battles. Children flocked to the streets, having great fun playing throwing bean bags, kicking the shuttlecock, and collecting firecracker shells. Dawa and Little Tashi, however, had to take care of the flock in turns and days passed quickly from the first day of the new year to the fifth. Beginning in the afternoon on the fifth day of the new year, a series of activities was held in monasteries, especially on the sixth day of the new year, the first day of the Great Prayer Festival established by Je Tsongkhapa (a famous teacher of Tibetan Buddhism whose activities led to the formation of the Gelug school of Tibetan Buddhism). Dungkar village and the monastery were separated by a stream, so adults in the village all went one after another to listen to sutras in the monastery and only some rebellious young men or children played on the streets, as the atmosphere of the new year slowly faded.

It was less than two months before the beginning of the spring and for Little Tashi, the flock in Lungser was more important than anything else, so from the sixth day of the new year, Dawa and Little Tashi stuck around with the flock together. Life in Lungser suddenly became much longer since they returned there; perhaps they had met too many people during the new year celebration which infused them with the joyous mood of the festival. They were very lonely and bored, on the mountain or in the sheep pen; they looked forward to something novel to change their tedious life, but the more you hope, the more disappointed you get, and their life in Lungser went on as usual. The sun rose from the east, sank in the west; the flock went out of the pen in the morning and came back from the mountain in the evening; the old dog walked around in circles beside the stake after his meals. All remained the same except one small change: the frozen stream at the bottom of the valley gradually became smaller as the weather changed. The stream sometimes froze over, sometimes with cracks or even small holes on the surface. To relieve the boredom of the long dull day, Dawa and Little Tashi would set off firecrackers on the open space in front of the pen or went skating on the frozen river whenever they had time.

One day after a heavy snowfall, Dawa drove the flock to the bushes at the bottom of the valley where the sheep could graze the dried grass, tree bark and the other plants that were available as long as their scissor-like mouths could get it. Little Tashi walked back and forth in the cabin, busy with the housework. When the two brothers went back to eat in the cabin, a strange but familiar cry of an animal burst out in the opposite forest. They listened to it carefully and Dawa recognised that it must be a musk deer, which, based on his experience, was probably trapped by wires set by the poachers. They walked out of the cabin and hastened toward the opposite forest after they finished their food.

They arrived at the bank of the stream, and the two brothers seemed to hear the bleat of a lamb too. They looked around and were relieved to find the flock scattered in the bushes at the bottom of the valley, grazing leisurely. Dawa and Little Tashi continued their exploration, crossing the frozen river, climbing up the opposite forest and heading for the crying musk deer. Dead leaves and branches accumulated on the forest floor in winter, on which a thin layer of snow rested silently. When Little Tashi and Dawa breathlessly climbed to the hillside, the plaintive cries of the musk deer were trailing off, off and on. Hearing the sound, Little Tashi and Dawa, burning with impatience, searched everywhere in the forest but found nothing.

All of a sudden, a small tail wagging in the bushes caught Little Tashi's eyes. He went closer to take a look and then called Dawa to join him. A musk deer was tied with an iron wire around its neck, the other end of the wire fastened beside the mountain road on a short shrub that happened to grow out of the steep rock. The poor fellow hanging over there was unable to move at all, very dangerous! Dawa, however, was very excited. If it was a male musk deer, the musk in his body would be worth a thousand yuan; it would be the most precious new year gift! He, like an experienced veteran hunter, examined the musk deer over and again and even patted it on its behind to determine whether it was a male one as he had thought. The disappointed look on his face told everything, but for this musk deer, nothing could be luckier than the arrival of the two brothers. Little Tashi and Dawa went all out to save it.

The steep rock was not high, but it was not easy to get the musk deer, hanging over there, out of the shrubs; they pulled hard for a long time, still unable to loosen it from the wire. Dawa realised the problem was with the vegetation to which the wire was tied, so he made a detour and climbed up close to the vegetation, trying his best to pull it out. The vegetation, though it looked tender and frail, had an extraordinarily strong root system, reaching deep into the frozen soil; 10 Dawas might not accomplish the task, let alone the present Dawa alone. Dawa made a gesture of head-chopping towards Little Tashi, signalling him to go back to the cabin and bring a dagger. Little Tashi understood tacitly and stumbled down the snow-covered forest as fast as he could.

He found the dagger in the cabin, held it in the palm of his hand, and hastened back to the hillside. Nobody knew how Dawa managed to start a fire in the frozen soil where the vegetation was rooted. Squatting on the rock, Dawa was busy adding some dried wood to the fire, alternating with digging the roots of the vegetation out with a stone with sharp points. Little Tashi noticed the musk deer didn't move at all, eyes rolling backwards, but he didn't tell this to Dawa; instead he stood close by, assisting him in an unhurried manner. He felt Dawa looked like a hero of the State of Ling in the story of *King Gesar*, and his heart brimmed over with great respect for his brother. When the vegetation was dug out of the rock, the musk deer fell off the rock to the ground below. Seeing the deer lying there quite still, Dawa jumped off the rock, ran to the deer and held the back of his hand above its nose for breaths, only to find that it had already died. Dawa sighed and said to himself, "Well, what a pity we haven't made it!"

"He had already died when I came back with the dagger, but I dare not tell you that," said Little Tashi regretfully.

Dawa blamed himself, "Alas, if we hadn't cared too much about whether it was a male or a female at the very beginning and saved it with our whole hearts, we might have saved it."

"Brother, it's alright! We have tried our best. The poachers who set up the wire on the rock surface should be the ones to blame for its death," Little Tashi comforted him, calmly.

"With things as such, nothing helps!" Dawa lamented as he untied the wire from its neck.

The wire around the musk deer's neck had worn out all the fur around its neck, a thin print of the wire left there still. The deer was dead, its corpse might attract wild wolves to come, so they dragged the deer down the snow-covered hill.

One in the front and the other in the back, they hauled the deer all the way to the entrance of the cabin, and the old dog greeted them with his tongue sticking out and licking the corner of his mouth, as if he knew he would have a big feast today. The corpse of the deer was somewhat frozen stiff, but a knife would do the skinning work still. Dawa skinned the deer, gutted it and fed the entrails to the old dog. The old fellow, who hadn't eaten meat for a long time, gobbled down his treat instantly, and kept licking the corner of his mouth then, as if he hadn't eaten to his heart's content.

Musk deer usually grazed on the most fresh and tender grass and moss in the forest or the bushes on the shaded slope; although their bodies are tiny, their meat tastes fresh, tender and juicy; once having some in your mouth, the aroma would linger for a long time. Dawa and Little Tashi hid in the cabin and had a big, wonderful meal of venison, even bones were cleaned like smooth bamboo. They belched all the way as they drove back the flock from different places inside Lungser, and it was almost evening when they returned to the sheep pen. When counting the flock, Dawa found there was one missing; Little Tashi said instinctively, "It must be Little Black Head!" though he didn't check the pen as if, like two hearts beating as one, he knew instinctively.

"Why?" Dawa asked surprisingly.

"Don't you remember the cry of a lamb under the frozen river when we hurried to save the musk deer at noon? I had a feeling that it was Little Black

Head's cry at that time." With these words, Little Tashi ran to the frozen stream.

Dawa was perplexed, "Wait a minute! I'd like to check on it one more time."

"No need! Come with me," said Little Tashi, as he was near the frozen stream.

"What could you do with your bare hands? I will bring the shovel," Dawa said, disapprovingly, as he ran back to the cabin and came out with one in his hand.

They arrived at the bank of the frozen stream one after another. The weather getting warmer, a crevasse and even holes could be seen on the surface; the cries of Little Black Head had long disappeared, and it was quiet except the sound of the babbling current flowing under the ice. They started digging through the ice with shovels. From the opposite side of the sheep pen, they chiselled and shovelled, and it was getting dark when they finished 100 metres away. They had to hurry up and find Little Black Head before night fell, or it would be 'mission impossible' for them to dig him out of the river within a couple of days when the stream froze again the next day. The two brothers dug frantically; in the twilight, everything was blurry, and barely could a silhouette be seen clearly. They found Little Black Head's body at last! That was too much for Little Tashi! Staring at the frozen dead body of Little Black Head, he wanted to cry but no tears came out. With great efforts, they dragged Little Black Head to the riverside and hauled him back to the cabin.

They remained silent along the way. Dawa was in deep remorse for his negligence as he turned everything over in his mind. He should have been more alert when he heard the bleat of the lamb at noon; he should have gone back and checked on it. That was 'burn the house to rid it of the mouse'! As for Little Tashi, memories of the wonderful time he had with Little Black Head stuck in his mind and replayed over and over again. The young fellow sleeping with him on the kang since he was born; the young fellow greeting him every day, bleating and circling around and the theft of his mum, Spotted Neck. Little Tashi couldn't help feeling a sudden pain in his heart as if it were pricked by a needle. It had been his fault to have let the sheep stealer into the pen; it was his fault, too, to let Little Black Head fall into the frozen river and lose his life. At the moment, it was too late for him to do anything. He had the agreement with his father and he could win the chance to go to school only if nothing should happen to the flock, but he now was the one who didn't keep the promise and how could his father send him to school as they had agreed? Little Tashi became sadder and sadder and he knew for certain there was not the slightest hope of realising his dream.

It was pitch dark in the cabin. Dawa, listless and languid, lit the oil lamp; instantly the wooden cabin was slightly illuminated, though appearing to be much gloomier than it used to be. Beside the cold stove Little Black Head lay still and Little Tashi couldn't hold back his tears anymore; his tears streamed down his face again. He said in great grief, "It must be our punishment because we didn't save the musk deer's life in time!"

"But we have done our best!" Dawa comforted him.

Little Tashi said, as he wiped his tears, "Little Black Head is dead and there is no chance for me to go to school."

"It isn't a big deal. Our parents will understand."

No moon hung in the sky and the bottom of the valley was shrouded by a gigantic black cloak that night. The sound of the frozen river softened a little; was it feeling guilty and remorseful for having taken life away from this innocent poor young fellow too? The sheep in the pen were surprisingly silent tonight, not even burps or the sound of chewing the cud could be heard; were they mourning Little Black Head or indifferent to what had happened to him? The prayer flag standing in front of the pen gate suddenly fluttered in the air, as if it gave way to emotions and began to recite Puwa scriptures to pray and help the spirit of Little Black Head move on.

30
ABSOLUTION OF THE DEAD

It was freezing cold, though there had been no snowfall for days. The sheep came out of the pen, pounded on the frozen ground as if beating a drum, dung droppings hit the ground, clear and sharp, the sheep's urine landed on the earth and froze to ice immediately and the sheep sneezed, making a big cloud in the air. The two brothers shivered all over with cold, on their heads, the shearling sheepskin hats Dekyi had made for them failed to keep them warm.

Suppose Little Black Head had been an ordinary lamb, they could eat its tender and fresh meat; they could make delicious mutton soup that was full of nutrition, they could even strip its skin to sell for money or make leather jackets for themselves, but in Dawa and Little Tashi's hearts, Little Black Head was more than an animal, no different to a human being. Since the day when he was born, he was so close to them like brothers, though he couldn't talk to them. It was the local custom that when a family member died, they would be kept at home during the first seven days, and after that he would be sent to a sky burial site. To mourn him, the brothers kept the body of Little Black Head in the cabin, melted a bar of butter and used it to fill a mud lamp, lit it and placed it on the crossbars over the dead body. Little Black Head lay beside the kang, and when his spirit went back to its body, it would not feel cold. Dawa and Little Tashi were unable to invite lamas in monastery to read scriptures for him, but they had their own special way to mourn him. Not only did they chant a six-character mantra for him, they also picked up pebbles from the frozen river and carved the mantra on the stones. On the seventh day, stones, large and small, were piled beside the river like a pagoda, making a mani stone pile at last.

They went to great pains to perform a funeral service for Little Black Head after the first seven days. Based on the local convention, children or juveniles would not be sent to a sky burial when they die, instead they would usually be buried in a grave in a secret place. Dawa and Little Tashi however, would, on no condition, dig a hole and hastily bury him underground where it was complete dark. Little Black Head had died of suffocation under the ice, his spirit would be suffocated and never rest in peace if he should be buried underground. Adults always said that prior to reincarnation, people will be reincarnated as a dog first, therefore sending a dog's corpse to the mountain top would accumulate good virtues. Little Black Head was not a dog, but in the brothers' eyes, he was smarter and more alert than a real dog, so they decided to send Little Black Head to the mountain top.

On the morning of the first seventh day, the sky was crystal blue as if it had been washed carefully. The dark valley, with slopes, rivers and forests on its sides, still presented a desolate scene, but when the golden rays beamed on the mountain top behind, the entire valley brimmed with a refreshing atmosphere. Dawa and Little Tashi got up early that morning. They drove the sheep out of the pen to the foot of the mountain and then went back to the cabin to do some housework. The sun at that time began to descend slowly from the top of the mountain, shining on the cabin and the sheep pen. The burial ceremony was a complicated practice but Dawa and Little Tashi decided to make it simpler, though their grief remained deeply felt. They wrapped Little Black Head's body in a leather jacket and prepared to climb from the foot of the mountain to the ridge. When they carried Little Black Head's body out of the cabin, the old dog kept walking around the stake, as if to say goodbye to him. Little Tashi said, "Brother, shall we take the old dog with us?"

"Nope. He will bite people if he gets lost," explained Dawa.

"No, he won't. Last time when you were in the remote grazing area, I took him to the mountain."

"The old dog is old, but he is a ferocious. How could you be so reckless?" Dawa scolded him.

Little Tashi explained, as he recalled his memories, "Brother, you may not know it but Little Black Head was bitten by a jackal on that day. If it hadn't been for the old dog bravely fighting the jackal, Little Black Head would have lost his life long ago."

"Alas, you boy! You always do wild things," Dawa's voice softened, though he did not show any approval.

Bearing Little Black Head on his back, Dawa started climbing the mountain. Little Tashi read Dawa's mind and ran at once to the old dog, untying him from the stake. The old fellow shuddered all over, shaking the dust from his body then, with Little Tashi, he headed for Dawa. The foot of the mountain behind was steep and thick with bushes, so they climbed slowly, the old dog, like a scout, walked ahead of Little Tashi for a while or at his heels for a change, wagging his tail along the way.

At this moment, Little Tashi's thoughts drifted back to the day when his mother had taken him from the pasture to his maternal grandparents' house after the news came that his maternal grandma had died. It happened a few years ago on a snowy day. When Father came back from the village and broke the bad news to Mother, she passed out at once. Father came towards her, pressed her philtrum, and luckily, she regained consciousness. She cried, "Good heavens! I have lost my mother forever!" Her cries resounded through the bottom of the valley in the winter pasture. After she had a good cry, she took Little Tashi with her and rushed to the village that very night. It was pitch dark along the way, big snowflakes were falling in the biting wind. Mother cried all the way, sometimes her voice choked in her throat, so she was barely audible, sometimes in her mouth showing great sorrow. Tashi was very young at that time and knew very little about sadness, but when he watched his mother crying so bitterly, he was terrified that his mother would collapse on the ground and leave him unattended.

They raced all the way, sweating profusely, the snowflakes on their heads melted and drifted down and their leather jackets were soaking wet. They arrived at Tashi's maternal grandpa's house at about 10 o'clock at night. The doorway of the house was ablaze with light; relatives coming to help with the funeral ceremony were bustling in and out, talking with each other with occasional laughter. Someone turned to the house and gave a shout. Little

Tashi's maternal grandpa came out with a grim look on his face but a smile hovering at the corner of his mouth. How strange it was! He gave his miserable daughter some comforting words; she however said nothing but turned around and leaned against the wall beside the door and wept for a long time. Then a relative came over and took him and his mother to the inner room. Little Tashi saw in the distance four lamas sitting cross-legged on the kang, swaying their heads, chanting mantras. A shrine, with many khatas on it, had been set up. Little Tashi worried that his mother would sob her heart out when she saw his maternal grandma placed in front of the shrine but when they came into the room, his mother didn't cry but knelt and kowtowed three times and then took from the shrine the small prayer wheel Grandma always used, chanting something as she sat on the floor, turning the pray wheel. Little Tashi sat beside his mother silently after he kowtowed, his eyes busy looking around as if to look for something. He was recollecting his memories about his maternal grandma. His maternal grandpa was known for his misery, but his maternal grandma often took Little Tashi home and secretly gave him some candies or scones to eat. Now she had died and there would be no chance for him to eat those delicious treats anymore. He suddenly felt hungry, but he dared not speak but forced himself to stay with his mother, listening to the endless chanting of the lamas.

Seven days later, they wrapped his maternal grandma's body in a white cloth bag, placed her on Blackhawk's back and sent her to a sky burial site. All the men in the family would attend the ceremony, including Little Tashi, who was the youngest and therefore was afraid to look at his maternal grandma's face. To his surprise, her face, though full of lines, hadn't changed much, it was as kind and beautiful and elegant as it used to be. Little Tashi didn't feel sad, instead he had the feeling that his maternal grandma had just gone to a remote place and she would be back soon. At noon, except for the man who was in charge of the sky burial ceremony, all the men in his maternal grandma's family went back to the village. When they looked back on their return trip, clouds of vultures were hovering over the sky burial site.

As Little Tashi was lost in his memories, they arrived at the ridge of the hillside behind them and stopped to take a rest on a smooth slope for a while. The sunlight had already moved to the bottom of the valley, the icy river crossed through the vegetation and wound towards the mouth of the valley like a white khata. Little Tashi suddenly remembered Grandpa Humpback's ram whose remains had been eaten by vultures after it had been bitten to death by wolves. Little Tashi rolled his eyes quickly and said, "Brother, let's place Little Black Head here."

"Didn't you always say that we should bring Little Black Head to the top of the mountain?" asked Dawa.

Little Tashi explained, "We could place Little Black Head here but vultures would come to eat him."

"This is not the sky burial site," retorted Dawa.

Little Tashi was impatient, "Brother, didn't you remember last time, when Sister Dekyi's ram was eaten by vultures right here?"

"I remember that, but…" Dawa was slow to react.

Little Tashi added eagerly, "Grandma always said after a man dies, vultures would come to eat his meat and bring his soul to a blissful world. Doesn't that mean Little Black Head's soul would go there too?"

"What if vultures don't come to eat him? Crows and sparrowhawks would come to peck his eyes out and wolves would come to eat him," said Dawa.

As predicted, a crow and an unknown big bird suddenly hovered in the sky. As a gust of cold wind roared past, a solitary cypress tree shivered in the wind and the short bushes made a whistling sound, spooky and gloomy as if it were indeed a sky burial site. Dawa felt quite uneasy, so he carried Little Black Head on and continued climbing towards the mountain top. Strangely enough, the old dog stood where he was, barking all the time as if he was unwilling to leave this place. Dawa had moved a couple of steps along the ridge, but the old fellow still barked at him strangely, as if telling him to put Little Black Head down, otherwise, he would not go on with them. Little Tashi said, "Brother, Mother said dogs are the most sensitive animal in the world. They could see ghosts and spirits we can't see. Since he doesn't want us to bring Little Black Head to the mountain top, let's put Little Black Head here."

"Not a good idea. What if vultures don't come to eat him?" said Dawa, with no confidence.

Little Tashi suggested earnestly, "We could have a try."

"If crows and sparrowhawks eat Little Black Head, you will be responsible for it," with these words, Dawa turned back and came over to them.

Dawa unloaded Little Black Head from his back and placed him in the open space on the ridge. The old dog wagged his tail happily as he walked around Dawa, as if he knew he had his wish fulfilled. Crows perched on the cypress branches, croaking loudly. Today, the flock was on the sunny slope and though scattering in different corners, they seemed to know today was no ordinary; it was the day of Little Black Head's funeral ceremony. Some affectionate ewes raised their heads towards them and bleated, as if they were lamenting the death of this miserable orphan and sending him off.

It is said that if there was no blood on the dead body, vultures would not come to eat. Dawa picked up a stone with a sharp point from nearby and scratched on Little Black Head's thigh, immediately blood poured out. The brothers hid inside the bushes nearby, looking up at the blue sky, waiting for vultures to swoop down. They waited for a few hours, but vultures did not come. The sun climbed up over head, the sunlight on the ridge became soft and weak, still no vultures. Dawa and Little Tashi felt hungry, so they decided to go back and have lunch. If there were still no vultures coming over, they would send Little Black Head to the mountain top. They climbed down the mountain with the old dog. When they were close to the ridge behind the cabin, they were attracted by the mani stone pile they had made for Little Black Head beside the icy river; the mani stone pile shone with every hue under the sunlight, filling their hearts with an unspeakable rarity and blessing.

They returned to the cabin, cooked on the stove, fed the old dog and ate their lunch too. Then the brothers went out of the cabin and came to a small road on the opposite of the stream, where they both turned back to gaze on the mountain ridge behind. A group of vultures had circled around Little Black Head. The head of them was invited to peck on the dead body first, then they all swarmed forward, and in a minute, there was only skeletal remains left on the ground.

At the moment, Little Tashi looked at the sky and found there was an auspicious white cloud on top of the mountain, which in his eyes resembled a Buddha. Little Tashi pointed to the sky and said to Dawa, "Brother, did you see a Buddha over there?"

"Buddha? No," said Dawa as he stared at the sky overhead.

Little Tashi explained eagerly, "I mean does that white cloud look like a Buddha?"

"Sort of but not really," said Dawa as he inspected the cloud again with a perplexed look on his face.

Little Tashi claimed with a firm tone, "It looks quite like a Buddha."

All of a sudden, the stream raised its voice and bickered under the icy water. Did it receive some blessings from Buddhas? Was it reading scriptures and praying for Little Black Head? It might be. Little Tashi and Dawa were inspired and they began to chant the six-character mantra aloud. Their voices resounded at the bottom of the valley and the entire Lungser brimmed with warm atmosphere and callings of holiness.

31
THE GREAT PRAYER FESTIVAL

The Great Prayer Festival in monasteries started on the afternoon of January 6th and ended on the morning of January 16th, 11 days all together. For Little Tashi and Dawa, January 13th to 16th was what they yearned for the most: a Buddha exhibition in the morning, horse racing in the afternoon of the 13th, a cham dance for a whole day on the 14th, Buddha worshipping during the day and an exhibition of butter sculpture presented by monasteries in front of the Great Hall on the night of the 15th and Lord Maitreya's turning prayer wheels on the morning of the 16th. For seniors and believers, the festival was a worship to prayers, but for young and beautiful boys and girls, as well as children who were innocent and ignorant, the festival was simply a visit, which meant quite different things to each one.

It was the coldest time of the year. The flock, especially the old ewes and young lambs, were comparatively weak, so they might easily fall into the ice caves or stumble down from the steep mountain if left unattended. To take care of the flock, the brothers had to visit the prayer festival in turns. Dawa chose the Dharma dance festival, the most holy and ceremonious one on the 14th while Little Tashi had to choose the Buddha Thangka display festival on the 13th.

On the morning of the 13th, Little Tashi set out early. It was not a clear day, snowflakes hid inside the grey and white clouds. When he passed across the small road at the bottom of the valley, vegetation on the roadside, though sparse and unappealing, could block the wind to a degree but at the mouth of Lungser, the cold wind roared through, biting his hands, nose and forehead: painful! He could see his breath. During the Buddha Thangka display festival, this year's living Buddha, abbots and Geyok Guard would appear in full costume in the festival, so villagers came to monasteries early to see them. Little Tashi trotted along the route and when he arrived at the village, all adults had already gone to the monasteries except Grandpa who was waiting for him at home. They ate a hasty meal, then one after another they came to the road leading to the monastery below the village. Far away at the foot of the mountain on the right of the monastery, the Buddha Thangka display festival had already begun. Amid the bustling crowds in front of the Buddhas and the chanting of *Praises to Gurus* by young lamas around the Buddha statues, the entire valley was filled with a sacred and solemn atmosphere. Usually when *Fraises to Gurus* was chanted, all the rituals were about to end, so Little Tashi ran ahead like a rolling stone, urging Grandpa, behind him to walk faster, even though he limped as if he were dancing. When they arrived at the cement bridge and took the turning, men and women, old and young, in festival costumes, hurried here from the upstream villages; sometimes motorcycles roared past them like a gust of wind, full of passengers, children and adults.

Little Tashi was anxious when those people behind them passed by again and again, but Grandpa had no choice but to walk slowly because of his legs. When they managed to squeeze into the crowd before the displayed Buddhas, the living Buddha, the abbot, and Geyok Guard of this year had all gone. It was indeed a great pity. All the people behind them lined up and raised their hands over their foreheads to worship the Buddha statue. Offerings were piled like a hill before the statue, khatas and money thrown by believers fell to the ground beside the statue like snowflakes.

Grandma was nowhere to be found in the crowd. Grandpa fumbled for a while with his black talisman around his neck, took out from it some worn paper money, handed some to Little Tashi and held the rest in his hands, waiting patiently in the line. When it was finally their turn to worship the Buddha, a lama in charge of maintaining order whipped them on their heads with a willow branch and literally shoved them out of the line. They had to line up again and after they had worshipped the statue and squeezed out of the crowd, they were numb and worn out. Grandpa rubbed his knees again and again; obviously he had another attack of leg pain. They wormed out of the crowd and took a rest in the open space outside. Young lamas, holding different corners of the statue, carried the statue slowly down the mountain, then like a snake they circled around the statue. All the young lamas chanted the scriptures as they held the statue of Buddha above their heads or on their shoulders to carry it away. Those who missed this would follow the procession that carried the statue, squeezed in between the young lamas and made kowtows.

After the statue of Buddha was sent away, the circumambulation was crowded with people coming to turn prayer wheels. Little Tashi and Grandpa joined them too. When they reached the back of the ruins of the Great Hall of Scripture above the monastery, someone in the crowd stopped to play with a few released goats that bathed in the sunshine beside the road. The goats were not frightened by the noisy crowd, instead they interacted with the crowd calmly and peacefully. Suddenly the goat released by Little Tashi's family saw Little Tashi and Grandpa and he bleated as he crossed through the crowd and ran to them, sniffing their sleeves and butting them softly with its horns like a naughty boy who had spotted his mum. People around were deeply moved by such a scene, some found their eyes moistening and some giving the thumbs up in praise. Little Tashi and Grandpa could have had a great reunion with the goat, but those who came to turn the prayer wheels behind them pushed the crowd forward like waves behind driving the waves ahead. The moving crowd tore them apart, but their released goat didn't bleat miserably; he stood beside the circumambulation, looking at the crowd silently.

Little Tashi and Grandpa turned prayer wheels all the way from the circumambulation and when they reached the mani Lhakhang donated by Third Uncle above the monastery, circumambulators started chatting in confusion. Some said the mani Lhakhang had a good position, some said the decoration was quite unique, some praised the fine workmanship of the big mani inside the mani Lhakhang. When Grandpa heard this, a smile appeared around the corners of his mouth, he winked at Little Tashi, as if to say how great your Third Uncle is to build such a magnificent Lhakhang in the monastery. They squeezed out of Third Uncle's mani Lhakhang and continued along the circumambulation. Little Tashi, however, felt uncomfortable without any reason when he heard Grandpa praise Third Uncle. He gazed at the mountain top on the opposite side, a little bit worriedly, faintly catching sight of the flock of his family there. Little Tashi felt happy again but when he was about to point it out to Grandpa, the crowd behind them pushed them forward again.

They finally arrived at Hayagriva Lhakhang below the monastery, where bones of cattle and sheep were hung on the Lhakhang inside and outside. Farmers would usually write scriptures on bones of those livestock they liked most to transmigrate them when they died. Little Tashi dare not tell his grandparents about the death of Little Black Head. That day when they offered Little Black Head to vultures, he went to the mountain ridge to collect his bones, but for vultures, Little Black Head was so tiny that they left nothing except a few hairs. Little Tashi spun his wool into a fine thread and placed it in his bosom and carried it all the time. He brought it here today and, when Grandpa did not notice, he tied the thread on the beam of the mani Lhakhang, praying for Little Black Head and hoped his soul would never be bullied in the underworld and he would reincarnated as soon as possible.

Grandpa and Little Tashi walked on along the circumambulation and when they reached the place right under the monastery, Grandpa asked Little Tashi to eat something in Second Uncle's abode. Little Tashi knew shaving his head and becoming a member of a monastery would usually be done on an auspicious day and the Great Prayer Festival was the peak time for people to become lamas. Second Uncle, though different from Third Uncle who pestered Little Tashi's grandparents every day, was the most influential person in the family; if he went to see him, he was sure to persuade him to be a lama. What if his grandparents felt it hard to decline Second Uncle and allow it to happen before his father came back from the remote grazing area? If so, there would be no chance for him to go to school anymore! Little Tashi did not follow his grandpa, instead he secretly hid in the crowd and then came to the town school at last. It was the winter holiday and the school gate was closed tightly. He wanted to look into the campus through the gate, but street vendors from other places crowded in front of the school with various fancy goods, so he could not get through. He stopped in front of a store selling stationery on the right side of the school. He stood at the doorway staring at the dazzling variety of goods, but he didn't have a penny on him. He had wanted to ask for some from his grandpa in the morning, but Grandpa had already given him one yuan as the offering to be used during the Buddha statue exhibition and he felt it would be hard for him to ask again. Little Tashi was simply standing at the doorway, staring intently. The shop owner came out and yelled at him angrily, "If you have money, come in and buy what you want; if not, don't stand in the way!" Feeling sad, Little Tashi reluctantly left the shop with regret.

At that moment there was a commotion in the crowd. People thronged to the roadside, gazing at the flat area below. Little Tashi knew horse racing was about to begin, but he couldn't get himself into the crowd and he could only reach the waist of an adults, even if he stood on his toes. He climbed up along the way and arrived at the platform in the town where visitors were comparatively sparse. He looked at the flat track, horses and their riders assembling at its lower reaches and people around him talking with each other excitedly.

Horse racing was co-sponsored by the monastery and local government. Every year all the horses in all villages in Bei Gu valley would participate in this event and it was said that every owner of the horse would do bsang in their village to worship mountain gods for blessings. Little Tashi looked back and saw the bsang smoke curling up above the platform in Dungkar village on the other side of the river. He knew Third Uncle would surely take Blackhawk to the race. Presently cadres wearing winter clothes and lamas in robes were keeping order on the track. They organised the crowd on the track into two groups on either side and drove all the horses to the lower reaches of the track, 300 horses this year in total. According to horse racing rules, 10 horses would be grouped into one team after drawing lots and the top three horses in a group in each round would qualify for the next round. All the selected top three would join the final race and a list of winners and results would be settled afterwards. The whistle blew and off went the first 10 horses and then the second batch. Blackhawk was in the seventh group. As he galloped into view as the leader in his group like an arrow, the audiences cheered and applauded his brilliance, some shouting excitedly, some whistling and some even taking off their hats and waving towards him.

The final round began. Some villagers around Little Tashi talked with each other enthusiastically. A man said, "Horse racing this year is fantastic!"

"I heard villages upstream have bought in a lot of horses from other places at a great cost in the past few years, that's why the final this year is really worth watching."

"But considering speed and endurance, Blackhawk is sure to be the winner this year!"

"Well, it is a blessing for such a small village like Dungkar to have such a great horse!"

"I heard Gold Teeth, the owner of Blackhawk loves the horse the way he loves his children. He feeds it with rice every day."

"If I had such a great horse like Blackhawk, I shall die without regret."

Little Tashi shivered in the cold on the platform. Gradually, dark clouds, mixed with white ones, moved away and a large hole appeared in the clouds overhead, from which the sun revealed its face and beamed down on the snow-covered track and the crowd, everyone's face was brimming with anticipation and happiness. Presently the final whistle blew, and a dozen horses dashed forward together from the lower stream. They reached the middle part of the flat track, no apparent winner yet, but when the riders reached the upstream part of the flat, the horses gradually began to pull apart. They were near the finishing line. Blackhawk and a bay dashed towards the finishing line, side by side. At the most exciting and tense moment, spectators on both sides of the track, including the crowd on the upper platform, all held their breath and fixed their eyes on the finishing line. Blackhawk and the bay almost crossed the finishing line at the same time. The crowd began talking about it again, some saying Blackhawk won while some were saying the bay was the winner, and no one knew the result except the referee.

When the sponsor awarded the prizes to the winners with silk prizes, a lot of people rushed over to see this glorious scene. Friends and relatives of the winners also presented khatas to the winning horses, some even stuffing money inside the khatas. Little Tashi did not join them, no matter whether Blackhawk won the first prize or the second, he simply stood among the people on the platform, watching. As the custom went, all the horses would run back to the track to show their charms one by one according to their ranking in the race. When each horse ran back to the track with a long and colourful silk ribbon behind, the bay was the first one while Blackhawk was the second. Suddenly a massive booing rose from the crowd and then all kinds of talk. A man said, "Hey, this bay was ranked eighth last year, how could it be first this year?"

"Something must have gone wrong! We don't accept this. It is obvious that Blackhawk won the race!"

"Well, we don't need to worry about this. The referees are at the finishing line and how couldn't they see this with their own eyes?"

"Gold Teeth is in his thirties but still rode the horse himself. Doesn't he have any children?"

"He has no son."

"Why not hire one?"

"Well, it is no use talking about this anymore. It is definitely a wrong decision!"

"Wrong decision is part of the competition."

Little Tashi felt he owed Third Uncle something when he heard this. He was seized with a sudden pain and prepared to sneak away from the crowd. At this time, he saw Dekyi in the crowd who was dressed in the festival costume but no red scarf on her head. What shocked him more was that Dekyi wore a sheepskin robe embroidered with pulu along its fringe and a green belt on her waist. Traditionally, a girl would tie a woollen belt around her waist before she got married and only when she was engaged or got married would she wear a cloth belt of different colours. Though Little Tashi felt sad, he decided to greet her. To his surprise, Dekyi disappeared into the crowd the moment he called her while a gruff voice of a woman beside him asked instead, "What's the matter?" Little Tashi knew there was a mistake and hurried to explain, "I am sorry. I am looking for another Sister Dekyi." The girl with the gruff voice thought Little Tashi was making fun of her; she pulled a long face and left. Little Tashi was feeling even worse after this; he didn't wait for his grandparents and went back to the village alone. When he reached the empty road down the village and looked back in the cold wind, the crowd on the flat under the monastery began to disperse slowly and randomly. Little Tashi didn't know whether it was the cold wind that irritated his eyes or the deep sorrow that he failed to suppress, but tears welled up inside. He stood stock still in the middle of the road, looked back again for a while and finally threw his shoulder back and headed for the village.

32
RED SCARF IN THE WIND

The Great Prayer Festival ended. The weather was gradually getting warmer, the ice on the surface of the stream melted at a different speed and only a thin layer of ice was left on the edge, the most obvious sign of the coming spring. Sheep droppings, piled up at the gate of the pen, had fermented under the warm sunshine and a faint smoke was rising from these droppings. On the vegetation around the sheep pen, all kinds of birds that had been silent for quite a long time restored their vitality and could not wait to fly again in the warm and vast sky. In another 10 days, Little Tashi's family's herd and flock would move back to the winter pastures in Dungkar village, so if Little Tashi and Dawa worked harder, they could drive the flock back to the spring pasture. Usually, the spring pasture was on the hillside of the winter pasture, which meant the spring pasture, like the autumn one, was another temporary transitioning area between the winter pasture and the summer pasture. From now on their flocks had to migrate according to changes in the seasons.

Little Tashi and Dawa drove the flock to the small ravine behind the cabin and the flock climbed to the mountain top. On the top of the blue mountain, the sheep and the white clouds became one and it was difficult to distinguish which was which. Along the mountain ridge, Little Tashi and Dawa ascended the mountain, step by step. The frozen grassland on the road started thawing, when you stepped on it, you could feel the life and vitality underfoot, which was indeed an unspeakable comfort. The brothers stood on the top of the mountain and saw the flock scattered like pearls on the top of the mountain; some of them had already roamed to the edge of Namtso. With the change of weather and season, Namtso would change accordingly like a magic mirror, sometimes larger and sometimes smaller. Look! The lake that used to be full and sparkling had now retreated to the heart of the lake. The yellow and withered bushes around the lake had also become sparse and leggy; a desolate scene indeed. Luckily the sunlight lay on the edge of Namtso and made it warm and pleasant still.

Little Tashi and Dawa played by the lake to kill time. An ugly frog suddenly crawled out of the lake. Dawa was surprised when he saw it. He said, "How can frogs come out during this season?"

"Yep, a bit weird."

"Its ugly appearance reminds me of a story Mum told me, *Frog Knight*."

"Brother, you haven't told me a story for a long time. Please tell me this one."

"Who will tell stories in the daytime? No."

"Please!"

"You boy! But remember, I will tell you this story only for the sake of your concern about me and Dekyi."

"Heh, heh."

"A long time ago there was a very old couple who had no children but later gave birth to a meatball. The old couple was frustrated and didn't know how to deal with it. Before long, the meatball changed into a frog, who could speak human language, which in a sense comforted the couple a little bit. Three years later, the frog boldly proposed to the head of the local people that he should marry one of his three daughters. How could the chief agree to marry his daughter to an ugly frog? The frog therefore laughed, cried and jumped to show its magical power. Exhausted by all his efforts, the chief had no choice but to agree to let him marry a daughter. His two elder daughters would rather die than consent to marry this ugly frog, so the kind, youngest daughter became his wife."

"Even a frog could marry the third daughter of a chief, so you are sure to marry Dekyi from Grandpa Humpback's family."

"Stop talking! The youngest daughter and the frog lived a happy life, but the frog often took off its skin and changed into a strong and handsome young knight when his wife was not at home. He went to take part in horse racing and, because he was so good at riding horses, he was often praised by the audience. When he came back from horse racing, he would change back from the young knight to a frog. Unexpectedly, his wife found his secret one day."

"Oh, the wife didn't want her frog husband, did she?"

"Yes! When the husband took off his skin and went to the horse races again, the wife found the skin and burned it secretly because this way her husband would not change into a frog anymore. When the young knight came back home, he was terrified to find his skin had been burnt. He told his wife he used to be the personification of Salgaer, the son of the goddess of the earth, the ancestral mother of all life. He told her that he had planned to do three things for the people when he had enough strength: there would be no difference between rich and poor, officials would no longer oppress the common people, and he would make a way to the land of the fairies…"

"What happened next?"

"Before his wife burned the skin, he could survive the cold winter using that magic frog skin, but now that he had lost that skin, it was impossible for him to live and he had to go back to his mother, the goddess of the earth. To save her frog husband, the wife went to the west, pleaded to the gods to help her husband complete the three tasks, so the world would become warm."

"What about the ending?"

"As the wife told the three things the gods had promised to the local people, door by door, her father heard about it and opposed it firmly, obstructing her by every means possible. At last, she failed to complete the three things and her husband died. After that, the wife was in deep remorse and turned to stone praying for happiness to the end of time."

"What a sad story! I hope you and Sister Dekyi will have a happy ending."

"I hope so too!"

Suddenly a layer of clouds covered the sky above the lake and presently the sun overhead disappeared. Little Tashi cupped his hands around his mouth and shouted towards the sky, "Cloud Grandma, please go back home and ask Grandpa Sun to come out!" He shouted several times and it seemed the clouds in the sky heard him and moved away in a minute. The warm sunlight once again shone through the gaps in the clouds on Namtso, on the flock beside the lake and on Little Tashi and Dawa as well. Bathed in the afternoon sunshine, the brothers felt so warm, in body and mind, but when Dawa told the story to Little Tashi, he kept looking behind him as if he couldn't control himself. Little Tashi knew what he thought and asked him voluntarily, "Brother, did you see Sister Dekyi at the Great Prayer Festival?"

"No. Did you see her?" asked Dawa.

Little Tashi replied with regret, "I did see her in the crowd when I was about to go back, but before I went to greet her, she was gone."

"Well, I haven't seen her for a few days!" Dawa sighed.

"Yes, I miss her singing too," Little Tashi taking on a yearning tone.

"Time flies! A year has passed by!" Dawa lamented.

"Brother, we are leaving this place soon. Don't you want to see her again?"

"I want to see her, but I just can't find her," Dawa said, sadly.

"Brother, let me call her for you," offered Little Tashi.

"Great," said Dawa as he jumped to his feet happily.

Two hawks suddenly appeared in the sky, which had not been seen for quite a long time; it seemed they had already known the lambing season had arrived. When the two hawks hovered overhead, the ewes beside Namtso bleated vigilantly as if worrying about their babies in their bellies. Little Tashi stood up, cupped his hands around his mouth and shouted towards Dekyi's sheep pen. There was no response, but the two hawks were frightened away instead. Little Tashi shouted louder a few more times, the veins standing out in his neck, but still no response at all. Sad and uncomfortable, Dawa said, "Forget about it! She didn't care about this. Let it be."

"Brother, you shouldn't say like this! I will try again," and with these words, Little Tashi shouted again.

Frustrated, Dawa said, "Tashi, forget about it! Let's go home."

"Brother, it is only noon, why are we going back so early?" reminded Little Tashi.

Dawa replied in a languid manner, "Out of sight, out of mind."

"Go away with your 'out of mind'! We are moving back in a few days, Brother, and if you give up now, there will be no chance for you to see her again," said Little Tashi, earnestly.

The sheep pen of Dekyi's family was out of sight, covered by the bushes and they couldn't see it, except for a corner of it, from the mountain top. Downhearted and depressed, Dawa explained, "I am talking about her sheep pen!"

"Brother, Sister Dekyi might not hear me. Let's go to her sheep pen," suggested Little Tashi.

Dawa frowned and said, "If Grandpa Humpback sees me, he will break my legs."

"Brother, hurry up, don't hesitate anymore!" Little Tashi urged firmly.

Little Tashi and Dawa headed for Dekyi's sheep pen from the mountain top. A small tornado suddenly formed on the quiet mountain top; dry grass and branches on the ground were picked up by the wind and whirled into the air. Dawa spat at the tornado though it had done nothing wrong while Little Tashi slipped into the bushes. The dry branches could not endure Little Tashi's intrusion and broke with cracks one after another. Little Tashi was close to Dekyi's sheep pen while Dawa followed behind at a distance, as if quite reluctant.

When they arrived at the pen, they found it empty, not even with fresh sheep droppings as if the flock had not been enclosed in the pen for a few days. They walked cautiously towards the cabin door below the sheep pen and saw the mother dog and her puppies were not there.

"Sister Dekyi? Sister Dekyi, is anybody home?" Little Tashi shouted a few times in the distance. No response. Dawa whispered in Little Tashi's ear, "Try Grandpa Humpback this time."

"Grandpa Humpback? Grandpa Humpback, are you in the cabin?" shouted Little Tashi a few more times but there was still no response, so the brothers went to the cabin door and found it was locked. They went to the window and looked inside. There was nothing in the cabin. They searched around the outside of the cabin and found a pile of tea dust in the corner of the cabin that Grandpa Humpback had left. Dawa bent down to smell a little bit and said, "They might have left a few days ago."

"Brother, look!" shouted Little Tashi as he looked up and saw a red scarf tied on to a pole where a prayer flag used to be hung, above the sheep pen.

Seeing this red scarf, Dawa was stunned into silence and he didn't even blink his eyes as if someone had pressed hard on one of his acupoints. Little Tashi knew something might have gone wrong. He ran to the pole, looked up at the red scarf, wondering whether he should untie it or leave it there. The tornado, as if being provoked by someone, followed them from the mountain top to Dekyi's sheep pen. The dried sheep droppings were picked up by the wind and whirled into the air; the red scarf tied on the pole was fluttering and was almost blown away. Presently, the tornado disappeared but the wind didn't stop blowing and the red scarf was still slightly flying. Hesitantly, Little Tashi lifted his hands to grab the corners of the red scarf while Dawa said, "Leave it there!"

"What's wrong? To leave it here is such a waste," murmured Little Tashi.

Dawa answered sadly, "Since Dekyi tied it here, she must have had some unutterable secrets. Leave it here for the time being."

"What if it is taken away by someone else?" Little Tashi asked with regret.

Dawa walked towards the mountain and then he turned back and said, "Anyway, whatever is yours will come to you and whatever is not coming was never yours. Let it be."

"Brother, wait for me."

Little Tashi ran after Dawa, but he kept a certain distance from him when he saw his shoulders were shaking. He knew Dawa was crying silently. He had never seen him cry before, nor did he want to.

When they reached the mountain top, the flock spontaneously went back to Lungser. Without saying a word, Dawa climbed down the mountain ridge to the valley. Standing on the mountain top, Little Tashi gazed at Dekyi's sheep pen, but the red scarf hanging on the pole was blocked from sight by the tall bushes, so he could only see a corner of her pen, nothing else. Many scenes flickered past in Little Tashi's memory: Dawa finding the red scarf on the road, the hawk taking the red scarf to the mountain top, Sister Dekyi finding the red scarf on the mountain and wearing it on her head and now the red scarf hanging on the pole all alone. So many emotions were surging through him and he couldn't calm himself down. Little Tashi developed some sympathy for Dawa; he felt guilty for his parents, for his Third Uncle, and now for his brother, and he felt guilty for everyone.

The sun had climbed to the top of the far west hill, the clouds in the sky turned red, like Sister Dekyi's red scarf. Little Tashi looked around with sadness because in a few days he would leave this place and maybe he would not come back here again, farming the sheep. He would never see Namtso, various birds or flowers and trees, and even if he could, he might not have the same feelings as he had now. What made it harder for him to accept was he would never have the chance to listen to Sister Dekyi's singing. The setting sun beamed on Little Tashi, who glowed like a statue of Buddha and the long shadow behind him had already lain on the grassland in the upper stream.

㉞ MIGRATION

A few days later, all the ice on the edge of the stream melted, the soil of the open space softened and the yellow and dry bushes remained almost the same, but some green buds with great vitality had already burst out. The chirping of wild thrushes inside the surrounding vegetation was clear and silvery and sparrows and other unknown birds scattered around the sheep pen, shook their necks excitedly for a while or lowered their heads for food. Silently, beautiful days arrived like this, without a whisper.

It was the first day of March. Little Tashi's family's flock would move back from the remote forest valley to the village that morning. Dawa got up before dawn to go to the remote grazing area, helping their parents. Little Tashi got up as usual, cleaned the cabin, lit the stove and took all the bags down from the roof. All the bags were almost empty. He mixed them together, black flour, zanba powder and coarse grain, spared a little bit for himself and then poured the rest all into the old dog's bowl, stirring it with boiling water. He carried the bowl to the old dog, a kind of treat for his hard work over the past year. It was no easy job for the old fellow to lick up the thick porridge but he still ate it with relish and presently his belly bulged like a barrel.

After Little Tashi finished his zanba, he cleared up the bedding on the kang and the other utensils in the cabin, then he went to the sheep pen preparing to drive the flock out. From the small road, covered from sight by the vegetation on the opposite of the stream, there suddenly came the voices of two people and Little Tashi knew his grandparents were coming the moment he heard them. He trotted to meet them. Indeed, when he reached the stream, his grandparents appeared in front of him, Grandpa supporting himself with a crutch and Grandma bearing a big bamboo basket on her back. They were almost the same age, but compared with Grandpa limping on the way, Grandma walked quickly and vigorously like a middle-aged woman.

Little Tashi escorted them into the cabin. The water was boiling on the stove and he wanted to cook something for them to eat but there was nothing to cook. Luckily, Grandma had brought enough food for their return trip in the bamboo basket, so Little Tashi poured each of them a bowl of hot water and they sat around the stove, chatting as they ate the food. Grandma looked around the cabin and said to herself, "Well, that is indeed the blessings of the Three Treasures as the shabby cabin didn't collapse and hurt them!"

"Yes, had it not been for my poor legs, the flock would have migrated to the pastures. They had a hard time in the past year, herding the flock and helping with the work in the village," said Grandpa as he took a pinch of snuff.

Little Tashi said, worriedly, "Grandpa and Grandma, we are alright, but I am afraid Father will scold me because we have lost Spotted Neck and Little Black Head."

"No, he won't," his grandparents comforted him at the same time.

At that moment, the sun shone on the cabin and the sheep pen; a layer of mist danced above the pen, flashing every hue of colour under the sun. Grandpa and Grandma started collecting up the only bedding and utensils they had in the cabin and placed them all in the bamboo basket. Little Tashi shovelled the unburned wood out of the stove and threw it on the open place in front of the pen gate; the smoke floated into the air immediately. The old dog barked and the prayer flag in front of the pen gate fluttered as if it knew the flock was about to migrate away. The sheep in the pen joined in the fun too, bleating one after another, among which a little sharp cry of a baby lamb could be heard.

Hearing the scream, Little Tashi was very excited. He went to the pen and looked inside through the fence. A ewe had just given birth to a baby lamb and the other sheep all moved to stand in the corner of the pen, making enough space for the mother and the baby. The mother ewe licked her baby and ate the foetal membrane. Presently the baby lamb wobbled up, looking for the ewe's nipple. Little Tashi felt the baby lamb looked very familiar and after he took another look, he found the new little one had a black head too, as if his Black Head that had been swallowed by the ice hole in the river had come back to the pen. Little Tashi shouted happily. He opened the gate, rushed into the pen, and held the new lamb in his arms. As he kept kissing the little fellow, the flock passed by him and slipped out of the pen in small groups.

Sheep are intelligent animals. They knew they would travel far today, so they all voluntarily peed and pooped at the pen gate, getting ready for the order from Little Tashi. The old dog was usually tied with the chain when they travelled on the road with him, but today Little Tashi would hold Little Black Head II, so he untied the old dog's chain from the stake and said to him, "Old dog, you got to behave yourself today or I won't let you get away with it easily." The old fellow nodded his head, as if he understood what Little Tashi meant. The moment Little Tashi removed the chain from the old dog's neck, the old fellow excitedly ran in circles in the open space. Grandma carried the bamboo basket, Grandpa held the pole used to hang the prayer flag on his shoulder and Little Tashi held the baby lamb in his arms; everything was ready.

When they were about to depart, the flock walked to the mountain road on the opposite of the stream spontaneously before Little Tashi gave any command. They headed for the Lungser along the winding path, and presently the flock arrived at the mouth of Lungser, where they huddled together, waiting. Little Tashi and Grandma reached the grass meadow at the mouth of Lungser, but Grandpa was still far behind. Little Tashi, therefore helped Grandma unload the basket and then they sat in the meadow, waiting for Grandpa. Grandma took the baby lamb from Little Tashi, stroked it and said, "What a poor little guy! Coming into the world like this."

"Grandma, it looks almost the same as Black Head who froze to death in the river," said Little Tashi.

Grandma said affectionately, "It might be the reincarnation of Little Black Head."

"But I didn't take good care of him, my parents will blame me for that," said Little Tashi as he took the baby lamb from Grandma and put it under the ewe for milk.

"Om ma ni bai," murmured Grandma as she took off the rosary from her neck, turning it in her hand and said, "No, they won't."

"I had an agreement with Dad. If I could help my brother and take good care of the flock, he would send me to school when he comes back, but now..." Little Tashi said, worriedly.

"To err is human. As long as you know what your mistakes are and correct them later, mistakes are good things. And, your father loves you and if you want to go to school, your father won't change his mind simply because you lost Spotted Neck and Little Black Head."

"But Third Uncle said he is going to adopt me. What if my father agrees out of anger?" asked Little Tashi.

"No, he..." Grandma wanted to say something, but she swallowed it back.

At this moment, crowds of white clouds floated overhead towards the depths of Lungser, as if guiding them where they should go. The flock scattered on the grass meadow at the mouth of the valley while some of them had already wandered to the side of the lake, drinking water. The old dog was overwhelmed with excitement. He slipped into the nearby bushes for a while or ran back to them and circled around, like turning the prayer wheel, as if he got lost and didn't know what he should do. Little Tashi gazed at the village and said, "Grandma, why didn't Third Uncle come over to help us move back?"

"Well, in the Great Prayer Festival, Blackhawk didn't win the first prize, so your Third Uncle felt sad for a couple of days," said Grandma dismally.

Little Tashi asked, "Where is he now?"

"He led Blackhawk to take part in horse racing in other villages, and he said he must earn back the honour of Blackhawk."

Confused, Little Tashi asked, "Why should Third Uncle do this?"

"Your Third Uncle is the youngest child in the family. All his brothers and sisters have taken good care of him since he was young, so he is fond of flaunting his superiority, and he is conceited too. He always tries to win first place for everything," explained Grandma with sincerity and affection.

Little Tashi said, "My Third Uncle has built a mani Lhakhang for the monastery, he offers food for the elders in the village, everyone knows about his famous Blackhawk and he has an adopted daughter. Why should it necessary for him to adopt me?"

"Well, your Third Uncle has no son, though he has a big ego, he has suffered a lot. I am his mother and I am the only one who understand him," Grandma said worriedly.

Little Tashi said firmly, "Grandma, I understand Third Uncle, but I really don't want to be his son, I want to go to school."

"Well, your Second Uncle wants you to be a lama in the monastery!"

"No, I will go to school!"

"They are all my sons and I believe your father has his own arrangement. Grandma wants you to grow happily and healthily, nothing else," said Grandma as she kissed his forehead.

Grandpa limped from behind the bushes, with the prayer flag on his shoulder. When he reached them, he untied the prayer flag from the pole, folded and handed it to Little Tashi, "Tashi, Grandpa has taken too much of your time, Grandma and I will go back to the village. You hurry up to meet your parents and brother in the pasture."

Holding Little Black Head II in his arms, Tashi shouted towards the flock. Obediently those scattered sheep gathered together. Little Tashi drove the flock on deep into Lungser. When he turned back halfway to take a look, Grandpa and Grandma still stood on the grass meadow at the mouth of Lungser watching him. The road at the bottom of Dungkar valley, though rocky and bumpy, was much wider than the small one in Gonpa; the flock walked fast and in a while they arrived in front of the water mill where his maternal grandpa had ground flour this summer. Now it looked like a lonely old man, standing in the deserted valley. The water under the mill was frozen into ice cubes and a black lock hung on the door. Little Tashi stopped to look at it for a while, thinking of the day when he ventured to go to the remote grazing area alone last summer, and how he had made a detour around the mountain road in order not to be found by his maternal grandpa. He himself might think that was too funny and too much, so he snorted with laughter. Then he drove the flock and continued his journey along the road.

The spring pasture of Little Tashi's family was in the innermost place in the spring pastures of the whole village, amid the summer pasture and winter pasture. Little Tashi knew he was sure to meet some other herdsmen or migrating caravans of yaks, so he drove the flock slowly in case the old dog might bite someone on the way. If that should happen, Little Tashi would be in big trouble; what's more, he couldn't arrive at the spring pasture before the night fell. Little Black Head II made a lot of trouble today, but the old dog kept his promise and tried his best to stay away from any passers-by. As the dark of night set in, they had reached the winter pasture while the spring pasture was on the hillside of the upper stream of the summer pasture. The flock entered the winter pasture, crossed through a long slope in the forest and scrambled forward to the hillside. Even the baby lamb stumbled after his mother when it was placed on the ground. The old dog who seemed to be somewhat exhausted, followed behind Little Tashi, his tongue hanging out.

Night fell. Little Tashi hurried to the spring pasture of his family through the small road in the forest. Along the way were forests, and at the hillside, smooth grassland appeared. It was the spring pasture of his family! When Little Tashi and the old dog were halfway along the road in the forest, the leading sheep might have already arrived at the spring pasture. Little Tashi could hear the cries of the cattle and sheep and of his family. It was dark when Little Tashi reached the place where a grass meadow below the spring pasture bordered the forest. Presently, the moon emerged from the mountain top. Although the moon was half covered from sight by the mountain, his family's tents, standing on the slope and cattle and flocks resting nearby, were already visible in the hazy moonlight.

It would take more than half an hour to arrive at the cattle ranch of his family, though it looked very close from here. When Little Tashi reached his destination breathlessly, cattle mooed, and flocks bleated to greet each other. Little Black Head II slipped into the flock with its mother, the old dog walked inside the herd merrily at first, then he ran to his stake, sitting there with his tail between his legs.

Little Tashi lifted his head to gaze at his family's tents. In the blurry moonlight, his father and brother were doing bsang at the upper side of the tent; father stood below the bsang, holding a sliver spoon as he prayed loudly for all the Naga and mountain gods and sprinkled milk in all directions while Dawa stood beside him, adding cypress leaves to the bsang. It was a cloudless and starry night. The crystal moon climbed leisurely overhead from the mountain top behind; silvery moonlight lay on the hillside, which shone brightly as if covered with white silk. The smoke of the bsang floated into the air and became a graceful solo dancer for tonight's show.

34

AN AUSPICIOUS CLOUD LANDS

"My sweet boy, it is a tiring trip, isn't it?"

When Little Tashi came to the door of the tent, Mother got to her feet from under a yattle beside the tent as she greeted him with a milk bucket in her hand. She held aside the door curtain and showed him in. Afraid of being scolded by his parents, Little Tashi wondered as he responded to his mother, "No, it is ok."

Mother placed the milk bucket beside the fire pit. By the firelight she looked at Little Tashi's face and said fondly, "Sweetheart, you are losing weight! But it is really amazing that today you have driven the flock back by yourself."

"Dad didn't blame me?" asked Little Tashi, since he was still wondering about this.

Mother smiled, "No, he didn't. He said you have grown up and you are a man."

The firewood was crackling inside the stones in the tent, flames were flaring up and shining on the bed on the left and milk barrels alike on the right. Living in the cabin with a kang for a year, Little Tashi felt somewhat uneasy when he was inside the tent. He sat on the crossbar at the edge of the bed and asked his mother, as he warmed his hands over the fire, "Mum, hasn't my brother told Dad that I didn't take good care of Little Black Head and its mother," asked Little Tashi, anxiously.

"Yes, he has. Your Dad didn't blame you for that," said Mother as she poured the milk into the pot.

"Then I can go to school, can I?" asked Little Tashi, cheerfully.

"Why not! Only if you want yo," said Mother as she added firewood to the fire pit.

Little Tashi could hardly contain his excitement and sprang to his feet, "So I will not be adopted by Third Uncle, will I?"

"Who ever said you will be adopted by Third Uncle?"

"Third Uncle said that. He said after you and Dad come back from the remote grazing area, he will adopt me, otherwise, he will break off relations with my father."

"Well, that is your Third Uncle. He has insisted on adopting you since you were very young. Later, your brother went to school, he didn't mention it again. He has been harbouring a grievance even though your second paternal aunt let him adopt Drolma. Now your sister has married and your brother has also dropped out of school, he is thinking about you again," said Mother, relating the whole story.

"I see." Little Tashi who had puzzled over it for quite a long time felt enlightened after Mother told him this. He asked, "Mum, do you want me to be adopted by Third Uncle?"

"Tashi, you are my son, how could a mother give her son to others so easily, right?" The milk in the pot was boiling. She continued as she poured milk into Little Tashi's bowl, "Drink it while it is still hot."

"Thanks Mum, you are so sweet!" Little Tashi smiled broadly, but he worried again as he held the bowl of delicious milk in his hand. "Mum, and my Second Uncle too, he has always wanted me to be a lama in the monastery. What should I do?"

"That is not your Second Uncle's problem. Your grandparents were particularly fond of you when you were a little boy and they want you to be a lama when you grow up."

Little Tashi asked, "Should I be a lama then?"

"I don't know. See how your father and your grandparents decide!" Mother added one more ladle of hot milk to Little Tashi's bowl.

At this time, Father and Dawa came back from outside the tent, still chanting in low voices. Father held aside the door curtain and shouted half-jokingly, "Look, people are always selfish. Only thinking about her son and totally forgetting about the old dog outside."

"Aha, yes! What a forgetful selfish devil I am!" Mother patted her thigh heavily and immediately cooked a pot of hot porridge and placed in front of the old dog.

When in spring pasture or summer pasture, they did not have a fixed ranch for the cattle and pen for the flock, so the animals could only crowd in the open places surrounding the tent in the silvery moonlight. Some old yaks began chewing cud noisily, which was obviously not from eating too much but was now a habit. The flock lay under the bushes on the right side of the tent, huddling together. The crystal moonlight beamed on the sheep, the reflection of the white light from them made these fellows look almost transparent.

The old dog, who was very old after all, still maintained his dignity and honour as the shepherd of herdsmen after he finished his meal. Standing beside the stake, he looked around vigilantly and barked from time to time, as if to warn those potential aggressors not to invade the territory he was protecting right now, or the consequences would be serious.

That night, laughter and cheers filled their tent and it seemed there was no need for Little Tashi to worry about the loss of Little Black Head and his mother. It was not until crowds of clouds appeared and sheltered the stars in the night sky that the lights in their tent were put out.

That night Father agreed to send Little Tashi to school, but it was almost half a month until term began while new pupils usually started school in September. Little Tashi however could not wait even for one day. The next day when he woke up, the prayer flag they had brought back from the cabin was tied to a pole and was fluttering in the wind, in front of the tent. He had no idea who had tied the prayer flag there. A yak was tied in front of the tent too. He had heard they were going to sell it to a merchant of Hui minority and the payment would be used for this year's expenditure. Grandpa's leg was getting worse and he needed to see a doctor, his sister was going to give birth to a baby, his brother needed a wife, and so on.

When the sun rose from behind the mountain and shone on the opposite mountain top, Father and Little Tashi went out on a yak. Dawa hurried to drive yaks to the mountain, then had to drive the flock to the foot of the mountain; there was no time to say goodbye to Little Tashi. The old dog was quite reluctant to let Little Tashi go, he kept wailing although he couldn't see him anymore. Mother went to see them off until they reached the place where grass hills bordered the forest. When they were about to wave goodbye, Mother was still murmuring something to him. The moment the yak entered the forest, Little Tashi looked back and saw Mother had lowered her head and was weeping there, which touched his cheerful heart and filled it with a little sorrow from a sentimental attachment.

Father was firm and steady though he was somewhat inarticulate. He was respected, not only in the family but also in the village, and as for important events like weddings and funerals in the family, they would even listen to Father's suggestions. His brother and sister never dared to speak in front of Father, let alone be unbridled. In Mother's words, whenever they saw Father, it was quite like the scene when mice saw the cat. But Little Tashi was the youngest son and Father always showed him tenderness. Whenever they met, they always had too much to chat about, but today, when his father brought him to the village and his dream was about to be realised, he was seized by a deep guilt as he thought of Little Black Head and Spotted Neck, so he remained silent all the way and prayed secretly in his heart hoping to arrive at the village soon, which might relieve his grievance a little bit. When they arrived at the village in the afternoon, a gale was suddenly blowing wildly in the entire valley, gusts of tornados were sweeping over the village with dust storms. Grandparents and Second Uncle were standing in the hallway under the roof, marvelling at the weird weather, when they reached the doorway. They went over to greet them when Little Tashi and his father entered the yard with the yak. Grandma unloaded the saddle from the yak and led it into the cowshed on the lower right corner of the yard while Grandpa and Second Uncle showed them into the inner room. Inside the inner room, Grandpa and Father invited Second Uncle to sit on the kang but he declined and walked back and forth before the shrine, preoccupied with thoughts.

Although it was not very easy for Grandpa to serve guests with his painful legs, he insisted on doing this himself even if his sons and grandsons came to visit because he always complained about Grandma's clumsiness. He asked Little Tashi and his father to sit beside the stove and brought them zanba and butter. Two porcelain bowls of different sizes were placed on the stove. He put some brown tea into the bowls and poured boiling water on it.

The room fell into complete silence except for the sound when Grandpa was moving around, serving the tea. At this time, Grandma came in. When she saw this, she said, "It's been a year since you saw each other last time, why do you all have long faces and keep silent like this? What's the matter?"

"Right, you brothers need to say something!" Grandpa agreed.

Second Uncle broke the silence. "Today I in fact had a Dharma assembly to attend, but when I heard Little Tashi and his father were back in the village, I asked for leave and came to see them. I just want to know, will Little Tashi be a lama or not?"

"No!" answered Little Tashi as he looked up from eating the zanba.

Father slapped his face and scolded, "Don't you know how to talk to your Second Uncle? He is a monk."

Little Tashi cried as he put his head in his hands.

Grandma cursed, "He did nothing wrong, why did you beat him like this?"

Second Uncle said, "Don't do that! What's the use of beating him? He has been regarded as a future monk in the family since he was born, and now you simply follow others when seeing the children of other families going to school. If so, why did you drag Dawa from school and ask him to stay at home? Well? I ask you!"

"Please excuse me. Children nowadays are not very obedient. You haven't seen through what he truly wants?" explained Father, a little submissively when he was faced with Second Uncle.

Second Uncle glared at him, "What? You just let him be wayward like this? Doing anything he wants?"

Father replied, "No, I am thinking even if he would be a lama, he should go to school to be educated first which would be good for his future learning of scriptures. It might be better for him to be a lama after he grows up a little bit."

"I think it is a good suggestion," said Grandpa.

"Father, you are sitting on the fence! You know when a man grows up and experiences all the things in the secular world, how could he get down to study scriptures?"

Grandpa explained, "This is not a problem. In history, many prestigious monks were not young when…"

"Come on! How could people nowadays be the same as people in the past?" argued Second Uncle who actually was a steady man and seldom lost control. He said sadly, "So many lamas in the monastery resume secular life!"

Grandpa said, "That's why we should be more careful since so many lamas resume secular life."

"Couldn't you all talk to each other nicely," interrupted Grandma with sadness.

"Father, please stop arguing," Little Tashi's father looked at Second Uncle and said insincerely, "Agu, how about this? You go back first and I will think about it later."

Second Uncle calmed down and then said, "All right. I have a Dharma event tonight anyway."

"Good! You two will have enough time to think about this," said Grandpa in a summary tone.

Second Uncle went out of the inner room and the rest of them followed him to the front gate, reverently. The gale had faded a little bit but the dust pervading above the village were still lingering in the sky. Second Uncle covered his head with one corner of his red robe and then said to them thoughtfully, "You all must make it clear what does it mean if Little Tashi is not going to be a lama!"

"Yes! Yes!" Grandpa, Grandma and Father all bowed and answered at the same time.

That afternoon, Second Uncle's strong intervention made everyone feel like cats on hot bricks, so when Second Uncle left, they all felt relieved, as if the sword of Damocles had been taken away from their heads. Second Uncle was the only monk in the family, and no one in the family dared to show objection to whatever he said and whatever he did, even his own father would have to show respect to him. The last words Second Uncle said were indeed thought provoking, but this did not discourage the grandparents. They were still overjoyed to see Little Tashi and his father and kept asking them all kinds of questions, but his father answered quite briefly, and it was Little Tashi who offered to give the details.

God knows whether it was grandparents who sent a message to Third Uncle or Third Uncle who guessed it himself but before they even had a few minutes' rest, Third Uncle came in a hurry. He grinned and asked Little Tashi's father, "Brother, when did you arrive?"

"What do you mean? Didn't you see the yak tied in the yard?" said Father, a little bit coldly.

"Flocks just migrated from the pastures in other villages. Why did you hurry back to the village?" asked Third Uncle surprised.

"Tomorrow I will go to school," Little Tashi interrupted.

"Go to school?" Third Uncle opened his eyes wide, "Brother, you have agreed to send him to school?"

"Why shouldn't I?" Father retorted.

The tornado was roaring outside again right now. Wind and dust upturned the world; even the two-storey wooden house creaked in the wind. Suddenly someone called outside, "Uncle Gold Teeth, the roof of your house has collapsed, and your wife wants you to go back quickly."

"What? The roof collapsed? Don't they have hands to do something?" said Third Uncle as he blinked at his parents. "Mum and Dad, haven't you told this to my big brother?"

"That is very urgent! Go back home as soon as possible!" said his parents at the same time.

"Brother, well, it's been quite a long time. You know…" said Third Uncle as he went to the door, looking back at the grandparents, "I will go back home first, then I come back at night."

"I know what you want to say. Go and repair your roof. I will come to your house later," said Father.

"That is great. We haven't seen each other for a whole year and you are my most honoured guest." With these words, Third Uncle rushed out of the door immediately.

The wind stopped outside but the dust in the air lingered above for a long time. After a while, Father went out in a hurry after he finished his meal. The tension inside the room was reduced a little bit, grandparents and Little Tashi all sighed with relief. But Father didn't come back home that night. As time went by, Little Tashi was overwhelmed with all kinds of uncertainties. What if quick-tongued Third Uncle had persuaded Father and adopted him at last? He feared more and more and he was afraid his life would be changed by a single line his father would say when he came back from Third Uncle's family. Grandpa was reading his scripture on the kang, Grandma was sitting on the edge of the kang, turning the prayer wheel beside the shrine. They looked very calm, but Little Tashi knew they were overwhelmed with strong emotions inwardly. Little Tashi drifted off to sleep amid the scripture chanting of Grandpa and the creaking sound of the prayer wheel by Grandma. Little Tashi had a lot of nightmares that night, but he forgot all about these dreams after he woke up the next day. When he woke up, his grandparents had already gone to the nearby monastery to turn the prayer wheels, father alone changed the holy water offering before the shrine. Little Tashi looked at his father from under his quilt and Father said slowly after he finished his work, "Tashi, get up quickly and wash your face."

"Okay." Little Tashi couldn't read anything from his father's expression and he got up from the kang uneasily.

"Put these new clothes on!" said Father as he grabbed a set of new clothes from a case and threw them on his pillow.

"Ok." Little Tashi became excited when he heard Father's words and he didn't even know how he managed to put the new clothes on.

Taking Little Tashi's hand, Father led Little Tashi out of the home. When they reached the corner at the far end of the village, at a road crossing a slope, a woman wearing a yellow scarf and carrying a full bucket of water, happened to pass by them. Little Tashi looked up at his tall father, whose face gleamed with one of his rare smiles. They walked on, crossed the village road and came to the cement bridge. The cold morning air braided Little Tashi's wet curls into thin threads, but he had never felt as warm and safe in his heart as this. People they met on the road seemed to smile at them too. When they turned in the direction of the school from the cement bridge, above the opposite forest, that is, above Namtso where he and his brother farmed the flock, a white cloud like the treasure vase in the Eight Auspicious Symbols suddenly came down and lingered. Little Tashi felt the auspicious white cloud was blessing him; he was seized with a surge of peace and ease. At that moment, the sudden silvery notes of a bell ringing pulled him into reality. He and his father had already arrived at the school gate! Little Tashi looked up and saw the green iron gate was wide open, as if welcoming him.

ABOUT THE AUTHOR

Chone Yum Tsering, (born in Zhuoni County, Gansu Province in 1977, Ph.D. from Sichuan University) is a Tibetan novelist, short story writer and essayist in China. As a bilingual writer involved in both literary creation and academic research, Dr Chone Yum Tsering has gained fruitful achievements. He is the author of many novels and story collections such as *Abstinence* (a collection of short stories and novellas in Tibetan), *Old House* (a collection of essays in Tibetan), and *Cloud Farming* (a novel in Tibetan and Chinese). Apart from literary creation, he has published an academic book, *A Study on Tibetan Classical Allegorical Novels*. Chone Yum Tsering has won numerous awards including the 5th Drang-char (sbrang-char) Tibetan Literature Prize for Best Work by a New Writer in 2007, the 9th National Minority Literature Horse Award in 2008, the New Talents Award of the 7th National Minority Literature Research Association in 2010, and the 3rd Tibetan Literature Award "Gangjian Cup" in 2015. He currently lives in Chengdu, a post-doctoral fellow in modern and contemporary Chinese literature at the College of Literature and Journalism of Sichuan University.